The JUNIOR CLASSICS

VOLUME FOUR · HERO TALES

Wilfred Jones

The hound rushed at him and drove him straight into the sea.

[See page 314]

The JUNIOR CLASSICS

Edited by MABEL WILLIAMS and MARCIA DALPHIN.

With Introduction by WILLIAM ALLAN NEILSON, Former

President of Smith College; Introduction to First Edition by

CHARLES W. ELIOT, Former President of Harvard University

Popular Edition

ILLUSTRATED

VOLUME
FOUR

HERO
TALES

P. F. COLLIER & SON CORPORATION

"The Departure of Telemachus," from "The Odyssey of Homer," copyright, 1884, 1891, 1912, by George Herbert Palmer; copyright, 1929, by Houghton Mifflin Company. "The Adventures of Odysseus," from "The Adventures of Odysseus, and the Tale of Troy," copyright, 1918, by The Macmillan Company. "Rustem and Sohrab," from "The Epic of Kings," copyright, 1926, by The Macmillan Company. "The Forging of the Sampo," from "The Sampo," copyright, 1912, by Charles Scribner's Sons. "Roland and Oliver," from "The Story of Roland," copyright, 1883, 1930, by Charles Scribner's Sons; copyright, 1911, by James Baldwin. "The Battle at Roncesvalles," from "The Song of Roland," copyright, 1904, by Houghton Mifflin Company; copyright, 1932, by Isabel Butler. "Stories from the Chronicle of the Cid," copyright, 1910, by Henry Holt & Company, Inc. "Beowulf Fights Grendel," "Beowulf Fights the Dragon," from "Beowulf," copyright, 1910, by Little, Brown & Company. "The Hunting of the Boar," from "The Island of the Mighty," copyright, 1924, by The Macmillan Company. "Robin Hood and Little John," "Robin Hood and Allen a Dale," "Robin Hood and the Curtal Friar," "Death of Robin Hood," from "English and Scottish Popular Ballads," copyright, 1904, 1932, by George Lyman Kittredge.

Acknowledgments of permissions given by authors and publishers for the use of copyright material appear in Volume X

CD

CONTENTS

v

CONTENTS

BEOWULF

KING ARTHUR

THE MABINOGION

CELTIC HEROES

ROBIN HOOD

From the Old English Ballads

(The sources of the stories in this volume will be found listed on page 377.)

The Odyssey of Homer

THE ODYSSEY OF HOMER

The great epic of Greek literature which tells the adventures of Odysseus on his way home from the siege of Troy.

THE DEPARTURE OF TELEMACHUS

Translated By
GEORGE HERBERT PALMER

Illustrations by John Flaxman

SOON as the early, rosy-fingered dawn appeared, the dear son of Odysseus rose from bed, put on his clothes, slung his sharp sword about his shoulder, under his shining feet bound his fair sandals, and came forth from his chamber in bearing like a god. Straightway he bade the clear-voiced heralds summon to an assembly the long-haired Achaeans. Those summoned, and these gathered very quickly. So when they were assembled and all had come together, he went himself to the assembly, holding in hand a brazen spear—yet not alone, two swift dogs followed after—and marvelous was the grace Athene cast about him, that all the people gazed as he drew near. He sat down in his father's seat; the elders made him way.

The first to speak was Lord Aegyptius, a man bowed down with age, who knew a thousand things. His dear son Antiphus, a spearman, had gone with godlike Odysseus in the hollow ships to Ilios, famed for horses. The savage Cyclops killed him in the deep cave and on him made a supper last of all. Three other sons there were; one joined the suitors—Eurynomus—and two still kept their father's farm. Yet not because of these did he forget to mourn and miss that other. With tears for him, he thus addressed the assembly, saying:

"Hearken now, men of Ithaca, to what I say. Never has our assembly once been held, no single session, since royal Odysseus went away in hollow ships. Who is it calls us now, in such a fashion? Who has such urgent need? Young or old is he? Has he heard tidings of the army's coming, which he would plainly tell to us as soon as he has learned? Or has he other public matter to announce and argue? At any rate, good seems the man to me—a blessed man. May Zeus accomplish all the good his mind intends!"

As thus he spoke, the dear son of Odysseus rejoiced at what was

3

said and kept his seat no longer. He burned to speak. He rose up in the midst of the assembly, and in his hand a herald placed the scepter—a herald named Peisenor, discreet of understanding. Then, turning first to the old man, he thus addressed him:

"Sire, not far off is he, as you full soon shall know, who called the people hither; for it is I especially whom grief befalls. No tidings of the army's coming have I heard, which I would plainly tell to you as soon as I have learned; nor have I other public matter to announce and argue. Rather it is my private need, ill falling on my house in twofold wise. For first I lost my noble father, who was formerly your king—kind father as e'er was—and now there comes a thing more grievous still, which soon will utterly destroy my home and quite cut off my substance. Suitors beset my mother sorely against her will, sons of the very men who are the leaders here. They shrink from going to the house of Icarius, her father, to let him count the bride-gifts of his daughter and give her then to whom he will, whoever meets his favor; but haunting this house of ours day after day, killing our oxen, sheep, and fatted goats, they hold high revel, drinking sparkling wine with little heed. Much goes to waste, for there is no man here fit like Odysseus to keep damage from our doors. We are not fit ourselves to guard the house; attempting it, we should be pitiful, unskilled in conflict. Guard it I would, if only strength were mine. For deeds are done not to be longer borne, and with no decency my house is plundered. Shame you should feel yourselves, and some respect as well for neighbors living near you, and awe before the anger of the gods, lest haply they may turn upon you, vexed with your evil courses. Nay, I entreat you by Olympian Zeus, and by that Justice which dissolves and gathers men's assemblies, forbear, my friends! Leave me to pine in bitter grief alone, unless indeed my father, good Odysseus, ever in malice wronged the mailed Achaeans, and in return for that you now with malice do me wrong, urging these people on. Better for me it were you should yourselves devour my stores and herds. If you devoured them, perhaps some day there might be payment made; for we would constantly pursue you through the town, demanding back our substance till all should be restored. Now, woes incurable you lay upon my heart."

In wrath he spoke, and dashed the scepter to the ground letting his tears burst forth, and pity fell on all the people. So all the rest were silent; no man dared to make Telemachus a bitter answer. Antinoüs alone made answer, saying:

"Telemachus, of the lofty tongue and the unbridled temper, what do you mean by putting us to shame? On us you would be glad to

John Flaxman

"We discovered her unraveling the splendid web."

fasten guilt: I tell you the Achaean suitors are not at all to blame; your mother is to blame, whose craft exceeds all women's. The third year is gone by, and fast the fourth is going since she began to mock the hearts in our Achaean breasts. To all she offers hopes, has promises for each, and sends us messages, but her mind has a different purpose. Here is the last pretext she cunningly devised. Within the hall she set up a great loom and went to weaving; fine was the web and very large; and then to us said she: 'Young men who are my suitors, though royal Odysseus is dead, forbear to urge my marriage till I complete this robe—its threads must not be wasted—a shroud for Lord Laërtes, against the time when the fell doom of death that lays men low shall overtake him. Achaean wives about the land, I fear, might give me blame if he should lie without a shroud, he who had great possessions.' Such were her words, and our high hearts assented. Then in the daytime would she weave at the great web, but in the night unravel, after her torch was set. Thus for three years she hid her craft and cheated the Achaeans. But when the fourth year came, as time rolled on, then at the last one of her maids, who knew full well, confessed, and we discovered her unraveling the splendid web; so then she finished it, against her will, perforce. Therefore, to you the suitors make this answer, that you yourself may understand in your own heart, and that the Achaeans all may understand. Send forth your mother! Bid her to marry whomever her father wills and him who pleases her! Or will she weary longer yet the sons of the Achaeans, mindful at heart of what Athene largely gave her, skill in fair works, a noble mind, and such a craft as we have never known in those of old, those who were long ago fair-haired Achaean women—Tyro, Alcmene, and crowned Mycene—no one of whom had judgment like Penelope; and yet, in truth, in this she judged not wisely. For just so long shall men devour your life and substance as she retains the mind the gods put in her breast at present. Great fame she brings herself, but brings on you the loss of large possessions; for we will never go to our estates, nor elsewhere either, till she shall marry an Achaean—whom she will."

Then answered him discreet Telemachus: "Antinoüs, against her will I cannot drive from home the one who bore me and who brought me up. My father is away—alive or dead—and hard it were to pay the heavy charges to Icarius which I needs must, if of my will alone I send my mother forth. For from her father's hand I shall meet ills, and Heaven will send me more, when my mother calls upon the dread Avengers as she forsakes the house; blame too will fall upon me from mankind. Therefore, that word I never will pronounce; and if your hearts chafe at your footing here, then quit my halls! Seek other tables and eat what is your own, changing from house to house! Or, if it seems to you more profitable and better to ruin the living of one man without amends, go wasting on! But I will call upon the gods that live forever and pray that Zeus may grant deeds of requital. Then, beyond all amends, here in this house you shall yourselves be ruined!"

So spoke Telemachus, and answering him far-seeing Zeus sent forth a pair of eagles, flying from a mountain peak on high. These for a time moved on along the wind, close by each other and with outstretched wings; but as they reached the middle of the many-voiced assembly, wheeling about they briskly flapped their wings, glared at the heads of all, and death was in their eyes. Then, with their claws tearing each other's cheek and neck, they darted to the right, across the town and houses. Men marveled at the birds, as they beheld, and pondered in their hearts what they might mean. And to the rest spoke old Lord Halitherses, the son of Mastor; for he surpassed all people of his time in understanding birds and telling words of fate. He with good will addressed them thus, and said:

"Hearken now, men of Ithaca, to what I say; and to the suitors especially I speak, for over them rolls a great wave of woe. Odysseus will not be long parted from his friends, but even now is near, sowing the seeds of death and doom for all men here. Aye, and on many others too shall sorrow fall, on many of us who live in far-seen Ithaca! But long ere that, let us consider how to check these men, or rather, let them check themselves; that shall be soon their gain. And not as inexpert I prophesy, but with sure knowledge. For this I say: all has come true which I declared that day the Argive host took ship for Ilios, and with them also wise Odysseus went. I said that, after suffering much, and losing all his men, unknown to all, in the twentieth year he should come home; and now it all comes true."

Then answered him Eurymachus, the son of Polybus: "Well, well, old man, go home and play the prophet to your children, or else they may have trouble in the days to come! About these matters I can prophesy much better than yourself. Plenty of birds flit in the sunshine, but not all are fateful. As for Odysseus, he died far away; and would that you had perished with him! You would not then be prating so of reading signs, nor would you, when Telemachus is wroth, thus press him on, looking for him to send your house some gift.

But this I tell you, and it shall be done; if you, who know all that an old man knows, delude this youth with talk and urge him on to anger, it shall be in the first place all the worse for him, and he shall accomplish nothing by aid of people here, while on yourself, old man, we will inflict a fine which it will grieve you to the soul to pay. Bitter indeed shall be your sorrow. And to Telemachus, here before all, I give this warning. Let him instruct his mother to go to her father's house. They there shall make the wedding and arrange the many gifts which should accompany a well-loved child; for not, I think, till then will the sons of the Achaeans quit their rough courtship. No fear have we of any man, not even of Telemachus, so full of talk. Nothing we care for auguries which you, old man, idly declare, making yourself the most detested. So now again, his substance shall be miserably devoured, and no return be made, so long as she delays the Achaeans with her marriage. Moreover, waiting here day after day, as rivals for her charms, we will not seek out other women whom it might well become a man to marry."

Then answered him discreet Telemachus: "Eurymachus, and all you other lordly suitors, this will I urge no longer; I have no more to say; for now the gods and all the Achaeans understand. But give me a swift ship with twenty comrades, to help me make a journey up and down the sea; for I will go to Sparta and to sandy Pylos, to learn about the coming home of my long-absent father. Perhaps some man may tell me, or I may catch a rumor sent from Zeus, which oftenest carries tidings. If I shall hear my father is alive and coming home, worn as I am, I might endure for one year more. But if I hear that he is dead—no longer with the living—I will at once return to my own native land, and pile his mound and pay the funeral rites, full many, as are due, and I will give my mother to a husband."

So saying, he sat down; and up rose Mentor, who was the friend of gallant Odysseus. On going with the ships, Odysseus gave him charge of all his house, that they should heed their elder and he keep all things secure. He with good will addressed them thus, and said:

"Hearken now, men of Ithaca, to what I say. Never again let sceptered king in all sincerity be kind and gentle, nor let him in his mind heed righteousness. Let him instead ever be stern, and work unrighteous deeds; since none remembers princely Odysseus among the people whom he ruled, kind father though he was. Yet I make no complaint against the haughty suitors for doing deeds of violence in insolence of heart; for they at hazard of their heads thus violently devour the household of Odysseus, saying he comes no more. But with the rest of the people I am wroth, because you all sit still, and, uttering not a word, you do not stop the suitors—they so few and you so many."

Then answered him Evenor's son, Leiocritus: "Infernal Mentor, crazy-witted, what do you mean by urging these to stop us? Hard would it be, for many more than we, to fight with us on question of our food! Indeed, should Ithacan Odysseus come himself upon us lordly suitors feasting in his house, and be resolved at heart to drive us from the hall, his wife would have no joy, however great her longing, over his coming; but here he should meet shameful death, fighting with more than he. You spoke unwisely! Come, people, then, turn to your own affairs! For this youth here, Mentor shall speed his voyage, and Halitherses too, for they are from of old his father's friends; but I suspect he still will sit about, gather his news in Ithaca, and never make the voyage."

He spoke, and hastily dissolved the assembly. So they dispersed, each to his house; but the suitors sought the house of princely Odysseus.

Telemachus, however, walked alone along the shore, and, washing his hands in the foaming water, prayed to Athene: "Hear me, thou god who camest yesterday here to our home, and badest me go on shipboard over the misty sea to ask about the coming home of my long-absent father. All thy commands the Achaeans hinder, the suitors most of all in wicked insolence."

So spoke he in his prayer, and near him came Athene, likened to Mentor in her form and voice, and speaking in winged words she said:

"Telemachus, henceforth you shall not be a base man nor a foolish, if in you stirs the brave soul of your father, and you like him can give effect to deed and word. Then shall this voyage not be vain and ineffective. But if you are no son of him and of Penelope, then am I hopeless of your gaining what you seek. Few sons are like their fathers; most are worse, few better than the father. Yet because you henceforth will not be base nor foolish, nor has the wisdom of Odysseus wholly failed you, therefore there is a hope you will one day accomplish all. Disregard, then, the thoughts and plans of the mad suitors, for they are in no way wise or upright men. Nothing they know of death and the dark doom which now is near, so that they all shall perish in a day. But for yourself, the journey you desire shall not be long delayed. So truly am I your father's friend, I will provide you a swift ship and be myself your comrade. But go you to the palace, mix with the suitors, and prepare the stores, securing all in vessels—wine in jars, and barley-meal, men's marrow, in tight skins —while I about the town will soon collect a willing crew. The ships are many in sea-girt Ithaca, ships new and old. Of these I will select the best, and quickly making ready we will sail the open sea."

So spoke Athene, daughter of Zeus. No longer then lingered Telemachus when he heard the goddess speak. He hastened to the house, though with a heavy heart, and at the palace found the haughty suitors flaying goats and singeing swine within the court. Antinoüs laughingly came forward to Telemachus, and holding him by the hand he spoke, and thus addressed him:

"Telemachus, of the lofty tongue and the unbridled temper, do not again grow sore in heart at what we do or say! No, eat and drink just as you used to do. All you have asked, of course, the Achaeans will provide—the ship and the picked crew—to help you quickly find your way to hallowed Pylos, seeking for tidings of your noble father."

Then answered him discreet Telemachus: "Antinoüs, it is not possible to sit at table quietly with you rude man and calmly take my ease. Was it not quite enough that in the days gone by you suitors wasted much good property of mine, while I was still a helpless child? But now that I am grown and hear and understand what people say, the spirit swells within me, and I will try to bring upon your heads an evil doom whether I go to Pylos or remain here in this land. But go I will—not vain shall be the voyage of which I speak—a passenger with others, since I can have command of neither ship nor crew. And this was what a while ago you judged was best."

He spoke, and from the hand of Antinoüs quietly drew his own. Meanwhile, the suitors in the house were busy at their meal. They mocked him, jeering at him in their talk, and a rude youth would say:

"Really, Telemachus is plotting for our ruin! He will bring champions from sandy Pylos, or even from Sparta, so deeply is he stirred; or else he means to go to Ephyra, that fruitful land, and fetch thence deadly drugs to drop into our wine-bowl and so destroy us all."

Then would another rude youth answer thus: "If he goes off upon a hollow ship and wanders far from friends, who knows but he too may be lost just as Odysseus was! And that would make us more ado; for all his goods we then must share, and to his mother give the house, for her to keep—her and the man who marries her."

So ran their talk. Meanwhile Telemachus passed down the house into his father's large and high-roofed chamber, where in a pile lay gold and bronze, clothing in chests, and stores of fragrant oil. Great jars of old delicious wine were standing there, holding within pure liquor fit for gods, in order ranged along the wall, in case Odysseus, after all his woes, ever came home again. Shut were the folding-doors, close-fitting, double; and here both night and day a housewife stayed, who in her watchful wisdom guarded all—Eurycleia, daughter of Ops, Peisenor's son. To her now spoke Telemachus, calling her to the room:

"Good nurse, come draw me wine in jars, sweet wine that is the choicest next to the wine you keep, thinking that ill-starred man will one day come—high-born Odysseus—safe from death and doom. Fill twelve and fit them all with covers. Then pour me barley into well-sewn sacks. Let there be twenty measures of ground barley-meal. None but yourself must know. Get all together, and I tonight will fetch them, so soon as my mother goes to her chamber seeking rest; for I am going to Sparta and to sandy Pylos, to try to learn of my dear father's coming."

As he said this, his dear nurse Eurycleia cried aloud and sorrowfully said in winged words: "Ah, my dear child, how came such notions in your mind? Where will you go through the wide world, our only one, our darling! High-born Odysseus is already dead, far from his home in some strange land. And now these men, the instant you are gone, will plot against you harm, that you by stealth may be cut off, and they thus share with one another all things here. No, stay you here at ease among your own! You have no need to suffer hardship, roaming over barren seas."

Then answered her discreet Telemachus: "Courage, good nurse! for not without God's warrant is my purpose. But swear to speak no word of this to my dear mother until the eleventh or twelfth day comes, or until she shall miss me and hear that I am gone, that so she may not stain her beautiful face with tears."

Thus did he speak, and the old woman swore by the gods a solemn oath. Then after she had sworn and ended all that oath, she straightway drew him wine in jars, and poured him barley into well-sewn sacks. Telemachus, meanwhile, passed to the house and joined the suitors.

Now a new plan the goddess formed, clear-eyed Athene. In likeness of Telemachus, she went through the town, and, approaching one and another man, gave them the word, bidding them meet by the swift ship at eventide. Noëmon next, the gallant son of Phronius, she begged for a swift ship; and this he freely promised.

Now the sun sank and all the ways grew dark. And now she drew the swift ship to the sea and put in all the gear that well-benched vessels carry; she moored her by the harbor's mouth; the good crew gathered roundabout, and the goddess gave them zeal.

Then a new plan the goddess formed, clear-eyed Athene. She hastened to the house of princely Odysseus, there on the suitors poured sweet sleep, confused them as they drank, and made the cups fall from their hands. They hurried off to rest throughout the town, and did not longer tarry, for sleep fell on their eyelids. Then to Telemachus spoke clear-eyed Athene, calling him forth before the stately hall, likened to Mentor in her form and voice:

"Telemachus, already your mailed comrades sit at the oar and wait your starting. Come, let us go, and not lose time upon the way."

Saying this, Pallas Athene led the way in haste, and he walked after in the footsteps of the goddess. But when they came to the ship and to the sea, they found upon the shore their long-haired comrades, to whom thus spoke revered Telemachus:

"Come, friends, and let us fetch the stores; all are collected at the hall. My mother knows of nothing, nor do the handmaids either. One alone had my orders."

John Flaxman

In guise of Mentor Athene led the way, and he followed after in the footsteps of the goddess.

So saying he led the way, the others followed after; and bringing all the stores into their well-benched ship they stowed them there, even as the dear son of Odysseus ordered. Then came Telemachus aboard; but Athene led the way, and at the vessel's stern she sat her down, while close at hand Telemachus was seated. The others loosed the cables, and coming aboard themselves took places at the pins. A favorable wind clear-eyed Athene sent, a brisk west wind that sang along the wine-dark sea. And now Telemachus, inspiriting his men, bade them lay hold upon the tackling, and they hearkened to his call. Raising the pinewood mast, they set it in the hollow socket, binding it firm with forestays, and tightened the white sail with twisted oxhide thongs. The wind swelled out the belly of the sail, and round the stem loudly the rippling water roared as the ship started. Onward she sped, forcing a passage through the waves. Making the tackling fast throughout the swift black ship, the men brought bowls brimming with wine, and to the gods that never die and never have been born, they poured it forth—chiefest of all to her, the clear-eyed child of Zeus. So through the night and early dawn did the ship cleave her way.

THE ADVENTURES OF ODYSSEUS

Retold by PADRIC COLUM

Illustrations by John Flaxman

I

EVER mindful was Pallas Athene of Odysseus although she might not help him openly because of a wrong he had done Poseidon, the god of the sea. But she spoke at the council of the

John Flaxman

Hermes, Zeus, and Athene in council.

gods, and she won from Zeus a pledge that Odysseus would now be permitted to return to his own land. On that day she went to Ithaca, and, appearing to Telemachus, moved him, as has been told, to go on the voyage in search of his father. And on that day, too, Hermes, by the will of Zeus, went to Ogygia—to that Island where, as the Ancient One of the sea had shown Menelaus, Odysseus was held by the nymph Calypso.

Beautiful indeed was that Island. All round the cave where Calypso lived was a blossoming wood—alder, poplar and cypress trees were there, and on their branches roosted long-winged birds—falcons

John Flaxman

Calypso knew Hermes and was pleased to see him.

and owls and chattering sea crows. Before the cave was a soft meadow in which thousands of violets bloomed, and with four fountains that gushed out of the ground and made clear streams through the grass. Across the cave grew a straggling vine, heavy with clusters of grapes. Calypso was within the cave, and as Hermes came near, he heard her singing one of her magic songs.

She was before a loom weaving the threads with a golden shuttle. Now she knew Hermes and was pleased to see him on her Island, but as soon as he spoke of Odysseus and how it was the will of Zeus that he should be permitted to leave the Island, her song ceased and the golden shuttle fell from her hand.

"Woe to me," she said, "and woe to any immortal who loves a mortal, for the gods are always jealous of their love. I do not hold him here because I hate Odysseus, but because I love him greatly, and would have him dwell with me here—more than this, Hermes, I would make him an immortal so that he would know neither old age nor death."

"He does not desire to be freed from old age and death," said Hermes, "he desires to return to his own land and to live with his dear wife, Penelope, and his son, Telemachus. And Zeus, the greatest of the gods, commands that you let him go upon his way."

"I have no ship to give him," said Calypso, "and I have no company of men to help him to cross the sea."

"He must leave the Island and cross the sea—Zeus commands it," Hermes said.

"I must help him to make his way across the sea if it must be so," Calypso said. Then she bowed her head and Hermes went from her.

Straightway Calypso left her cave and went down to the sea. By the shore Odysseus stayed, looking across the wide sea with tears in his eyes.

She came to him and she said, "Be not sorrowful any more, Odysseus. The time has come when thou mayst depart from my Island. Come now. I will show how I can help thee on thy way."

She brought him to the side of the Island where great trees grew and she put in his hands a double-edged ax and an adze. Then Odysseus started to hew down the timber. Twenty trees he felled with his ax of bronze, and he smoothed them and made straight the line. Calypso came to him at the dawn of the next day; she brought augers for boring and he made the beams fast. He built a raft, making it very broad, and set a mast upon it and fixed a rudder to guide it. To make it more secure, he wove out of osier rods a fence that went from stem to stern as a bulwark against the waves, and he strengthened the bulwark with wood placed behind. Calypso wove him a web of cloth for sails, and these he made very skillfully. Then he fastened the braces and the halyards and sheets, and he pushed the raft with levers down to the sea.

That was on the fourth day. On the fifth Calypso gave him garments for the journey and brought provision down to the raft—two skins of wine and a great skin of water; corn and many dainties. She showed Odysseus how to guide his course by the star that some call the Bear and others the Wain, and she bade farewell to him. He took his place on the raft and set his sail to the breeze and he sailed away from Ogygia, the island where Calypso had held him for so long.

But not easily or safely did he make his way across the sea. The winds blew upon his raft and the waves dashed against it; a fierce blast came and broke the mast in the middle; the sail and the arm-yard fell into the deep. Then Odysseus was flung down on the bottom of the raft. For a long time he lay there overwhelmed by the water that broke over him. The winds drove the raft to and fro—the South wind tossed it to the North to bear it along, and the East wind tossed it to the West to chase.

In the depths of the sea there was a Nymph who saw his toils and his troubles and who had pity upon him. Ino was her name. She rose from the waves in the likeness of a sea gull and she sat upon the raft and she spoke to Odysseus in words.

"Hapless man," she said, "Poseidon, the god of the sea, is still wroth with thee. It may be that the waters will destroy the raft upon which thou sailest. Then there would be no hope for thee. But do what I bid thee and thou shall yet escape. Strip off thy garments and take this veil from me and wind it around thy breast. As long as it is upon thee thou canst not drown. But when thou reachest the mainland loose the veil and cast it into the sea so that it may come back to me."

She gave him the veil, and then, in the likeness of a sea gull, she dived into the sea and the waves closed over her. Odysseus took the veil and wound it around his breast, but he would not leave the raft as long at its timbers held together.

Then a great wave came and shattered the raft. He held himself on a single beam as one holds himself on a horse, and then, with the veil bound across his breast, he threw himself into the waves.

For two nights and two days he was tossed about on the waters. When on the third day the dawn came and the winds fell he saw land very near. He swam eagerly toward it. But when he drew nearer he heard the crash of waves as they struck against rocks that were all covered with foam. Then indeed was Odysseus afraid.

A great wave took hold of him and flung him toward the shore. Now would his bone have been broken upon the rocks if he had not been ready-minded enough to rush toward a rock and to cling to it with both hands until the wave dashed by. Its backward drag took him and carried him back to the deep with the skin stripped from his hands. The waves closed over him. When he rose again he swam round looking for a place where there might be, not rocks, but some easy opening into the land.

At last he saw the mouth of a river. He swam toward it until he felt its stream flowing through the water of the sea. Then in his heart he prayed to the river. "Hear me, O River," was what he said, "I am come to thee as a suppliant, fleeing from the anger of Poseidon, god of the sea. Even by the gods is the man pitied who comes to them as a wanderer and a hapless man. I am thy suppliant, O River; pity me and help me in my need."

Now the river water was smooth for his swimming, and he came safely to its mouth. He came to a place where he might land, but with his flesh swollen and streams of salt water gushing from his mouth and nostrils. He lay on the ground without breath or speech, swooning with the terrible weariness that was upon him. But in a while his breath came back to him and his courage rose. He remembered the veil that the Sea-nymph had given him and he loosened it and let it fall back into the flowing river. A wave came and bore it back to Ino who caught it in her hands.

But Odysseus was still fearful, and he said in his heart, "Ah, me! what is to befall me now? Here am I, naked and forlorn, and I know not amongst what people I am come. And what shall I do with myself when night comes on? If I lie by the river in the frost and dew I may perish of the cold. And if I climb up yonder to the woods and seek refuge in the thickets I may become the prey of wild beasts."

He went from the cold of the river up to the woods, and he found two olive trees growing side by side, twining together so that they made a shelter against the winds. He went and lay between them upon a bed of leaves, and with leaves he covered himself over. There in that shelter, and with that warmth he lay, and sleep came on him, and at last he rested from perils and toils.

II

And while he rested, the goddess, Pallas Athene, went to the City of the Phæacians, to whose land Odysseus had now come.

She came to the palace of the King, and, passing through all the doors, came to the chamber where the King's daughter, Nausicaa slept. She entered into Nausicaa's dream, appearing to her in it as one of her girl-comrades. And in the dream she spoke to the Princess:

"Nausicaa," she said, "the garments of your household are all uncared for, and the time is near when, more than ever, you have need to have much and beautiful raiment. Your marriage day will be soon. You will have to have many garments ready by that time— garments to bring with you to your husband's house, and garments to give to those who will attend you at your wedding. There is much to be done, Nausicaa. Be ready at the break of day, and take your maidens with you, and bring the garments of your household to the river to be washed. I will be your mate in the toil. Beg your father to give you a wagon with mules to carry all the garments that we have need to wash."

So in her dream Pallas Athene spoke to the Princess in the likeness of her girl-comrade. Having put the task of washing into her mind, the goddess left the Palace of the King and the country of the Phæacians.

Nausicaa, when she rose, thought upon her dream, and she went through the Palace and found her father. He was going to the assembly of the Phæacians. She came to him, but she was shy about

speaking of that which had been in her dream—her marriage day—
since her parents had not spoken to her about such a thing. Saying
that she was going to the river to wash the garments of the household, she asked for a wagon and for mules. "So many garments
have I lying soiled," she said. "Yea, and thou too, my father, would
have fresh raiment when you go forth to the assembly of the Phæacians. And in our house are the two unwedded youths, my brothers,
who are always eager for new washed garments wherein to go to
dances." Her father smiled on her and said, "The mules and wagon
thou mayst have, Nausicaa, and the servants shall get them ready for
thee now."

He called to the servants and bade them get ready the mules and
the wagon. Then Nausicaa gathered her maids together and they
brought the soiled garments of the household to the wagon. And
her mother, so that Nausicaa and her maids might eat while they
were from home, put in a basket filled with dainties and a skin of
wine. Also she gave them a jar of olive-oil so that they might rub
themselves with oil when bathing in the river.

Young Nausicaa herself drove the wagon. She mounted it and
took the whip in her hands and started the mules, and then went
through fields and by farms and came to the river bank.

The girls brought the garments to the stream, and leaving them
in the shallow parts trod them with their bare feet. The wagon was
unharnessed and the mules were left to graze along the river side.

Now when they had washed the garments they took them to the
seashore and left them on the clean pebbles to dry in the sun. Then
Nausicaa and her companions went into the river and bathed and
sported in the water.

When they had bathed they sat down and ate the meal that had
been put on the wagon for them. The garments were not yet dried
and Nausicaa called on her companions to play. Straightway they
took a ball and threw it from one to the other, each singing a song
that went with the game. And as they played on the meadow they
made a lovely company, and the Princess Nausicaa was the tallest
and fairest and noblest of them all.

Before they left the river side to load the wagon they played a last

game. The Princess threw the ball, and the girl whose turn it was
to catch missed it. The ball went into the river and was carried
down the stream. At that they all raised a cry. It was this cry that
woke up Odysseus who, covered over with leaves, was then sleeping
in the shelter of the two olive trees.

John Flaxman

And as they played they made a lovely company.

He crept out from the under the thicket, covering his nakedness
with leafy boughs that he broke off the trees. And when he saw
the girls in the meadow he wanted to go to them to beg for their
help. But when they looked at him they were terribly frightened
and they ran this way and that way and hid themselves. Only
Nausicaa stood still, for Pallas Athene had taken fear from her mind.

Odysseus stood a little way from her and spoke to her in a be-
seeching voice. "I supplicate thee, lady, to help me in my bitter need.
I would kneel to thee and clasp thy knees only I fear thine anger.
Have pity upon me. Yesterday was the twentieth day that I was
upon the sea, driven hither and thither by the waves and the winds."

And still Nausicaa stood, and Odysseus looking upon her was
filled with reverence for her, so noble she seemed. "I know not as I

look upon thee," he said, "whether thou art a goddess or a mortal maiden. If thou art a mortal maiden, happy must thy father be and thy mother and thy brothers. Surely they must be proud and glad to see thee in the dance, for thou art the very flower of maidens. And happy above all will he be who will lead thee to his home as his bride. Never have my eyes beheld one who had such beauty and such nobleness. I think thou art like to the young palm tree I once saw springing up by the altar of Apollo in Delos—a tree that many marveled to look at. O lady, after many and sore trials, to thee, first of all the people, have I come. I know that thou wilt be gracious to me. Show me the way to the town. Give me an old garment to cast about me. And may the gods grant thee thy wish and heart's desire —a noble husband who will cherish thee."

She spoke to him as a Princess should, seeing that in spite of the evil plight he was in, he was a man of worth. "Stranger," she said, "since thou hast come to our land, thou shalt not lack for raiment nor aught else that is given to a suppliant. I will show thee the way to the town also."

He asked what land he was in. "This, stranger," she said, "is the land of the Phæacians, and Alcinoüs is King over them. And I am the King's daughter, Nausicaa."

Then she called to her companions. "Do not hide yourselves," she said. "This is not an enemy, but a helpless and an unfriended man. We must befriend him, for it is well said that the stranger and the beggar are from God."

The girls came back and they brought Odysseus to a sheltered place and they made him sit down and laid a garment beside him. One brought the jar of olive oil that he might clean himself when he bathed in the river. And Odysseus was very glad to get this oil, for his back and shoulders were all crusted over with flakes of brine. He went into the river and bathed and rubbed himself with the oil. Then he put on the garment that had been brought him. So well he looked that when he came toward them again the Princess said to the maids:

"Look now on the man who a while ago seemed so terrifying! He is most handsome and stately. Would that we might see more of him. Now, my maidens, bring the stranger meat and drink."

They came to him and they served him with meat and drink and he ate and drank eagerly, for it was long since he had tasted food. And while he ate, Nausicaa and her companions went down to the seashore and gathered the garments that were now dried, singing songs the while. They harnessed the mules and folded the garments and left them on the wagon.

When they were ready to go Nausicaa went to Odysseus and said to him, "Stranger, if thou wouldst make thy way into the city, come with us now, so that we may guide thee. But first listen to what I would say. While we are going through the fields and by the farms

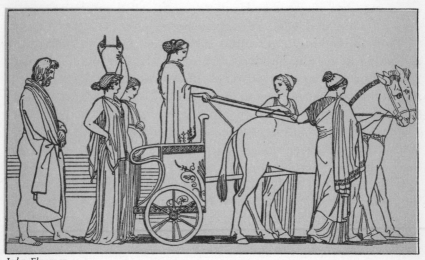

John Flaxman

Odysseus walked behind with the maids.

walk thou behind, keeping near the wagon. But when we enter the ways of the City, go no farther with us. People might speak unkindly of me if they saw me with a stranger such as thou. They might say, 'Whom does Nausicaa bring to her father's house? Someone she would like to make her husband most likely.' So that we may not meet with such rudeness I would have thee come alone to my father's house. Listen now and I will tell thee how thou mayst do this.

"There is a grove kept for the goddess Pallas Athene within a man's shout of the city. In that grove is a spring, and when we come near I would have thee go and rest thyself by it. Then when thou dost think we have come to my father's house, enter the City and ask thy way to the palace of the King. When thou hast come to it, pass quickly through the court and through the great chamber and come to where my mother sits weaving yarn by the light of the fire. My father will be sitting near, drinking his wine in the evening. Pass by his seat and come to my mother, and clasp your hands about her knees and ask for her aid. If she become friendly to thee thou wilt be helped by our people and wilt be given the means of returning to thine own land."

So Nausicaa bade him. Then she touched the mules with the whip and the wagon went on. Odysseus walked with the maids behind. As the sun set they came to the grove that was outside the City—the grove of Pallas Athene. Odysseus went into it and sat by the spring. And while he was in her grove he prayed to the goddess, "Hear me, Pallas Athene, and grant that I may come before the King of this land as one well worthy of his pity and his help."

III

About the time that the maiden Nausicaa had come to her father's house, Odysseus rose up from where he sat by the spring in the grove of Pallas Athene and went into the City. There he met one who showed him the way to the palace of King Alcinoüs. The doors of that place were golden and the doorposts were of silver. And there was a garden by the great door filled with fruitful trees—pear trees and pomegranates; apple trees and trees bearing figs and olives. Below it was a vineyard showing clusters of grapes. That orchard and that vineyard were marvels, for in them never fruit fell or was gathered but other fruit ripened to take its place; from season to season there was fruit for the gathering in the king's close.

Odysseus stood before the threshold of bronze and many thoughts were in his mind. But at last with a prayer to Zeus he crossed the threshold and went through the great hall. Now on that evening the Captains and the Councilors of the Phæacians sat drinking wine with the King. Odysseus passed by them, and stayed not at the King's chair, but went where Arete, the Queen, sat. And he knelt before her and clasped her knees with his hands and spoke in supplication:

"Arete, Queen! After many toils and perils I am come to thee and to thy husband, and to these, thy guests! May the gods give all who are here a happy life and may each see his children in safe possession of his halls. I have come to beg that thou put me on my way to my own land, for long have I suffered far from my friends."

Then, having spoken, Odysseus went and sat down in the ashes of the hearth with his head bowed. No one spoke for long. Then an aged Councilor who was there spoke to the King.

"O Alcinoüs," he said, "it is not right that a stranger should sit in the ashes by thy hearth. Bid the stranger rise now and let a chair be given him and supper set before him."

Then Alcinoüs took Odysseus by the hand, and raised him from where he sat, and bade his son Laodamas give place to him. He sat on a chair inlaid with silver and the house-dame brought him bread and wine and dainties. He ate, and King Alcinoüs spoke to the company and said: "Tomorrow I shall call you together and we will entertain this stranger with a feast in our halls, and we shall take counsel to see in what way we can convoy him to his own land."

The Captains and Councilors assented to this, and then each one arose and went to his own house. Odysseus was left alone in the hall with the King and the Queen. Now Arete, looking closely at Odysseus, recognized the mantle he wore, for she herself had wrought it with her handmaids. And when all the company had gone she spoke to Odysseus and said: "Stranger, who art thou? Didst thou not speak of coming to us from across the deep? And if thou didst come that way, who gave thee the raiment that thou hast on?"

Said Odysseus, "Lady, for seven and ten days I sailed across the deep, and on the eighteenth day I sighted the hills of thy land. But my woes were not yet ended. The storm winds shattered my raft, and when I strove to land the waves overwhelmed me and dashed me against great rocks in a desolate place. At length I came to a river, and I swam through its mouth and I found a shelter from the wind. There I lay amongst the leaves all the night long and from dawn to midday. Then came thy daughter down to the river. I was aware of her playing with her friends, and to her I made my supplication. She gave me bread and wine, and she bestowed these garments upon me, and she showed an understanding far beyond her years."

Then said Alcinoüs the King, "Our daughter did not do well when she did not bring thee straight to our house."

Odysseus said, "My Lord, do not blame the maiden. She bade me follow with her company, and she was only careful that no one should have cause to make ill-judged remarks upon the stranger whom she found."

Then Alcinoüs, the King, praised Odysseus and said that he should like such a man to abide in his house and that he would give him land and wealth, in the country of the Phæacians. "But if it is not thy will to abide with us," he said. "I shall give thee a ship and a company of men to take thee to thy own land, even if that land be as far as Eubœa, which, our men say, is the farthest of all lands." As he said this Odysseus uttered a prayer in his heart, "O Father Zeus, grant that Alcinoüs the King may fulfill all that he has promised—and for that may his fame never be quenched—and that I may come to my own land."

Arete now bade the maids prepare a bed for Odysseus. This they did, casting warm coverlets and purple blankets upon it. And when Odysseus came to the bed and lay in it, after the tossing of the waves, rest in it seemed wonderfully good.

At dawn of day he went with the King to the assembly of the Phæacians. When the Princes and Captains and Councilors were gathered together, Alcinoüs spoke to them saying:

"Princes and Captains and Councilors of the Phæacians! This stranger has come to my house in his wanderings, and he desires us to give him a ship and a company of men, so that he may cross the sea and come to his own land. Let us, as in times past we have done for others, help him in his journey. Nay, let us even now draw down a black ship to the sea, and put two and fifty of our noblest youths upon it, and let us make it ready for the voyage. But before he departs from amongst us, come all of you to a feast that I shall give to this stranger in my house. And moreover, let us take with us the minstrel of our land, blind Demodocus, that his songs may make us glad at the feast."

So the King spoke, and the Princes, Captains and Councilors of the Phæacians went with him to the palace. And at the same time two and fifty youths went down to the shore of the sea, and drew down a ship and placed the masts and sails upon it, and left the oars in their leathern loops. Having done all this they went to the palace where the feast was being given and where many men had gathered.

The henchman led in the minstrel, blind Demodocus. To him the gods had given a good and an evil fortune—the gift of song with the lack of sight. The henchman led him through the company, and placed him on a seat inlaid with silver, and hung his lyre on the pillar above his seat.

When the guests and the minstrel had feasted, blind Demodocus took down the lyre and sang of things that were already famous— of the deeds of Achilles and Odysseus.

Now when he heard the words that the minstrel uttered, Odysseus caught up his purple cloak and drew it over his head. Tears were falling down his cheeks and he was ashamed of their being seen. No one marked his weeping except the King, and the King wondered why his guest should be so moved by what the minstrel related.

When they had feasted and the minstrel had sung to them, Alcinoüs said, "Let us go forth now and engage in games and sports so that our stranger guest may tell his friends when he is amongst them what our young men can do."

All went out from the palace to the place where the games were played. There was a foot race, and there was a boxing-match, and there was wrestling and weight-throwing. All the youths present went into the games. And when the sports were ending Laodamas, the son of King Alcinoüs, said to his friends:

"Come, my friends, and let us ask the stranger whether he is skilled or practised in any sport." And saying this he went to Odysseus and said, "Friend and stranger, come now and try thy skill in the games. Cast care away from thee, for thy journey shall not be long delayed. Even now the ship is drawn down to the sea, and we have with us the company of youths that is ready to help thee to thine own land."

Said Odysseus, "Sorrow is nearer to my heart than sport, for much have I endured in times that are not far past."

Then a youth who was with Laodamas, Euryalus, who had won in the wrestling bout, said insolently, "Laodamas is surely mistaken in thinking that thou shouldst be proficient in sports. As I look at thee I think that thou art one who makes voyages for gain—a trader whose only thought is for his cargo and his gains."

Then said Odysseus with anger. "Thou hast not spoken well, young man. Thou hast beauty surely, but thou hast not grace of manner nor speech. And thou hast stirred the spirit in my breast by speaking to me in such words."

Thereupon, clad as he was in his mantle, Odysseus sprang up and took a weight that was larger than any yet lifted, and with one whirl he flung it from his hands. Beyond all marks it flew, and one who was standing far off cried out, "Even a blind man, stranger, might know that thy weight need not be confused with the others, but lies far beyond them. In this bout none of the Phæacians can surpass thee."

And Odysseus, turning to the youths, said, "Let who will, pass that throw. And if any of you would try with me in boxing or wrestling or even in the foot race, let him stand forward—anyone except Laodamas, for he is of the house that has befriended me. A rude man he would surely be who should strive with his host."

All kept silence. Then Alcinoüs the King said, "So that thou shalt have something to tell thy friends when thou are in thine own land, we shall show thee the games in which we are most skillful. For we Phæacians are not perfect boxers or wrestlers, but we excel all in running and in dancing and in pulling with the oar. Lo, now, ye dancers! Come forward and show your nimbleness, so that the stranger may tell his friends, when he is amongst them, how far we surpass all men in dancing as well as in seamanship and speed of foot."

A place was leveled for the dance, and the blind minstrel, Demodocus, took the lyre in his hands and made music, while youths skilled in the dance struck the ground with their feet. Odysseus as he watched them marveled at their grace and their spirit. When the dance was ended he said to the King, "My Lord Alcinoüs, thou didst boast thy dancers to be the best in the world, and thy word is not to be denied. I wonder as I look upon them."

At the end of the day Alcinoüs spoke to his people and said, "This stranger, in all that he does and says, shows himself to be a wise and a mighty man. Let each of us now give him the stranger's gift. Here there are twelve princes of the Phæacians and I am the thirteenth. Let each of us give him a worthy gift, and then let us go back to my house and sit down to supper. As for Euryalus, let him make amends to the stranger for his rudeness of speech as he offers him his gift."

All assented to the King's words, and Euryalus went to Odysseus and said, "Stranger, if I have spoken aught that offended thee, may the storm winds snatch it and bear it away. May the gods grant that thou shalt see thy wife and come to thine own country. Too long hast thou endured afflictions away from thy friends."

So saying, Euryalus gave Odysseus a sword of bronze with a silver hilt and a sheath of ivory. Odysseus took it and said, "And to you, my friend, may the gods grant all happiness, and mayst thou never miss the sword that thou hast given me. Thy gracious speech hath made full amends."

Each of the twelve princes gave gifts to Odysseus, and the gifts were brought to the palace and left by the side of the Queen. And Arete herself gave Odysseus a beautiful coffer with raiment and gold in it, and Alcinoüs, the King, gave him a beautiful cup, all of gold.

In the palace the bath was prepared for Odysseus, and he entered it and was glad of the warm water, for not since he had left the Island of Calypso did he have a warm bath. He came from the bath and put on the beautiful raiment that had been given him and he walked through the hall, looking a king amongst men.

Now the maiden, Nausicaa, stood by a pillar as he passed, and she knew that she had never looked upon a man who was more splendid. She had thought that the stranger whom she had saved would have stayed in her father's house, and that one day he would be her husband. But now she knew that by no means would he abide in the land of the Phæacians. As he passed by, she spoke to him and said, "Farewell, O Stranger! And when thou art in thine own country, think sometimes of me, Nausicaa, who helped thee." Odysseus took her hand and said to her, "Farewell, daughter of King Alcinoüs! May Zeus grant that I may return to my own land. There every day shall I pay homage to my memory of thee, to whom I owe my life."

He passed on and he came to where the Princes and Captains and Councilors of the Phæacians sat. His seat was beside the King's. Then the henchman brought in the minstrel, blind Demodocus, and placed him on a seat by a pillar. And when supper was served Odysseus sent to Demodocus a portion of his own meat. He spoke, too, in praise of the minstrel saying, "Right well dost thou sing of the Greeks and all they wrought and suffered—as well, methinks, as if thou hadst been present at the war of Troy. I would ask if thou canst sing of the Wooden Horse—that brought destruction to the Trojans. If thou canst, I shall be a witness amongst all men how the gods have surely given thee the gift of song."

Demodocus took down the lyre and sang. His song told how one part of the Greeks sailed away in their ships and how others with Odysseus to lead them were now in the center of Priam's City all hidden in the great Wooden Horse which the Trojans themselves had dragged across their broken wall. So the Wooden Horse stood, and the people gathered around talked of what should be done with so wonderful a thing—whether to break open its timbers, or drag it to a steep hill and hurl it down on the rocks, or leave it there as an offering to the gods. As an offering to the gods it was left at last. Then the minstrel sang how Odysseus and his comrades poured forth from the hollow of the horse and took the City.

As the minstrel sang, the heart of Odysseus melted within him and tears fell down his cheeks. None of the company saw him weeping except Alcinoüs the King. But the King cried out to the company saying, "Let the minstrel cease, for there is one amongst us to whom his song is not pleasing. Ever since it began the stranger here has wept with tears flowing down his cheeks."

The minstrel ceased, and all the company looked in surprise at Odysseus, who sat with his head bowed and his mantle wrapped around his head. Why did he weep? each man asked. No one had asked of him his name, for each thought it was more noble to serve a stranger without knowing his name.

Said the King, speaking again, "In a brother's place stands the stranger and the suppliant, and as a brother art thou to us, O unknown guest. But wilt thou not be brotherly to us? Tell us by what name they call thee in thine own land. Tell us, too, of thy land and thy city. And tell us, too, where thou wert borne on thy wanderings, and to what lands and peoples thou camest. And as a brother tell us why thou dost weep and mourn in spirit over the tale of the going forth of the Greeks to the war of Troy. Didst thou have a kinsman who fell before Priam's City—a daughter's husband, or a wife's father, or someone nearer by blood? Or didst thou have a loving friend who fell there—one with an understanding heart who was to thee as a brother?"

Such questions the King asked, and Odysseus taking the mantle from around his head turned round to the company.

IV

Then Odysseus spoke before the company and said, "O Alcinoüs, famous King, it is good to listen to a minstrel such as Demodocus is. And as for me, I know of no greater delight than when men feast together with open hearts, when tables are plentifully spread, when wine-bearers pour out good wine into cups, and when a minstrel sings to them noble songs. This seems to me to be happiness indeed. But thou hast asked me to speak of my wanderings and my toils. Ah, where can I begin that tale? For the gods have given me more woes than a man can speak of!

"But first of all I will declare to you my name and my country. I am ODYSSEUS, SON OF LAERTES, and my land is Ithaca, an island around which many islands lie. Ithaca is a rugged isle, but a good nurse of hardy men, and I, for one, have found that there is no place fairer than a man's own land. But now I will tell thee, King, and tell the Princes and Captains and Councilors of the Phæacians, the tale of my wanderings.

"The wind bore my ships from the coast of Troy, and with our white sails hoisted we came to the cape that is called Malea. Now if we had been able to double this cape we should soon have come to our own country, all unhurt. But the north wind came and swept us from our course and drove us wandering past Cythera.

"Then for nine days we were borne onward by terrible winds, and away from all known lands. On the tenth day we came to a strange country. Many of my men landed there. The people of that land were harmless and friendly, but the land itself was most danger-ous. For there grew there the honey-sweet fruit of the lotus that makes all men forgetful of their past and neglectful of their future. And those of my men who ate the lotus that the dwellers of that land offered them became forgetful of their country and of the way before them. They wanted to abide forever in the land of the lotus. They wept when they thought of all the toils before them and of all they had endured. I led them back to the ships, and I had to place them beneath the benches and leave them in bonds. And I com-manded those who had not eaten of the lotus to go at once aboard the ships. Then, when I had got all my men upon the ships, we made haste to sail away.

"Later we came to the land of the Cyclopes, a giant people. There is a waste island outside the harbor of their land, and on it there is a well of bright water that has poplars growing round it. We came to that empty island, and we beached our ships and took down our sails.

"As soon as the dawn came we went through the empty island, starting the wild goats that were there in flocks, and shooting them with our arrows. We killed so many wild goats there that we had nine for each ship. Afterwards we looked across to the land of the Cyclopes, and we heard the sound of voices and saw the smoke of fires and heard the bleating of flocks of sheep and goats.

"I called my companions together and I said, 'It would be well for some of us to go to that other island. With my own ship and with the company that is on it I shall go there. The rest of you abide here. I will find out what manner of men live there, and whether they will treat us kindly and give us gifts that are due to strangers—gifts of provisions for our voyage.'

"We embarked and we came to the land. There was a cave near the sea, and round the cave there were mighty flocks of sheep and goats. I took twelve men with me and I left the rest to guard the ship. We went into the cave and found no man there. There were baskets filled with cheeses, and vessels of whey, and pails and bowls of milk. My men wanted me to take some of the cheeses and drive off some of the lambs and kids and come away. But this I would not do, for I would rather that he who owned the stores would give us of his own free will the offerings that were due to strangers.

"While we were in the cave, he whose dwelling it was returned to it. He carried on his shoulder a great pile of wood for his fire. Never in our lives did we see a creature so frightful as this Cyclops was. He was a giant in size, and, what made him terrible to behold, he had but one eye, and that single eye was in his forehead. He cast down on the ground the pile of wood that he carried, making such a din that we fled in terror into the corners and recesses of the cave. Next he drove his flocks into the cave and began to milk his ewes and goats. And when he had the flocks within, he took up a stone that not all our strengths could move and set it as a door to the mouth of the cave.

"The Cyclops kindled his fire, and when it blazed up he saw us in the corners and recesses. He spoke to us. We knew not what he said, but our hearts were shaken with terror at the sound of his deep voice.

"I spoke to him saying that we were Agamemnon's men on our way home from the taking of Priam's City, and I begged him to deal with us kindly, for the sake of Zeus who is ever in the company of strangers and suppliants. But he answered me saying, 'We Cyclopes pay no heed to Zeus, nor to any of thy gods. In our strength and our power we deem that we are mightier than they. I will not spare thee, neither will I give thee aught for the sake of Zeus, but only as my own spirit bids me. And first I would have thee tell me how thou camest to our land.'

"I knew it would be better not to let the Cyclops know that my ship and my companions were at the harbor of the island. Therefore I spoke to him guilefully, telling him that my ship had been broken on the rocks, and that I and the men with me were the only ones who had escaped utter doom.

"I begged him again that he would deal with us as just men deal with strangers and suppliants, but he, without saying a word, laid hands upon two of my men, and swinging them by the legs, dashed their brains out on the earth. He then cut them to pieces and ate them before our very eyes. We wept and we prayed to Zeus as we witnessed a deed so terrible.

"Next the Cyclops stretched himself amongst his sheep and went to sleep beside the fire. Then I debated whether I should take my sharp sword in my hand, and feeling where his heart was, stab him there. But second thoughts held me back from doing this. I might be able to kill him as he slept, but not even with my companions could I roll away the great stone that closed the mouth of the cave.

"Dawn came, and the Cyclops awakened, kindled his fire and milked his flocks. Then he seized two others of my men and made ready for his midday meal. And now he rolled away the great stone and drove his flocks out of the cave.

"I had pondered on a way of escape, and I had thought of something that might be done to baffle the Cyclops. I had with me a great skin of sweet wine, and I thought that if I could make him drunken with wine I and my companions might be able for him. But there were other preparations to be made first. On the floor of the cave there was a great beam of olive wood which the Cyclops had cut to make a club when the wood would be seasoned. It was yet green. I and my companions went and cut off a fathom's length of the wood, and sharpened it to a point and took it to the fire and hardened it in the glow. Then I hid the beam in a recess of the cave.

"The Cyclops came back in the evening, and opening up the cave drove in his flocks. Then he closed the cave again with the stone and went and milked his ewes and his goats. Again he seized two of my companions. I went to the terrible creature with a bowl of wine in my hands. He took it and drank it and cried out, 'Give me another bowl of this, and tell me thy name that I may give thee gifts for bringing me this honey-tasting drink.'

"Again I spoke to him guilefully and said, 'No-man is my name. No-man my father and my mother call me.'

"'Give me more of the drink, No-man,' he shouted. 'And the gift that I shall give to thee is that I shall make thee the last of thy fellows to be eaten.'

John Flaxman

"Give me more of the drink, No-man," he shouted.

"I gave him wine again, and when he had taken the third bowl he sank backwards with his face upturned, and sleep came upon him. Then I, with four companions, took that beam of olive wood, now made into a hard and pointed stake, and thrust it into the ashes of the fire. When the pointed end began to glow we drew it out of the flame. Then I and my companions laid hold of the great stake and, dashing at the Cyclops, thrust it into his eye. He raised a terrible cry that made the rocks ring and we dashed away into the recesses of the cave.

"His cries brought other Cyclopes to the mouth of the cave, and they, naming him as Polyphemus, called out and asked him what ailed him to cry. 'No-man,' he shrieked out, 'No-man is slaying me by guile.' They answered him saying, 'If no man is slaying thee, there is nothing we can do for thee, Polyphemus. What ails thee has been sent to thee by the gods.' Saying this, they went away from the mouth of the cave without attempting to move away the stone.

"Polyphemus then, groaning with pain, rolled away the stone and sat before the mouth of the cave with his hands outstretched, thinking that he would catch us as we dashed out. I showed my companions how we might pass by him. I laid hands on certain rams of the flock and I lashed three of them together with supple rods. Then on the middle ram I put a man of my company. Thus every three rams carried a man. As soon as the dawn had come the rams hastened out to the pasture, and, as they passed, Polyphemus laid hands on the first and third of each three that went by. They passed out and Polyphemus did not guess that a ram that he did not touch carried out a man.

"For myself, I took a ram that was the strongest and fleeciest of the whole flock and I placed myself under him, clinging to the wool of his belly. As this ram, the best of all his flock, went by, Polyphemus, laying his hands upon him, said, 'Would that you, the best of my flock, were endowed with speech, so that you might tell me where No-man, who has blinded me, has hidden himself.' The ram went by him, and when he had gone a little way from the cave I loosed myself from him and went and set my companions free.

"We gathered together many of Polyphemus' sheep and we drove them down to our ship. The men we had left behind would have wept when they heard what had happened to six of their companions. But I bade them take on board the sheep we had brought and pull the ship away from that land. Then when we had drawn a certain distance from the shore I could not forbear to shout my taunts into the cave of Polyphemus.

"Cyclops," I cried, 'you thought that you had the company of a fool and a weakling to eat. But you have been worsted by me, and your evil deeds have been punished.'

"So I shouted, and Polyphemus came to the mouth of the cave with great anger in his heart. He took up rocks and cast them at the ship and they fell before the prow. The men bent to the oars and pulled the ship away or it would have been broken by the rocks he cast. And when we were farther away I shouted to him:

" 'Cyclops, if any man should ask who it was set his mark upon you, say that he was Odysseus, the son of Laertes.'

"Then I heard Polyphemus cry out, 'I call upon Poseidon, the god of the sea, whose son I am, to avenge me upon you, Odysseus. I call upon Poseidon to grant that you, Odysseus, may never come to your home, or if the gods have ordained your return, that you come to it after much toil and suffering, in an evil plight and in a stranger's ship, to find sorrow in your home.'

"So Polyphemus prayed, and, to my evil fortune, Poseidon heard his prayer. But we went on in our ship rejoicing at our escape. We came to the waste island where my other ships were. All the company rejoiced to see us, although they had to mourn for their six companions slain by Polyphemus. We divided amongst the ships the sheep we had taken from Polyphemus' flock and we sacrificed to the gods. At the dawn of the next day we raised the sails on each ship and we sailed away.

V

"We came to the island where Æolus, the Lord of the Winds, he who can give mariners a good or a bad wind, has his dwelling. With his six sons and his six daughters Æolus lives on a floating island that has all around it a wall of bronze. And when we came to his island, the Lord of the Winds treated us kindly and kept us at his dwelling for a month. Now when the time came for us to leave, Æolus did not try to hold us on the island. And to me, when I was going down to the ships, he gave a bag made from the hide of an ox, and in that bag were all the winds that blow. He made the mouth of the bag fast with a silver thong, so that no wind that might drive us from our course could escape. Then he sent the West Wind to blow on our sails that we might reach our own land as quickly as a ship might go.

"For nine days we sailed with the West Wind driving us, and on the tenth day we came in sight of Ithaca, our own land. We saw its coast and the beacon fires upon the coast and the people tending the fires. Then I thought that the curse of the Cyclops was vain and could bring no harm to us. Sleep that I had kept from me for long I let weigh me down, and I no longer kept watch.

"Then even as I slept, the misfortune that I had watched against fell upon me. For now my men spoke together and said, 'There is our native land, and we come back to it after ten years' struggles and toils, with empty hands. Different is it with our lord, Odysseus. He brings gold and silver from Priam's treasure-chamber in Troy. And Æolus, too, has given him a treasure in an ox-hide bag. But let us take something out of that bag while he sleeps.'

"So they spoke, and they unloosed the mouth of the bag, and behold! all the winds that were tied in it burst out. Then the winds drove our ship toward the high seas and away from our land. What became of the other ships I know not. I awoke and I found that we were being driven here and there by the winds. I did not know whether I should spring into the sea and so end all my troubles, or whether I should endure this terrible misfortune. I muffled my head in my cloak and lay on the deck of my ship.

"The winds brought us back again to the floating island. We landed and I went to the dwelling of the Lord of the Winds. I sat by the pillars of his threshold and he came out and spoke to me. 'How now, Odysseus?' said he. 'How is it thou hast returned so soon? Did I not give thee a fair wind to take thee to thine own country, and did I not tie up all the winds that might be contrary to thee?'

"'My evil companions,' I said, 'have been my bane. They have undone all the good that thou didst for me, O King of the Winds. They opened the bag and let all the winds fly out. And now help me, O Lord Æolus, once again.'

"But Æolus said to me, 'Far be it from me to help such a man as thou—a man surely accursed by the gods. Go from my Island, for nothing will I do for thee.' Then I went from his dwelling and took my way down to the ship.

"We sailed away from the Island of Æolus with heavy hearts. Next we came to the Æean Island, where we met with Circe, the Enchantress. For two days and two nights we were on that island without seeing the sign of a habitation. On the third day I saw smoke rising up from some hearth. I spoke of it to my men, and it seemed good to us that part of our company should go to see were there people there who might help us. We drew lots to find out who should go, and it fell to the lot of Eurylochus to go with part of the company, while I remained with the other part.

"So Eurylochus went with two and twenty men. In the forest glades they came upon a house built of polished stones. All around that house wild beasts roamed—wolves and lions. But these beasts were not fierce. As Eurylochus and his men went toward the house the lions and wolves fawned upon them like house dogs.

"But the men were affrighted and stood round the outer gate of the court. They heard a voice within the house singing, and it seemed to them to be the voice of a woman, singing as she went to and fro before a web she was weaving on a loom. The men shouted, and she who had been singing opened the polished doors and came out of the dwelling. She was very fair to see. As she opened the doors of the house she asked the men to come within and they went into her halls.

"But Eurylochus tarried behind. He watched the woman and he saw her give food to the men. But he saw that she mixed a drug with what she gave them to eat and with the wine she gave them to drink. No sooner had they eaten the food and drunk the wine than she struck them with a wand, and behold! the men turned into swine. Then the woman drove them out of the house and put them in the swine-pens and gave them acorns and mast and the fruit of the cornel tree to eat.

"Eurylochus, when he saw these happenings, ran back through

the forest and told me all. Then I cast about my shoulder my good sword of bronze, and, bidding Eurylochus to stay by the ships, I went through the forest and came to the house of the enchantress. I stood at the outer court and called out. Then Circe the Enchantress flung wide the shining doors, and called to me to come within. I entered her dwelling and she brought me to a chair and put a foot-stool under my feet. Then she brought me in a golden cup the wine into which she had cast a harmful drug.

"As she handed me the cup I drew my sword and sprang at her as one eager to slay her. She shrank back from me and cried out, 'Who art thou who art able to guess at my enchantments? Verily, thou art Odysseus, of whom Hermes told me. Nay, put up thy sword and let us two be friendly to each other. In all things I will treat thee kindly.'

"But I said to her, 'Nay, Circe, thou must swear to me first that thou wilt not treat me guilefully.'

"She swore by the gods that she would not treat me guilefully, and I put up my sword. Then the handmaidens of Circe prepared a bath, and I bathed and rubbed myself with olive oil, and Circe gave me a new mantle and doublet. The handmaidens brought out silver tables, and on them set golden baskets with bread and meat in them, and others brought cups of honey-tasting wine. I sat before a silver table but I had no pleasure in the food before me.

"When Circe saw me sitting silent and troubled she said, 'Why, Odysseus, dost thou sit like a speechless man? Dost thou think there is a drug in this food? But I have sworn that I will not treat thee guilefully, and that oath I shall keep.'

"And I said to her, 'O Circe, Enchantress, what man of good heart could take meat and drink while his companions are as swine in swine-pens? If thou wouldst have me eat and drink, first let me see my companions in their own forms.'

"Circe, when she heard me say this, went to the swine-pen and anointed each of the swine that was there with a charm. As she did, the bristles dropped away and the limbs of the man were seen. My companions became men again, and were even taller and handsomer than they had been before.

"After that we lived on Circe's island in friendship with the enchantress. She did not treat us guilefully again and we feasted in her house for a year.

John Flaxman
"Why, Odysseus, dost thou sit speechless? Dost thou think there is a drug in this food?"

"But in all of us there was a longing to return to our own land. And my men came to me and craved that I should ask Circe to let us go on our homeward way. She gave us leave to go and she told us of the many dangers we should meet on our voyage.

VI

"When the sun sank and darkness came on, my men went to lie by the hawsers on the ship. Then Circe the Enchantress took my hand, and making me sit down by her, told me of the voyage that was before us.

"'To the Sirens first you shall come,' she said, 'to the Sirens, who sit in their field of flowers and bewitch all men who come near them. He who comes near the Sirens without knowing their ways and hears the sound of their voices—never again shall that man see wife or child, or have joy of his home-coming. All round where the Sirens sit are great heaps of the bones of men. But I will tell thee, Odysseus, how thou mayst pass them.

" 'When thou comest near put wax over the ears of thy company lest any of them hear the Sirens' song. But if thou thyself art minded to hear, let thy company bind thee hand and foot to the mast. And if thou shalt beseech them to loose thee, then must they bind thee with tighter bonds. When thy companions have driven the ship past where the Sirens sing then thou canst be unbound.

" 'Past where the Sirens sit there is a dangerous place indeed. On one side there are great rocks which the gods call the Rocks Wandering. No ship ever escapes that goes that way. And round these rocks the planks of ships and the bodies of men are tossed by waves of the sea and storms of fire. One ship only ever passed that way, Jason's ship, the Argo, and that ship would have been broken on the rocks if Hera the goddess had not helped it to pass, because of her love for the hero Jason.

" 'On the other side of the Rocks Wandering are two peaks through which thou wilt have to take thy ship. One peak is smooth and sheer and goes up to the clouds of heaven. In the middle of it there is a cave, and that cave is the den of a monster named Scylla. This monster has six necks and on each neck there is a hideous head. She holds her heads over the gulf, seeking for prey and yelping horribly. No ship has ever passed that way without Scylla seizing and carrying off in each mouth of her six heads the body of a man.

" 'The other peak is near. Thou couldst send an arrow across to it from Scylla's den. Out of the peak a fig tree grows, and below that fig tree Charybdis has her den. She sits there sucking down the water and spouting it forth. Mayst thou not be near when she sucks the water down, for then nothing could save thee. Keep nearer to Scylla's than to Charybdis' rock. It is better to lose six of your company than to lose thy ship and all thy company. Keep near Scylla's rock and drive right on.

" 'If thou shouldst win past the deadly rocks guarded by Scylla

and Charybdis thou wilt come to the Island of Thrinacia. There the
Cattle of the Sun graze with immortal nymphs to guard them. If
thou comest to that Island, do no hurt to those herds. If thou doest
hurt to them I foresee ruin for thy ship and thy men, even though
thou thyself shouldst escape.'

"So Circe spoke to me, and having told me such things she took
her way up the island. Then I went to the ship and roused my men.
Speedily they went aboard, and, having taken their seats upon the
benches, struck the water with their oars. Then the sails were hoisted
and a breeze came and we sailed away from the Isle of Circe, the
Enchantress.

"I told my companions what Circe had told me about the Sirens
in their field of flowers. I took a great piece of wax and broke it and
kneaded it until it was soft. Then I covered the ears of my men, and
they bound me upright to the mast of the ship. The wind dropped
and the sea became calm as though a god had stilled the waters.
My company took their oars and pulled away. When the ship was
within a man's shout from the land we had come near, the Sirens
espied us and raised their song.

"'Come hither, come hither, O Odysseus,' the Sirens sang, 'stay
thy bark and listen to our song. None hath ever gone this way in
his ship until he hath heard from our own lips the voice sweet as
a honeycomb, and hath joy of it, and gone on his way a wiser man.
We know all things—all the travail the Greeks had in the war of
Troy, and we know all that hereafter shall be upon the earth.
Odysseus, Odysseus, come to our field of flowers, and hear the song
that we shall sing to thee.'

"My heart was mad to listen to the Sirens. I nodded my head to
the company commanding them to unloose me, but they bound me
the tighter, and bent to their oars and rowed on. When we had gone
past the place of the Sirens the men took the wax from off their ears
and loosed me from the mast.

"But no sooner had we passed the Island than I saw smoke arising
and heard the roaring of the sea. My company threw down their
oars in terror. I went amongst them to hearten them, and I made
them remember how, by my device, we had escaped from the Cave

of the Cyclops. I told them nothing of the monster Scylla, lest the fear of her should break their hearts. And now we began to drive through the narrow strait. On one side was Scylla and on the other Charybdis. Fear gripped the men when they saw Charybdis gulping down the sea. But as we drove by, the monster Scylla seized six of my company—the hardiest of the men who were with me. As they were lifted up in the mouths of her six heads they called to me in their agony. But I could do nothing to aid them. They were carried up to be devoured in the monster's den. Of all the sights I have seen on the ways of the water, that sight was the most pitiful.

"Having passed the rocks of Scylla and Charybdis we came to the Island of Thrinacia. While we were yet on the ship I heard the lowing of the Cattle of the Sun. I spoke to my company and told them that we should drive past that Island and not venture to go upon it.

"The hearts of my men were broken within them at that sentence, and Eurylochus answered me, speaking sadly.

"'It is easy for thee, O Odysseus, to speak like that, for thou art never weary, and thou hast strength beyond measure. But is thy heart, too, of iron that thou wilt not suffer thy companions to set foot upon shore where they may rest themselves from the sea and prepare their supper at their ease?'

"So Eurylochus spoke and the rest of the company joined in what he said. Their force was greater than mine. Then said I, 'Swear to me a mighty oath, one and all of you, that if we go upon this Island none of you will slay the cattle out of any herd.'

"They swore the oath that I gave them. We brought our ship to a harbor, and landed near a spring of fresh water, and the men got their supper ready. Having eaten their supper they fell to weeping, for they thought upon their comrades that Scylla had devoured. Then they slept.

"The dawn came, but we found that we could not take our ship out of the harbor, for the North Wind and the East Wind blew a hurricane. So we stayed upon the Island and the days and the weeks went by. When the corn we had brought in the ship was all

eaten the men went through the island fishing and hunting. Little
they got to stay their hunger.

"One day while I slept, Eurylochus gave the men a most evil
counsel. 'Every death,' he said, 'is hateful to man, but death by
hunger is by far the worst. Rather than die of hunger let us drive off
the best cattle from the herds of the Sun. Then, if the gods would
wreck us on the sea for the deed, let them do it. I would rather
perish on the waves than die in the pangs of hunger.'

"So he spoke, and the rest of the men approved of what he said.
They slaughtered them and roasted their flesh. It was then that I
awakened from my sleep. As I came down to the ship the smell of
the roasting flesh came to me. Then I knew that a terrible deed had
been committed and that a dreadful thing would befall all of us.

"For six days my company feasted on the best of the cattle. On
the seventh day the winds ceased to blow. Then we went to the ship
and set up the mast and the sails and fared out again on the deep.

"But, having left that island, no other land appeared, and only
sky and sea were to be seen. A cloud stayed always above our ship
and beneath that cloud the sea was darkened. The West Wind came
in a rush, and the mast broke, and, in breaking, struck off the head
of the pilot, and he fell straight down into the sea. A thunderbolt
struck the ship and the men were swept from the deck. Never a man
of my company did I see again.

"The West Wind ceased to blow but the South Wind came and
it drove the ship back on its course. It rushed toward the terrible
rocks of Scylla and Charybdis. All night long I was borne on, and,
at the rising of the sun, I found myself near Charybdis. My ship was
sucked down. But I caught the branches of the fig tree that grew out
of the rock and hung to it like a bat. There I stayed until the timbers
of my ship were cast up again by Charybdis. I dropped down on
them. Sitting on the boards I rowed with my hands and passed the
rock of Scylla without the monster seeing me.

"Then for nine days I was borne along by the waves, and on the
tenth day I came to Ogygia where the nymph Calypso dwells. She
took me to her dwelling and treated me kindly. But why tell the
remainder of my toils? To thee, O King, and to thy noble wife I

told how I came from Calypso's Island, and I am not one to repeat a plain-told tale."

VII

Odysseus finished, and the company in the hall sat silent, like men enchanted. Then King Alcinoüs spoke and said, "Never, as far as we Phæacians are concerned, wilt thou, Odysseus, be driven from thy homeward way. Tomorrow we will give thee a ship and an escort, and we will land thee in Ithaca, thine own country." The Princes, Captains and Councilors, marveling that they had met the renowned Odysseus, went each to his own home. When the dawn had come, each carried down to the ship on which Odysseus was to sail, gifts for him.

When the sun was near its setting they all came back to the King's hall to take farewell of him. The King poured out a great bowl of wine as an offering to the gods. Then Odysseus rose up and placed in the Queen's hands a two-handled cup, and he said, "Farewell to thee, O Queen! Mayst thou long rejoice in thy house and thy children, and in thy husband, Alcinoüs, the renowned King."

He passed over the threshold of the King's house, and he went down to the ship. He went aboard and lay down on the deck on a sheet and rug that had been spread for him. Straightway the mariners took to their oars, and hoisted their sails, and the ship sped on like a strong sea bird. Odysseus slept. And lightly the ship sped on, bearing that man who had suffered so much sorrow of heart in passing through wars of men and through troublous seas——the ship sped on, and he slept, and was forgetful of all he had passed through.

When the dawn came the ship was near to the Island of Ithaca. The mariners drove to a harbor near which there was a great cave. They ran the ship ashore and lifted out Odysseus, wrapped in the sheet and the rugs, and still sleeping. They left him on the sandy shore of his own land. Then they took the gifts which the King and Queen, the Princes, Captains and Councilors of the Phæacians had given him, and they set them by an olive tree, a little apart from the road, so that no wandering person might come upon them before

Odysseus had awakened. Then they went back to their ship and departed from Ithaca for their own land.

Odysseus awakened on the beach of his own land. A mist lay over all, and he did not know what land he had come to. He thought that the Phæacians had left him forsaken on a strange shore. As he looked around him in his bewilderment he saw one who was like a King's son approaching.

Now the one who came near him was not a young man, but the goddess, Pallas Athene, who had made herself look like a young man. Odysseus arose, and questioned her as to the land he had come to. The goddess answered him and said, "This is Ithaca, a land good for goats and cattle, a land of woods and wells."

Even as she spoke she changed from the semblance of a young man and was seen by Odysseus as a woman tall and fair. "Dost thou not know me, Pallas Athene, the daughter of Zeus, who has always helped thee?" the goddess said. "I would have been more often by thy side, only I did not want to go openly against my brother, Poseidon, the god of the sea, whose son, Polyphemus, thou didst blind." As the goddess spoke the mist that lay on the land scattered and Odysseus saw that he was indeed in Ithaca, his own country—he knew the harbor and the cave, and the hill Neriton all covered with its forest. And knowing them he knelt down on the ground and kissed the earth of his country.

Then the goddess helped him to lay his goods within the cave— the gold and the bronze and the woven raiment that the Phæacians had given him. She made him sit beside her under the olive tree while she told him of the things that were happening in his house.

"There is trouble in thy halls, Odysseus," she said, "and it would be well for thee not to make thyself known for a time. Harden thy heart, that thou mayst endure for a while longer ill treatment at the hands of men." She told him about the wooers of his wife, who filled his halls all day, and wasted his substance, and who would slay him, lest he should punish them for their insolence. "So that the doom of Agamemnon shall not befall thee—thy slaying within thine own halls—I will change thine appearance that no man shall know thee," the goddess said.

Then she made a change in his appearance that would have been evil but that it was to last for a while only. She made his skin wither, and she dimmed his shining eyes. She made his yellow hair gray and scanty. Then she changed his raiment to a beggar's wrap, torn and stained with smoke. Over his shoulder she cast the hide of deer, and she put into his hands a beggar's staff, with a tattered bag and a cord to hang it by. And when she had made this change in his appearance the goddess left Odysseus and went from Ithaca.

It was then that she came to Telemachus in Sparta and counseled him to leave the house of Menelaus and Helen; and it has been told how he went with Peisistratus, the son of Nestor, and came to his own ship. His ship was hailed by a man who was flying from those who would slay him, and this man Telemachus took aboard. The stranger's name was Theoclymenus, and he was a soothsayer and a second-sighted man.

And Telemachus, returning to Ithaca, was in peril of his life. The wooers of his mother had discovered that he had gone from Ithaca in a ship. Two of the wooers, Antinoüs and Eurymachus, were greatly angered at the daring act of the youth. "He has gone to Sparta for help," Antinoüs said, "and if he finds that there are those who will help him we will not be able to stand against his pride. He will make us suffer for what we have wasted in his house. But let us too act. I will take a ship with twenty men, and lie in wait for him in a strait between Ithaca and Samos, and put an end to his search for his father."

Thereupon Antinoüs took twenty men to a ship, and fixing mast and sails they went over the sea. There is a little isle between Ithaca and Samos—Asteris it is called—and in the harbor of that isle he and his men lay in wait for Telemachus.

VIII

Near the place where Odysseus had landed there lived an old man who was a faithful servant in his house. Eumæus was his name, and he was a swineherd. He had made for himself a dwelling in the wildest part of the island, and had built a wall round it, and had made for the swine pens in the courtyard—twelve pens, and in each pen there were fifty swine. Old Eumæus lived in this place tending the swine with three young men to help him. The swine-pens were guarded by four dogs that were as fierce as the beasts of the forest.

As he came near, the dogs dashed at him, yelping and snapping; and Odysseus might have suffered foul hurt if the swineherd had not run out of the courtyard and driven the fierce dogs away. Seeing before him one who looked an ancient beggar, Eumæus said, "Old man, it is well that my dogs did not tear thee, for they might have brought upon me the shame of thy death. I have grief and pains enough, the gods know, without such a happening. Here I sit, mourning for my noble master, and fattening hogs for others to eat, while he, mayhap, is wandering in hunger through some friendless city. But come in, old man. I have bread and wine to give thee."

The swineherd led the seeming beggar into the courtyard, and he let him sit down on a heap of brushwood, and spread for him a shaggy goat-skin. Odysseus was glad of his servant's welcome, and he said, "May Zeus and all the other gods grant thee thy heart's dearest wish for the welcome that thou hast given to me."

Said Eumæus the swineherd, "A good man looks on all strangers and beggars as being from Zeus himself. And my heart's dearest wish is that my master Odysseus should return. Ah, if Odysseus were here, he would give me something which I could hold as mine own—a piece of ground to till, and a wife to comfort me. But my master will not return, and we thralls must go in fear when young lords come to rule it over them."

He went to the swine pens and brought out two suckling pigs; he slaughtered them and cut them small and roasted the meat. When all was cooked, he brought portions to Odysseus sprinkled with barley meal, and he brought him, too, wine in a deep bowl of ivy wood. And when Odysseus had eaten and drunken, Eumæus the swineherd said to him:

"Old man, no wanderer ever comes to this land but that our lady Penelope sends for him, and gives him entertainment, hoping that he will have something to tell her of her lord, Odysseus. They all do as thou wouldst do if thou camest to her—tell her a tale of having seen or of having heard of her lord, to win her ear. But as for Odysseus, no matter what wanderers or vagrants say, he will never return—dogs, or wild birds, or the fishes of the deep have devoured his body ere this. Never again shall I find so good a lord, nor would I find one so kind even if I were back in my own land, and saw the faces of my father and my mother. But not so much for them do I mourn as for the loss of my master."

Said Odysseus, "Thou sayst that thy master will never return, but I notice that thou are slow to believe thine own words. Now I tell thee that Odysseus will return and in this same year. And as sure as the old moon wanes and the young moon is born, he will take vengeance on those whom you have spoken of—those who eat his substance and dishonor his wife and son. I say that, and I swear it with an oath."

"I do not heed thine oath," said Eumæus the swineherd. "I do not listen to vagrants' tales about my master since a stranger came here and cheated us with a story. He told us that he had seen Odysseus in the land of the Cretans, in the house of the hero Idomeneus, mending his ships that had been broken by the storm, and that he would be here by summer or by harvest time, bringing with him much wealth."

As they were speaking the younger swineherds came back from the woods, bringing the drove of swine into the courtyard. There was a mighty din whilst the swine were being put into their pens. Supper time came on, and Eumæus and Odysseus and the younger swineherds sat down to a meal. Eumæus carved the swineflesh, giving the best portion to Odysseus whom he treated as the guest of honor. And Odysseus said, "Eumæus, surely thou are counseled by Zeus, seeing thou dost give the best of the meat even to such a one as I."

And Eumæus, thinking Odysseus was praising him for treating a stranger kindly, said, "Eat, stranger, and make merry with such fare as is here."

The night came on cold with rain. Then Odysseus, to test the kindliness of the swineherd, said, "O that I were young and could endure this bitter night! O that I were better off! Then would one of you swineherds give me a wrap to cover myself from the wind and rain! But now, verily, I am an outcast because of my sorry raiment."

Then Eumæus sprang up and made a bed for Odysseus near the fire. Odysseus lay down, and the swineherd covered him with a mantle he kept for a covering when great storms should arise. Then, that he might better guard the swine, Eumæus, wrapping himself up in a cloak, and taking with him a sword and javelin, to drive off wild beasts should they come near, went to lie nearer to the pens.

When morning came, Odysseus said, "I am going to the town to beg, so that I need take nothing more from thee. Send someone with me to be a guide. I would go to the house of Odysseus, and see if I can earn a little from the wooers who are there. Right well could I serve them if they would take me on. There could be no better serving-man then I, when it comes to splitting fagots, and kindling a fire and carving meat."

"Nay, nay," said Eumæus, "do not go there, stranger. None here are at a loss by thy presence. Stay until the son of Odysseus, Telemachus, returns, and he will do something for thee. Go not near the wooers. It is not such a one as thee that they would have to serve them. Stay this day with us."

Odysseus did not go to the town but stayed all day with Eumæus. And at night, when he and Eumæus and the younger swineherds were seated at the fire, Odysseus said, "Thou, too, Eumæus, hast wandered far and hast had many sorrows. Tell us how thou camest to be a slave and a swineherd."

THE STORY OF EUMÆUS THE SWINEHERD

"There is," said Eumæus, "a certain island over against Ortygia. That island has two cities, and my father was king over them both.

"There came to the city where my father dwelt, a ship with merchants from the land of the Phœnicians. I was a child then, and there was in my father's house a Phœnician slave-woman who nursed me. Once, when she was washing clothes, one of the sailors from the Phœnician ship spoke to her and asked her would she like to go back with them to their own land.

"She spoke to that sailor and told him her story. 'I am from Sidon in the Phœnician land,' she said, 'and my father was named Artybas, and was famous for his riches. Sea robbers caught me one day as I was crossing the fields, and they stole me away, and brought me here, and sold me to the master of yonder house.'

"Then the sailor said to her, 'Thy father and mother are still alive, I know, and they have lost none of their wealth. Wilt thou not come with us and see them again?'

"Then the woman made the sailors swear that they would bring her safely to the city of Sidon. She told them that when their ship was ready she would come down to it, and that she would bring what gold she could lay her hands on away from her master's house, and that she would also bring the child whom she nursed. 'He is a wise child,' she said, 'and you can sell him for a slave when you come to a foreign land.'

When the Phœnician ship was ready to depart they sent a message to the woman. The sailor who brought the message brought too a chain of gold with amber beads strung here and there, for my mother to buy. And, while my mother and her handmaids were handling the chain, the sailor nodded to the woman, and she went out, taking with her three cups of gold, and leading me by the hand.

"The sun sank and all the ways were darkened. But the Phœnician woman went down to the harbor and came to the ship and went aboard it. And when the sailor who had gone to my father's house came back, they raised the mast and sails, and took the oars in their hands, and drew the ship away from our land. We sailed away and I was left stricken at heart. For six days we sailed over the sea, and on the seventh day the woman died and her body was cast into the deep. The wind and the waves bore us to Ithaca, and there the merchants sold me to Laertes, the father of Odysseus.

"The wife of Laertes reared me kindly, and I grew up with the youngest of her daughters, the lovely Ctimene. But Ctimene went to Same, and was married to one of the princes of that island. Afterwards Laertes' lady sent me to work in the fields. But always she treated me kindly. Now Laertes' lady is dead—she wasted away from grief when she heard no tidings of her only son, Odysseus. Laertes yet lives, but since the death of his noble wife he never leaves his house. All day he sits by his fire, they say, and thinks upon his son's doom, and how his son's substance is being wasted, and how his son's son will have but little to inherit."

So Odysseus passed part of the night, Eumæus telling him of his wanderings and his sorrows. And while they were speaking, Telemachus, the son of Odysseus, came to Ithaca in his good ship. Antinoüs had lain in wait for him, and had posted sentinels to watch for his ship; nevertheless Telemachus had passed by without being seen by his enemies. And having come to Ithaca, he bade one of his comrades bring the ship into the wharf of the city while he himself went to another place. Leaving the ship he came to the dwelling of the servant he most trusted—to the dwelling of Eumæus, the swineherd.

IX

On the morning of his fourth day in Ithaca, as he and the swineherd were eating a meal together, Odysseus heard the sound of footsteps approaching the hut. The fierce dogs were outside and he expected to hear them yelping against the stranger's approach. No sound came from them. Then he saw a young man come to the entrance of the courtyard, the swineherd's dogs fawning upon him.

When Eumæus saw this young man he let fall the vessels he was carrying, and running to him, kissed his head and his eyes and his hands. While he was kissing and weeping over him, Odysseus heard the swineherd saying:

"Telemachus, art thou come back to us? Like a light in the darkness thou hast appeared! I thought that never again should we see thee when I heard that thou hadst taken a ship to Pylos! Come in, dear son, come in, that I may see thee once again in mine house."

Odysseus raised his head and looked at his son. As a lion might look over his cub so he looked over Telemachus. But neither the swineherd nor Telemachus was aware of Odysseus' gaze.

"I have come to see thee, friend Eumæus," said Telemachus, "for before I go into the City I would know whether my mother is still in the house of Odysseus, or whether one of the wooers has at last taken her as a wife to his own house."

"Thy mother is still in thy father's house," Eumæus answered. Then Telemachus came within the courtyard. Odysseus in the guise of the old beggar rose from his seat, but the young man said to him courteously: "Be seated, friend. Another seat can be found for me."

Eumæus strewed green brushwood and spread a fleece upon it, and Telemachus seated himself. Next Eumæus fetched a meal for him—oaten cakes and swine flesh and wine. While they were eating, the swineherd said:

"We have here a stranger who has wandered through many countries, and who has come to my house as a suppliant. Wilt thou take him for thy man, Telemachus?"

Said Telemachus, "How can I support any man? I have not the strength of hand to defend mine own house. But for this stranger I will do what I can. I will give him a mantle and doublet, with shoes for his feet and a sword to defend himself, and I will send him on whatever way he wants to go. But, Eumæus, I would not have him go near my father's house. The wooers grow more insolent each day, and they might mock the stranger if he went amongst them."

Then said Odysseus, speaking for the first time, "Young sir, what thou hast said seems strange to me. Dost thou willingly submit to insolence in thine own father's house? But perhaps it is that the people of the city hate thee and will not help thee against thine enemies. Ah, if I had such youth as I have spirit, or if I were the son of Odysseus, I should go amongst them this very day, and make myself the bane of each man of them. I would rather die in mine own halls than see such shame as is reported—strangers mocked at, and servants injured, and wine and food wasted."

Said Telemachus, "The people of the City do not hate me, and they would help me if they could. But the wooers of my mother are powerful men—men to make the City folk afraid. And if I should oppose them I would assuredly be slain in my father's house, for how could I hope to overcome so many?"

"What wouldst thou have me do for thee, Telemachus?" said the swineherd.

"I would have thee go to my mother, friend Eumæus," Telemachus said, "and let her know that I am safe returned from Pylos."

Eumæus at once put sandals upon his feet and took his staff in his hands. He begged Telemachus to rest himself in the hut, and then he left the courtyard and went toward the City.

Telemachus lay down on his seat and closed his eyes in weariness. He saw, while thinking that he only dreamt it, a woman come to the gate of the courtyard. She was fair and tall and splendid, and the dogs shrank away from her presence with a whine. She touched the beggar with a golden wand. As she did the marks of age and beggary fell from him and the man stood up as tall and noble looking.

"Who art thou?" cried Telemachus, starting up. "Even a moment ago thou didst look aged and a beggar! Now thou dost look a chief of men! Art thou one of the divine ones?"

Odysseus looked upon him and said, "My son, do not speak so to me. I am Odysseus, thy father. After much suffering and much wandering I have come to my own country." He kissed his son with tears flowing down his cheeks, and Telemachus threw his arms around his father's neck, but scarce believing that the father he had searched for was indeed before him.

But no doubt was left as Odysseus talked to him, and told him how he had come to Ithaca in a ship and how he had brought with him gifts of bronze and raiment that were hidden in the cave, and told him, too, how Pallas Athene had changed his appearance into that of an old beggar.

And when his own story was finished he said, "Come, my son, tell me of the wooers who waste the substance of our house—tell me how many they number, and who they are, so that we may prepare a way of dealing with them."

"Even though thou art a great warrior, my father, thou and I cannot hope to deal with them. They have come, not from Ithaca alone, but from all the islands around—from Dulichium and Same and Zacynthus. We two cannot deal with such a throng."

Said Odysseus, "I shall make a plan to deal with them. Go thou home, and keep company with the wooers. Later in the day the swincherd will lead me into the city, and I shall go into the house in the likeness of an old beggar. And if thou shouldst see any of the wooers ill-treat me, harden thine heart to endure it—even if they drag me by the feet to the door of the house, keep quiet thou. And let no one—not even thy mother, Penelope—nor my father Laertes—know that Odysseus hath returned."

Telemachus said, "My father, thou shalt learn soon what spirit is in me and what wisdom I have."

While they talked together the ship that Antinoüs had taken, when he went to lie in wait for Telemachus, returned. The wooers, assembled and debated whether they should kill Telemachus, for now there was danger that he would draw the people to his side, and so make up a force that could drive the wooers out of Ithaca. But they did not agree to kill him then, for there was one amongst them who was against the deed.

Eumæus brought the news to Telemachus and Odysseus of the return of Antinoüs' ship. He came back to the hut in the afternoon. Pallas Athene had again given Odysseus the appearance of an ancient beggar-man and the swineherd saw no change in his guest.

X

It was time for Telemachus to go into the City. He put his sandals on his feet, and took his spear in his hand, and then speaking to the swineherd he said:

"Friend Eumæus, I am now going into the City to show myself to my mother, and to let her hear from my own lips the tale of my journey. And I have an order to leave with thee. Take this stranger into the City, that he may go about as he desires, asking alms from the people."

Odysseus in the guise of a beggar said, "I thank thee, lord Telemachus. I would not stay here, for I am not of an age to wait about a hut and courtyard, obeying the orders of a master, even if that master be as good a man as thy swineherd. Go thy way, lord Telemachus, and Eumæus, as thou hast bidden him, will lead me into the City."

Telemachus then passed out of the courtyard and went the ways until he came into the City. When he went into the house, the first person he saw was his nurse, old Eurycleia, who welcomed him with joy. To Eurycleia he spoke of the guest who had come on his ship, Theoclymenus. He told her that this guest would be in the house that day, and that he was to be treated with all honor and reverence. The wooers came into the hall and crowded around him, with fair words in their mouths. Then all sat down at tables, and Eurycleia brought wheaten bread and wine and dainties.

Just at that time Odysseus and Eumæus were journeying toward the City. Odysseus, in the guise of a beggar, had a ragged bag across his shoulders and he carried a staff that the swineherd had given him to help him over the slippery ground. They went by a rugged path and they came to a place where a spring flowed into a basin made for its water, and where there was an altar to the Nymphs, at which men made offerings.

As Eumæus and Odysseus were resting at the spring, a servant from Odysseus' house came along. He was a goatherd, and Melanthius was his name. He was leading a flock of goats for the wooers to kill, and when he saw the swineherd with the seeming beggar he cried out:

"Now we see the vile leading the vile. Say, swineherd, whither art thou leading this wretch? It is easy to see the sort of fellow he is! He is the sort to rub shoulders against many doorposts, begging for scraps. Nothing else is he good for. But if thou wouldst give him to me, swineherd, I would make him watch my fields, and sweep out my stalls, and carry fresh water to the kids. He'd have his dish of whey from me. But a fellow like this doesn't want an honest job—he wants to lounge through the country, filling his belly without doing anything for the people who feed him up. If he goes to the house of Odysseus, I pray that he be pelted from the door."

He said all this as he came up to them with his flock of goats. And as he went by he gave a kick to Odysseus.

Odysseus took thought whether he should strike the fellow with his staff or fling him upon the ground. But in the end he hardened his heart to endure the insult, and let the goatherd go on his way. But turning to the altar that was by the spring, he prayed:

"Nymphs of the Well! If ever Odysseus made offerings to you, fulfill for me this wish—that he—even Odysseus—may come to his own home, and have power to chastise the insolence that gathers around his house."

They journeyed on, and when they came near they heard the sound of the lyre within the house. The wooers were now feasting, and Phemius the minstrel was singing to them. And when Odysseus came before his own house, he caught the swineherd by the hand suddenly and with a hard grip, and he said:

"Lo now, I who have wandered in many lands and have walked in pain through many Cities have come at last to the house of Odysseus. There it is, standing as of old, with building beyond building; with its walls and its battlements; its courts and its doors. The house of Odysseus, verily! And lo! unwelcome men keep revel within it, and the smoke of their feast rises up and the sound of the lyre is heard playing for them."

Said Eumæus, "What wilt thou have me do for thee, friend? Shall I bring thee into the hall and before the company of wooers, whilst I remain here, or wouldst thou have me go in before thee?"

"I would have thee go in before me," Odysseus said.

Now as they went through the courtyard a thing happened that dashed Odysseus' eyes with tears. A hound lay in the dirt of the yard, a hound that was very old. All uncared for he lay in the dirt, old and feeble. But he had been a famous hound, and Odysseus himself had trained him before he went to the wars of Troy. Argos was his name. Now as Odysseus came near, the hound Argos knew him, and stood up before him and whined and dropped his ears, but had no strength to come near him. Odysseus knew the hound and

stopped and gazed at him. "A good hound lies there," said he to
Eumæus, "once, I think, he was so swift that no beast in the deep
places of the wood could flee from him." Then he went on, and the
hound Argos lay down in the dirt of the yard, and that same day
the life passed from him.

Behind Eumæus, the swineherd, he came into his own hall, in
the appearance of a beggar, wretchedly clad and leaning on an old
man's staff. Odysseus looked upon the young lords who wooed his
wife, and then he sat down upon the threshold and went no farther
into the hall.

Telemachus was there. Seeing Eumæus he called to him and gave
the swineherd bread and meat, and said, "Take these, and give them
to the stranger at the doorway, and tell him that he may go amongst
the company and crave an alms from each."

Odysseus ate whilst the minstrel was finishing his song. When it
was finished he rose up, and went into the hall, craving an alms
from each of the wooers.

Seeing him, Antinoüs, the most insolent of the wooers, cried out,
"O notorious swineherd, why didst thou bring this fellow here?
Have we not enough vagabonds? Is it nothing to thee that worthless
fellows come here and devour thy master's substance?"

Hearing such a speech from Antinoüs, Telemachus had to say,
"Antinoüs, I see that thou hast good care for me and mine. I marvel
that thou hast such good care. But wouldst thou have me drive a
stranger from the door? The gods forbid I should do this. Nay,
Antinoüs, give the stranger something for the sake of the house."

"If all the company gives him as much as I, he will have something to keep him from beggary for a three months' space," said
Antinoüs, meaning that he would work some hurt upon the
beggar.

Odysseus came before him. "They say that thou art the noblest of
all the wooers," he said, "and for that reason thou shouldst give me a
better thing than any of the others have given me. Look upon me.
I too had a house of mine own, and was accounted wealthy amongst
men, and I had servants to wait upon me. And many a time would
I make welcome the wanderer and give him something.

"Stand away from my table, thou wretched fellow," said Antinoüs.

Then said Odysseus, "Thou hast beauty, lord Antinoüs, but thou hast not wisdom. Out of thine own house thou wouldst not give a grain of salt to a suppliant. And even whilst thou dost sit at another man's table thou dost not find it in thy heart to give something out of the plenty that is before thee."

So Odysseus spoke and Antinoüs became terribly angered. He caught up a footstool, and with it he struck Odysseus in the back, at the base of the right shoulder. Such a blow would have knocked another man over, but Odysseus stood steadfast under it. He gave one look at Antinoüs, and then without a word he went over and sat down again upon the threshold.

Telemachus had in his heart a mighty rage for the stroke that had been given his father. But he let no tear fall from his eyes and he sat very still, brooding in his heart evil for the wooers. Odysseus, after a while, lifted his head and spoke:

"Wooers of the renowned queen," he said, "hear what the spirit within me bids me say to you. There is neither pain nor shame in the blow that a man may get in battle. But in the blow that Antinoüs has given me—a blow aimed at a beggar—there is pain and there is shame. And now I call upon that god who is the avenger of the insult to the poor, to bring, not a wedding to Antinoüs, but death."

"Sit there and eat thy meat in quiet." Antinoüs called out, "or else thou wilt be dragged through the house by thy heels, and the flesh will be stripped off thy bones."

And now the lady Penelope had come into the hall. Hearing that a stranger was there, she sent for Eumæus and bade the swineherd bring him to her, that she might question him as to what he had heard about Odysseus. Eumæus came and told him of Penelope's request. But Odysseus said, "Eumæus, right willing am I to tell the truth about Odysseus to the fair and wise Penelope. But now I may not speak to her. Go to her and tell her that when the wooers have gone I will speak to her. And ask her to give me a seat near the fire, that I may sit and warm myself as I speak, for the clothes I wear are comfortless."

As Eumæus gave the message to the lady Penelope, one who was there, Theoclymenus, the guest who had come in Telemachus' ship, said, "O wife of the renowned Odysseus, be sure that thy lord will return to his house. As I came here on the ship of Telemachus, thy son, I saw a happening that is an omen of the return of Odysseus. A bird flew out on the right, a hawk. In his talons he held a dove, and plucked her and shed the feathers down on the ship. By that omen I know that the lord of this high house will return, and strike here in his anger."

Penelope left the hall and went back to her own chamber. Next Eumæus went away to look after his swine. But still the wooers continued the feast, and still Odysseus sat in the guise of a beggar on the threshold of his own house.

XI

There was in Ithaca a common beggar; he was a most greedy fellow, and he was nicknamed Irus because he used to run errands for the servants of Odysseus' house. He came in the evening, and seeing a seeming beggar seated on the threshold, he flew into a rage and shouted at him:

"Get away from here, old fellow, lest you be dragged away by the hand or foot. Look you! The lords within the house are giving me the wink to turn you out. But I can't demean myself by touching the like of you. Get up now and go while I'm easy with you."

Odysseus looked at the fellow and said, "I have not harmed you in deed or word, and I do not grudge you anything of what you may get in this house. The threshold I sit on is wide enough for two."

"What words this fellow has!" said Irus the beggar. "He talks like an old sit-by-the-fire. I'll not waste more words on him. Get up now, heavy paunch, and strip for the fight, for I'm going to show all the lords that I can keep the door for them."

"Do not provoke me," said Odysseus. "Old as I seem, I may be able to draw your blood."

But Irus kept on shouting. "I'll knock the teeth out of your jaws."
"I'll trounce you." Antinoüs, the most insolent of the wooers, saw the

squabble, and he laughed to see the pair defying each other. "Friends," said he, "the gods are good to us, and don't fail to send us amusement. The strange beggar and our own Irus are threatening each other. Let us see that they don't draw back from the fight. Let us match one against the other."

All the wooers trooped to the threshold and stood round the ragged men. Antinoüs thought of something to make the game more merry. "There are two great puddings in the larder," he said. "Let us offer them for a prize to these pugilists. Come, Irus. Come, stranger. A choice of puddings for whichever of you wins the match. Aye, and more than that. Whoever wins shall have leave to eat every day in this hall, and no other beggar shall be let come near the house. Go to it now, ye mighty men." All the wooers crowded round and clapped the men on to the fight.

Odysseus said, "Friends, an old man like me cannot fight one who is younger and abler."

But they cried to him, "Go on, go on. Get into the fight or else take stripes upon your body."

Then said Odysseus, "Swear to me all of you, that none of you will show favor to Irus nor deal me a foul blow."

All the wooers cried out that none would favor Irus or deal his opponent a foul blow. And Telemachus, who was there, said, "The man who strikes thee, stranger, will have to take reckoning from me."

Straightway Odysseus girt up his rags. When his great arms and shoulders and thighs were seen, the wooers were amazed and Irus was frightened. He would have slipped away if Antinoüs had not caught him and said to him, "You lubber, you! If you do not stand up before this man I will have you flung on my ship and sent over to King Echetus, who will cut off your nose and ears and give your flesh to the dogs to eat." He took hold of Irus and dragged him into the ring.

The fighters faced each other. But Odysseus with his hands up-raised stood for long without striking, for he was pondering whether he should strike Irus a hard or a light blow. It seemed to him better to strike him lightly, so that his strength should not be made a matter for the wooers to note and wonder at. Irus struck first. He struck Odysseus on the shoulder. Then Odysseus aimed a blow at his neck, just below the ear, and the beggar fell to the ground, with the blood gushing from his mouth and nose.

The wooers were not sorry for Irus. They laughed until they were ready to fall backward. Then Odysseus seized Irus by the feet, and dragged him out of the house, and to the gate of the courtyard. He lifted him up and put him standing against the wall. Placing the staff in the beggar's hands, he said, "Sit there, and scare off the dogs and swine, and do not let such a one as you lord it over strangers. A worse thing might have befallen you."

Then back he went to the hall, with his beggar's bag on his shoulder and his clothes more ragged than ever. Back he went, and when the wooers saw him they burst into peals of laughter and shouted out:

"May Zeus, O stranger, give thee thy dearest wish and thy heart's desire. Thou only shalt be beggar in Ithaca." They laughed and laughed again when Antinoüs brought out the great pudding that was the prize. Odysseus took it from him. And another of the wooers pledged him in a golden cup, saying, "May you come to your own, O beggar, and may happiness be yours in time to come."

While these things were happening, the wife of Odysseus, the lady Penelope, called to Eurycleia, and said, "This evening I will go into the hall of our house and speak to my son, Telemachus. Bid my two handmaidens make ready to come with me, for I shrink from going amongst the wooers alone."

Eurycleia went to tell the handmaidens and Penelope washed off her cheeks the traces of tears that she had wept that day. Then she sat down to wait for the handmaidens to come to her. As she waited she fell into a deep sleep. And as she slept, the goddess Pallas Athene bathed her face in the Water of Beauty and took all weariness away from her body, and restored all her youthfulness to her. The sound of the handmaidens' voices as they came in awakened her, and Penelope rose up to go into the hall.

Now when she came amongst them with her two handmaidens, one standing each side of her, the wooers were amazed, for they had never seen one so beautiful. The hearts of all were enchanted with love for her, and each prayed that he might have her for his wife.

Penelope did not look on any of the wooers, but she went to her son, Telemachus, and spoke to him.

"Telemachus," she said, "I have heard that a stranger has been ill-treated in this house. How, my child, didst thou permit such a thing to happen?"

Telemachus said, "My lady mother, thou hast no right to be angered at what took place in this hall."

So they spoke to one another, mother and son. Now one of the wooers, Eurymachus by name, spoke to Penelope, saying:

"Lady, if any more than we beheld thee in the beauty thou hast now, by so many more wouldst thou have wooers tomorrow."

"Speak not so to me, lord Eurymachus," said Penelope, "speak not of my beauty, which departed in the grief I felt when my lord went to the wars of Troy."

Odysseus stood up, and gazed upon his wife who was standing amongst her wooers. Eurymachus noted him and going to him, said, "Stranger, wouldst thou be my hireling? If thou wouldst work on my upland farm, I should give thee food and clothes. But I think thou art practised only in shifts and dodges, and that thou wouldst prefer to go begging thy way through the country."

Odysseus, standing there, said to that proud wooer, "Lord Eurymachus, if there might be a trial of labor between us two, I know which of us would come out the better man. I would that we two stood together, a scythe in the hands of each, and a good swath of meadow to be mown—then would I match with thee, fasting from dawn until evening's dark. Or would that we were set plowing together. Then thou shouldst see who would plow the longest and the best furrow! Or would that we two were in the ways of war! Then shouldst thou see who would be in the front rank of battle. Thou dost think thyself a great man. But if Odysseus should return, that door, wide as it is, would be too narrow for thy flight."

So angry was Eurymachus at this speech that he would have struck Odysseus if Telemachus had not come amongst the wooers, saying, "That man must not be struck again in this hall. Sirs, if you have finished feasting, and if the time has come for you, go to your own homes, go in peace I pray you."

All were astonished that Telemachus should speak so boldly. No one answered him back, for one said to the other, "What he has said is proper. We have nothing to say against it. To misuse a stranger in the house of Odysseus is a shame. Now let us pour out a libation of wine to the gods, and then let each man go to his home."

The wine was poured out and the wooers departed. Then Penelope and her handmaidens went to her own chamber and Telemachus was left with his father, Odysseus.

XII

To Telemachus Odysseus said, "My son, we must now get the weapons out of the hall. Take them down from the walls." Telemachus and his father took down the helmets and shields and sharp-pointed spears. Then said Odysseus as they carried them out, "Tomorrow, when the wooers miss the weapons and say, 'Why have they been taken?' answer them, saying, 'The smoke of the fire dulled them, and they no longer looked the weapons that my father left behind him when he went to the wars of Troy. Besides, I am fearful lest some day the company in the hall come to a quarrel, one with the other, and snatch the weapons in anger. Strife has come here already. And iron draws iron, men say.'"

Telemachus carried the armor and weapons out of the hall and hid them in the women's apartment. Then when the hall was cleared he went to his own chamber.

It was then that Penelope came back to the hall to speak to the stranger. One of her handmaidens, Melantho by name, was there, and she was speaking angrily to him. Now this Melantho was proud and hard of heart because Antinoüs often conversed with her. As Penelope came near she was saying: "Stranger, art thou still here, prying things out and spying on the servants? Be thankful for the supper thou hast gotten and betake thyself out of this."

Odysseus, looking fiercely at her, said, "Why shouldst thou speak to me in such a way? If I go in ragged clothes and beg through the land it is because of my necessity. Once I had a house with servants and much substance, and the stranger who came was not abused."

The lady Penelope called to the handmaiden and said, "Thou Mclantho, didst hear it from my own lips that I was minded to speak to this stranger and ask him if he had tidings of my lord. Therefore, it does not become thee to revile him." She spoke to the old nurse who was with her, and said, "Eurycleia, bring to the fire a bench, with a fleece on it, that this stranger may sit and tell his story."

Eurycleia brought over the bench, and Odysseus sat down near the fire. Then said the lady Penelope, "First, stranger, wilt thou tell me who thou art, what is thy name, thy race and country?"

Said Odysseus, "Ask me all thou wilt, lady, but inquire not concerning my name, or race, or country, lest thou should fill my heart with more pains than I am able to endure. Verily I am a man of grief. But hast thou no tale to tell me? We know of thee, Penelope, for thy fame goes up to heaven, and no one of mortal men can find fault with thee."

Then said Penelope, "What excellence I had of face or form departed from me when my lord Odysseus went from this hall to the wars of Troy. And since he went a host of ills has beset me. Ah, would that he were here to watch over my life! The lords of all the islands around—Dulichium and Same and Zacynthus; and the lords of the land of Ithaca, have come here and are wooing me against my will. They devour the substance of this house and my son is being impoverished.

"Long ago a god put into my mind a device to keep marriage with any of them away from me. I set up a great web upon my loom and I spoke to the wooers, saying, 'Odysseus is assuredly dead, but I crave that you be not eager to speed on this marriage with me. Wait until I finish the web I am weaving. It is a shroud for Odysseus' father, and I make it against the day when death shall come to him. There will be no woman to care for Laertes when I have left his son's house, and I would not have such a hero lie without a shroud, lest the women of our land should blame me for neglect of my husband's father in his last days.'

"So I spoke, and they agreed to wait until the web was woven.

In the daytime I wove it, but at night I unraveled the web. So three years passed away. Then the fourth year came, and my wooers were hard to deal with. My treacherous handmaidens brought them upon me as I was unraveling the web. And now I cannot devise any other plan to keep the marriage away from me. My parents command me to marry one of my wooers. My son cannot long endure to see the substance of his house and field being wasted, and the wealth that should be his destroyed. He too would·wish that I should marry. And there is no reason why I should not be wed again, for surely Odysseus, my lord, is dead."

Said Odysseus, "Thy lord was known to me. On his way to Troy he came to my land, for the wind blew him out of his course, sending him wandering past Malea. For twelve days he stayed in my city, and I gave him good entertainment, and saw that he lacked for nothing in cattle, or wine, or barley meal."

When Odysseus was spoken of, the heart of Penelope melted, and tears ran down her cheeks. Odysseus had pity for his wife when he saw her weeping for the man who was even then sitting by her. Tears would have run down his cheeks but that he was strong enough and able to hold them back.

Said Penelope, "Stranger, I cannot help but question thee about Odysseus. What raiment had he on when thou didst see him? And what men were with him?"

Said Odysseus, "Lady, it is hard for one so long parted from him to tell thee what thou hast asked. It is now twenty years since I saw Odysseus. He wore a purple mantle that was fastened with a brooch. And this brooch had on it the image of a hound holding a fawn between its forepaws. All the people marveled at this brooch, for it was of gold, and the fawn and the hound were done to the life. And I remember that there was a henchman with Odysseus—he was a man somewhat older than his master, round-shouldered and black-skinned and curly headed. His name was Eurybates, and Odysseus honored him above the rest of his company."

When he spoke, giving such tokens of Odysseus, Penelope wept again. And when she had wept for a long time she said:

"Stranger, thou wert made welcome, but now thou shalt be honored in this hall. Thou dost speak of the garments that Odysseus wore. It was I who gave him these garments, folding them myself and bringing them out of the chamber. And it was I who gave him the brooch that thou hast described. Ah, it was an evil fate that took him from me, bringing him to Troy, that place too evil to be named by me."

Odysseus leaned toward her, and said, "Do not waste thy heart with endless weeping, lady. Cease from lamentation, and lay up in thy mind the word I give thee. Odysseus is near. He has lost all his companions, and he knows not how to come into this house, whether openly or by stealth. I swear it. By the hearth of Odysseus to which I am come, I swear that Odysseus himself will stand up here before the old moon wanes and the new moon is born."

"Ah, no," said Penelope. "Often before have wanderers told me such comfortable things, and I believed them. I know now that thy word cannot be accomplished. But it is time for thee to rest thyself, stranger. My handmaidens will make a bed for thee in the vestibule, and then come to thee and bathe thy feet."

Said Odysseus, "Thy handmaidens would be loath to touch the feet of a wanderer such as I. But if there is in the house some old wife who has borne such troubles as I have borne, I would have my feet bathed by her."

Said Penelope, "Here is an ancient woman who nursed and tended that hapless man, Odysseus. She took him in her arms in the very hour he was born. Eurycleia, wash the feet of this man, who knew thy lord and mine."

Thereupon the nurse, old Eurycleia, fetched water, both hot and cold, and brought the bath to the hearth. And standing before Odysseus in the flickering light of the fire, she said, "I will wash thy feet, both for Penelope's sake and for thine own. The heart within me is moved at the sight of thee. Many strangers have come into this hall, but I have never seen one so like as thou art to Odysseus."

Said Odysseus, "Many people have said that Odysseus and I favor each other."

His feet were in the water, and she put her hand upon one of them. As she did so, Odysseus turned his face away to the darkness, for it suddenly came into his mind that his nurse, old Eurycleia, might recognize the scar that was upon that foot.

How came it there, that scar? It had been made long ago when a boar's tusk had ripped up the flesh of his foot. Odysseus was then a youth, and he had gone to the mountain Parnassus to visit there his mother's father.

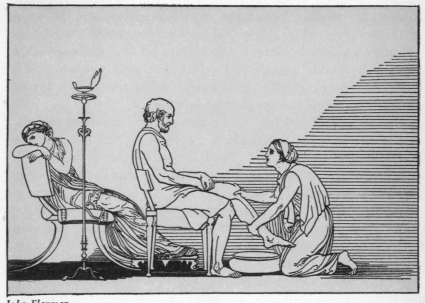

John Flaxman

"Thou art Odysseus!"

One morning, with his uncles, young Odysseus went up the slope of the mountain Parnassus, to hunt with hounds. In a thick lair a mighty boar was lying. When the sound of the men's trampling came near him, he sprang up with gleaming eyes and stood before them all. Odysseus, holding his spear in his hands, rushed upon him. But before he could strike him, the boar charged, ripping deep into his flesh with his tusk. Then Odysseus speared him through the shoulder and the boar was slain. His uncles staunched the wound and he stayed with them on the mountain Parnassus, in his grandfather's house, until the wound was healed.

And now, as Eurycleia, his old nurse, passed her hands along the leg, she let his foot drop suddenly. His knee struck against the bath, and the vessel of water was overturned. The nurse touched the chin of Odysseus and she said, "Thou art Odysseus."

She looked to where Penelope was sitting, so that she might make a sign to her. But Penelope had her eyes turned away. Odysseus put his hand on Eurycleia's mouth, and with the other hand he drew her to him.

"Woman," he whispered. "Say nothing. Be silent, lest mine enemies learn what thou knowest now."

"Silent I'll be," said the nurse Eurycleia. "Thou knowest me. Firm and unyielding I am, and by no sign will I let anyone know that thou hast come under this roof."

So saying she went out of the hall to fetch water in the place of that which had been spilt. She came back and finished bathing his feet. Then Odysseus arranged the rags around his leg to hide the scar, and he drew the bench closer to the fire.

Penelope turned to him again. "Wise thou art, my guest," she said, "and it may be that thou art just such a man as can interpret a dream that comes to me constantly. I have twenty geese in the yard outside. In my dream I see them, and then a great eagle flies down from the mountains, and breaks their necks and kills them all, and lays them in a heap in this hall. I weep and lament for my geese, but then the eagle comes back, and perching on a beam of the roof speaks to me in the voice of a man. 'Take heart, O wife of Odysseus,' the eagle says, 'this is no dream but a true vision. For the geese that thou hast seen are thy wooers, and I, that appeared as an eagle, am thy husband who will swiftly bring death to the wooers.' Then the dream goes, and I waken and look out on the daylight and see my geese in the courtyard pecking at the wheat in the trough. Canst thou interpret this dream?"

"Lady," said Odysseus, "the dream interprets itself. All will come about as thou hast dreamed."

"Ah," said Penelope, "but it cannot now, for the day of my woe is at hand. I am being forced by my parents to choose a husband from the wooers, and depart from the house of Odysseus."

"And how wilt thou choose from amongst them?" said Odysseus.

"In this way will I make choice," said Penelope. "My husband's great bow is still in the house. The one who can bend that bow, and shoot an arrow through the holes in the backs of twelve axes set one behind the other—him will I choose for my husband."

Said Odysseus, "Thy device is good, Penelope, and some god hath instructed thee to do this. But delay no longer the contest of the bow. Let it be tomorrow."

"Is that thy counsel, O stranger?" said Penelope.

"It is my counsel," said Odysseus.

"I thank thee for thy counsel," she said. "And now farewell, for I must go to my rest. And do thou lie down in the vestibule, in the bed that has been made for thee."

So Penelope spoke, and then she went to her chamber with her handmaidens. And in her bed she thought over all the stranger had told her of Odysseus, and she wept again for him.

XIII

All night Odysseus lay awake, tossing this side and that as he pondered on how he might slay the wooers and save his house from them. As soon the dawn came, he went into the open air and, lifting up his hands, prayed to Zeus, the greatest of the gods, that he might be shown some sign, as to whether he would win victory or meet with defeat.

And then, as he was going within the house, he heard the voice of a woman who ground barley-meal between stones. She was one of twelve, but the other women had fallen asleep by the quern-stones. She was an ancient, wretched woman, covered all over with the dust of the grain, and, as Odysseus came near her, she lifted up her hands and prayed in a weak voice:

"O Zeus, even for miserable me, fulfill a prayer! May this be the last day that the wooers make their feast in the house of Odysseus! They have loosened my knees with the cruel toil they have made me undergo, grinding for them the barley for the bread they eat. O Zeus, may they today sup their last!"

Thus the quern-woman spoke, as Odysseus crossed his threshold. He was glad of her speech, for it seemed to him her words were an omen from Zeus, and that vengeance would soon be wrought upon the proud and hard-hearted men who wasted the goods of the house and oppressed the servants.

And now the maids came into the hall from the women's apartment, and some cleaned the tables and others took pitchers and went to the well for water. Then men-servants came in and split the fagots for the fire. Other servants came into the courtyard—Eumæus the swineherd, driving fatted swine, the best of his drove, and Philœtius the cattleherd bringing a calf. The goatherd Melanthius, him whom Odysseus and Eumæus had met on the road the day before, also came, bringing the best goats of his flock to be killed for the wooers' feast.

When the cattleherd, Philœtius, saw a stranger in the guise of a beggar, he called out as he tethered the calf in the yard, "Hail, stranger friend! My eyes fill with tears as I look on thee. For even now, clad as thou art in rags, thou dost make me think of my master Odysseus, who may be a wanderer such as thou in friendless lands. Ah, that he might return and make a scattering of the wooers in his hall." Eumæus the swineherd came up to Philœtius and made the same prayer. These two, and the ancient woman at the quern, were the only ones of his servants whom he heard pray for his return.

And now the wooers came into the hall. Philœtius the cattleherd, and Melanthius the evil goatherd, went amongst them, handing them bread and meat and wine. Odysseus stood outside the hall until Telemachus went to him and brought him within.

Now there was amongst the wooers a man named Ctesippus, and he was the rudest and the roughest of them all. When he saw Telemachus bringing Odysseus within he shouted out, "Here is a guest of Telemachus to whom some gift is due from us. It will be unseemly if he should get nothing today. Therefore I will bestow this upon him as a token."

Saying this, Ctesippus took up the foot of a slaughtered ox and flung it full at Odysseus. Odysseus drew back, and the ox's foot struck the wall. Then did Odysseus smile grimly upon the wooers.

Said Telemachus, "Verily, Ctesippus, the cast turned out happily for thyself. For if thou shouldst have struck my guest, there would have been a funeral feast instead of a wedding banquet in thy father's house. I should have driven my spear through thee."

All the wooers were silent when Telemachus spoke these bold words. But soon they fell laughing at something one of their number said. The guest from Telemachus' ship, Theoclymenus, was there, and he started up and went to leave the hall.

"Why dost thou go, my guest?" said Telemachus.

"I see the walls and the beams of the roof sprinkled with blood," said Theoclymenus, the second-sighted man. "I hear the voice of wailing. I see cheeks wet with tears. The men before me have shrouds upon them. The courtyard is filled with ghosts."

So Theoclymenus spoke, and all the wooers laughed at the second-sighted man, for he stumbled about the hall as if it were in darkness. Then said one of the wooers:

"Lead that man out of the house, for surely he cannot tell day from night."

"I will go from the place," said Theoclymenus. "I see death approaching. Not one of all the company before me will be able to avoid it."

So saying, the second-sighted man went out of the hall. The wooers looking at each other laughed again, and one of them said:

"Telemachus has no luck in his guests. One is a dirty beggar, who thinks of nothing but what he can put from his hand into his mouth, and the other wants to stand up here and play the seer." So the wooers spake in mockery, but neither Telemachus nor Odysseus paid heed to their words, for their minds were bent upon the time when they should take vengeance upon them.

XIV

In the treasure-chamber of the house Odysseus' great bow was kept. That bow had been given to him by a hero named Iphitus long ago. Odysseus had not taken it with him when he went to the wars of Troy.

To the treasure-chamber Penelope went. She carried in her hand the great key that opened the door—a key all of bronze with a handle of ivory. Now as she thrust the key into the locks, the doors groaned as a bull groans. She went within, and saw the great bow upon its peg. She took it down and laid it upon her knees, and thought long upon the man who had bent it.

Beside the bow was its quiver full of bronze-weighted arrows. The servant took the quiver and Penelope took the bow, and they

John Flaxman

They went from the treasure-chamber into the hall.

went from the treasure-chamber into the hall where the wooers were.

When she came in she spoke to the company and said: "Lords of Ithaca and of the islands around: You have come here, each desiring that I should wed him. Now the time has come for me to make my choice of a man from amongst you. Here is how I shall make choice.

"This is the bow of Odysseus, my lord who is no more. Whosoever amongst you who can bend this bow and shoot an arrow from it through the holes in the backs of twelve axes which I shall have set up, him will I wed, and to his house I will go, forsaking the house of my wedlock, this house so filled with treasure and substance, this house which I shall remember in my dreams."

As she spoke, Telemachus took the twelve axes and set them upright in an even line, so that one could shoot an arrow through the hole in the back of each ax head. Then Eumæus the swineherd took the bow of Odysseus, and laid it before the wooers.

One of the wooers took up the bow and tried to bend it. But he could not bend it, and he laid it down at the doorway with the arrow beside it. The others took up the bow, and warmed it at the fire, and rubbed it with lard to make it more pliable. As they were doing this, Eumæus, the swineherd, and Philœtius, the cattleherd, passed out of the hall.

Odysseus followed them into the courtyard. He laid a hand on each and said, "Swineherd and cattleherd, I have a word to say to you. But will you keep it to yourselves, the word I say? And first, what would you do to help Odysseus if he should return? Would you stand on his side, or on the side of the wooers? Answer me now from your hearts."

Said Philœtius the cattleherd, "May Zeus fulfill my wish and bring Odysseus back! Then thou shouldst know on whose side I would stand." And Eumæus said, "If Odysseus should return I would be on his side, and that with all the strength that is in me."

When they said this, Odysseus declared himself. Lifting up his hand to heaven he said, "I am your master, Odysseus. After twenty years I have come back to my own country, and I find that of all my servants, by you two alone is my homecoming desired. If you need see a token that I am indeed Odysseus, look down on my foot. See there the mark the wild boar left on me in my youth."

Straightway he drew the rags from the scar, and the swineherd and the cattleherd saw it and marked it well. Knowing that it was indeed Odysseus who stood before them, they cast their arms around him and kissed him on the head and shoulders. And Odysseus was moved by their tears, and he kissed their heads and their hands.

As they went back to the hall, he told Eumæus to bring the bow to him as he was bearing it through the hall. He told him, too, to

order Eurycleia, the faithful nurse, to bar the doors of the women's
apartment at the end of the hall, and to bid the women, even if they
heard a groaning and a din, not to come into the hall. And he
charged the cattleherd Philœtius to bar the gates of the courtyard.

As he went into the hall, one of the wooers, Eurymachus, was
striving to bend the bow. As he struggled to do so he groaned aloud:

"Not because I may not marry Penelope do I groan, but because
we youths of today are shown to be weaklings beside Odysseus,
whose bow we can in no way bend."

Then Antinoüs, the proudest of the wooers, made answer and
said, "Why should we strive to bend the bow today? Nay, lay the
bow aside, Eurymachus, and let the wine-bearers pour us out a cup-
ful each. In the morning let us make sacrifice to the Archer-god, and
pray that the bow be fitted to some of our hands."

Then Odysseus came forward and said, "Sirs, you do well to
lay the bow aside for today. But will you not put the bow into my
hands, that I may try to bend it, and judge for myself whether I
have any of the strength that once was mine?"

All the wooers were angry that a seeming beggar should attempt
to bend the bow that none of their company were able to bend;
Antinoüs spoke to him sharply and said:

"Thou wretched beggar! Is it not enough that thou are let into
this high hall to pick up scraps, but thou must listen to our speech
and join in our conversation? If thou shouldst bend that bow we
will make short shrift of thee, I promise. We will put thee on a ship
and send thee over to King Echetus, who will cut thee to pieces and
give thy flesh to his hounds."

Old Eumæus had taken up the bow. As he went with it to Odysseus some of them shouted to him, "Where are thou going with the
bow, thou crazy fellow? Put it down." Eumæus was confused by
their shouts, and he put down the bow.

Then Telemachus spoke to him and said, "Eumæus, beware of
being the man who served many masters." Eumæus, hearing these
words, took it up again and brought it to Odysseus, and put the
bow into his hands.

As Odysseus stood in the doorway of the hall, the bow in his hands, and with the arrows scattered at his feet, Eumæus went to Eurycleia, and told her to bar the door of the women's apartment at the back. Then Philœtius, the cattleherd, went out of the hall and barred the gates leading out of the courtyard.

For long Odysseus stood with the bow in his hands, handling it as a minstrel handles a lyre when he stretches a cord or tightens a peg. Then he bent the great bow; he bent it without an effort, and at his touch the bowstring made a sound that was like the cry of a swallow. The wooers seeing him bend that mighty bow felt, every man of them, a sharp pain at the heart. They saw Odysseus take up an arrow and fit it to the string. He held the notch, and he drew the string, and he shot the bronze-weighted arrow straight through the holes in the back of the ax heads.

Then as Eumæus took up the axes, and brought them outside, Odysseus said:

"Thou seest, lord Telemachus, that thy guest does not shame thee through foolish boasting. I have bent the bow of Odysseus, and I have shot the arrow aright. But now it is time to provide the feast for the lords who woo thy lady mother. While it is yet light, the feast must be served to them, and with the feast they must have music and the dance."

Saying this he nodded to Telemachus, bending his terrible brows. Telemachus instantly girt his sword upon him and took his spear in his hand. Outside was heard the thunder of Zeus. And now Odysseus had stripped his rags from him and was standing upright, looking a master of men. The mighty bow was in his hands, and at his feet were scattered many bronze-weighted arrows.

XV

"It is ended," Odysseus said, "My trial is ended. Now will I have another mark." Saying this, he put the bronze-weighted arrow against the string of the bow, and shot at the first of his enemies.

It was at Antinoüs he pointed the arrow—at Antinoüs who was even then lifting up a golden cup filled with wine, and who was smiling, with death far from his thoughts. Odysseus aimed at him, and smote him with the arrow in the throat and the point passed out clean through his neck. The wine cup fell from his hands and Antinoüs fell dead across the table. Then did all the wooers raise a shout, threatening Odysseus for sending an arrow astray. It did not come into their minds that this stranger-beggar had aimed to kill Antinoüs.

John Flaxman

Odysseus slaying the wooers.

But Odysseus shouted back to them, "Ye dogs, ye that said in your hearts that Odysseus would never return to his home, ye that wasted my substance, and troubled my wife, and injured my servants; ye who showed no fear of heaven, nor of the just judgments of men; behold Odysseus returned, and know that death is loosed on you!"

Then Eurymachus shouted out, "Friends, this man will not hold his hands, nor cease from shooting with the bow, until all of us are slain. Now must we enter into the battle with him. Draw your swords and hold up the tables before you for shields and advance upon him."

But even as he spoke Odysseus, with a terrible cry, loosed an arrow at him and shot Eurymachus through the breast. He let the sword fall from his hand, and he too fell dead upon the floor.

One of the band rushed straight at Odysseus with his sword in hand. But Telemachus was at hand, and he drove his spear through this man's shoulders. Then Telemachus ran quickly to a chamber where there were weapons and armor lying. The swineherd and the cattleherd joined him, and all three put armor upon them. Odysseus, as long as he had arrows to defend himself, kept shooting at and smiting the wooers. When all the arrows were gone, he put the helmet on his head and took up the shield that Telemachus had brought, and the two great spears.

But now Melanthius, the goatherd—he who was the enemy of Odysseus, got into the chamber where the arms were kept, and brought out spears and shields and helmets, and gave them to the wooers. Seeing the goatherd go back for more arms, Telemachus and Eumæus dashed into the chamber, and caught him and bound him with a rope, and dragged him up near the roof-beams, and left him hanging there. Then they closed and bolted the door, and stood on guard.

Many of the wooers lay dead upon the floor of the hall. Now one who was called Agelaus stood forward, and directed the wooers to cast spears at Odyessus. But not one of the spears they cast struck him, for Odysseus was able to avoid them all.

And now he directed Telemachus and Eumæus and Philœtius to cast their spears. When they cast them with Odysseus, each one struck a man, and four of the wooers fell down. And again Odysseus directed his following to cast their spears, and again they cast them, and slew their men. They drove those who remained from one end of the hall to the other, and slew them all.

Straightway the doors of the women's apartment were flung open, and Eurycleia appeared. She saw Odysseus amongst the bodies of the dead, all stained with blood. She would have cried out in triumph if Odysseus had not restrained her. "Rejoice within thine own heart," he said, "but do not cry aloud, for it is an unholy thing to triumph over men lying dead. These men the gods themselves have overcome, because of their own hard and unjust hearts."

As he spoke the women came out of their chambers, carrying torches in their hands. They fell upon Odysseus and embraced him and clasped and kissed his hands. A longing came over him to weep, for he remembered them from of old—every one of the servants who were there.

XVI

Eurycleia, the old nurse, went to the upper chamber where Penelope lay in her bed. She bent over her and called out, "Awake, Penelope, dear child. Come down and see with thine own eyes what hath happened. The wooers are overthrown. And he whom thou hast ever longed to see hath come back. Odysseus, thy husband, hath returned. He hath slain the proud wooers who have troubled thee for so long." But Penelope only looked at the nurse, for she thought that her brain had been turned.

Still Eurycleia kept on saying, "In very deed Odysseus is here. He is that guest whom all the wooers dishonor in the hall."

Then hearing Eurycleia say these words, Penelope sprang out of bed and put her arms round the nurse's neck. "O tell me—if what thou dost say be true—tell me how this stranger slew the wooers, who were so many."

"I did not see the slaying," Eurycleia said, "but I heard the groaning of the men as they were slain. And then I found Odysseus standing amongst many dead men, and it comforted my heart to see him standing there like a lion aroused. Come with me now, lady, that you may both enter into your heart's delight—you that have suffered so much of affliction. Thy lord hath come alive to his own hearth, and he hath found his wife and his son alive and well."

"Ah, no!" said Penelope, "ah, no, Odysseus hath not returned. He who hath slain the wooers is one of the deathless gods, come down to punish them for their injustice and their hardheartedness. Odysseus long ago lost the way of his returning, and he is lying dead in some far-off land."

"No, no," said Eurycleia. "I can show thee that it is Odysseus indeed who is in the hall. On his foot is the scar that the tusk of a boar gave him in the old days. I spied it when I was washing his feet last night, and I would have told thee of it, but he clapped a hand across my mouth to stop my speech. Lo, I stake my life that it is Odysseus, and none other who is in the hall below."

Saying this she took Penelope by the hand and led her from the upper chamber into the hall. Odysseus was standing by a tall pillar. He waited there for his wife to come and speak to him. But Penelope stood still, and gazed long upon him, and made no step toward him.

Then said Telemachus, "Mother, can it be that thy heart is so hard? Here is my father, and thou wilt not go to him nor question him at all."

Said Penelope, "My mind is amazed and I have no strength to speak, nor to ask him aught, nor even to look on him face to face. If this is indeed Odysseus who hath come home, a place has to be prepared for him."

Then Odysseus spoke to Telemachus and said, "Go now to the bath, and make thyself clean of the stains of battle. I will stay and speak with thy lady mother."

"Strange lady," said he to Penelope, "is thy heart indeed so hard? No other woman in the world, I think, would stand so aloof from her husband who, after so much toil and so many trials, has come back after twenty years to his own hearth. Is there no place for me here, and must I again sleep in the stranger's bed?"

Said Penelope, "In no stranger's bed wilt thou lie, my lord. Come, Eurycleia. Set up for him his own bedstead outside his bed-chamber."

Then Odysseus said to her, speaking in anger: "How comes it that my bed can be moved to this place and that? Not a bed of that kind was the bed I built for myself. Knowest thou not how I built my bed? First, there grew up in the courtyard an olive tree. Round that olive tree I built a chamber, and I roofed it well and I set doors to it. Then I sheared off all the light wood on the growing olive tree, and I rough-hewed the trunk with the adze, and I made the tree into a bedpost. Beginning with this bedpost I wrought a bedstead, and when I finished it, I inlaid it with silver and ivory. Such was the bed I built for myself, and such a bed could not be moved to this place or that."

Then did Penelope know assuredly that the man who stood before her was indeed her husband, the steadfast Odysseus—none other knew of where the bed was placed, and how it had been built, Penelope fell a-weeping and she put her arms round his neck.

"O Odysseus, my lord," she said, "be not angry with thy wife. Always the fear was in my heart that some guileful stranger should come here professing to be Odysseus, and that I should take him to me as my husband. How terrible such a thing would be! But now my heart is freed from all doubts. Be not angry with me, Odysseus, for not throwing myself on thy neck, as the women of the house did."

Then husband and wife wept together, and Penelope said, "It was the gods did this to us, Odysseus—the gods who grudged that we should have joy of the days of our youth."

Next they told each other of things that happened in the twenty years they were apart; Odysseus speaking of his own toils and sorrows, and Penelope telling what she had endured at the hands of the wooers. And as they told tales, one to the other, slumber came upon them, and the dawn found them sleeping side by side.

XVII

And still many dangers had to be faced. The wooers whom Odysseus had slain were the richest and the most powerful of the lords of Ithaca and the Islands; all of them had fathers and brothers who would fain avenge them upon their slayer.

Now before anyone in the City knew that he had returned, Odysseus went forth to the farm that Laertes, his old father, stayed at. As he drew near he saw an old man working in the vineyard, digging round a plant. When he came to him he saw that this old man was not a slave nor a servant, but Laertes, his own father.

When he saw him, wasted with age and all uncared for, Odysseus stood still, leaning his hand against a pear tree and sorrowing in his heart. Old Laertes kept his head down as he stood digging at the plant, and he did not see Odysseus until he stood before him and said:

"Old man, thou dost care for this garden well and all things here are flourishing—fig tree, and vine, and olive, and pear. But, if a stranger may say it, thine ownself is not cared for well."

"Who art thou that dost speak to me like this?" old Laertes said, lifting his head.

"I am a stranger in Ithaca," said Odysseus. "I seek a man whom I once kindly treated—a man whose name was Odysseus. A stranger, he came to me, and he declared that he was of Ithaca, and that one day he would give me entertainment for the entertainment I had given him. I know not if this man be still alive."

Old Laertes wept before Odysseus. "Ah," said he, "if thou hadst been able to find him here, the gifts thou gavest him would not have been bestowed in vain. True hospitality thou wouldst have received from Odysseus, my son. But he has perished—far from his country's soil he has perished, the hapless man, and his mother wept not over him, nor his wife, nor me, his father."

So he spake and then with his hands he took up the dust of the ground, and he strewed it over his head in his sorrow. The heart of Odysseus was moved with grief. He sprang forward and fell on his father's neck and he kissed him, saying:

"Behold I am here, even I, my father. I, Odysseus, have come back to mine own country. Cease thy lamentation until I tell thee of the things that have happened. I have slain the wooers in mine hall, and I have avenged all their injuries and all their wrongful doings. Dost thou not believe this, my father? Then look on what I will show thee. Behold on my foot the mark of the boar's tusk—there it is from the days of my youth."

Laertes looked down on the bare foot, and he saw the scar, but still his mind was clouded by doubt. But then Odysseus took him through the garden, and he told him of the fruit trees that Laertes had set for him when he, Odysseus, was a little child, following his father about the garden—thirteen pear trees, and ten apple trees, and forty fig trees.

When Odysseus showed him these Laertes knew that it was his son indeed who stood before him—his son come back after twenty years' wandering. He cast his arms around his neck, and Odysseus caught him fainting to his breast, and led him into the house.

Within the house were Telemachus, and Eumæus the swineherd and Philœtius the cattleherd. They all clasped the hand of Laertes and their words raised his spirits. Then he was bathed, and when he came from the bath, rubbed with olive oil, he looked hale and strong. Odysseus said to him, "Father, surely one of the gods has made thee goodlier and greater than thou wert a while ago."

Said the old hero Laertes: "Ah, my son, would that I had such might as when, long before thou wert born, I took the Castle of Nericus there upon the Foreland. Would that in such might, and with such mail upon my shoulders, I stood with thee yesterday when thou didst fight with the wooers."

While they were speaking in this way the rumor of the slaying of the wooers went through the City. Then those who were related to the men slain went into the courtyard of Odysseus' house, and brought forth the bodies. Those who belonged to Ithaca they buried, and those who belonged to the Islands they put upon ships, and sent them with fisherfolk, each to his own home. Many were wroth with Odysseus for the slaying of a friend. He who was the most wroth was Eupeithes, the father of Antinoüs.

There was an assembly of the men of the country, and Eupeithes spake in it, and all who were there pitied him. He told how Odysseus had led away the best of the men of Ithaca, and how he had lost them in his ships. And he told them how, when he returned, he slew the noblest of the men of Ithaca and the Islands in his own hall. He called upon them to slay Odysseus saying, "If we avenge not ourselves on the slayer of our kin we will be scorned for all time as weak and cowardly men. As for me, life will be no more sweet to me. I would rather die straightway and be with the departed. Up now, and let us attack Odysseus and his followers before they take ship and escape across the sea."

Many in that assembly put on their armor and went out with old Eupeithes. And as they went through the town they met with Odysseus and his following as they were coming from the house of Laertes.

Now as the two bands came close to each other—Odysseus with

Telemachus and Laertes; with the swineherd and the cattleherd; with Dolius, Laertes' servant, and with the six sons of Dolius—and Eupeithes with his friends—a great figure came between. It was the figure of a tall, fair and splendid woman. Odysseus knew her for the goddess Pallas Athene.

"Hold your hands from fierce fighting, ye men of Ithaca," the goddess called out in a terrible voice. "Hold your hands." Straightway the arms fell from each man's hands. Then the goddess called them together, and she made them enter into a covenant that all bloodshed and wrong would be forgotten, and that Odysseus would be left to rule Ithaca as a King, in peace.

So ends the story of Odysseus who went with King Agamemnon to the wars of Troy; who made the plan of the Wooden Horse by which Priam's City was taken at last; who missed the way of his return, and came to the Land of the Lotus-eaters; who came to the Country of the dread Cyclopes, to the Island of Æolus and to the house of Circe, the Enchantress; who heard the song of the Sirens, and came to the Rocks Wandering, and to the terrible Charybdis, and the Scylla, past whom no other man had won scatheless; who landed on the Island where the Cattle of the Sun grazed, and who stayed upon Ogygia, the home of the nymph Calypso; so ends the story of Odysseus, who would have been made deathless and ageless by Calypso if he had not yearned always to come back to his own hearth and his own land. And spite of all his troubles and his toils he was fortunate, for he found a constant wife and a dutiful son and a father still alive to weep over him.

The Epic of Kings

THE EPIC OF KINGS

Hero Tales of Ancient Persia, retold from Firdusi's "Shah-Nameh."

RUSTEM AND SOHRAB

Retold by HELEN ZIMMERN

Illustration by Wilfred Jones

GIVE ear unto the combat of Sohrab against Rustem, though it be a tale replete with tears.

It came about that on a certain day Rustem arose from his couch, and his mind was filled with forebodings. He bethought him therefore to go out to the chase. So he saddled Rakush and made ready his quiver with arrows. Then he turned him unto the wilds that lie near Turan, even in the direction of the city of Samengan. And when he was come nigh unto it, he started a herd of asses and made sport among them till that he was weary of the hunt. Then he caught one and slew it and roasted it for his meal, and when he had eaten it and broken the bones for the marrow, he laid himself down to slumber, and Rakush cropped the pasture beside him.

Now while the hero was sleeping, there passed by seven knights of Turan, and they beheld Rakush and coveted him. So they threw their cords at him to ensnare him. But Rakush, when he beheld their design, pawed the ground in anger, and fell upon them as he had fallen upon the lion. And of one man he bit off the head, and another he struck down under his hoofs, and he would have overcome them all, but they were too many. So they ensnared him and led him into the city, thinking in their hearts, "Verily a goodly capture have we made." But Rustem when he awoke from his slumbers was downcast and sore grieved when he saw not his steed, and he said unto himself:

"How can I stand against the Turks, and how can I traverse the desert alone?"

And his heart was full of trouble. Then he sought for the traces of the horse's hoofs, and he followed them, and they led him even unto the gates of the city. Now when those within beheld Rustem, and that he came before them on foot, the King and the nobles came forth to greet him, and inquired of him how this was come about. Then Rustem told them how Rakush was vanished while he slumbered, and how he had followed his track even unto these gates. And he sware a great oath, and vowed that if his courser were not restored unto him many heads should quit their trunks. Then the King of Samengan, when he saw that Rustem was beside himself with anger, spoke words of soothing, and said that none of his people should do wrong unto the hero; and he begged him that he would enter into his house and abide with him until that search had been made, saying:

"Surely Rakush cannot be hid."

And Rustem was satisfied at these words, and cast suspicion from his spirit, and entered the house of the King, and feasted with him, and beguiled the hours with wine. And the King rejoiced in his guest, and encompassed him with sweet singers and all honor. And when the night was fallen the King himself led Rustem unto a couch perfumed with musk and roses, and he bade him slumber sweetly until the morning. And he declared to him yet again that all was well for him and for his steed.

Now when a portion of the night was spent, and the star of morning stood high in the arch of heaven, the door of Rustem's chamber was opened, and a murmur of soft voices came in from the threshold. And there stepped within a slave bearing a lamp perfumed with amber, and a woman whose beauty was veiled came after her. And as she moved musk was scattered from her robes. And the woman came nigh unto the bed of the hero heavy with wine and slumber. And he was amazed when he saw them. And when he had roused him somewhat he spake and said:

"Who art thou, and what is thy name and thy desire, and what seekest thou from me in the dark night?"

Then the Peri-faced answered him, saying, "I am Tahmineh, the daughter of the King of Samengan, of the race of the leopard and the lion, and none of the princes of this earth are worthy of my hand, neither hath any man seen me unveiled. But my heart is torn with anguish, and my spirit is tossed with desire, for I have heard of thy deeds of prowess, and how thou fearest neither Deev nor lion, neither leopard nor crocodile, and how thy hand is swift to strike, and how thou didst venture alone into Mazinderan, and how wild asses are devoured of thee, and how the earth groaneth under the tread of thy feet, and how men perish at thy blows, and how even the eagle dareth not swoop down upon her prey when she beholdeth thy sword. These things and more have they told unto me, and mine eyes have yearned to look upon thy face. And now hath God brought thee within the gates of my father, and I am come to say unto thee that I am thine if thou wilt hear me, and if thou wilt not, none other will I espouse. And consider, O Pehliva, how that love hath obscured mine understanding and withdrawn me from the bosom of discretion, yet peradventure God will grant unto me a son like to thee for strength and valor, to whom shall be given the empire of the world. And if thou will listen unto me, I will lead forth before thee Rakush thy steed, and I will place under thy feet the land of Samengan."

Now while this moon of beauty was yet speaking, Rustem regarded her. And he saw that she was fair, and that wisdom abode in her mind; and when he heard of Rakush, his spirit was decided within him, and he held that this adventure could not end save gloriously. So he sent a Mubid unto the King and demanded the hand of Tahmineh from her father. And the King, when he heard the news, was rejoiced, and gave his daughter unto the Pehliva, and they concluded an alliance according to custom and the rites. And all men, young and old, within the house and city of the King were glad at this alliance, and called down blessings upon Rustem.

Now Rustem, when he was alone with the Peri-faced, took from his arm an onyx that was known unto all the world. And he gave it to her, and said:

"Cherish this jewel, and if Heaven cause thee to give birth unto a daughter, fasten it within her locks, and it will shield her from evil; but if it be granted unto thee to bring forth a son, fasten it upon his arm, that he may wear it like his father. And he shall be strong as Keriman, of stature like unto Saum the son of Neriman, and of grace of speech like unto Zal, my father."

The Peri-faced, when she had heard these words, was glad in his presence. But when the day was passed there came in unto them the King her father, and he told Rustem how that tidings of Rakush were come unto his ears, and how that the courser would shortly be within the gates. And Rustem, when he heard it, was filled with longing after his steed, and when he knew that he was come he hastened forth to caress him. And with his own hands he fastened the saddle, and gave thanks unto Ormuzd, who had restored his joy between his hands. Then he knew that the time to depart was come. And he opened his arms and took unto his heart Tahmineh the fair of face, and he bathed her cheek with his tears and covered her hair with kisses. Then he flung him upon Rakush, and the swift-footed bare him quickly from out of her sight. And Tahmineh was sorrowful exceedingly, and Rustem too was filled with thoughts as he turned him back into Zaboulistan. And he pondered this adventure in his heart, but to no man did he speak of what he had seen or done.

Now when nine moons had run their course there was born unto Tahmineh a son in the likeness of his father, a babe whose mouth was filled with smiles, and wherefore men called him Sohrab. And when he numbered but one month he was like unto a child of twelve, and when he numbered five years he was skilled in arms and all the arts of war, and when ten years were rolled above his head there was none in the land that could resist him in games of strength. Then he came before his mother and spake words of daring. And he said:

"Since I am taller and stouter than my peers, teach unto me my race and lineage, and what I shall say when men ask me the name of my sire. But if thou refuse an answer unto my demands, I will strike thee out from the rolls of the living."

When Tahmineh beheld the ardor of her son, she smiled in her spirit because that his fire was like to that of his father. And she opened her mouth and said:

"Hear my words, O my son, and be glad in thine heart, neither give way in thy spirit to anger. For thou art the offspring of Rustem, thou art descended from the seed of Saum and Zal, and Neriman was thy forefather. And since God made the world it hath held none like unto Rustem, thy sire."

Then she showed to him a letter written by the Pehliva, and gave to him the gold and jewels Rustem had sent at his birth. And she spake and said:

"Cherish these gifts with gratitude, for it is thy father who hath sent them. Yet remember, O my son, that thou close thy lips concerning these things; for Turan groaneth under the hand of Afrasiyab, and he is foe unto Rustem the glorious. If, therefore, he should learn of thee, he would seek to destroy the son for hatred of the sire. Moreover, O my boy, if Rustem learned that thou wert become a mountain of valor, perchance he would demand thee at my hands, and the sorrow of thy loss would crush the heart of thy mother."

But Sohrab replied, "Nought can be hidden upon earth for aye. To all men are known the deeds of Rustem, and since my birth be thus noble, wherefore hast thou kept it dark from me so long? I will go forth with an army of brave Turks and lead them unto Iran, I will cast Kai Kaous from off his throne, I will give to Rustem the crown of the Kaianides, and together we will subdue the land of Turan, and Afrasiyab shall be slain by my hands. Then will I mount the throne in his stead. But thou shalt be called Queen of Iran, for since Rustem is my father and I am his son no other kings shall rule in this world, for to us alone behooveth it to wear the crowns of might. And I pant in longing after the battlefield, and I desire that the world should behold my prowess. But a horse is needful unto me, a steed tall and strong of power to bear me, for it beseemeth me not to go on foot before mine enemies."

Now Tahmineh, when she had heard the words of this boy, rejoiced in her soul at his courage. So she bade the guardians of the flocks lead out the horses before Sohrab her son. And they did as she had bidden, and Sohrab surveyed the steeds, and tested their strength like as his father had done before him of old, and he bowed them under his hand, and he could not be satisfied. And thus for many days did he seek a worthy steed. Then one came before him and told of a foal sprung from Rakush, the swift of foot. When Sohrab heard the tidings he smiled, and bade that the foal be led before him. And he tested it and found it to be strong. So he saddled it and sprang upon its back and cried, saying,

"Now that I own a horse like thee, the world shall be made dark to many."

Then he made ready for war against Iran, and the nobles and warriors flocked around him. And when all was in order Sohrab came before his grandsire and craved his counsel and his aid to go forth into the land of Iran and seek out his father. And the King of Samengan, when he heard these wishes, deemed them to be just, and he opened the doors of his treasures without stint and gave unto Sohrab of his wealth, for he was filled with pleasure at this boy. And he invested Sohrab with all the honors of a King, and he bestowed on him all the marks of his good pleasure.

Meantime a certain man brought news unto Afrasiyab that Sohrab was making ready an army to fall upon Iran, and to cast Kai Kaous from off his throne. And he told Afrasiyab how the courage and valor of Sohrab exceeded words. And Afrasiyab, when he heard this, hid not his contentment, and he called before him Human and Barman, the doughty. Then he bade them gather together an army and join the ranks of Sohrab, and he confided to them his secret purpose, but he enjoined them to tell no man thereof. For he said:

"Into our hands hath it been given to settle the course of the world. For it is known unto me that Sohrab is sprung from Rustem the Pehliva, but from Rustem must it be hidden who it is that goeth out against him, then peradventure he will perish by the hands of this young lion, and Iran, devoid of Rustem, will fall a prey into my hands. Then will we subdue Sohrab also, and all the world will be ours. But if it be written that Sohrab fall under the hand of Tehemten, then the grief he shall endure when he shall learn that he hath slain his son will bring him to the grave for sorrow."

So spake Afrasiyab in his guile, and when he had done unveiling his black heart he bade the warriors depart unto Samengan. And they bare with them gifts of great price to pour before the face of Sohrab. And they bare also a letter filled with soft words. And in the letter Afrasiyab lauded Sohrab for his resolve, and told him how that if Iran be subdued the world would henceforth know peace, for

upon his own head would he place the crown of the Kaianides; and
Turan, Iran, and Samengan should be as one land.

When Sohrab had read this letter, and saw the gifts and the aid
sent out to him, he rejoiced aloud, for he deemed that now none
could withstand his might. So he caused the cymbals of departure
to be clashed, and the army made them ready to go forth. Then
Sohrab led them into the land of Iran. And their track was marked
by desolation and destruction, for they spared nothing that they
passed. And they spread fire and dismay abroad, and they marched
on unstayed until they came unto the White Castle, the fortress
wherein Iran put its trust.

Now the guardian of the castle was named Hujir, and there lived
with him Gustahem the brave, but he was grown old, and could aid
no longer save with his counsels. And there abode also his daughter
Gurdafrid, a warlike maid, firm in the saddle, and practised in the
fight. Now when Hujir beheld from afar a dusty cloud of armed
men he came forth to meet them. And Sohrab, when he saw him,
drew his sword, and demanded his name, and bade him prepare to
meet his end. And he taunted him with rashness that he was come
forth thus unaided to stand against a lion. But Hujir answered Sohrab with taunts again, and vowed that he would sever his head from
his trunk and send it for a trophy unto the Shah. Yet Sohrab only
smiled when he heard these words, and he challenged Hujir to come
near. And they met in combat, and wrestled sore one with another,
and stalwart were their strokes and strong; but Sohrab overcame
Hujir as though he were an infant, and he bound him and sent him
captive unto Human.

But when those within the castle learned that their chief was
bound they raised great lamentation, and their fears were sore. And
Gurdafrid, too, when she learned it, was grieved, but she was
ashamed also for the fate of Hujir. So she took forth burnished mail
and clad herself therein, and she hid her tresses under a helmet of
Roum, and she mounted a steed of battle and came forth before the
walls like to a warrior. And she uttered a cry of thunder, and flung
it amid the ranks of Turan, and she defied the champions to come
forth to single combat. And none came, for they beheld her how

she was strong, and they knew not that it was a woman, and they were afraid. But Sohrab, when he saw it, stepped forth and said:

"I will accept thy challenge, and a second prize will fall into my hands."

Then he girded himself and made ready for the fight. And the maid, when she saw he was ready, rained arrows upon him with art, and they fell quick like hail, and whizzed about his head; and Sohrab, when he saw it, could not defend himself, and was angry and ashamed. Then he covered his head with a shield and ran at the maid. But she, when she saw him approach, dropped her bow and couched a lance, and thrust at Sohrab with vigor, and shook him mightily, and it wanted little and she would have thrown him from his seat. And Sohrab was amazed, and his wrath knew no bounds. Then he ran at Gurdafrid with fury, and seized the reins of her steed, and caught her by the waist, and tore her armor, and threw her upon the ground. Yet ere he could raise his hand to strike her, she drew her sword and shivered his lance in twain, and leaped again upon her steed. And when she saw that the day was hers, she was weary of further combat, and she sped back unto the fortress. But Sohrab gave rein unto his horse, and followed after her in his great anger. And he caught her, and seized her, and tore the helmet from off her head, for he desired to look upon the face of the man who could withstand the son of Rustem. And lo! when he had done so, there rolled forth from the helmet coils of dusky hue, and Sohrab beheld it was a woman that had overcome him in the fight. And he was confounded. But when he had found speech he said:

"If the daughters of Iran are like to thee, and go forth unto battle, none can stand against this land."

Then he took his cord and threw it about her, and bound her in its snare, saying:

"Seek not to escape me, O moon of beauty, for never hath prey like unto thee fallen between my hands."

Then Gurdafrid, full of wile, turned unto him her face that was unveiled, for she beheld no other means of safety, and she said unto him:

"O hero without flaw, is it well that thou shouldst seek to make me captive, and show me unto the army? For they have beheld our combat, and that I overcame thee, and surely now they will gibe when they learn that thy strength was withstood by a woman. Better would it beseem thee to hide this adventure, lest thy cheeks have cause to blush because of me. Therefore let us conclude a peace together. The castle shall be thine, and all it holds; follow after me then, and take possession of thine own."

Now Sohrab, when he had listened, was beguiled by her words and her beauty, and he said:

"Thou dost wisely to make peace with me, for verily these walls could not resist my might."

And he followed after her unto the heights of the castle, and he stood with her before its gates. And Gustahem, when he saw them, opened the portal, and Gurdafrid stepped within the threshold, but when Sohrab would have followed after her she shut the door upon him. Then Sohrab saw that she had befooled him, and his fury knew no bounds. But ere he was recovered from his surprise she came out upon the battlements and scoffed at him, and counseled him to go back whence he was come; for surely, since he could not stand against a woman, he would fall an easy prey before Rustem, when the Pehliva should have learned that robbers from Turan were broken into the land. And Sohrab was made yet madder for her words, and he departed from the walls in his wrath, and rode far in his anger, and spread terror in his path. And he vowed that he would yet bring the maid into subjection.

In the meantime Gustahem the aged called before him a scribe, and bade him write unto Kai Kaous all that was come about, and how an army was come forth from Turan, at whose head rode a chief that was a child in years, a lion in strength and stature. And he told how Hujir had been bound, and how the fortress was like to fall into the hands of the enemy; for there were none to defend it save only his daughter and himself and he craved the Shah to come to their aid.

Albeit when the day had followed yet again upon the night, Sohrab made ready his host to fall upon the castle. But when he came near thereto he found it was empty, and the doors thereof stood open, and no warriors appeared upon its walls. And he was surprised, for he knew not that in the darkness the inmates were fled by a passage that was hidden under the earth. And he searched the building for Gurdafrid, for his heart yearned after her in love, and he cried aloud:

"Woe, woe is me that this moon is vanished behind the clouds!"

Now when Kai Kaous had gotten the writing of Gustahem, he was sore afflicted and much afraid, and he called about him his nobles and asked their counsels. And he said:

"Who shall stand against this Turk? For Gustahem doth liken him in power unto Rustem, and saith he resembleth the seed of Neriman." Then the warriors cried with one accord, "Unto Rustem alone can we look in this danger!"

And Kai Kaous hearkened to their voice, and he called for a scribe and dictated unto him a letter. And he wrote unto his Pehliva, and invoked the blessings of Heaven upon his head, and he told him all that was come to pass, and how new dangers threatened Iran, and how to Rustem alone could he look for help in his trouble. And he recalled unto Tehemten all that he had done for him in the days that were gone by, and he entreated him once again to be his refuge. And he said:

"When thou shalt receive this letter, stay not to speak the word that hangeth upon thy lips; and if thou bearest roses in thy hands, stop not to smell them, but haste thee to help us in our need."

Then Kai Kaous sent forth Gew with this writing unto Zaboulistan, and bade him neither rest nor tarry until he should stand before the face of Rustem. And he said:

"When thou hast done my behest, turn thee again unto me; neither abide within the courts of the Pehliva, nor linger by the roadside."

And Gew did as the Shah commanded, and took neither food nor rest till he set foot within the gates of Rustem. And Rustem greeted him kindly, and asked him of his mission; and when he had read the writing of the Shah, he questioned Gew concerning Sohrab. For he said:

"I should not marvel if such a hero arose in Iran; but that a warrior of renown should come forth from amid the Turks, I cannot believe it. But thou sayest none knoweth whence cometh this knight. I have myself a son in Samengan, but he is yet an infant, and his mother writeth to me that he rejoiceth in the sports of his age, and though he be like to become a hero among men, his time is not yet come to lead forth an army. And that which thou sayest hath been done, surely it is not the work of a babe. But enter, I pray thee, into my house, and we will confer together concerning this adventure."

Then Rustem bade his cooks make ready a banquet, and he feasted Gew, and troubled his head with wine, and caused him to forget cares and time. But when morn was come Gew remembered the commands of the Shah that he tarry not, but return with all speed, and he spake thereof to Rustem, and prayed him to make known his resolve. But Rustem spake, saying:

"Disquiet not thyself, for death will surely fall upon these men of Turan. Stay with me yet another day and rest, and water thy lips that are parched. For though this Sohrab be a hero like to Saum and Zal and Neriman, verily he shall fall by my hands."

And he made ready yet another banquet, and three days they caroused without ceasing. But on the fourth Gew uprose with resolve, and came before Rustem girt for departure. And he said:

"It behooveth me to return, O Pehliva, for I bethink me how Kai Kaous is a man hard and choleric, and the fear of Sohrab weigheth upon his heart, and his soul burneth with impatience, and he hath lost sleep, and hath hunger and thirst on this account. And he will be wroth against us if we delay yet longer to do his behest."

Then Rustem said, "Fear not, for none on earth dare be angered with me."

But he did as Gew desired, and made ready his army, and saddled Rakush, and set forth from Zaboulistan, and a great train followed after him.

Now when they came nigh unto the courts of the Shah, the nobles came forth to meet them, and do homage before Rustem. And when they were come in, Rustem got him from Rakush and hastened into the presence of his lord. But Kai Kaous, when he beheld him, was

angry, and spake not, and his brows were knit with fury; and when
Rustem had done obeisance before him, he unlocked the doors of
his mouth, and words of folly escaped his lips. And he said:

"Who is Rustem, that he defieth my power and disregardeth my
commands? If I had a sword within my grasp I would split his
head like to an orange. Seize him, I command, and hang him upon
the nearest gallows, and let his name be never spoken in my presence."

When he heard these words Gew trembled in his heart, but he
said, "Dost thou put forth thy hand against Rustem?"

And the Shah when he heard it was beside himself, and he cried
with a loud voice that Gew be hanged together with the other; and
he bade Tus lead them forth. And Tus would have led them out,
for he hoped the anger of the Shah would be appeased; but Rustem
broke from his grasp and stood before Kai Kaous, and all the nobles
were filled with fear when they saw his anger. And he flung reproaches at Kai Kaous, and he recalled to him his follies, and the
march into Mazinderan and Hamaveran, and his flight into Heaven;
and he reminded him how that but for Rustem he would not now be
seated upon the throne of light. And he bade him threaten Sohrab
the Turk with his gallows, and he said:

"I am a free man and no slave, and am servant alone unto God;
and without Rustem, Kai Kaous is as nothing. And the world is
subject unto me, and Rakush is my throne, and my sword is my seal,
and my helmet my crown. And but for me, who called forth Kai
Kobad, thine eyes had never looked upon this throne. And had I
desired it I could have sat upon its seat. But now am I weary of thy
follies, and I will turn me away from Iran, and when this Turk shall
have put you under his yoke I shall not learn thereof."

Then he turned him and strode from out the presence-chamber.
And he sprang upon Rakush, who waited without, and he was vanished from before their eyes ere yet the nobles had rallied from their
astonishment. And they were downcast and oppressed with boding
cares, and they held counsel among themselves what to do; for
Rustem was their mainstay, and they knew that bereft of his arm
and counsel they could not stand against this Turk. And they

blamed Kai Kaous, and counted over the good deeds that Rustem had done for him, and they pondered and spake long. And in the end they resolved to send a messenger unto Kai Kaous, and they chose from their midst Gudarz the aged, and bade him stand before the Shah. And Gudarz did as they desired, and he spake long and without fear, and he counted over each deed that had been done by Rustem; and he reproached the Shah with his ingratitude, and he said how Rustem was the shepherd, and how the flock could not be led without its leader. And Kai Kaous heard him unto the end, and he knew that his words were the words of reason and truth, and he was ashamed of that which he had done, and confounded when he beheld his acts thus naked before him. And he humbled himself before Gudarz, and said:

"That which thou sayest, surely it is right."

And he entreated Gudarz to go forth and seek Rustem, and bid him forget the evil words of his Shah, and bring him back to the succor of Iran. And Gudarz hastened forth to do as Kai Kaous desired, and he told the nobles of his mission and they joined themselves unto him, and all the chiefs of Iran went forth in quest of Rustem. And when they had found him, they prostrated themselves into the dust before him, and Gudarz told him of his mission, and he prayed him to remember that Kai Kaous was a man devoid of understanding, whose thoughts flowed over like to new wine that fermenteth. And he said:

"Though Rustem be angered against the King, yet hath the land of Iran done no wrong that it should perish at his hands. Yet, if Rustem save it not, surely it will fall under this Turk."

But Rustem said, "My patience hath an end, and I fear none but God. What is this Kai Kaous that he should anger me? and what am I that I have need of him? I have not deserved the evil words that he spake unto me, but now will I think of them no longer, but cast aside all thoughts of Iran."

When the nobles heard these words they grew pale, and fear took hold on their hearts. But Gudarz, full of wisdom, opened his mouth and said:

"O Pehliva! the land, when it shall learn of this, will deem that

Rustem is fled before the face of this Turk; and when men shall believe that Tehemten is afraid, they will cease to combat, and Iran will be downtrodden at his hands. Turn thee not, therefore, at this hour from thy allegiance to the Shah, and tarnish not thy glory by this retreat, neither suffer that the downfall of Iran rest upon thy head. Put from thee, therefore, the words that Kai Kaous spake in his empty anger, and lead us forth to battle against this Turk. For it must not be spoken that Rustem feared to fight a beardless boy."

And Rustem listened and pondered these words in his heart, and knew that they were good. But he said:

"Fear hath never been known of me, neither hath Rustem shunned the din of arms, and I depart not because of Sohrab, but because that scorn and insult have been my recompense."

Yet when he had pondered a while longer, he saw that he must return unto the Shah. So he did that which he knew to be right, and he rode till he came unto the gates of Kai Kaous, and he strode with a proud step into his presence.

Now when the Shah beheld Rustem from afar, he stepped down from off his throne and came before his Pehliva, and craved his pardon for that which was come about. And he said how he had been angered because Rustem had tarried in his coming, and how haste was his birthright, and how he had forgotten himself in his vexation. But now was his mouth filled with the dust of repentance. And Rustem said:

"The world is the Shah's, and it behooveth thee to do as beseemeth thee best with thy servants. And until old age shall my loins be girt in fealty unto thee. And may power and majesty be thine forever!"

And Kai Kaous answered and said, "O my Pehliva, may thy days be blessed unto the end!"

Then he invited him to feast with him, and they drank wine till far into the night, and held counsel together how they should act; and slaves poured rich gifts before Rustem, and the nobles rejoiced, and all was well again within the gates of the King.

Then when the sun had risen and clothed the world with love, the clarions of war were sounded throughout the city, and men made them ready to go forth in enmity before the Turks. And the legions of Persia came forth at the behest of their Shah, and their countless thousands hid the earth under their feet, and the air was darkened by their spears. And when they were come unto the plains where stood the fortress of Hujir, they set up their tents as was their manner. So the watchman saw them from the battlements, and he set up a great cry. And Sohrab heard the cry, and questioned the man wherefore he shouted; and when he learned that the enemy were come, he rejoiced, and demanded a cup of wine, and drank to their destruction. Then he called forth Human and showed him the army, and bade him be of good cheer, for he said that he saw within its ranks no hero of mighty mace who could stand against himself. So he bade his warriors to a banquet of wine, and he said that they would feast until the time was come to meet their foes in battle. And they did as Sohrab said.

Now when night had thrown her mantle over the earth, Rustem came before the Shah and craved that he would suffer him to go forth beyond the camp that he might see what manner of man was this stripling. And Kai Kaous granted his request, and said that it was worthy a Pehliva of renown. Then Rustem went forth disguised in the garb of a Turk, and he entered the castle in secret, and he came within the chamber where Sohrab held his feast. Now when he had looked upon the boy he saw that he was like to a tall cypress of good sap, and that his arms were sinewy and strong like the flanks of a camel, and that his stature was that of a hero. And he saw that round about him stood brave warriors. And slaves with golden bugles poured wine before them, and they were all glad, neither did they dream of sorrow. Then it came about that while Rustem regarded them, Zindeh changed his seat and came nigh unto the spot where Rustem was watching. Now Zindeh was brother unto Tahmineh, and she had sent him forth with her son that he might point out to him his father, whom he alone knew of all the army, and she did it that harm might not befall if the heroes should meet in battle. Now Zindeh, when he had changed his seat, thought that he espied a watcher, and he strode toward the place where Rustem was hid, and he came before him and said:

"Who are thou? Come forth into the light that I may behold thy face."

But ere he could speak further, Rustem had lifted up his hand and struck him, and laid him dead upon the ground.

Now Sohrab, when he saw that Zindeh was gone out, was disquieted, and he asked of his slaves wherefore the hero returned not unto the banquet. So they went forth to seek him, and when they had found him in his blood, they came and told Sohrab what they had seen. But Sohrab would not believe it; so he ran to the spot and bade them bring torches, and all the warriors and singing girls followed after him. Then when Sohrab saw that it was true he was sore grieved; but he suffered not that the banquet be ended, for he would not that the spirits of his men be damped with pity. So they went back yet again to the feast.

Meanwhile Rustem returned him to the camp, and as he would have entered the lines he encountered Gew, who went around to see that all was safe. And Gew, when he saw a tall man clad in the garb of a Turk, drew his sword and held himself ready for combat. But Rustem smiled and opened his mouth, and Gew knew his voice, and came to him and questioned him what he did without in the darkness. And Rustem told him. Then he went before Kai Kaous also and related what he had seen, and how no man like unto Sohrab was yet come forth from amid the Turks. And he likened him unto Saum, the son of Neriman.

Now when the morning was come, Sohrab put on his armor. Then he went unto a height whence he could look down over the camp of the Iranians. And he took with him Hujir, and spake to him, saying:

"Seek not to deceive me, nor swerve from the paths of truth. For if thou reply unto my questions with sincerity, I will loosen thy bands and give thee treasures; but if thou deceive me, thou shalt languish till death in thy chains."

And Hujir said, "I will give answer unto thee according to my knowledge."

Then Sohrab said, "I am about to question thee concerning the nobles whose camps are spread beneath our feet, and thou shalt name unto me those whom I point out. Behold yon tent of gold brocade, adorned with skins of leopard, before whose doors stand a hundred elephants of war. Within its gates is a throne of turquoise, and over it floateth a standard of violet with a moon and sun worked in its center. Tell unto me now whose is this pavilion that standeth thus in the midst of the whole camp?"

And Hujir replied, "It pertaineth unto the Shah of Iran."

Then Sohrab said, "I behold on its right hand yet another tent draped in the colors of mourning, and above it floateth a standard whereon is worked an elephant."

And Hujir said, "It is the tent of Tus, the son of Nuder, for he beareth an elephant as his ensign."

Then Sohrab said, "Whose is the camp in which stand many warriors clad in rich armor? A flag of gold with a lion worked upon it waveth along its field."

And Hujir said, "It belongeth unto Gudarz the brave. And those who stand about it are his sons, for eighty men of might are sprung from his loins."

Then Sohrab said, "To whom belongeth the tent draped with green tissues? Before its doors is planted the flag of Kawah. I see upon its throne a Pehliva, nobler of mien than all his fellows, whose head striketh the stars. And beside him standeth a steed tall as he, and his standard showeth a lion and a writhing dragon."

When Hujir heard this question he thought within himself, "If I tell unto this lion the signs whereby he may know Rustem the Pehliva, surely he will fall upon him and seek to destroy him. It will beseem me better, therefore, to keep silent, and to omit his name from the list of the heroes." So he said unto Sohrab:

"This is some ally who is come unto Kai Kaous from far Cathay, and his name is not known unto me."

And Sohrab when he heard it was downcast, and his heart was sad that he could nowhere discover Rustem; and though it seemed unto him that he beheld the marks whereby his mother said that he would know him, he could not credit the words of his eyes against the words of Hujir. Still he asked yet again the name of the warrior, and yet again Hujir denied it unto him, for it was written that

that should come to pass which had been decreed. But Sohrab ceased not from his questionings. And he asked:

"Who dwelleth beneath the standard with the head of a wolf?"

And Hujir said, "It is Gew, the son of Gudarz, who dwelleth within that tent, and men call him Gew the valiant."

Then Sohrab said, "Whose is the seat over which are raised awnings and brocades of Roum, that glisten with gold in the sunlight?"

And Hujir said, "It is the throne of Fraburz, the son of the Shah."

Then Sohrab said, "It beseemeth the son of a Shah to surround himself with such splendor."

And he pointed unto a tent with trappings of yellow that was encircled by flags of many colors. And he questioned of its owner.

And Hujir said, "Guraz the lion-hearted is master therein."

Then Sohrab, when he could not learn the tent of his father, questioned Hujir concerning Rustem, and he asked yet a third time of the green tent. Yet Hujir ever replied that he knew not the name of its master. And when Sohrab pressed him concerning Rustem, he said that Rustem lingered in Zaboulistan, for it was the feast of roses. But Sohrab refused to give ear unto the thought that Kai Kaous should go forth to battle without the aid of Rustem, whose might none could match. So he said unto Hujir:

"An thou show not unto me the tents of Rustem, I will strike thy head from off thy shoulders, and the world shall fade before thine eyes. Choose, therefore, the truth or thy life."

And Hujir thought within himself, "Though five score men cannot withstand Rustem when he be roused to battle-fury, my mind misgiveth me that he may have found his equal in this boy. And, for that the stripling is younger, it might come about that he subdue the Pehliva. What recketh my life against the weal of Iran? I will therefore abandon me into his hands rather than show unto him the marks of Rustem the Pehliva." So he said:

"Why seekest thou to know Rustem the Pehliva? Surely thou wilt know him in battle, and he shall strike thee dumb, and quell thy pride of youth. Yet I will not show him unto thee."

When Sohrab heard these words he raised his sword and smote Hujir, and made an end of him with a great blow. Then he made himself ready for fight, and leaped upon his steed of battle, and he rode till he came unto the camp of the Iranians, and he broke down the barriers with his spear, and fear seized upon all men when they beheld his stalwart form and majesty of mien and action. Then Sohrab opened his mouth, and his voice of thunder was heard even unto the far ends of the camp. And he spake words of pride, and called forth the Shah to do battle with him, and he sware with a loud voice that the blood of Zindeh should be avenged. Now when Sohrab's voice had rung throughout the camp, confusion spread within its borders, and none of those who stood about the throne would accept his challenge for the Shah. And with one accord they said that Rustem was their sole support, and that his sword alone could cause the sun to weep. And Tus sped him within the courts of Rustem. And Rustem said:

"The hardest tasks doth Kai Kaous ever lay upon me."

But the nobles would not suffer him to linger, neither to waste time in words, and they buckled upon him his armor, and they threw his leopard-skin about him, and they saddled Rakush, and made ready the hero for the strife. And they pushed him forth, and called after him.

"Haste, haste, for no common combat awaiteth thee, for verily Ahriman standeth before us."

Now when Rustem was come before Sohrab, and beheld the youth, brave and strong, with a breast like unto Saum, he said to him:

"Let us go apart from hence, and step forth from out the lines of the armies."

For there was a zone between the two camps that none might pass. And Sohrab assented to the demand of Rustem, and they stepped out into it, and made them ready for single combat. But when Sohrab would have fallen upon him, the soul of Rustem melted with compassion, and he desired to save a boy thus fair and valiant. So he said unto him:

"O young man, the air is warm and soft, but the earth is cold. I have pity upon thee, and would not take from thee the boon of life. Yet if we combat together, surely thou wilt fall by my hands, for none have withstood my power, neither men nor Deevs nor dragons. Desist, therefore, from this enterprise, and quit the ranks of Turan, for Iran hath need of heroes like unto thee."

Now while Rustem spake thus, the heart of Sohrab went out to him. And he looked at him wistfully, and said:

"O hero, I am about to put unto thee a question, and I entreat of thee that thou reply to me according to the truth. Tell unto me thy name, that my heart may rejoice in thy words, for it seemeth unto me that thou art none other than Rustem, the son of Zal, the son of Saum, the son of Neriman."

But Rustem replied, "Thou errest, I am not Rustem, neither am I sprung from the race of Neriman. Rustem is a Pehliva, but I, I am a slave, and own neither a crown nor a throne."

These words spake Rustem that Sohrab might be afraid when he beheld his prowess, and deem that yet greater might was hidden in the camp of his enemy. But Sohrab when he heard these words was sad, and his hopes that were risen so high were shattered, and the day that had looked so bright was made dark unto his eyes. Then he made him ready for the combat, and they fought until their spears were shivered and their swords hacked like unto saws. And when all their weapons were bent, they betook them unto clubs and they waged war with these until they were broken. Then they strove until their mail was torn and their horses spent with exhaustion, and even then they could not desist, but wrestled with one another with their hands till that the sweat and blood ran down from their bodies. And they contended until their throats were parched and their bodies weary, and to neither was given the victory. Then they stayed them a while to rest, and Rustem thought within his mind how all his days he had not coped with such a hero. And it seemed to him that his contest with the White Deev had been as nought to this.

Now when they had rested a while they fell to, again, and they fought with arrows, but still none could surpass the other. Then Rustem strove to hurl Sohrab from his steed, but it availed him nought, and he could shake him no more than the mountain can be moved from its seat. So they betook themselves again unto clubs, and Sohrab aimed at Rustem with might and smote him, and Rustem reeled beneath the stroke, and bit his lips in agony. Then Sohrab vaunted his advantage, and bade Rustem go and measure him with his equals; for though his strength be great, he could not stand against a youth. So they went their ways, and Rustem fell upon the men of Turan, and spread confusion far and wide among their ranks; and Sohrab raged along the lines of Iran, and men and horses fell under his hands. And Rustem was sad in his soul, and he turned with sorrow into his camp. But when he saw the destruction Sohrab had wrought his anger was kindled, and he reproached the youth, and challenged him to come forth yet again to single combat. But because that the day was far spent they resolved to rest until the morrow.

Then Rustem went before Kai Kaous and told him of this boy of valor, and he prayed unto Ormuzd that he would give him strength to vanquish his foe. Yet he made ready also his house lest he should fall in the fight, and he commanded that a tender message be borne unto Rudabeh, and he sent words of comfort unto Zal, his father. And Sohrab, too, in his camp lauded the might of Rustem, and he said how the battle had been sore, and how his mind had misgiven him of the issue. And he spake unto Human, saying:

"My mind is filled with thoughts of this aged man, mine adversary, for it would seem unto me that his stature is like unto mine, and that I behold about him the tokens that my mother recounted unto me. And my heart goeth out toward him, and I muse if it be Rustem, my father. For it behooveth me not to combat him. Wherefore, I beseech thee, tell unto me how this may be."

But Human answered and said, "Oft have I looked upon the face of Rustem in battle, and mine eyes have beheld his deeds of valor; but this man in no wise resembleth him, nor is his manner of wielding his club the same."

These things spake Human in his vileness, because that Afrasiyab had enjoined him to lead Sohrab into destruction, And Sohrab held his peace, but he was not wholly satisfied.

Now when the day had begun to lighten the sky and clear away the shadows, Rustem and Sohrab strode forth unto the midway spot that stretched between the armies. And Sohrab bare in his hands a mighty club, and the garb of battle was upon him; but his mouth was full of smiles, and he asked of Rustem how he had rested, and he said:

"Wherefore hast thou prepared thy heart for battle? Cast from thee, I beg, this mace and sword of vengeance, and let us doff our armor, and seat ourselves together in amity, and let wine soften our angry deeds. For it seemeth unto me that this conflict is impure. And if thou wilt listen to my desires, my heart shall speak to thee of love, and I will make the tears of shame spring up into thine eyes. And for this cause I ask thee yet again, tell me thy name, neither hide it any longer, for I behold that thou art of noble race. And it would seem unto me that thou art Rustem, the chosen one, the Lord of Zaboulistan, the son of Zal, the son of Saum the hero."

But Rustem answered, "O hero of tender age, we are not come forth to parley but to combat, and mine ears are sealed against thy words of lure. I am an old man, and thou art young, but we are girded for battle, and the Master of the world shall decide between us."

Then Sohrab said, "O man of many years, wherefore wilt thou not listen to the counsel of a stripling? I desired that thy soul should leave thee upon thy bed, but thou hast elected to perish in the combat. That which is ordained it must be done, therefore let us make ready for the conflict."

So they made them ready, and when they had bound their steeds they fell upon each other and the crash of their encounter was heard like thunder throughout the camps. And they measured their strength from the morning until the setting of the sun. And when the day was about to vanish, Sohrab seized upon Rustem by the girdle and threw him upon the ground, and kneeled upon him, and drew forth his sword from his scabbard, and would have severed his head from his trunk. Then Rustem knew that only wile could save him. So he opened his mouth and said:

"O young man, thou knowest not the customs of the combat. It is written in the laws of honor that he who overthroweth a brave man for the first time should not destroy him, but preserve him for

Wilfred Jones

Rustem hurled him unto the earth.

[See page 112]

fight a second time, then only is it given unto him to kill his adversary."

And Sohrab listened to Rustem's words of craft and stayed his hand, and he let the warrior go, and because that the day was ended he sought to fight no more, but turned him aside and chased the deer until the night was spent. Then came to him Human, and asked of the adventures of the day. And Sohrab told him how he had vanquished the tall man, and how he had granted him freedom. And Human reproached him with his folly, and said:

"Alas, young man, thou didst fall into a snare, for this is not the custom among the brave. And now perchance thou wilt yet fall under the hands of this warrior."

Sohrab was abashed when he heard the words of Human, but he said:

"Be not grieved, for in an hour we meet again in battle, and verily he will not stand a third time against my youthful strength."

Now while Sohrab was thus doing, Rustem was gone beside a running brook, and laved his limbs, and prayed to God in his distress. And he entreated of Ormuzd that he would grant him such strength that the victory must be his. And Ormuzd heard him, and gave to him such strength that the rock whereon Rustem stood gave way under his feet, because it had not the power to bear him. Then Rustem saw it was too much, and he prayed yet again that part thereof be taken from him. And once more Ormuzd listened to his voice. Then when the time for combat was come, Rustem turned him to the meeting-place, and his heart was full of cares and his face of fears. But Sohrab came forth like a giant refreshed, and he ran at Rustem like to a mad elephant, and he cried with a voice of thunder:

"O thou who didst flee from battle, wherefore art thou come out once more against me? But I say unto thee, this time shall thy words of guile avail thee nought."

And Rustem, when he heard him, and looked upon him, was seized with misgiving, and he learned to know fear. So he prayed to Ormuzd that he would restore to him the power he had taken back. But he suffered not Sohrab to behold his fears, and they made them ready for the fight. And he closed upon Sohrab with all his new-found might, and shook him terribly, and though Sohrab returned his attacks with vigor, the hour of his overthrow was come. For Rustem took him by the girdle and hurled him unto the earth, and he broke his back like to a reed, and he drew forth his sword to sever his body. Then Sohrab knew it was the end, and he gave a great sigh, and writhed in his agony, and he said:

"That which is come about, it is my fault, and henceforward will my youth be a theme of derision among the people. But I sped not forth for empty glory, but I went out to seek my father; for my mother had told me by what tokens I should know him, and I perish for longing after him. And now have my pains been fruitless, for it hath not been given unto me to look upon his face. Yet I say unto thee, if shouldest become a fish that swimmeth in the depths of the ocean, if thou shouldest change into a star that is concealed in the farthest heaven, my father would draw thee forth from thy hiding-place, and avenge my death upon thee when he shall learn that the earth is become my bed. For my father is Rustem the Pehliva, and it shall be told unto him how that Sohrab his son perished in the quest after his face."

When Rustem heard these words his sword fell from out of his grasp, and he was shaken with dismay. And there broke from his heart a groan as of one whose heart was racked with anguish. And the earth became dark before his eyes, and he sank down lifeless beside his son. But when he opened his eyes once more, he cried unto Sohrab in the agony of his spirit. And he said:

"Bearest thou about thee a token of Rustem, that I may know that the words which thou speakest are true? For I am Rustem the unhappy, and may my name be struck from the lists of men!"

When Sohrab heard these words his misery was boundless, and he cried:

"If thou art indeed my father, then hast thou stained thy sword in the lifeblood of thy son. And thou didst it of thine obstinacy. For I sought to turn thee unto love, and I implored of thee thy name, for I thought to behold in thee the tokens recounted of my mother.

But I appealed unto thy heart in vain, and now is the time gone by for meeting. Yet open, I beseech thee, mine armor, and regard the jewel upon mine arm. For it is an onyx given unto me by my father, as a token whereby he should know me."

Then Rustem did as Sohrab bade him, and he opened his mail and saw the onyx; and when he had seen it he tore his clothes in his distress, and he covered his head with ashes. And the tears of penitence ran from his eyes, and he roared aloud in his sorrow. But Sohrab said:

"It is in vain, there is no remedy. Weep not, therefore, for doubtless it is written that this should be.

Now when the sun was set, and Rustem returned not to the camp, the nobles of Iran were afraid, and they went forth to seek him. And when they were gone but a little way they came upon Rakush, and when they saw that he was alone they raised a wailing, for they deemed that of a surety Rustem was perished. And they went and told Kai Kaous thereof, and he said:

"Let us go forth and see if this indeed be so, and if Rustem be truly fallen, let the drums call men unto battle that we may avenge him upon this Turk."

Now Sohrab, when he beheld afar off the men that were come out to seek Rustem, turned to his father and said:

"I entreat of thee that thou do unto me an act of love. Let not the Shah fall upon the men of Turan, for they came not forth in enmity to him but to do my desire, and on my head alone resteth this expedition. Wherefore I desire not that they should perish when I can defend them no longer. As for me, I came like the thunder and I vanish like the wind, but perchance it is given unto us to meet again above."

Then Rustem promised to do the desires of Sohrab. And he went before the men of Iran, and when they beheld him yet alive they set up a great shout, but when they saw that his clothes were torn, and that he bare about him the marks of sorrow, they asked of him what was come to pass. Then he told them how he had caused a noble son to perish. And they were grieved for him, and joined in his wailing. Then he bade one among them go forth into the camp of

Turan, and deliver this message unto Human. And he sent word unto him, saying:

"The sword of vengeance must slumber in the scabbard. Thou art now leader of the host; return, therefore, whence thou camest, and depart across the river ere many days be fallen. As for me, I will fight no more, yet neither will I speak unto thee again, for thou didst hide from my son the tokens of his father, of thine iniquity thou didst lead him into this pit."

Then when he had thus spoken, Rustem turned him yet again unto his son. And the nobles went with him, and they beheld Sohrab, and heard his groans of pain. And Rustem, when he saw the agony of the boy, was beside himself, and would have made an end of his own life, but the nobles suffered it not, and stayed his hand. Then Rustem remembered him that Kai Kaous had a balm mighty to heal. And he prayed Gudarz go before the Shah, and bear unto him a message of entreaty from Rustem his servant. And he said:

"O Shah, if ever I have done that which was good in thy sight, if ever my hand have been of avail unto thee, recall now my benefits in the hour of my need, and have pity upon my dire distress. Send unto me, I pray thee, of the balm that is among thy treasures, that my son may be healed by thy grace."

And Gudarz outstripped the whirlwind in his speed to bear unto the Shah this message. But the heart of Kai Kaous was hardened, and he remembered not the benefits he had received from Rustem, and he recalled only the proud words that he had spoken before him. And he was afraid lest the might of Sohrab be joined to that of his father, and that together they prove mightier than he, and turn upon him. So he shut his ear unto the cry of his Pehliva. And Gudarz bore back the answer of the Shah, and he said:

"The heart of Kai Kaous is flinty, and his evil nature is like to a bitter gourd that ceaseth never to bear fruit. Yet I counsel thee, go before him thyself, and see if peradventure thou soften this rock."

And Rustem in his grief did as Gudarz counseled, and turned to go before the Shah, but he was not come before him ere a messenger overtook him, and told unto him that Sohrab was departed from the world. Then Rustem set up a wailing such as the earth had not heard the like of, and he heaped reproaches upon himself, and he could not cease from plaining the son that was fallen by his hands. And he cried continually:

"I that am old have killed my son. I that am strong have uprooted this mighty boy. I have torn the heart of my child, I have laid low the head of a Pehliva."

Then he made a great fire, and flung into it his tent of many colors, and his trappings of Roum, his saddle, and his leopard-skin, his armor well tried in battle, and all the appurtenances of his throne. And he stood by and looked on to see his pride laid in the dust. And he tore his flesh, and cried aloud:

"My heart is sick unto death."

Then he commanded that Sohrab be swathed in rich brocades of gold worthy of his body. And when they had enfolded him, and Rustem learned that the Turanians had quitted the borders, he made ready his army to return unto Zaboulistan. And the nobles marched before the bier, and their heads were covered with ashes, and their garments were torn. And the drums of the war-elephants were shattered, and the cymbals broken, and the tails of the horses were shorn to the root, and all the signs of mourning were abroad.

Now Zal, when he saw the host returning thus in sorrow, marveled what was come about; for he beheld Rustem at their head, wherefore he knew that the wailing was not for his son. And he came before Rustem and questioned him. And Rustem led him unto the bier and showed unto him the youth that was like in feature and in might unto Saum the son of Neriman, and he told him all that was come to pass, and how this was his son, who in years was but an infant, but a hero in battle. And Rudabeh too came out to behold the child, and she joined her lamentations unto theirs. Then they built for Sohrab a tomb like to a horse's hoof, and Rustem laid him therein in a chamber of gold perfumed with ambergris. And he covered him with brocades of gold. And when it was done, the house of Rustem grew like to a grave, and its courts were filled with the voice of sorrow. And no joy would enter into the heart of Rustem, and it was long before he held high his head.

Meantime the news spread even unto Turan, and there too did all men grieve and weep for the child of prowess that was fallen in his bloom. And the King of Samengan tore his vestments, but when his daughter learned it she was beside herself with affliction. And Tahmineh cried after her son, and bewailed the evil fate that had befallen him, and she heaped black earth upon her head, and tore her hair, and wrung her hands, and rolled on the ground in her agony. And her mouth was never weary of plaining. Then she caused the garments of Sohrab to be brought unto her, and his throne and his steed. And she regarded them, and stroked the courser and poured tears upon his hoofs, and she cherished the robes as though they yet contained her boy, and she pressed the head of the palfrey unto her breast, and she kissed the helmet that Sohrab had worn. Then with his sword she cut off the tail of his steed and set fire unto the house of Sohrab, and she gave his gold and jewels unto the poor. And when a year had thus rolled over her bitterness, the breath departed from out her body, and her spirit went forth after Sohrab her son.

The Kalevala

THE KALEVALA

The old mythological traditions of the Finnish people told in the form of epic songs.

THE FORGING OF THE SAMPO

By JAMES BALDWIN

THE RECIPE

SMITH ILMARINEN stood thoughtfully, silently, beside the fire. The low, dark hall was full of shadows; dim figures lurked in the corners and danced among the rafters; the air was grimy with smoke; the flames burned blue and fitfully on the ash-strewn hearth.

Out-of-doors the storm was raging. The winds whooped and howled in savage combat. They reached their chilly fingers down demons; he heard the hail pelting upon the roof and the rain dashing and splashing upon the half-frozen ground; he heard the sea through the chimney hole as though they would snatch up the luckless Smith and bear him still farther away into regions untraversed and unknown.

He stood and listened. He heard the shrieking of the tempest roaring fearfully in the darkness and the mad waves pounding upon the dumb and patient shore.

"In such a storm as this, any shelter is sweet," he said; and he stirred the fire logs till the sparks shot upward and filled the hall with the sound of their merry snapping. Then the thought came to him of his own fireside at home—of his mother and sister and the friends whom he loved—and he groaned aloud in anguish.

"O Wainamoinen, prince of Minstrels!" he moaned. "Why have you treated me so unkindly? Why have you betrayed me—me your friend and brother? Never could I have believed that your magic power was so much greater than my own. Never——"

He paused suddenly, for he heard a rustling which was not the rustling of leaves, a breathing which was not the breathing of the South Wind, a pitty-pat of soft footsteps upon the floor. He turned and looked, and lo! a radiant vision appeared before him in the firelight. It was the Maid of Beauty, the peerless daughter of the grim Mistress of Pohyola. Right winsomely she came forward to greet him, her cheeks blushing red, her eyes sparkling and joyous. The Smith's heart was beating hard and fast, like a sledge hammer beneath his waistcoat. He trembled and grew pale. Never had he seen, never had he imagined, a maiden so wondrously fair.

"O prince of Smiths," she said in tones more sweet than the warble of birds, "I welcome you to our pleasant land of Pohyola."

Not even when the storm winds seized him had Ilmarinen felt so helpless and utterly overcome. He could scarcely say a word in answer; he could hardly lift his eyes; his hands hung as though palsied at his side; his feet were rooted to the floor. Then, ere he could recover from his confusion, he saw the Mistress herself advancing—the grim and toothless Mistress of the Frozen Land. She spoke, and her voice was cracked and harsh and grating.

"O master of Smiths," she said, "this is my daughter, the fairest of all maidens. Now say, will you not forge the Sampo? Will you not hang its weights, adjust its levers? Will you not hammer its lid of many colors, even as your brother, the Minstrel, assured me you would?"

"Yes, yes, yes!" stammered the poor Smith, scarcely knowing what he said. "I will do anything, everything that lies in my power. But I have never seen a Sampo, and I know not what it is. Tell me what it is like; tell me of its various uses."

"The Sampo," answered the Maid of Beauty—and her voice was like the ripple of wavelets on the shore of the summer sea—"the Sampo is the mill of fortune—the magic grinder that will grind whatever its owner most desires: money, houses, ships, silver, flour, salt—everything!"

"Silver, flour, salt—everything!" echoed the Smith.

"Yes. Do you think that you have the skill to forge it?"

"Well, I have done greater things than that," he answered boastingly. "Long ago, when the world was young, I found Iron, ruddy Iron, hiding in the bogs, skulking in the woods, basking in the sunlight of the hills. I caught him and subdued him; I taught him to serve me; I gave him to the world to be a joy forever."

"We have often heard of your skill, and your praise is in all men's mouths," said the eager Mistress. "But the Sampo can be forged only by a great master of magic. Your friend, the Minstrel, although he was able to do many very wonderful things, would not undertake a task so difficult."

"Truly, I have performed harder tasks," answered the boaster. "Why, it was I that forged the blue sky that bends over the earth in summer. I hammered it out of a single piece of metal. I fashioned it into a dome-shaped lid to shut down over the earth and air. I painted it pale blue and azure and murky brown. Nothing is too great for my magic. Give me but one hint regarding its shape and nature, and I will make the Sampo—yes, a hundred Sampos—for you."

Toothless though she was, the wise old Mistress smiled—she smiled fearfully, cunningly, as one pleased and plotting.

"I cannot describe its shape," she answered, "for it is still uncreated and therefore formless; but its composition is quite simple and its ingredients are of the commonest kind. If by your power in magic you can mix these ingredients properly, the mill is made—it will do its work. But talk not of a hundred Sampos; the world can never hold but one."

"And I promise that with my magic skill I will put that one together," said the Smith; "but what can you tell me about its ingredients? Tell me all you know about its composition."

"I have a recipe which has come down through the ages," said the woman, "a recipe for making the Sampo; but no magician has ever yet been wise enough, strong enough to make use of it. Here it is, written in runes on a white whalebone:

> " 'Take the tips of two swan feathers;
> Add the milk of a young heifer;
> Add a single grain of barley;
> Mix and stir with wool of lambskin;
> Heat the mixture, quickly, rightly;
> In a magic caldron boil it;
> On a magic anvil beat it;
> Hammer its lid of many colors;

> Furnish it with wheels and levers;
> Set it up, and start it going.' "

Ilmarinen listened. "The directions are plain and easily followed," he said. "To a Smith who has shaped the mountains and hammered out the sky it will be an easy task, the pleasant pastime of a few fleeting days. But it must not be undertaken in the winter time. We must wait till the sky is clear and the sun shines warm on land and sea."

"And will you then forge the much-desired Sampo?" inquired the Mistress.

"I promise you," answered the Smith.

Thus the boasting Ilmarinen, having come suddenly, unexpectedly, unwillingly to the land of Pohyola, was conquered by the power of beauty. And thus he promised, not once alone, but thrice, promised solemnly on his honor, that he with his magic power would forge the wondrous mill of fortune and shape its lid of rainbow colors. And the cunning Mistress grimly smiled and joyfully gave him a home in her broad, low dwelling—she gave him food and lodging, the softest seat beside her hearth, the warmest bed beneath her rafters. And he, forgetful of his home and kinsmen, sat content in the glow of the blazing fire logs, and counted the days till the storm should pass, the weeks till the winter should end.

THE CALDRON

All through the long and dreary winter, Ilmarinen waited idly by old Louhi's hearth-side. "No great thing in magic can be done in stormy weather," he said. "Summer and fair days of sunshine are the wizard's time for action."

The wise men of the North Land came often to see him. Herdsmen from the frozen meadows, savage fellows from the forest, fishermen from the icy inlets—these also came to hear the words of the wizard Smith and be taught by him. They came on snowshoes and in reindeer sledges, battling with the wintry storm winds and heeding not the cold. Singly and by twos and threes they came and squatted round Dame Louhi's fireplace, rubbing their hands together, warming their shins, and staring into the face of the marvelous stranger. And Ilmarinen sat in their midst and told them many tales of wonder, chiefly tales of his own rare skill and cunning.

He told them how he had broken the mountains with his hammer, how he had conquered wild Iron and imprisoned him in his smithy, and how, from a single lump of metal, he had hammered out the sky and set it up as a lid to cover the land and the sea. "All these things," said he, "were done by me—me, the prince of Smiths, me, the skillfulest of men."

Then all his listeners, wise men, herdsmen, fishermen, wild men, looked at him with awe and admiration. They drew up closer to the fire, they threw fresh logs into the flames, they turned their faces toward him and asked a thousand curious questions.

"Who painted the sky and gave it its blue and friendly color?" asked the wise men.

"I painted it—I, the first of Smiths," answered Ilmarinen. "And when I swept my brush across from east to west, some drops of blue fell into the sea and colored it also."

"What are the stars that glitter so brightly above us when the nights are clear?" asked the herdsmen.

"They are the sparks from my forge," was the answer. "I caught them and fixed them securely in their places; I welded them into the vast sky-lid so they should never fall out nor fly away."

"Where is the home of the Great Pike, the mightiest of all the creatures that swim in the water?" asked the fishermen.

"The Great Pike lurks in the hidden places of the deep sea," said Ilmarinen; "for he knows that I have forged a hook of iron that will some day be the cause of his undoing."

"Ah! ah! ah!" muttered the wild men. Their mouths were open and their eyes were staring at the rafters where hung long rows of smoked salmon, slabs of bacon, and dried herbs of magic power. "Ah! ah! ah! What shall we do when we are hungry and there are no nuts to be gathered, no roots to be digged, no small beasts to be captured, no food of any kind? Ah! ah! ah!"

"Forget today, think only of tomorrow—for then there will be plenty," answered Ilmarinen. "Go back to your old haunts in the forest, and tomorrow I will send you so many nuts and roots and small beasts that you shall grow fat with the eating of them."

Thus, all through the wintry weather, Ilmarinen dispensed wisdom to the inquiring men who desired it, and there was no question which he could not answer, no want which he could not satisfy. And at length, when every mind was filled with knowledge, and every stomach with food from Dame Louhi's bountiful stores, the visitors departed. Singly, or by twos and threes, in sledges, on snow shoes, on foot, they returned to their respective haunts and homes. "We have seen him, and there is nothing more to be desired," they said.

And now the snow was melting, the grass was green on the hillsides, the reeds were springing up in the marshes, and the birds were twittering under the eaves.

Forthwith, brave Ilmarinen sallied out to find a smithy. Ten men, willing and strong, followed him, prepared to do any sort of labor, to undergo any sort of privation. Long did he seek, and far and wide did he travel, and many were the vain inquiries which he made; but nowhere in all the Frozen Land did he discover forge or chimney, bellows or tongs, anvil or hammer. In that dismal, snowy country men had never needed iron; they had no tools save tools of fishbone; they had no weapons save sticks and stones and fists and feet. What wonder, then, that they had no smithy?

Some men would have given up in despair, but not so Ilmarinen. "Women may lose their courage," he said; "fools may give up a task because it is hard; but heroes persevere, wizards and smiths conquer."

So, still followed by his serving-men, he set out to find a fit place in which to build a smithy. For nine days he sought—yes, for ten long summer days he wandered over the brown meadows and among the gloomy hills of Pohyola. At length, deep in the silent forest he found a great stone all streaked and striped in colors of the rainbow.

"This is the place," he said, never doubting; and he gave orders to build his smithy there.

The first day's task was to build the furnace and the forge with yawning mouth and towering chimney. On the second day he framed the bellows and covered it with stout reindeer hide. On the third he set up his anvil, a block of hardest granite heavy for ten men to roll.

Then he made his tools. For a hammer he took a smooth stone from the brook; for tongs he cut a green sapling and bent it in the middle, forcing the two ends together. Thus his smithy was completed; but how was he to forge the magic Sampo? With what was he to form its iridescent lid?

"Only weaklings say, 'I cannot,'" said he. "Only want-wits say, 'It is too difficult.' Heroes never give up. Nothing is impossible to a true Smith."

Then from a secret pocket he drew the things most needful for his forging. He counted them over, giving to each a magic number —two tips of white swan feathers, a bottle of milk from a young red heifer, a grain of barley grown in a land beyond the sea, and the fleece of a lambkin not one day old. These he mixed in a magic caldron, throwing upon them many bits of precious metals, with strange wild herbs and rank poisons and sweet honey dew. And all the while, he kept muttering harshly the spells and charms which none but smiths and skillful wizards understand.

At length the mixture was completed. Ilmarinen set the caldron firmly in the furnace, he pushed it far into the yawning cavern. Then he kindled the fire, he heaped on fuel, he closed the furnace door and bade the serving-men set the bellows to blowing.

Tirelessly the ten men toiled, taking turns, five by five, at the mighty lever. Like the fierce North Wind sweeping over the hills and rushing through the piney forest, the heaving bellows roared. The flames leaped up and filled the furnace and the forge. The black smoke poured from the chimney and rose in cloudlike, inky masses to the sky. Ilmarinen heaped on more fuel, he opened the draughts of the furnace, he danced like a madman in the light of the flames, he shouted strange words of magic meaning. Thus, for three long summer days and three brief summer nights, the fire glowed and the furnace roared and the men toiled and watched unceasingly. And round about the feet of the workmen lichens and leafy plants grew up, and in the crannies of the rocks wild flowers bloomed, nourished by the warmth from the magic forge.

On the fourth day, the wizard Smith bade the workmen pause while he stooped down and looked into the caldron far within the fire-filled furnace. He wished to see whether anything had begun to shape itself from the magic mixture, whether anything had been brought forth by the mighty heat.

As he looked, lo! a crossbow rose from out the caldron—a crossbow, perfect in form and carved with figures fantastical and beautiful. On each side it was inlaid with precious gold, and the tips were balls of silver. The shaft was made of copper, and the whole bow was wondrously strong. "This is a beautiful thing," said Ilmarinen, "but it is not the Sampo."

Forthwith the crossbow leaped from the caldron; it flew out of the furnace; it stood humbly bowing before the wizard Smith.

"Hail, my master!" it said. "Here I am, ready to serve you as you command. My task is to kill, and I love it, I love it! Send me forth quickly, and let me begin. On every workday I'll kill at least one. On every holiday I'll kill more—sometimes two, and sometimes very many. Oh, yes, I will kill, I will kill!"

"What will you kill?" asked Ilmarinen.

"In war, men; in peace, singing birds and timid deer. Oh, I can kill, I can kill!"

And having said this, the crossbow began to shoot arrows recklessly about to the great peril of the ten serving-men. This made Ilmarinen angry. "You are bad!" he cried. "You love only evil. I have no use for you!" and he seized the bow and threw it back into the boiling caldron. Then he bade the workmen blow the bellows as before; and he heaped on more fuel and more fuel, singing meanwhile a wild, weird song which made the flames leap out from the very top of the chimney.

All day, all night, the bellows roared; all day again, and again all night, the furnace glowed, white-hot, and furious. Then, just at sunrise, the Smith called to the bellows-men. "Halt!" He stooped down and gazed steadfastly, curiously, into the magic caldron. As the flames subsided and the furnace began to grow cool, behold a ship rose from the mixture—a ship complete with pointed beak and oars and sails, all ready to be launched upon the sea. Its hull was painted blue and yellow, its ribs were golden, its prow was of copper, and its sails were of white linen whereon were depicted most wonderful figures of dragons and savage beasts; and on its deck and within its hold were all manner of weapons of war—axes and spears, bows and arrows, sharp daggers and gleaming swords.

"Here I am, my master!" said the ship. "I am ready for your service, if you please. You see that I am well fitted for war, well fitted to plunder and rob the seaports of other lands. Send me out, that I may help you slay your enemies and make your name a terror throughout the world."

The wizard Smith drew the ship toward him. Beautiful and well-laden though it was, he was by no means pleased with it. "I like you not!" he cried. "You are a destroyer and not a builder. You love evil, and I will have no part nor parcel of you," and he broke the ship into a thousand pieces, and threw the fragments back into the caldron. Then he bade the serving-men blow the bellows with all their might, while he heaped fresh fuel upon the flames and sang wild songs of wizardry and enchantment.

On the fourth morning Ilmarinen looked again into the caldron. "Surely something good has been formed by this time," he said.

From the caldron a mist was slowly rising, hot, pungent, foglike; within it, the magic mixture could be heard bubbling, seething, hissing. The Smith looked long ere he could see what was forming. Then suddenly the mist cleared away and a beautiful young heifer sprang out into the sunlight. Her color was golden, her neck and legs were like the wild deer's, her horns were ivory, her eyes were wondrous large, and on her forehead was a disc of steely sunshine.

The Smith was delighted, his heart was filled with admiration. "Beautiful, beautiful creature!" he cried. "Surely, she will be of use to mankind."

Scarcely had he spoken when the heifer rushed out of the smithy, pausing not a moment to salute her master. She ran swiftly into the forest, bellowing, horning, fighting, spurning everything that came in her way.

"Ah, me!" sighed the Smith, "she, too, has an evil nature. Alas, that one so wickedly inclined should be blessed with so beautiful a form!"

Then he bade the serving-men bring her back to the smithy; and when, with infinite labor, they had done this, he cut her in pieces and threw her back into the caldron. And now the bellows was set to blowing again, and it roared like a tempest in a forest of pines; the smoke rolled darkly from the chimney; and the fire glowed hotter than before around the seething caldron. And all that day, and through the midsummer night, the master and his men toiled unceasingly.

At sunrise on the fifth day, Ilmarinen looked again into the caldron. As he stooped and gazed, a plow rose suddenly from the magic mixture. Like a thing of life it glided softly through the furnace door, bowed low before the wizard Smith, and waited to receive his judgment. It had been shaped and put together with great skill, and every line was a line of beauty. The frame was of copper, the share was of gold, the handles were tipped with silver.

"Here I am, my master," it said. "Send me forth to do your bidding."

"What good thing can you do?" asked Ilmarinen.

"I can turn things over, tear things up," answered the plow. "Nothing in the fields can stand against me. I will overturn the sod, I will uproot all growing things whether good or bad. I will go into gardens, meadows, cornfields, and stir the soil; and woe to the plant that comes in my way, for I will destroy it."

"You are beautiful and you are useful," said the Smith; "but you are rude and unkind. You do not know how to discriminate between the evil and the good. You give pain, you cause death, and therefore I do not love you."

He waited not for the plow's answer, but struck it with his hammer and broke it into a thousand fragments; then he threw the fragments back into the magic caldron and closed the door of the furnace.

Long and thoughtfully he sat, silent but not despairing. His elbows rested upon his knees, his head was bowed upon his hands.

And he repeated to himself his favorite saying: "None but cowards say, 'I cannot,' none but weaklings say, 'Impossible,' none but women weep for failure."

At length he rose and called to his serving-men; he dismissed them, every one, and summoned the winds to come and be his helpers.

THE FORGING

The four winds heard the magic call of Ilmarinen, and they hastened from the corners of the sky to do his bidding. First came the East Wind, riding over the sea, combing the crests of the waves with his clammy fingers, and rushing with chilly breath through the dank marshes and across the lonely meadows. He knocked at the door of the smithy, he rattled the latch, and shrieked down the chimney:

"Master of Wizards and prince of all Smiths, what will you have me do?"

And Ilmarinen answered, "Set my bellows to blowing that I may forge the wondrous Sampo."

Next there was heard a joyous whistling among the pine trees, and a whir-whirring as of the wings of a thousand birds; and there was a fragrance in the air like the fragrance of countless wildflowers, and a soft breathing like the breath of a sleeping child. The South Wind crept softly up to the smithy door, it peeped slyly in, and said merrily:

"What now, old friend and companion? What will you have me do?"

And Ilmarinen answered, "Blow into my furnace, and blow hard, that I may forge the wondrous Sampo."

Then came the jolly West Wind, roaring among the mountains, dancing in the valleys, playing among the willows and the reeds, and frolicking with the growing grass. He laughed as he lifted the roof of the smithy and peered down at the furnace and the forge and the tools of the Smith.

"Ha, ha!" he called. "Have you some work for me? Let me get at it at once."

And Ilmarinen answered, "Feed my fire, so that I may forge the wondrous Sampo."

He had scarcely spoken when the sky was overcast and heavy gray clouds obscured the sun. The North Wind, like an untamed monster, came hurtling over the land, howling and shrieking, as fierce as a thousand wolves, as fleet as the swiftest reindeer. He filled the air with snowflakes, he covered the hills with a coating of ice. The pine trees shivered and moaned because of his chilly breath, and the brooks and waterfalls were frozen with fear.

"What do you wish, master of wizards?" he called from every corner of the smithy. "Tell me how I can serve you."

And Ilmarinen answered, "Fan the flames around my magic caldron, so that I may forge the wondrous Sampo."

So, the chilling East Wind, the whistling South Wind, the laughing West Wind, and the blustering North Wind, joined together in giving aid to the wizard Smith. From morning till evening, from evening till another morning, they worked with right good will, as their master directed them. The great bellows puffed and groaned and shook the very ground with its roaring. The flames filled the furnace; they wrapped themselves around the caldron; they burst out through a thousand cracks and crevices; they leaped, in tongues of fire, through the windows of the smithy. Showers of red sparks issued from the chimney and flew upward to the sky. The smoke rose in clouds of ink-like blackness and floated in vast masses over the mountains and the sea.

For three anxious days and three sleepless nights the winds toiled and paused not; and Ilmarinen sang magic incantations, and heaped fresh fuel upon the fire, and cheered his helpers with shouts and cries and words of enchantment which wizards alone can speak.

On the fourth day he bade the winds cease their blowing. He knelt down and looked into the furnace. He pushed the cinders aside; he uncovered the caldron and lifted the lid, slowly, cautiously. How strange and beautiful was the sight that rose before him! Colors of the rainbows, forms and figures without number, precious metals, floating vapors—all these were mingled in the caldron.

Ilmarinen drew the vessel quickly out of the furnace. He thrust his tongs into the mixture, and seized it with the grip of a giant. He pulled it bodily from the caldron, writhing, creeping, struggling, but unable to escape him. He twirled it in the air as blacksmiths sometimes twirl small masses of half-molten iron; then he held it firmly on his anvil of granite, while with quick and steady strokes he beat it with his heavy hammer. He turned it and twisted it and shaped it, and put each delicate part in its proper place. All night and all day, from starlight till starlight, he labored tirelessly and without ceasing.

Slowly, piece by piece and part by part, the magic Sampo with its wheels and levers grew into being. The wizard workman forged it with infinite skill and patience, for well he knew that one false stroke would undo all his labor, would be fatal to all his hopes. He scanned it from every side; he touched up the more delicate parts; he readjusted its springs and wheels; he tested its strength and the speed of its running. Finally, after the mill itself was proved satisfactory, he forged the lid to cover it; and the lid was the most marvelous part of all—as many-colored as the rainbow and embossed with gold and lined with silver and ornamented with beautiful pictures.

At length everything was finished. The fire in the furnace was dead; the caldron was empty and void; the bellows was silent; the anvil of granite was idle. Ilmarinen called to his ten serving-men and put the precious Sampo upon their shoulders. "Carry this to your Mistress," he said, "and beware that you touch not the lid of magic colors."

Then, leaving the smithy and all his tools in the silence of the forest, he followed the laborers to Pohyola, proud of his great performance, but pale and wan and well-nigh exhausted from long labor and ceaseless anxiety.

The Wise Woman was standing in the doorway of her smoke-begrimed dwelling. She smiled grimly as she saw the working men returning. She welcomed Ilmarinen not unkindly, and he placed before her the result of his long and arduous labors.

"Behold, I bring you the magic Sampo!" he said. "In all the world there is no other wizard that could have formed it, no other smith that could have welded its parts together or forged its lid of many colors. You have only to whisper your wishes into the small orifice on the top of the mill, and it will begin to run—you can hear its wheels buzzing and its levers creaking. Lay it on this side and it will grind flour—flour for your kitchen, flour for your neighbors, flour for the market. Turn the mill over, thus, and it will grind salt—salt for seasoning, salt for the reindeer, salt for everything. But the third side is the best. Lay the mill on that side and whisper, 'Money.' Ah! then you will see what comes out—pieces of gold, pieces of silver, pieces of copper, treasures fit for a king!"

The Mistress of Pohyola was overcome with joy. Her toothless face expanded into a smile—a smile that was grim and altogether ill-favored. She tried to express her feelings in words, but her voice was cracked and broken, and her speech sounded like the yelping of a gray wolf in the frozen marshes. Without delay she set the mill to grinding; and wonderful was the way in which it obeyed her wishes. She filled her house with flour; she filled her barns with salt; she filled all her strong boxes with gold and silver.

"Enough! enough!" she cried, at length. "Stop your grinding! I want no more."

The tireless Sampo heard not nor heeded. It kept on grinding, grinding; no matter on which side it was placed, its wheels kept running, and flour, or salt, or gold and silver kept pouring out in endless streams.

"We shall all be buried!" shouted the Mistress in dismay. "Enough is good, but too much is embarrassment. Take the mill to some safe place and confine it within strong walls, lest it overwhelm us with prosperity."

Forthwith she caused the Sampo to be taken with becoming care to a strong-built chamber underneath a hill of copper. There she imprisoned it behind nine strong doors of toughest granite, each of which was held fast shut by nine strong locks of hardest metal. Then she laughed a laugh of triumph, and said: "Lie there, sweet mill, until I have need of you again. Grind flour, grind salt, grind wealth, grind all things good for Pohyola, but do not smother us with your bounties."

They closed the strong doors and bolted them and left the Sampo alone in its dark prison-house; but through the keyhole of the ninth lock of the ninth door there issued a sweet delightful whirring sound as of wheels rapidly turning. The Sampo was grinding treasures for Dame Louhi's people, and laying them up for future uses—richness for the land, golden sap for the trees, and warm and balmy breezes to make all things flourish.

Meanwhile Ilmarinen sat silent and alone in the Mistress's hall, thinking of many things, but mostly of the reward which he hoped to receive for his labor. For an hour he sat there, waiting—yes, for a day of sunlight he remained there, his eyes downcast, his head uncovered.

Suddenly Dame Louhi, the Wise Woman, came out of the darkening shadows and stood before him. The flames which darted up, flickering, from the half-burned fagots, lighted her grim features and shone yellow and red upon her gray head and her flour-whitened face. Very unlovely, even fearful, did she seem to Ilmarinen. She spoke, and her voice was gruff and unkind.

"Why do you sit here idle by my hearth-stone?" she asked. "Why, indeed, do you tarry so long in Pohyola, wearing out your welcome, and wearying us all with your presence?"

The Smith answered her gently, politely, as men should always answer women: "Have I not forged the Sampo for you—the wondrous Sampo which you so much desired? Have I not hammered its lid of rainbow colors? Have I not made you rich—rich in flour, in salt, in silver and gold? I am now waiting only for my reward—for the prize which you promised."

"Never have I promised you any reward," cried the Mistress angrily. "Never have I offered to give you a prize"; and her gaunt form and gruesome features seemed truly terrible in their ugliness.

But Ilmarinen did not forget himself; the master of magic did not falter. "I have a friend whose name is Wainamoinen," he said. "He is the first of all Minstrels, a singer of sweet songs, a man of honor, old and truthful. Did you not say to him that you would richly reward the hero who should forge the magic Sampo—that you would give him your daughter, the Maid of Beauty, to be his wife?"

"Ah, but that was said to him and not to you," said the Mistress, and she laughed until her toothless mouth seemed to cover the whole of her misshapen face.

"But a promise is a promise," gently returned the Smith; "and so I demand of you to fulfill it."

The features of the unlovely Mistress softened, they lost somewhat of their grimness as she answered: "Willingly would I fulfill it, prince of Wizards and of Smiths; but I cannot. Since Wainamoinen's visit, the Maid of Beauty has become of age. She is her own mistress, she must speak for herself. I cannot give her away as a reward or prize—she does not belong to me. If you wish her to go to the Land of Heroes with you, ask her. She has a mind of her own! she will do as she pleases."

She ceased speaking. The firelight grew brighter and then suddenly died away, and the room became dark.

"I will see her in the morning," said Ilmarinen.

THE HOMESICK HERO

The sunlight was streaming white and yellow, over sea and land. The wild geese were honking among the reeds. The swallows were twittering under the eaves. The maids were milking the reindeer in the paddock behind Dame Louhi's dwelling. Ilmarinen had slept late. He rose hurriedly and hastened to go out, not to listen to the varied sounds of the morning, but to ponder concerning the great problem that was soon to be solved.

He opened the door, but quickly started back, trembling, and pale. What had he seen to give him pause, to cause him to be frightened? Right before him, so near that he might have touched her with his hand, stood the Maid of Beauty. Her cheeks were like the dawn of a summer's morning; her lips were like two ripe, red berries with rows of pearls between; her eyes were like glorious suns, shining softly in the midst of heaven. Who would not have trembled in the presence of such marvelous beauty?

Ilmarinen was overcome with bashfulness. He stammered, he paused, he looked into those wonderful eyes and was covered with confusion. Then he spoke to his own heart and said, "Why am I so cowardly—I who have hitherto feared nothing under the sun? I will be brave. I will ask her the momentous question and abide by her answer."

So, with quivering lips and downcast eyes he spoke: "Fairest of maidens, my task is done. I have forged the Sampo, I have hammered its marvelous lid, I have proved myself worthy to be called the prince of Smiths. Will you not now go with me to my far distant home—to the Land of Heroes in the sunny south? There you shall be my queen; you shall rule my house, keep my kitchen, sit at the head of the table. O Maid of Beauty, it was for you that I forged the Sampo and performed those acts of magic which no other man would dare to undertake. Be kind, and disappoint me not."

The maiden answered softly, and she blushed as she spoke: "Why should I leave my own sweet home to go and live with strangers, to be a poor man's wife in a poor and distant land? My mother's hall would be desolate; her kitchen would be cold and ill-cared for were I to go away. She herself would grieve and die of loneliness."

"Nay," said Ilmarinen, "she is not the sort of woman to feel sorrow; her heart is too hard to be crushed so easily."

"But there are others who would miss me," said the maiden softly. "If I should go away, who would feed the reindeer at the break of day? Who, in the early springtime, would welcome the cuckoo and answer his joyous song? Who, in the short summer, would caress the wild-flowers in the wooded nooks and sing to the violets in the meadows? Who, in the autumn, would pick the red cranberries in our marshes? Who, at winter's beginning, would tell the songbirds to fly southward, and who would cheer the wild geese on their way to summer lands?"

The Smith had now grown bolder, and he answered wisely: "The cuckoo comes to my country as well as yours. There are flowers in the forests of Wainola more beautiful than any in this chilly land.

There are cranberries in our marshes also, redder and larger than any you have ever picked. The songbirds live in the Land of Heroes half of every year, and the wild geese tarry there and build their nests in the sedgy inlets."

"All that may be true," said the Maid of Beauty, "but your cuckoo is not my cuckoo, and so how could I welcome it in the spring-time? All things in Wainola would be strangers to me, while all things in Pohyola are friends. The North Country, the Frozen Land as you call it, would be very lonely if I were to leave it; the meadows would be joyless, the hills would be forlorn, the shores would be desolate. Were I not here to paint the rainbow, the storm clouds would never vanish. Were I not here to note the change of seasons, the songbirds would surely forget to come, the flowers would neglect to bloom, the cranberries would perish ungathered. No, Ilmarinen, I must not go with you. You are skillful, you are wise, you are brave, you are the prince of Wizards and of Smiths—but I love my native land. Say no more; I will not go with you."

The Smith was speechless; his tongue was motionless, and he could not make reply. He turned slowly away, and with head bowed down and cap pulled over his eyes, he sought his favorite place by the side of the smouldering hearth-fire.

All day he sat there, pondering, wondering how now by any makeshift he could escape from Pohyola and return to his native land. The longer he thought, the larger his troubles appeared. He had no boat to sail by sea, no sledge nor reindeer to travel by land, no money in his purse, no knowledge of the road. Would not magic avail him? Could he not call upon the winds to carry him, as they had once done against his will? Alas, no! All his magic lore, all his magic power, had been exhausted in the forging of the Sampo; he was utterly bankrupt.

While he sat thus, homesick, disappointed, and forlorn, Dame Louhi came suddenly into the hall. She was white with flour and laden with silver, and she wore a look of triumph on her grim and unlovely face.

"Ha! forger of the Sampo!" she cried. "Why do you sit here moping day after day? What ails you—you, who hammered out the sky and set the stars in their places—you, the prince of Wizards, the king of Boasters?"

Ilmarinen groaned and pulled his cap still lower over his eyebrows; but he answered not a word.

The Mistress went on with her bantering; she laid salt on the poor man's wounds and briskly rubbed it in. "Why do you groan so like an ice floe breaking up at the end of winter? Why do you weep salt tears, extinguishing the fire on my hearth? Have you the toothache, earache, heartache, stomach-ache? Did you eat too much at dinner? Surely the prince of Wizards ought to curb his appetite."

The Smith's heart was filled with anger; his brain burned, his cheeks were flushed with shame. Much had he suffered from this woman's greed and cunning; painfully was he stung by her bitter words. Yet he answered her with becoming gentleness—for was she not the mother of the Maid of Beauty?

"I have no ache nor bodily pain," he said; "but I am sick of this wretched country, this Frozen Land. I am sick of its mists, of its storms, of its long nights and its cheerless days. And, most of all, I am sick of its thankless people."

"Ah! I understand," answered the woman; and she closed her toothless jaws tightly, restraining her anger. "In other words, you are homesick; your heart is filled with longing for your own country and your own fireside."

"You speak rightly," answered Ilmarinen. "My heart is in the South Land, in the Land of Heroes. Unwillingly did I come to your bleak and chilly Pohyola; unwillingly have I remained here, cheered by a single hope which has at last been blasted. And now my only wish is to return home, to see once more the friends whom I love, to cheer my mother in her loneliness."

"Surely, the lad who cries for his mother should be comforted," said the Mistress derisively. "At what moment would you like to start on your homeward journey?"

"At the break of day?" answered the Smith, his face brightening as his hopes were strengthened.

"It shall be as you wish," said the woman, and her tones were uncommonly tender and kind. "I will see that everything is in readiness. At the break of day a boat will be waiting for you at the landing. Delay not a moment, but go on board and ask no questions. You shall be safely carried to the haven that is so dear to you."

Ilmarinen stammered his thanks. His eyes grew brighter, his heart was cheered with hope.

Very impatiently the hero waited through the short hours of night, and gladly did he hail the first gray streak of dawn that heralded the morning.

He hastened out to the shore. The promised boat was there, moored to the landing by a hempen rope. It was a small vessel, but roomy enough for one passenger who would also be captain and crew. Its hull was of cedar and the trimmings were of maple. Its prow was tipped with copper, sharp and strong. The oar also was of copper, and the sail was painted red and yellow.

In the boat a great store of food was packed—deer meat, smoked herring, cakes of barley, toothsome victuals enough for many days.

Ilmarinen asked no man any questions, although many persons were gathered on the shore, wondering whence came the strange vessel and whither it was going. He climbed over the polished gunwales and stepped boldly on board. Then, as the sun was peeping out of the sea, he raised the square sail of red and yellow. He cut the mooring rope, and took the copper paddle in his hands; he sat down in the stern to do the steering.

A gentle wind filled the sail, and the boat glided smoothly, swiftly away from the land. Ilmarinen looked back; he saw all the folk of Pohyola standing along the shore, and he heard them shouting their good-byes and bidding him God-speed. He looked again, and saw the Maid of Beauty among them; she was waving her hand, and her face seemed to him tenfold more beautiful than before; her cheeks were wet with tears, and there was a look of great regret in her wonderful eyes.

And there also stood the Mistress of Pohyola, gray and grim and toothless, but noble in mien and of queenly appearance. She lifted her arms, she raised her eyes toward heaven, and called to the North Wind to prosper the voyage for her departing guest:

> "Come, thou North Wind, great and strong,
>   Guide this hero to his home;
> Gently drive his boat along
>   O'er the dashing white sea-foam.
>
> "Push him with your mighty hand;
>   Blow him o'er the blue-backed sea;
> Carry him safe to Hero Land,
>   And let him ne'er come back to me."

The North Wind heard her, and he came, strong, swift, and steady. Like a waterfowl in some sheltered cove, the boat glided with incredible smoothness over the chilly waters. Joyfully the prince of Smiths handled the oar, and loudly he shouted to the wind as he saw the red prow cleaving the waves and knew that he was speeding homeward.

Three days the voyage lasted. As the morning of the fourth was dawning, Ilmarinen beheld on his left the lofty headland and pleasant shore of his native land, green with summer-leafing trees and odorous with the breath of wildflowers. The sun rose above the eastern hills, and then his eyes were rejoiced with the sight of the weather-stained roofs of Wainola, and curling clouds of smoke rising from the hearths of many well-known dwellings.

Gently, then, the glad voyager guided his boat into the harbor. He dismissed the North Wind with warm thanks for his friendly service; and then with a few skillful strokes of the oar, he drove his stanch little boat high up on the sloping beach.

"Home! Home at last!" he cried as he leaped out. He paused not a moment, he took no care to tie his little vessel to the mooring-post, but with eager, impatient feet he hastened toward the village.

Scarcely had he walked halfway to the nearest dwelling, when a man stepped suddenly into the road before him. It was Wainamoinen, the cunning wizard, the first of all Minstrels.

"O Ilmarinen, dearest of brothers!" shouted the aged man, so wise, so truthful, so skilled in tricks of magic. "How delighted I am to behold your face again! Where have you been hiding through all these anxious months?"

The Smith answered curtly, coldly, yet politely: "You know quite well my hiding-place, for it was you who sent me thither. I thank you for the journey; but it will be long ere I climb another one of your magic trees."

"Wisest and skillfulest of metal workers, why do you speak in riddles?" said the Minstrel, appearing to be hurt. "Never have I sought to harm you; but all that I did was for your own good. Now, I welcome you back to Wainola. Let us be brothers as in the days of yore. Come! here is my hand; let us forgive and forget!"

The generous Smith could not cherish ill-feeling in his heart. He loved the aged Minstrel as he would have loved a father. So he grasped the proffered hand, gently, warmly; he embraced his friend twice, three times, as had been his wont whenever fondness prompted his warm heart. Then he said, "I forgive you, sweetest of Minstrels."

Side by side, arm in arm, the two old comrades walked homeward.

"Tell me, Ilmarinen," said the Minstrel, "did you perform my errand? Did you fulfill my promise and forge the magic Sampo? Did you win the prize?"

"Yes, I forged the Sampo," answered Ilmarinen; "and I hammered its rainbow cover. Therefore your debt is paid, and you are freed from your promise. But as for me—well, as you see, I have not won the Maid of Beauty."

The Song of Roland

THE SONG OF ROLAND

The greatest of the hero poems of France.

ROLAND AND OLIVER

By JAMES BALDWIN

Illustrations by Reginald Birch

THE VOW OF BROTHERHOOD

ONE summer afternoon rather more than eleven hundred years ago, the boy Roland was sitting in the cleft of a broken rock that forms the crest of one of the hills in the neighborhood of Sutri. Above him was the deep blue sky of Italy, unflecked by any cloud; on either side of him stretched a dull, uneven plain, broken here and there by wet marshes and long lines of low hills. A mile or more to the south, and partly hidden behind the brow of the hill, could be seen the old town with its strong castle, and its half-ruined amphitheatre, and its white-walled monastery. Directly beneath him was the dusty highroad, which, after winding among the straggling vineyards and the little farms that dotted the plain, was lost to sight in a strip of dusky woodland a league and more to the northward. Along that road King Charlemagne with the flower of his great army was hourly expected to pass, marching on his way to the castle of Sutri, where he was to be entertained for a time as a guest; and it was for this reason that the lad sat so still, and watched so long, in his half-hidden perch on the hilltop.

Everything, as if awed by the near coming of the hero king, seemed strangely still that afternoon. Scarcely a sign of life was to be seen; and the places which at other times had been noisy with busy workers were now silent and deserted. The reapers, who yesterday had made the wheat fields ring with their gay jests and their rude songs, had left their sickles in the fields and stolen silently away. The young girls who had been gleaning the fallen grain, and whose laughter had awakened the echoes among the hills, were nowhere to be seen today, although the eagle eyes of Roland sought them on every hand. Along the highroad, which at other times seemed alive with the busy folk coming and going between Sutri and Viterbo, neither man, woman, nor beast was stirring. But off toward Sutri the boy could see that things were quite different. The town seemed to be decked in holiday attire: the governor's castle was draped with gay bunting, and flags and banners floated from the turret-tops. Companies of knights dressed in rich livery rode hither and thither, impatiently waiting the word from the watchman above the gates to go out and meet the kingly guest. The streets were crowded with hurrying, eager folk, who knew not whether to hail the coming of Charlemagne and his host as a blessing, or to look upon it as a calamity.

Now and then the sound of voices from the town or the cries of the soldiers in the garrison came to Roland's ears; and anon he heard the monks in the monastery drowsily chanting their prayers. And there he sat, waiting and wondering, and anxiously watching for any sign of the coming host. The fair face of the lad, and the long flaxen hair which fell in glistening waves upon his bare shoulders, showed his kinship to the hardy races of the North. And there was something in the piercing look of his eye, in the proud curl of his lip, in the haughty turn of his head, which made him seem like a young king among men, and which often had caused those who met him to doff the hat in humble courtesy. He was very poorly clad: his head and limbs were bare; and the thin, scant clothing which covered his body was naught but rags and shreds. Yet he bore himself proudly, as one who knew his own worth, and who, having a blameless heart, had nothing of which to feel ashamed.

And now the sun began to slope toward the west; and, with each moment that passed, the lad's eagerness seemed to grow greater. By and by another boy came over the crest of the hill and stood in the cleft of the rock by the side of Roland, and with him gazed down the deserted road. He seemed to be of about the same age as Roland, and, like him, was tall and sparely built. His dark hair and over-hanging brows, his ruddy face and flashing eyes, betokened an equal kinship with the danger-daring North-folk and the leisure-loving people of the South. He wore the rich dress of a court page, and carried himself with a lofty grace such as only those who bear brave hearts can ever show.

"I feared you were not coming, Oliver," said Roland offering his hand, but not once turning his head, or taking his eyes from the distant woodland.

"It was indeed hard for me to get leave," answered the other. "But the ladies at the castle are very kind, and here I am; and I mean to be, with you, the first to see the great king and his valiant knights. Yet he is late."

"I think I see him coming now," said Roland. "There is a glimmering of light among the trees, which I think must be the flashing of the sun upon their armor. And it grows brighter, and seems to come nearer."

He had scarcely finished speaking when the clear notes of a bugle were heard, borne faintly to them on the breeze. And soon they heard a sound like the distant dashing of waves against the seashore, the rustling of myriads of dry leaves in the autumn woods, the faint rumbling of a faraway storm cloud. They knew that it was nought but the noise made by the trampling of many feet, the heavy tread of war horses, the rattling of arms and armor. Then a great cloud of dust was seen rising like a mist above the treetops; and the rainbow-hued banners of the coming host hove in sight.

Presently the edge of the wood seemed ablaze with flashing shields and glittering war coats. The boy Roland leaped to his feet. He stood on tiptoe, and strained himself eagerly forward; his face beamed with delight; and his eyes sparkled with that strange wild fire which in after-days, in the midst of the battle's din, was wont to strike his foes with terror. Oliver climbed to the highest point of the rock, and gazed with an eagerness half mixed with fear at the wonderful array of steel-clad warriors, who now could be plainly seen issuing from the woodland. Like a torrent of rolling, flashing waters, the host of Charlemagne came moving along the line of the highway, and spreading across the plain. They came not, however, in all the array of battle, nor with their terrible engines of war, nor, indeed, as enemies bent on pillage, or seeking revenge; but they came, rather, as an army of peace, with music sounding, and banners flying, and

Reginald Birch

Roland and Oliver view the host of Charlemagne.

words of good will and friendship to all. For Charlemagne, having left off fighting with the Lombards, was on his way to Rome with the best and bravest of his warriors to receive the homage and the blessing of the Pope.

The vanguard of the procession drew rapidly nearer. In front rode four and twenty knights, the heralds of the king, bearing aloft the silken banner of France and the golden eagle of Rome. They were clad in rich armor, which glittered like gold in the sunlight; their shields were inlaid with many priceless gems, and polished as bright as mirrors; and the sharp points of their long lances flashed around them like the restless gleams of lightning in the van of a summer storm cloud. They were mounted on milk-white horses trapped with white cloth-of-gold, with gold-red saddles, and housings of bluest silk.

The boy Roland had never seen anything so beautiful or so grand, and he thought that one of these knights must surely be Charlemagne. And as they drew very near to the foot of the hill, and he could look down almost upon the heads of the brilliant company, he called to Oliver, and asked:

"Which of these knights is the great Charles? Is it not he who rides nearest the standard-bearer? He, surely, is the noblest warrior of them all; and he rides with a grace which well becomes a king."

But this scene which filled the mind of Roland with such astonishment was not altogether new to Oliver. Not many months before, his father, the governor of Sutri, had taken him on a visit to the court of Charlemagne; and there he had witnessed the splendor of the king's surroundings, and had heard of the fearful might of his warriors.

"No," he answered. "The great king is not one of these. They are but heralds and messengers, who ride before to my father's castle to see that everything is in readiness for their master. They are right courtly fellows, I ween, fair of speech, and comely of form; but I doubt if any of them would be ranked among his bravest knights."

Following the heralds came a body of guards—a thousand men of giant stature, and muscles of iron—incased from head to foot in strongest armor, and riding heavy war-steeds trapped with steel. After these came a long line of bishops and abbots and monks and priests, most of them dressed in the garb of their office or profession, and riding on the backs of palfreys or of mules.

"See you the tall bishop, dressed partly in armor, and carrying a crucifix in one hand, while with the other he toys with his sword-hilt?" asked Oliver. "That is the brave Turpin, one of the peers of Charlemagne. He is at home in the battlefield as well as before the altar, and many an unbelieving Pagan has felt the thrust of his lance. But see! here comes the king himself!"

The whole highway and the fields before them now seemed filled with steel-coated men, and horses clothed in steel trappings; and the long lances in the hands of the knights seemed as thickset as the blades of grass in an autumn meadow. Everywhere were seen the gleam of polished steel and the waving of gay plumes and many-colored pennons; and here and there were banners of varied shapes and every hue, on which were emblazoned mottoes, and the strange devices of the warriors who bore them. First and foremost in this company was Charlemagne himself, clad in steel from head to foot, and riding a horse of the color of steel and the strength of steel. Roland, as soon as he saw him, knew that this must be the king; for there was no other man who seemed so kingly, or who bore himself with so lordly a grace. The noblest knight among his followers seemed but a weak stripling when seen by the side of the matchless Charlemagne. In his left hand he carried a lance of steel of wondrous length, while his right hand held the reins of his fiery steed. His head was bare, for he had laid aside his helmet; and his long hair fell in waves upon his steel-covered shoulders. His broad shield, which was carried by an attendant knight, was of plated steel of three thicknesses bound together with iron bolts. His thighs were encircled with plates of steel, and his hands were garnished with steel gauntlets. On his kingly face a smile lingered; and from his gleaming gray eyes sparks of fire seemed to shoot; and under a weight of armor which would have borne down a common man he carried himself erect and proud, like one who was every inch a king.

With wonder, rather than with awe, Roland kept his eyes fixed upon the noble figure of Charlemagne; and he did not withdraw his gaze until a sudden turn of the road around the hill toward Sutri hid the steel-clad company from his sight. He did not care to see that part of the host which followed. He had no thought for the throng of squires and pages, and the crowd of common soldiers and grooms, who brought up the rear with the baggage and the camp equipage and the led horses of the knights. He had seen the great Charles, and that was all he wished. He beckoned to Oliver; and the two boys climbed down from their well-hidden lookout, and started homeward.

To keep out of the way of the soldiery, and to shun other hindrances, they followed a narrow pathway which led them over the hill and down the slope on the other side from that where the highway ran. Not a word did either speak until they reached the level fields; but here they paused, for here they must needs part. The path which Oliver was to take led southward to the lordly castle of Sutri, where, that night and the following day, Charlemagne and his warriors were to rest and be entertained. But Roland's way lay across the lonely fields to a far different dwelling among the barren hills. Before they parted, each took the other's hand; and both stood for some time in silence, their hearts full of thoughts too big to find utterance in speech. Roland spoke first.

"Some day, Oliver," said he, "we, too, shall be knights, and we shall ride with Charlemagne and his peers as proud as the proudest warriors we have seen today."

"Yes," answered Oliver, his face beaming with delight. "And boldly will we fare over land and sea, fighting the Pagan folk, and doing worthy deeds for the honor of God, the king, and the ladies."

"My mother has often told me," said Roland, "that the day when I should first see Charlemagne would be to me the beginning of a new life. I know not why she said it; but I have seen the great king, and I feel that a wonderful change has come to me, and that I shall no longer be a mere beggar boy. I must soon be up and away, doing my part in this busy world. Let us now, like real knights, pledge ourselves as brothers-in-arms. Next to my mother, you are my dearest friend. Let me call you my brother."

"You are indeed my brother, Roland," answered Oliver earnestly. "You are my brother. Don't you remember, that, since the day when you gave me such a well-deserved drubbing for laughing at your ragged clothing, we have been sworn brothers-in-arms? Did anyone ever apologize for a fault more heartily than I did then? And did anyone ever forgive with freer grace than you forgave me? And have any two persons ever loved with a truer love than that which binds us together?"

"But we are only boys," said Roland. "You are a page and a prince. I am a beggar and a prince: at least so I have been told in my dreams. The next time we meet, we may both be knights. Let us pledge ourselves that, let that meeting be when it may, it shall be a meeting between brothers-in-arms."

Without more words, the two boys, still holding each other's hands, knelt together by the roadside. And they vowed to be true to each other so long as life should last; to share together whatever fortune might betide, whether it should be good or ill; to meet all dangers together, and to undertake all great enterprises in company; to rejoice together in success, and grieve together when sorrow should come; to devote their lives to the succor of the helpless and to the defense of the right; and, if need be, to die for each other.

"And now," said Oliver, as they rose to their feet, "let us, like true knights, seal our vow of brotherhood by exchanging tokens."

And with the word he took from his girdle a little dagger with long gleaming blade and a handle of ivory richly carved, and inlaid with gold. It was a gift from his grandfather, Gerard of Viana, and had once belonged to the Pagan king of Morocco. It was the dearest of Oliver's possessions, and hence the fittest token to present to his brother-in-arms. As Roland took it from his hand, and gazed with pleased eyes upon its razor edges, gleaming like lines of silver light, tears stood in his eyes, for he knew how highly its owner prized it. Then from the folds of his ragged garment he drew the short, broken fragment of an old sword-blade, dimmed with age and much rust, and dull with many notches.

"My token," said he, "is but a poor return for the beautiful keepsake you have given me. But it is very dear to me, and I know that it will also be dear to you. It is all that was left of my father's sword, when, hemmed in by Pagan foes, he sold his life dearly in fight and died for the honor of the king and the church."

Oliver took the proffered token reverently, for he already knew its story. He gazed a moment at the curious letters carved on its sides, and at its hacked and battered edge; and then he placed it carefully in his girdle. And the two boys, after many earnest words and many kind good-byes, turned away, and each hastened toward his own home.

By this time the sun had gone down, and the short twilight was fast giving place to darkness. With hasty steps Roland made his way across the fields toward the low line of yellow hills, which now could be scarcely seen, lying more than a league away, dimly outlined against the west horizon. It was quite dark long before he reached them. But he knew the way well, and a light shining in the door of his mother's dwelling helped to guide his steps across the uneven ground. And what kind of a dwelling was it that Roland called his home? It was nothing more than a little cave hollowed out of the rocky hillside, where, long before, a holy hermit had made himself a quiet cell in which to live, and worship God. The narrow entrance to the cave was in great part hidden by flowering vines, which Roland's mother had with daily care coaxed to grow in the barren soil and had trained to cling to the rough rocks and twine among the crevices overhead. Inside, every thing betokened poverty. A single stool, a broken table, a few earthen dishes, the simple articles which the hermit had left—these were the only pieces of furniture. In one corner of the room hung an old set of armor, dinted with many a lance-thrust and hacked in many a battle, but still kept bright against the day when Roland should become a knight. Near it leaned a long, broken lance which had done duty in more than one tourney; and beneath it was a battered shield on which were emblazoned the arms of Charlemagne. The stone floor was bare, and the rough stone walls were grimed with smoke, and the low ceilings were damp with moisture. Few were the comforts of home in that humble dwelling; and but for the kind welcome of his queenlike mother, the Lady Bertha, small would have been the cheer that Roland would have found there.

"I have seen him, mother!" he cried, rushing into her arms. "I have seen the great Charles and his glorious army and his gallant peers. Would that I were a man, that I, too, might ride forth with the king, the bravest of the brave!"

Then the gentle Bertha took the lad's hand in her own, and the two sat down together in their lowly dwelling, and Roland told her of all that he had seen that memorable afternoon; but he talked most of the noble Charlemagne, and of his kingly grace and bearing. Then he spoke again of his own hopes and of his high ambition, and of the time when he should be a knight, and, mayhap, one of the peers of the king.

"And now, dear mother," said he, "the time has come for me to learn the great secret of my life. Today I am twelve years old—old enough to be a page; today I have seen Charlemagne; and today you have promised to tell me all about my kinsfolk and myself, and the great destiny which lies before me."

Then the Lady Bertha drew the lad close to her, and told him the story of her own life and his—a story so full of strange surprises to Roland, that, when he heard it, he wept for joy and for the big thoughts that came welling up from his heart. She told him that the great king whom he had seen that day, and whose fame was known in every land, was his uncle and her own brother. She told him how she, the spoiled and petted daughter of Pepin, had been brought up at the French court; and how, after her father's death, she had lived in her brother's kingly palace at Aix, loved and honored next to Charlemagne himself. Then she told, how, on a time, there came to Charlemagne's court a worthy knight named Milon—a warrior poor and needy, but brave, and without reproach. "Milon boasted that his kin had been the noblest heroes of all time. Through his father he traced his descent from the Greeks; and he wore the arms of Trojan Hector engraved upon his shield; and he numbered among his ancestors the godlike hero Hercules. On his mother's side he claimed kinship with the fair-haired heroes of the North, with the fearless Vikings, with Siegfried the dragon-slayer, with the mighty Thor, and the matchless Odin.

"And when your mother, then the Princess Bertha, saw the gallant Count Milon, and heard of his nobleness and learned his true worth, she loved him. And your uncle Charlemagne hated him, and banished him from France, and sought even to take his life; for he wished to wed his sister to Duke Ganelon of Mayence, one of his peers. But when Milon fled from the king's court at Aix, he went not alone; he took me, the Princess Bertha, with him as his wife: for the good Archbishop Turpin had secretly married us, and given us his blessing and promised to help us on our way to Italy. When Charlemagne heard how he had been outwitted, he was very angry, and he swore that he would do his uttermost to ruin Count Milon, and to bring me back to France, and make me the wife of the hated Ganelon. And so, to escape his anger, we dressed ourselves in the guise of beggars, and wandered on foot from town to town and through many countries, begging our bread. And wherever we went we met the spies of Charlemagne seeking for Milon, and offering a price for his head. At last we came to Sutri, tired and footsore, and unable to go any farther. And, when none would take us into their houses, we found shelter in this wretched cave, which we fitted up the best that we could, to serve as a home until we could soften the anger of Charlemagne, and obtain his forgiveness. But soon after you were born, Roland, the Pagan folk crossed the sea, and came into Italy and threatened Rome itself. Then your father, the gallant Milon, remembering his knightly vows, once more donned his armor; and, taking his lance and his shield, he went out to do battle for the king and for the holy church. You know the rest. You know how bravely he fought, and how he died as heroes die, with his face toward the foe. All this I have told you often. And you know how we have lived these long, weary years in this wretched hermit cell, dependent on our kind neighbors for food, and hoping always for brighter and better days.

"And now you have learned the story of your birth and your kinship, and you know the destiny that is yours if you but do your part. The blood that flows in your veins is the blood of heroes, and it will not belie itself. You have seen Charlemagne, and today is the turning point in your life. Before the king leaves Sutri, he must acknowledge you as his nephew and take you as a page into his court."

Then mother and son sat long together in the quiet cell, talking of the past so fraught with distress and poverty and wretchedness, and of the unknown future with its vague promises and uncertain hopes. But so great was the lad's trust in his own strength, and so firm was the mother's faith in her son, that not once did clouds of doubt darken the bright pictures which their fancy painted of the good fortune yet in store for them. And the little candle which lighted the humble room burned down and left them in darkness; and the moon rose over the hills, and peeped in through the doorway, and sloped downward toward the west; and the stars, one by one, looked in between the vines, and then went onward in their endless journey around the world; and at length the eastern sky began to brighten and then to blush at the coming of the sun; and still the Lady Bertha and the boy Roland sat, unmindful of the passing hours, and talked of the new life which they felt must soon be theirs. But when the morning had fairly come, and the first rays of the sun shot in upon them, Roland, as if suddenly awakened, sprang to his feet, and cried,

"Mother, the night is past, and the day has dawned—the first day in the great new life which is mine! I will go at once to my uncle, the king, and demand my rights and yours."

And with his mother's blessing and many a word of advice well fixed in his memory, the lad hurried away, walking rapidly across the fields toward Sutri.

THE KING'S GUEST

It was a great day in Sutri. Never since the old Roman days had so brilliant a company of warriors and noblemen been seen in that quiet town. In the governor's castle the king and the peers of the realm were being entertained and feasted. The chambers and halls and courts were full of knights and squires; and everyone talked of the noble order of chivalry, and of war, and of arms and armor, and of the king's progress on the morrow to Rome. In the broad feast hall, Charlemagne and his peers were dining. On the dais, by the side of the king, sat Count Rainier, the governor of Sutri. Around them stood many of the noblest knights, attentive to their slightest wishes. Next below the king sat Turpin, the warrior bishop, clad today, not in his war coat of steel, but in his rich official robes, and looking much more the priest than the knight. Next to him sat Duke Namon of Bavaria, the king's counselor, gray-bearded and sage, strong in fight, and wise in statesmanship—the oldest and most trusted of all the peers. On the other side was Malagis, the cunning dwarf, who, it was said, had power over the unseen creatures of the air, and by means of witchery could sometimes foretell the things that were about to befall. Next to him was old Ganelon of Mayence, at heart a vile traitor, the smile of a hypocrite resting on his thin lips, and his serpent-eyes twinkling with an evil light. On either side of the long table below sat many worthy knights, the most trusted warriors of Charlemagne, and the doughtiest heroes in Christendom. I doubt if ever more valor was seen in the castle hall.

Mirth and revelry ruled the hour; and the long, low hall rang with the sound of the harp and the flute and the glad voices of the singers. The great oaken table groaned beneath its weight of good cheer. The lordly Count Rainier had provided for this feast everything that was pleasant to the taste, or that could add zest to the appetite. The richest meats and the rarest fruits, sparkling wine and foaming ale, the whitest bread and the most tempting sweetmeats— all were offered in generous profusion as if on purpose to make the knights forgetful of their vows of temperance. In the courtyard, around the open door, stood numbers of the poor people of the town, listening to the music, and waiting for the morsels that would be left after the feast. Suddenly a young boy, ragged and barefooted, appeared among them. All stood aside for him, as, with proud step and flashing eyes, he entered the great hall. With the air of a lord he pushed his way through the crowd of attendant knights and squires, and walked boldly to the table. Then, without a word, he seized upon a basket of rare fruit and a loaf of bread placed before the king.

"Indeed," said Charlemagne, "that is a bold boy. He will make a brave knight." But those who stood around were so awed by the lad's proud bearing and by the strange flash of his eyes, that they dared not touch him; nor did they think of placing any hindrance in his way until he had seized the golden wine-cup which Charlemagne was on the point of lifting to his lips.

"Stop!" cried the king. "How dare you be so rude?"

But Roland held fast to his prize; and fearless as a young eagle he gazed into the face of the king. Charlemagne tried hard to appear angry; but, in spite of himself, a pleasant smile played upon his face, and his eyes twinkled merrily.

"My boy," said he, "the forest is a fitter place than this banquet hall for such as you. You would do better picking nuts from the trees than snatching dishes from the king's table; and the wine which you have taken from my hand is not nearly so good for you as the water in the flowing brook."

"The peasant drinks from the brook," answered Roland proudly; "the slave gathers nuts in the forest. But to my mother belong the best things that your table affords."

"Ha!" cried the king. "Your mother must indeed be a noble lady! And I suppose you will tell me that she lives in a lordly castle, with scores of brave knights and gentle dames about her, and that she sits daily in her great feast hall at a table loaded with delicacies. How many servants has she? Who is her carver? Who her cupbearer?"

"My right hand is her carver," answered Roland; "and my left hand is her cupbearer."

"And has she soldiers and watchmen and minstrels, this wonderful mother of yours?"

"Indeed she has. These two arms are her soldiers; these eyes are her watchmen; these lips are her minstrels."

"That is a numerous household and a worthy one," answered the king, now very much amused. "But your good mother has strange taste in the matter of livery for her servants. I see they are all bareheaded and barefooted; and their clothing is made of all the colors of the rainbow. How came she to furnish you with a robe so rich and rare?"

"My robe is of my own furnishing," answered Roland. "Eight boys in the town do me homage; and they pay me tribute in cloth, each a different color. And now, my lord, since you have learned all about my mother, will you not visit her in her castle?"

Before the king could answer, the boy had turned on his heel, and, with the basket of food and the cup of wine in his hands, he fearlessly walked out of the hall. Charlemagne was surprised at the bold-ness of the lad, and delighted with his witty answers. "Let him go," said he. "A braver lad I have never seen; and he well deserves his prize. He will yet become the noblest knight in Christendom."

Then, turning to Duke Namon, he whispered, "Saw you the strange flash in his eye? Was there ever a fairer countenance, or a more kinglike form? Tell me truly, did he not remind you of some-one?"

"He did, my lord," answered Namon. "He reminded me of your worthy father, the great Pepin. He has the same noble features, the same broad brow, the same clear gray eyes flashing with a strange light. He reminded me, too, of yourself. Had he been clothed in a garb befitting a prince, I should have imagined that I saw you again as you appeared when a boy. But he reminded me most of your lost sister, the fair Princess Bertha. The same gentleness of manner, the same proud carriage of the head, the same curl of the lip—qualities that we once admired so much in the Lady Bertha—may all be seen in this wonderful boy."

"I dreamed last night," said the king, "that my darling sister came to me, leading just such a boy as this. And I thought that he grew tall and strong, and that the whole world looked up to him as a pattern of knightly valor and courtesy, and that he carried my whole kingdom upon his shoulders. Now this boy is no common lad; and the mother of whom he speaks can be no common beggar. My heart tells me that she is the long-lost, long-forgiven Bertha."

"Your heart speaks rightly," answered Namon. "The son of no other lady could bear so perfect a likeness to the Pepins. I am sure that we have found her at last."

Then Charlemagne turned to the dwarf Malagis. "What say you, sir wizard?" he asked. "You have the gift of foresight, and you can read that which lies hidden to the eyes of others. What think you of a boy who comes thus boldly, and levies mail as if it were his right?"

The dwarf twisted and writhed about in his seat: he smiled, as only wizards can smile, and then he humbly but wisely answered:

"My lord, the lad is no beggar. The blood of heroes flows in his veins. Kings are his kinsmen. Great deeds await his coming into manhood. Harm him not, but have him sought out, and brought again before you. I have read in the stars that somehow the woof of your life is strangely interwoven with that of a lad like this."

Charlemagne at once ordered a dozen squires to follow the boy secretly to find where he dwelt, and then, without harming him, to bring both him and his mother to the castle. And then the feasting, which had been so strangely broken off, was begun again. And the wassail bowl went round, and many a weak-souled knight forgot his solemn vows of temperance; and the old hall again resounded with music and with uproarious mirth; and the boy was for a time forgotten.

Very anxiously did the fair Bertha in the lonely hermit cell await the return of her son that day. He had left her in the morning, determined to make himself known to Charlemagne, and to demand the forgiveness of his mother and her reinstatement in the king's palace. He had promised to be back very soon, with a palfrey for his mother to ride upon and a company of knights and squires to escort her to the castle. But hour after hour had passed by; and it was now high noon, and still the boy did not come. Could it be possible that he had been too rash, and had been imprisoned or otherwise severely punished for his boldness? Another hour went by; and Bertha was about to despair of his return, when Roland suddenly appeared around the foot of the hill, carrying on his left arm a basket of food and in his right hand a golden goblet of wine.

"Mother," he cried, as he set his burden down in the doorway of the grotto, "mother, I have brought you some share of the feast. You shall not starve while your brother, who is no better than you, eats and drinks and has such plenty of other luxuries that he knows not what to do with them."

Then he placed before her the bread and the wine, and a delicately baked fowl, and the rare fruits; and, while she ate, he told her all that had happened to him since he had left her in the morning. He had waited a long time about the palace doors, trying in vain to be allowed to see the king. The guards said that he was sleeping and would not be disturbed. If he could only have found his friend Oliver, all would have been well. But the page was nowhere to be seen; and a squire whom he asked said that he had gone that morning with a company of knights and dames to Rome, and that it would be long ere he returned again to Sutri. At length, by the merest chance, he had peeped in through the open door of the banquet hall, and had seen the king himself seated at the table.

"I could not bear," he said, "to see so great plenty of all that was good, and to hear the mirth of the greedy revelers, and know that you were here in this wretched cave without a morsel of food. I walked right in and took the best, nor did I regard that I was robbing the king. He talked to me and seemed not a bit angry; and I feel sure he will send for me to come again, and then I will tell him all."

"Ah, Roland," said the Lady Bertha doubtfully, "you do not know your kingly uncle. He is hot-tempered and violent; and he may yet punish you for your rashness, and listen to no word of explanation or excuse. Many an innocent man has suffered from his unreasoning anger."

"I am not afraid," answered the boy. "He was altogether too jolly to be angry. And I expect, ere this time tomorrow, to be installed as a page to the king or to one of his peers."

He had scarcely spoken these words, when the squires who had been sent in search of him came around the foot of the hill and halted only a few yards from the entrance to the grotto. Some were on foot, some on horseback; and all were armed with sticks, and more or less under the influence of the strong ale which they had drunk at the banquet. As soon as they saw Roland, they called out loudly to him, ordering him to surrender himself as their prisoner.

"Come along at once, my little one," cried the leader. "The king wants you for robbing his table."

Had the squires approached Roland in a respectful manner, he would have gone with them gladly. But their insolence maddened him. "Tell the king," he answered, "that I am holding high court at home today and that if he wants me he must come after me himself."

"But you must come with us," cried the squires. "You and your mother the beggar woman must come with us to Sutri, and lose no time."

"Beggar woman, indeed!" cried Roland, overflowing with rage. "How dare you speak thus of the sister of Charlemagne? Go back to the king, and tell him that his nephew is not wont to do the bidding of squires and churls. Tell him that only by the worthiest of his peers will my mother and I be taken into his presence."

At this boastful speech of one whom they looked upon as only a beggar, the squires laughed heartily; and one or two of them shook their sticks in a threatening manner, and made as if they would seize upon the boy. Roland ran quickly into the grotto, and soon came out again, bearing the long, broken lance in his hands. But it was a heavy weapon, and, as he found it, an unwieldy one. The squires closed in upon him from every side; and, as the great length of the lance prevented him from turning it quickly enough to guard himself at all points, he was obliged to drop it to the ground. In its stead, he seized a stout, light club that lay in his way, and then, taking his stand in the doorway, he dared his assailants to come within his reach. "You shall see," said he, "whether I cannot defend my mother's castle."

The squires, astonished at the quickness and the pluck of the boy, fell back, and began trying to persuade him to go with them peaceably. But Roland stood warily in the doorway of his castle, and answered them only by swinging his club in the faces of the nearest, and by withering glances of defiance. It is uncertain how long this scene would have lasted, or how it would have ended, had it not been unexpectedly interrupted. A knight, unarmed, and mounted on a coal-black steed, rode suddenly around the hill and reined up in the midst of the excited crowd. His long hair and flowing beard were white with age, and his pleasant face beamed with kindliness, and was lighted up with lines of far-seeing wisdom.

"Ha, my brave men!" he cried in tones of merriment. "What have we here? Twelve gallant squires in combat with a single boy! And the boy holds his castle against them all. Surely this is chivalry! What does it all mean?"

"It means," answered Roland, "that these fellows want to take me by force to the king at Sutri, and they have insulted me and my mother. Were they knights, or even gentlemen, I would go with them; but they are neither. They are mere churls and hangers-on about the governor's court, and they know nought of honor and knightly courtesy. It will be long ere they are worthy to wear the golden spurs."

The knight was amused at the boy's earnestness; and he said, "I cannot blame you for refusing to be taken by them. Yet I know that the king wishes very much to see you and your good mother, and he has sent me to hasten your coming. I am Namon, Duke of Bavaria, and I am sometimes known as one of Charlemagne's peers. Perhaps you will be willing to go with me if I send these squires away."

Roland, without a word of dissent, dropped his club to the ground, and promised to go with the good knight at once if he would only find some means by which his mother might be helped to reach Sutri castle without the fatigue of walking so far. Duke Namon dismounted from his steed, and, having sent the squires away, went with Roland into the little cavern. There he was welcomed heartily by the Lady Bertha, who remembered him as a firm, kind friend in former days, when both were inmates of Charlemagne's palace at Aix. And the fair lady and the noble knight talked long together of things that had happened since then in France—of the gallant deeds of her brother the king, and of his many triumphs at home and abroad; of the death of the gallant Milon, and of the long years of wretchedness and want that had since dragged by. And the knight told her how Charlemagne had sought in every land for her, and had sent messengers beyond the sea to inquire for her, in order that he might grant her his forgiveness, and make some amends for his former harshness. But all in vain. The messengers had brought back word that Milon was dead, but they could find no traces of his noble wife; and Charlemagne mourned her as lost. And then Namon told her of Roland's strange, daring deed in the feast hall at Sutri castle that day, and of the thoughts that he and the king had had about the boy; and lastly he spoke of the king's desire that she should appear at once before him, and, if she were indeed the lost

Princess Bertha, she should be restored to her old place in his court and in his affections.

And toward evening the noble duke, with the Lady Bertha mounted behind him on a pillion, rode gayly over the fields to Sutri; while Roland, proud and happy, and carrying his father's broken lance on his shoulder, followed them on foot. Glad indeed was the greeting with which the king welcomed his sister; but not a word could the fair Bertha speak, so overwhelmed was she with gratitude. Roland, still wearing his livery of many-colored rags, but holding himself erect and haughty as a prince, raised his wondrous gray eyes until they met Charlemagne's gaze.

"Sister," said the king, "for this boy's sake, if for nought else, all shall be forgiven. Let the past be forgotten in the joy of the present hour."

"Dear brother," said fair Bertha, "your kindness shall not go unrewarded. Roland will not disappoint you. He will grow up to be, next to you, the pattern of all heroes and the type of all manly virtues."

And the next day a great feast was held in the banquet hall of Count Rainier's castle, in honor of the fair princess and her gallant little son. And not only the bravest warriors in Charlemagne's service, but also many noble ladies and many knights from Rome and the country round about, sat down with the king at the festal board. And this time Roland was not an uninvited guest; but he sat in the place of honor at the king's right hand, while squires and servitors waited his call, and hastened to do his bidding. And Charlemagne rested two days longer at Sutri before proceeding on his march; and then he sent his sister, the princess, with a guard of trustworthy knights, back to France and to the pleasant palace and halls of Aix. But Roland was made a page in the service of good Duke Namon; and, when the grand army moved on again toward Rome, he bade good-bye to his humble friends in Sutri and made ready to go too. No happier, prouder heart beat in Italy that day than Roland's. Dressed in a rich gown of green velvet bordered with crimson and gold, and mounted on a white palfrey most handsomely harnessed, he seemed not like the barefooted beggar to whom the boys of Sutri had been wont to do homage. But it needed not that one should look closely to recognize that same noble form, those wonderful gray eyes, that proud but kindly face. And he rode not with the rout of squires and soldiers and hangers-on who brought up the rear of the army, but by the side of Duke Namon, and in company with the bravest knights and the peers of the realm.

All along the road the people of the towns, the castles, and the countryside, crowded to see the conquering hero; and they welcomed him with shouts and glad songs as the guardian of Italy and the champion of all Christendom. Three miles this side of Rome all the noblest men of the city came out, with music playing and banners waving, to escort the grand army through the gates. At a mile from the walls the children of the schools met them, bearing palm leaves and olive branches in their hands, and strewing flowers in the way, and singing hymns in honor of the hero king. Charlemagne had laid aside his arms and his armor; and, dressed in his kingly robes, he rode by the side of the good Archbishop Turpin. His mantle was wrought of the finest purple, bordered with gold and ermine; upon his feet were sandals sparkling with priceless gems; upon his head was a coronet of pearls and flashing jewels. His horse was harnessed in the most goodly fashion, with trappings of purple damask bordered with ermine and white cloth-of-gold.

At the gate of the city the procession was met by a company of priests and monks bearing the standard of the cross, which was never taken out save on the most solemn and magnificent occasions. When Charlemagne saw the cross, he and his peers alighted from their horses, and went humbly on foot to the steps of St. Peter's Church. There he was met by the Pope, the bishops, and a great retinue of priests and monks, dressed in their richest vestments, who welcomed him to Rome, and blessed him. And on every side, in the streets and in the church, loud shouts rent the air, and the people joined in singing the chant, "Blessed is he that cometh in the name of the Lord."

The boy Roland, having never seen such grandeur, was filled with wonder and astonishment. "Surely," said he, "this is the happy vale of paradise, of which my mother has so often told me, where every Christian knight hopes one day to find a home."

"It is not that vale," answered good Duke Namon; "but it is the beginning of the road which leads thither."

Not many days did Charlemagne remain at Rome. Messengers came to him from France, who said that the Saxons and other Pagan folk had crossed the Rhine, and were carrying fire and sword into the fairest portions of the land; and they begged him to hasten to return to his own country, that he might protect his people from the ravages of their barbarous foes. So, having received the homage and the blessing of the Pope, and having been crowned with the iron crown of the Lombards, he marshaled all his forces, and set out on his journey back to France. And late that same autumn, Roland saw for the first time the noble city of Aix, and was formally installed as page in Duke Namon's household.

A ROLAND FOR AN OLIVER

Years later, when Roland had come to manhood, Charlemagne held high festival at Paris. It was in thanksgiving for the victories with which his arms had everywhere been blessed. Once more the foes of Christendom had been driven from Christian soil; once more did peace and prosperity seem to smile upon France. And the King had summoned the worthiest barons and warriors of his realm to award to each some fitting recompense for his services and good faith.

Among the knights who had come to Paris was old Count Gerard, the grandfather of Oliver, and one of the most powerful barons of France. He had come to renew his homage for his ancient fief of Viana; and he hoped that the king, as a reward for his lifelong services, would grant him now the vacant fief of Burgundy. But from some reason best known to himself Charlemagne failed to invest him with the wished-for dukedom. Count Gerard rebelled against the king, and declared, that, for the affront which Charlemagne had offered him, he would no longer be his man, nor pay him tribute. He shut himself up in the stronghold of Viana, which he victualed and strengthened with great care and made ready for a long and a close siege. He sent also to his brother Miles of Apulia and to his son Rainier of Genoa, craving their help. Miles came with a thousand men bearing shields; and Rainier with two thousand crossbow-men. With Rainier came also his son Oliver, boldest of warriors, and his daughter Alda, beautiful as a Persian peri, brave as a Saxon valkyrie.

Great indeed was the siege which Charlemagne placed around Viana: none ever saw the like before. And he vowed that he would never leave it, nor give up the contest, until the proud Gerard should be humbled in the dust before him.

Week after week passed by, and still the wearisome siege continued. Some say that Charlemagne was encamped around Viana for seven years, but I think it could not have been more than seven months. Nevertheless, the whole country, for leagues on every side, was laid waste; and what had once been a blooming garden was now in a fair way to become a desert. The vineyards had been destroyed; the orchards had been cut down; the houses of the country-folk had been burned and destroyed. Great, indeed, was the distress caused by this quarrel between the king and the count; but the distress fell upon neither king nor count, but upon the innocent and the helpless. Ah, how cruel is war!

The king allowed neither wind nor rain to turn him aside from his purpose, or to make him forget his vow; and all winter long his men sat by their camp fires, and surlily guarded the approaches to Viana. At length, however, Eastertide drew on apace; and the woods began to grow green again, and the flowers sprang up in the meadows, and the birds sang soft and sweet. And many knights bethought them then how idly and vainly their time was being spent in this fruitless war against one of their own number; and they longed to ride away in quest of other and more worthy adventures. The king tried hard to press the siege and to bring it to a speedy close, but in vain. The watchful and valiant crossbow-men held the besiegers at bay and obliged them to keep their accustomed goodly distance from the walls.

One day a party of strange knights rode into the camp and asked to see the king without delay. They came from the mountain land which borders France on the south; and they brought stirring news

—news which aroused the zeal of every loyal Christian warrior. Marsilius, the Pagan king of Spain, they said, had crossed the Pyrenees with a great host of Saracens, and was carrying fire and sword and dire distress into the fairest provinces of southern France. Unless Charlemagne should come quickly to the help of his people, all Aquitaine and Gascony would be lost and the Pagans would possess the richest portion of his kingdom.

The king was much troubled when he heard these tidings, and he called his peers together to ask their advice. All declared at once in favor of raising the siege of Viana, of making some sort of peace with Gerard, and marching without delay against the invaders. But Charlemagne remembered, that, before undertaking the siege of Viana, he had vowed not to desist until Count Gerard was humbled in the dust at his feet.

"I have an oath in heaven," said he, "and I must not break it. This traitor Gerard shall not be spared."

"Which were better," asked Duke Ganelon mildly—"to forget a vow which was made too hastily, or to sit here helpless, and see all Christendom trodden under the feet of accursed Saracens?"

"It seems to me," said sage Duke Namon, "that the present business might be speedily ended by leaving it to the judgment of God. Count Gerard knows nothing of the straits that you are in: he cannot have heard of this invasion by the Saracens; and he will gladly agree to any arrangement that will bring your quarrel with him to an honorable end. Let two knights be chosen by lot, one from each party, and let the combat between them decide the question between you and Count Gerard."

Charlemagne and his peers were much pleased with this plan; and a messenger with a truce-flag was sent into the fortress to propose the same to Count Gerard. The men of Viana were not only heartily tired of fighting against the king, but they foresaw that if the siege were kept up much longer they would be obliged to surrender for want of food; for their provisions were already beginning to run low. So they very gladly agreed to leave the whole matter to the decision of Heaven; and, as they numbered among them some of the bravest and most skillful swordsmen in Christendom, they had little doubt but that the judgment would be in their favor.

When the messenger came back to Charlemagne with Count Gerard's answer, the king and his peers at once drew lots in order to determine which one of their number should be their champion. The lot fell upon Roland; and to him was assigned the danger and the honor of maintaining the dignity and authority of the king, and of deciding a question which many months of warfare had failed to settle.

Early the next morning Roland was ferried over to an island meadow in the Rhone, where the knight of the Red Plume who had been chosen by the Vianese folk to oppose him was already waiting. Roland was well armed; but instead of his own shield he carried another, which the king had given him—one wide and thick, but new and untried; yet his good sword, Durendal the terror, slept in its sheath by his side, and with it alone he would have felt sure of victory. The Knight of the Red Plume had armed himself with the greatest care. His war coat had been wrought by the famed smith, the good Jew Joachim, and was said to be proof against the stroke of the best-tempered sword. The hauberk which he wore was the one which King Æneas, ages before, had won from the Greeks on the plains of Troy. His buckler was of fishskin from the great salt sea, stretched on a frame of iron, and hard enough to turn the edge of any common sword.

On one bank of the river stood the friends of Roland, anxious to see how the young hero would acquit himself, and yet not at all fearful of the result. On the other side were Count Gerard and Miles and Rainier, and the bravest knights and the fairest ladies of Viana. And among these last, the fairest of all was Alda, the daughter of Rainier, and the sister of Oliver. Very beautiful was she to look upon. A coronet of pearls encircled her brows; golden was her hair, which fell in rich ringlets on her shoulders; blue were her eyes as the eyes of moulted falcon; fresh was her face, and rosy as dawn of a summer's day; white were her hands, her fingers long and slender; her feet were well shaped and small. The red blood had risen to her face. Eagerly she waited the beginning of the fray.

Roland, when he saw her, trembled as he had never trembled before an enemy.

The signal for the onset is given. The two knights put spurs to their steeds, and dash toward each other with the fury of tigers and the speed of the wind. The lances of both are shivered in pieces against the opposing shields, but neither is moved from his place in his saddle. Quickly, then, they dismount and draw their swords. How Durendal flashes in the light of the morning sun! Now does the helmet which the good Jew Joachim made do good service for the red-plumed knight. The fair Alda is overcome with fear. She hastens back to the castle. She goes to the chapel to pray, and falls fainting at the foot of the altar.

Never before has there been so equal a fight. For more than two hours the two knights thrust and parry, ward and strike; but neither gains the better of the other. At last, however, the sword of the red-plumed knight is broken by a too lusty blow upon Roland's helmet: his shield, too, is split from top to bottom. He has neither wherewith to fight nor to defend himself, yet he has made up his mind to die rather than to be vanquished, and he stands ready to fight with his fists. Roland is pleased to see such pluck, and he scorns to take advantage of his foe's ill plight.

"Friend," said he right courteously, "full great is your pride, and I love you for it. You have lost your sword and your shield, while my good Durendal has neither notch nor blemish. Nephew am I to the king of France, and his champion I am today. Great shame would be upon me were I to slay an unarmed man when he is in my power. Choose you now another sword—one to your own liking —and a more trusty shield, and meet me again as my equal."

Roland sat down upon the grass and rested himself, while the red-plumed knight bade his squires bring him another sword from the castle. Three swords were sent over to him—that of Count Gerard, that of Rainier the Genoese, and Hauteclere, a blade which the Jew Joachim had made, and which in old times had been the sword of Closamont the emperor.

The knight chose Hauteclere. Roland rose from the grass, and the fierce fight began again. Never were weapons wielded with

greater skill; never was there a nobler combat. The sun rose high in
the heavens, and the noontide hour came; and still each knight stood
firmly in his place, thrusting and parrying, striking and warding,
and gaining no vantage over his foe. After a time, however, the
patience of the red-plumed knight gave out. He grew furious. He
was anxious to bring the combat to an end. He struck savagely at
Roland; but the stroke was skillfully warded, and Hauteclere
snapped short off near the handle. At the same time Durendal, coming down with the force of a thunderbolt, buried itself so deeply
in the shield of the red-plumed knight, that Roland could not withdraw it.

Both knights were thus made weaponless; but neither was vanquished. Wrathfully they rushed together to seize each other, to

Reginald Birch

They rushed into each other's arms.

throw each other down. Moved by the same thought, each snatched
the other's helmet, and lifted it from his head. Some saw that a
bright cloud and an angel came down between them, and bade
them cease their strife; but I know not whether this be true, for, as

they stood there, bareheaded, and face to face, memories of their boyhood came back to them. Both were struck dumb with astonishment for a moment. Roland saw before him his loved brother-in-arms, Oliver. Oliver, now no longer the red-plumed knight, recognized his old friend Roland. Then they rushed into each other's arms.

"I yield me!" cried Roland.

"I yield me!" cried Oliver.

Great was the wonder of Charlemagne and his peers when they saw their champion thus giving up the fight when victory seemed assured. Equally great was the astonishment of the Vianese and of Oliver's kinsmen. Knights and warriors from both sides of the river hastened to cross to the island. They were eager to know the meaning of conduct seemingly so unknightly. But when they came nearer, and saw the men, who had fought each other so long and so valiantly, now standing hand in hand, and pledging anew their faith as brothers-in-arms, everything was made clear. And with one voice all joined in declaring that both were equally deserving of the victory.

THE BATTLE AT RONCESVALLES

From THE SONG OF ROLAND

Translated by ISABEL BUTLER

Illustration by Reginald Birch

CHARLES THE GREAT has laid waste all Spain; he has taken its castles and sacked its cities. But now the war is ended, so saith the King, and he rides on toward fair France, leaving behind him Roland and Oliver in the passes of the Pyrenees, with twenty thousand Franks as a vanguard against the Saracen host.

Oliver has fared up the mountain, and from the summit thereof he sees all the kingdom of Spain and the great host of the Saracens. Wondrous is the shine of helmets studded with gold, of shields and broidered hauberks, of lances and gonfanons. The battles are without number, and no man may give count thereof, so great is the multitude. Oliver was all astonished at the sight; he got him down the hill as best he might, and came to the Franks, and gave them his tidings.

"I have seen the paynims," said Oliver; "never was so great a multitude seen of living men. Those of the vanguard are upon a hundred thousand, all armed with shields and helmets, and clad in white hauberks; right straight are the shafts of their lances, and bright the points thereof. Such a battle we shall have as was never before seen of man. Ye lords of France, may God give you might! And stand ye firm that we be not overcome." "Foul fall him who flees!" then say the Franks, "for no peril of death will we fail thee."

"Great is the host of the heathen," saith Oliver, "and few is our fellowship. Roland, fair comrade, I pray thee sound thy horn of ivory that Charles may hear it and return again with all his host." "That were but folly," quoth Roland, "and thereby would I lose all fame in sweet France. Rather will I strike good blows and great with Durendal, that the blade thereof shall be blooded even unto the hilt. Woe worth the paynims that they came into the passes! I pledge thee my faith short life shall be theirs."

Saith Oliver: "I see no shame herein. I have seen the Saracens of Spain, they cover the hills and the valleys, the heaths and the plains. Great are the hosts of this hostile folk, and ours is but a little fellowship." And Roland makes answer: "My desire is the greater thereby. May God and his most holy angels forfend that France should lose aught of worship through me. Liefer had I die than bring dishonor upon me. The Emperor loves us for dealing stout blows."

Roland is brave, and Oliver is wise, and both are good men of their hands; once armed and a-horseback, rather would they die than flee the battle. Hardy are the Counts and high their speech. The felon paynims ride on in great wrath. Saith Oliver: "Roland, prithee look. They are close upon us, but Charles is afar off. Thou wouldst not deign to sound your horn of ivory; but were the King here we should suffer no hurt. Look up toward the passes of Aspre and thou shalt see the woeful rearguard; they who are of it will do no more service henceforth." But Roland answers him: "Speak not so cowardly. Cursed be the heart that turns coward in the breast! Hold we the field, and ours be the buffets and the slaughter."

When Roland sees that the battle is close upon them he waxes fiercer than lion or leopard. He calls to the Franks, and he saith to Oliver: "Comrade, friend, say not so. When the Emperor left us his Franks he set apart such a twenty thousand of men that, certes, among them is no coward. For his liege lord a man ought to suffer all hardship, and endure great heat and great cold, and give both his blood and his body. Lay on with thy lance, and I will smite with Durendal, my good sword that the King gave me. If I die here may he to whom it shall fall, say, 'This was the sword of goodly vassal.'"

Roland rides through the passes of Spain on Veillantif, his good horse and swift. He is clad in his harness, right well it becomes him, and as he rides he brandishes his spear, turning its point toward heaven; and to its top is bound a gonfanon of pure white, whereof the golden fringes fall down even unto his hands. Well fashioned is his body, and his face fair and laughing; close behind him rides his comrade, and all the Franks claim him as their champion. Full haughtily he looks on the Saracens, but gently and mildly on the Franks, and he speaks to them courteously, saying: "Lords, barons, ride on softly. The paynims come seeking destruction, and this day we shall have plunder so goodly and great that no King of France hath ever taken any of so great price." At these words the two hosts come together.

Saith Oliver: "I have no mind for more words. Thou wouldst not deign to sound thy horn of ivory, and no help shalt thou get from Charles, nought he knows of our case, nor is the wrong his, the baron. They who are beyond the mountains are no wise to blame. Now ride on with what might ye may. Lords, barons, hold ye the field! And in God's name I pray you bethink you both how to deal good blows and how to take them. And let us not forget the device of our King." At these words all the Franks cried out together, and whosoever may have heard that cry of Montjoy must call to mind valor and worth. Then they rode forward, God! how proudly, spur-ing their horses for the more speed, and fell a-smiting—how else should they do? But no whit adread were the Saracens. And lo you, Franks and paynims come together in battle.

Dread and sore is the battle. Roland and Oliver lay on valiantly, and the Archbishop deals more than a thousand buffets, nor are the Twelve Peers backward, and all the Franks smite as a man. The paynims are slain by hundreds and thousands, whosoever does not flee has no surety from death, but will he, nill he, must take his end. But the Franks lose their goodliest arms and many a valiant knight. Never again shall they see father or kindred, or Charles their liege lord who abides for them in the passes.

Meantime, in France, a wondrous tempest broke forth, a mighty storm of wind and lightning, with rain and hail out of all measure, and bolts of thunder that fell ever and again; and verily therewith came a quaking of the earth that ran through all the land from Saint Michael of the Peril, even unto *Xanten,* and from Besançon to the port of Guitsand; and there was not a dwelling whose walls were not rent asunder. And at noon fell a shadow of great darkness, nor was there any light save as the heavens opened. They that saw these things were sore afraid, and many a one said: "This is the day of judgment and the end of the world is at hand." But they were deceived, and knew not whereof they spoke; it was the great mourning for the death of Roland.

When Count Roland is ware of the great slaughter of his men, he turns to Oliver, saying: "Sir comrade, as God may save thee, see how many a good man of arms lies on the ground; we may well have pity on sweet France, the fair, that must now be desolate of such barons. Ah, King and friend, would thou wert here! Oliver, my brother, what shall we do? How shall we send him tidings?" "Nay, I know not how to seek him," saith Oliver; "but liefer had I die than bring dishonor upon me."

Then saith Roland: "I will sound my horn of ivory, and Charles, as he passes the mountains, will hear it; and I pledge thee my faith the Franks will return again." Then saith Oliver: "Therein would be great shame for thee, and dishonor for all thy kindred, a reproach that would last all the days of their life. Thou wouldst not sound it when I bid thee, and now thou shalt not by my counsel."

Then saith Roland: "Wherefore art thou wroth with me?" And Oliver answers him, saying: "Comrade, thou thyself art to blame. Wise courage is not madness, and measure is better than rashness. Through thy folly these Franks have come to their death; nevermore shall Charles the King have service at our hands. Hadst thou taken my counsel, my liege lord had been here, and this battle had been ended, and King Marsila had been or taken or slain. Woe worth thy prowess, Roland! Henceforth Charles shall get no help of thee; never till God's judgment day shall there be such another man; but thou must die, and France shall be shamed thereby. And this day our loyal fellowship shall have an end; before this evening grievously shall we be parted."

The Archbishop, hearing them dispute together, spurs his horse with his spurs of pure gold, and comes unto them and rebukes them, saying: "Sir Roland, and thou, Sir Oliver, in God's name I pray ye, let be this strife. Little help shall we now have of thy horn; and yet it were better to sound it; if the King come, he will revenge us, and the paynims shall not go hence rejoicing. Our Franks will light off their horses, and find us dead and maimed, and they will lay us on biers, on the backs of sumpters, and will weep for us with dole and pity; and they will bury us in the courts of churches, that our bones may not be eaten by wolves and swine and dogs." "Sir, thou speakest well and truly," quoth Roland.

And therewith he sets his ivory horn to his lips, grasps it well and blows it with all the might he hath. High are the hills, and the sound echoes far, and for thirty full leagues they hear it resound. Charles and all his host hear it, and the King saith: "Our men are at battle." But Count Ganelon, the treacherous stepfather of Roland, denies it, saying: "Had any other said so, we had deemed it great falsehood."

With dolor and pain, and in sore torment, Count Roland blows his horn of ivory, that the bright blood springs out of his mouth, and the temples of his brain are broken. Mighty is the blast of the horn, and Charles, passing the mountains, hears it, and Naymes hears it, and all the Franks listen and hear. Then saith the King: "I hear the horn of Roland; never would he sound it, an he were not at battle." But Ganelon answers him, saying: "Battle there is none; thou art old and white and hoary, and thy words are those of a child. Well thou knowest the great pride of Roland;—a marvel it is that God hath suffered it thus long. Aforetime he took Noples against thy commandment, and when the Saracens came out of the city and set upon Roland the good knight, (he slew them with Durendal his sword;) thereafter with water he washed away the blood which stained the meadow, that none might know of what he had done. And for a single hare he will blow his horn all day long; and now he but boasts among his fellows, for there is no folk on earth would dare do him battle. I prithee ride on. Why tarry we? The Great Land still lies far before us."

Count Roland's mouth has burst out a-bleeding, and the temples of his brain are broken. In dolor and pain he sounds his horn of ivory; but Charles hears it and the Franks hear it. Saith the King: "Long drawn is the blast of that horn." "Yea," Naymes answers, "for in sore need is the baron who blows it. Certes, our men are at battle; and he who now dissembles hath betrayed Roland. Take your arms and cry your war cry, and succor the men of your house. Dost thou not hear Roland's call?"

The Emperor has commanded that his trumpets be sounded, and now the Franks light down from their horses and arm themselves with hauberks and helms and swords adorned with gold; fair are their shields, and goodly and great their lances, and their gonfanons are scarlet and white and blue. Then all the baron of the host get them to horse and spur through the passes; and each saith to other: "And we may but see Roland a living man, we will strike good blows at his side." But what avails it? for they have abode too long.

High are the hills and great and dark, deep the valleys, and swift the waters. To answer Roland's horn all the trumpets are sounded, both rear and van. The Emperor rides on in wrath, and the Franks are full of care and foreboding; there is not a man but weepeth and maketh sore lament, praying to God that he spare Roland until they come unto the field, that at his side they may deal good blows. But what avails it? They tarried too long and may not be in time.

Roland looks abroad over hill and heath and sees the great multitude of the Frankish dead, and he weeps for them as beseems a gentle knight, saying: "Lords and barons, now may God have mercy upon you, and grant Paradise to all your souls, that ye may rest among the blessed flowers. Man never saw better men of arms than ye were. Long and well, year in and year out, have ye served me, and many wide lands have ye won for the glory of Charles. Was it to such an end that he nourished you? O France, fair land, today art thou made desolate by rude slaughter. Ye Frankish barons, I see ye die through me, yet I can do naught to save or defend you. May God, who knows no lie, aid you! Oliver, my brother, I must not fail thee; yet I shall die of grief, and I be not slain by the sword. Sir comrade, let us get into battle."

Now when the paynims see how few are the Franks, they have great pride and joy thereof; and one saith to another: "Certes, the Emperor is in the wrong." The Caliph bestrides a sorrel horse, he pricks him on with his spurs of gold, and smites Oliver from behind, amid the back, that he drives the mails of his white hauberk into his body, and his lance passes out through his breast: "Now hast thou got a good buffet," quoth the Caliph. "On an ill day Charles the Great left thee in the passes; much wrong hath he done us, yet he shall not boast thereof, for on thee alone have I well revenged us."

Oliver feels that he is wounded unto death; in his hand he holds Hauteclere, bright was its blade, and with it he smites the Caliph on his golden pointed helmet, that its flowers and gems fall to earth, and he cleaves the head even unto the teeth, and with the force of the blow smote him dead to earth, and said: "Foul fall thee, paynim! *Say not that I am come to my death through Charles;* and neither to thy wife, nor any other dame, shalt thou ever boast in the land from which thou art come, that thou hast taken from me so much as one farthing's worth, or hast done any hurt to me or to others." And thereafter he called to Roland for succor.

Roland looks Oliver in the face, pale it is and livid and all discolored; the bright blood flows down from amid his body and falls in streams to the ground. "God," saith the Count, "now I know not what to do. Sir comrade, woe worth thy valor! Never shall the world see again a man of thy might. Alas, fair France, today art thou stripped of goodly vassals, and fallen and undone. The Emperor will suffer great loss thereby." And so speaking he swoons upon his horse.

Lo, Roland has swooned as he sits his horse, and Oliver is wounded unto death, so much has he bled that his sight is darkened, and he can no longer distinguish any living man whether far off or near at hand; and now, as he meets his comrade, he smites him upon the helm set with gold and gems, and cleaves it down to the nasal, but does not come unto the head. At the blow Roland looks up at him, and asks him full softly and gently: "Comrade, does thou this wittingly? I am Roland who so loves thee. Never yet hast thou mistrusted me." Then saith Oliver: "Now I hear thee speak, but I cannot see thee; may the Lord God guard thee. I have struck thee, but I pray thy pardon." "Thou hast done me no hurt," Roland answers him; "I pardon thee before God, as here and now." So speaking each leans forward toward other, and lo, in such friendship they are disparted.

When Count Roland sees his friend lie prone and dead, facing the

East, gently he begins to lament him: "Sir comrade, woe worth thy hardiness! We twain have held together for years and days, never didst thou me wrong or I thee. Since thou art dead, alack that I yet live." So speaking, the Count swoons as he sits Veillantif his horse, but his golden spurs hold him firm, and let him go where he will, he cannot fall.

So as soon as Roland comes to his senses and is restored from his swoon, he is aware of the great slaughter about him.

Count Roland fights right nobly, but all his body is a-sweat and burning hot, and in his head he hath great pain and torment, for when he sounded his horn he rent his temples. But he would fain know that Charles were coming, and he takes his horn of ivory, and feebly he sounds it. The Emperor stops to listen: "Lords," he saith, "now has great woe come upon us, this day shall we lose Roland my nephew, I wot from the blast of his horn that he is nigh to death. Let him who would reach the field ride fast. Now sound ye all the trumpets of the host." Then they blew sixty thousand, so loud that the mountains resound and the valleys give answer.

"In an evil hour," say the paynims, "were we born; woeful is the day that has dawned for us! We have lost our lords and our peers. Charles the valiant cometh hither again with his great host, we hear the clear trumpets of those of France, and great is the noise of their cry of Montjoy. Count Roland is of such might he cannot be vanquished by any mortal man. Let us hurl our missiles upon him, and then leave him." Even so they did; and cast upon him many a dart and javelin, and spears and lances and feathered arrows. They broke and rent the shield of Roland, tore open and unmailed his hauberk, but did not pierce his body; but Veillantif was wounded in thirty places, and fell from under the Count, dead. Then the paynims flee, and leave him; Count Roland is left alone and on foot.

The paynims flee in anger and wrath, and in all haste they fare toward Spain. Count Roland did not pursue after them, for he has lost his horse Veillantif, and whether he will or no, is left on foot. He went to the help of Archbishop Turpin, and unlaced his golden helm from his head, and took off his white hauberk of fine mail, and he tore his tunic into strips and with the pieces bound his great wounds. Then he gathers him in his arms, and lays him down full softly upon the green grass. and gently he beseeches him: "O gracious baron, I pray thy leave. Our comrades whom we so loved are slain, and it is not meet to leave them thus. I would go seek and find them, and range them before thee." "Go and return again," quoth the Archbishop. "Thank God, this field is thine and mine."

Roland turns away and fares on alone through the field; he searches the valleys and the hills. One by one he hath taken up the barons, and hath come with them unto the Archbishop, and places them in rank before him. The Archbishop cannot help but weep; he raises his hand and gives them benediction, and thereafter saith: "Alas for ye, lords! May God the Glorious receive your souls, and bring them into Paradise among the blessed flowers. And now my own death torments me sore; never again shall I see the great Emperor."

Again Roland turned away to search the field; and when he found Oliver his comrade, he gathered him close against his breast, and as best he might returned again unto the Archbishop, and laid his comrade upon a shield beside the others; and the Archbishop absolved and blessed him. Then their sorrow and pity broke forth again, and Roland saith: "Oliver, fair comrade, thou wert son of the great Duke Rainier, who held the Marches of Rivier and Genoa; for the breaking of lances or the piercing of shields, for vanquishing and affrighting the proud, for upholding and counseling the good, never in any land was there a better knight."

When Roland sees the peers, and Oliver whom he so loved, lying dead, pity takes him and he begins to weep; and his face is all discolored; so great is his grief he cannot stand upright, but will he, nill he, falls to the ground in a swoon.

Now Roland feels that death is near him; he prays to the Lord God for his peers that He will receive them, and he prays to the Angel Gabriel for himself. That he may be free from all reproach, he takes his horn of ivory in the one hand, and Durendal, his sword, in the other, and farther than a crossbow can cast an arrow, through a cornfield he goeth on toward Spain.

At the crest of a hill, beneath two fair trees, are four stairs of marble; there he falls down on the green grass in a swoon, for death is close upon him.

High are the hills and very tall are the trees; the four stones are of shining marble; and there Count Roland swoons upon the green grass. Meantime a Saracen is watching him; he has stained his face and body with blood, and feigning death, he lies still among his fellows; but now he springs to his feet and hastens forward. Fair he was, and strong, and of good courage; and in his pride he breaks out into mighty wrath, and seizes upon Roland, both him and his arms, and he cries: "Now is the nephew of Charles overthrown. This his sword I will carry into Arabia." But at his touch the Count recovered his senses.

Roland feels that his sword hath been taken from him, he opens his eyes, and saith. "Certes, thou art not one of our men." He holds his horn of ivory which he never lets out of his grasp, and he smites the Saracen upon the helm which was studded with gold and gems, and he breaks steel and head and bones, and he falls down dead at his feet. Then saith Roland: "Coward, what made thee so bold to lay hands upon me, whether right or wrong? No man shall hear it but shall hold thee a fool. Now is my horn of ivory broken in the bell, and its gold and its crystals have fallen."

Now Roland feels that his sight is gone from him. With much striving he gets upon his feet; the color has gone from his face; before him lies a brown stone, and in his sorrow and wrath he smites ten blows upon it. The sword grates upon the rock, but neither breaks nor splinters; and the Count saith: "Holy Mary, help me now! Ah, Durendal, alas for your goodness! *Now am I near to death, and have no more need of you.* Many a fight in the field have I won with you, many a wide land have I conquered with you, lands now ruled by Charles with the white beard. May the man who would flee before another, never possess you. For many a day have you been held by a right good lord, never will there be such another in France the free."

And again Roland smote upon the brown stone and beyond all telling shattered it; the sword grates, but springs back again into the air and is neither dinted nor broken. And when the Count sees he

Reginald Birch

The death of Roland.

may in no wise break it, he laments, saying: "O Durendal, how fair and holy a thing thou art! It is not meet that thou fall into the hands of the paynims; only Christians should wield thee. May no coward ever possess thee! Many wide lands have I conquered with thee, lands which Charles of the white beard rules; and thereby is the Emperor great and mighty."

Now Roland feels that death has come upon him, and that it creeps down from his head to his heart. In all haste he fares under a pine tree, and hath cast himself down upon his face on the green grass. Under him he laid his sword and his horn of ivory; and he turned his face toward the paynim folk, for he would that Charles and all his men should say that the gentle Count had died a conqueror. Speedily and full often he confesses his sins, and in atonement he offers his glove to God.

Roland lies on a high peak looking toward Spain; he feels that his time is spent, and with one hand he beats upon his breast: "O God, I have sinned; forgive me through Thy might the wrongs, both great and small, which I have done from the day I was born even to this day on which I was smitten." With his right hand he holds out his glove to God; and lo, the angels of heaven come down to him.

Count Roland lay under the pine tree; he has turned his face toward Spain, and he begins to call many things to remembrance— all the lands he had won by his valor, and sweet France, and the men of his lineage, and Charles, his liege lord, who had brought him up in his household; and he cannot help but weep. But he would not wholly forget himself, and again he confesses his sins and begs forgiveness of God: "Our Father, who art truth, who raised up Lazarus from the dead, and who defended Daniel from the lions, save thou my soul from the perils to which it is brought through the sins I wrought in my life days." With his right hand he offers his glove to God, and Saint Gabriel has taken it from his hand. Then his head sinks on his arm, and with clasped hands he hath gone to his end. And God sent him his cherubim, and Saint Michael of the Seas, and with them went Saint Gabriel, and they carried the soul of the Count into Paradise.

The Chronicle of the Cid

THE CHRONICLE OF THE CID

Tales about the great Spanish hero, Don Rodrigo Diaz of Vivar (Rodrigo, or Ruy, Diaz de Bivar), called the Cid.

STORIES FROM THE CHRONICLE OF THE CID

By MARY WRIGHT PLUMMER

Illustrations by D. J. Luis Pellicer

THE YOUTH AND MARRIAGE OF THE CID

RODRIGO DIAZ DE BIVAR was the name by which our hero was christened in the church of St. Martin at Burgos, Spain, in the year 1026; but he is frequently called Ruy Diaz as a sort of contraction. He gained other titles as he went through life, such as the Cid, or Chief, and Campeador, the Champion, and in many places we find him mentioned as "The Perfect One," "he who was born in a good hour," etc. He was of good family, almost as good as that of the King Don Ferrando, ruler of Castile and Leon, and his father, Don Diego, was high in honor at court.

Diego, at the time the *Chronicle of the Cid* begins, was an old man, weak and infirm in body, though he kept the high Castilian spirit that would not brook the slightest insult, and was very sensitive about his honor. It happened that he fell into a dispute with the Count Don Gomez, Lord of Gormaz, a powerful warrior in the prime of his years, and the Count in a moment of cowardly anger struck him on the cheek. The old courtier was too feeble to avenge himself for this the first affront that had ever been offered to one of his race, and he retired to his home to brood in solitude.

Rodrigo at this time was a mere youth, not at all a match for the Count Don Gomez, but he felt deeply the affront offered to his house, and knew that upon him alone could his father depend for vengeance. So, the *Chronicle* says, "he asked nothing but justice of heaven, and of man he asked only a fair field." Taking his father's sword, he went out and fought with the Count and killed him, thus wiping out, as he thought, the insult done to his father.

Don Diego felt himself avenged, and placed his son above him at table as a sign that Rodrigo was now head of the house and must uphold its honor. Soon after this the old courtier died, and his son was in reality the chief of his family.

It was at about this time that Rodrigo displayed great valor in his first sallies against the Moors, who were ravaging and plundering the country, and took prisoner five Moorish kings, with many of their followers and much spoil.

D. J. Luis Pelliger

Thus he wiped out the insult done to his father.

He brought the kings to his aged mother, who must have been very proud of her son's prowess, but prouder still of the generosity which led him to send them back to their own country without a ransom. The kings themselves showed that they appreciated this treatment by sending him tribute afterwards and of their own will declaring themselves his vassals, or subjects. It was they who gave him the name of El Seid, or the Cid, the name by which he is best known to this day.

And now we come to the most curious episode in the life of our hero—his marriage to Doña Ximena Gomez, the daughter of the Count whom he had slain. The most curious part of it is that the lady herself went to King Don Ferrando, who, like most kings in those days, could control the marriages of his subjects, and begged him to marry her to Rodrigo. The reasons she gave for wishing this were, first, that she believed Rodrigo was destined to be one of the first men of the land, and second, that she desired to show forgiveness, a most Christian virtue, toward the man who had killed her father, and thus to end the feud between the two houses. Shocking as this marriage appears to us, it seems to have struck the King as a very happy arrangement of the difficulties between the two noble families; and he agreed to broach the matter to the Cid. Rodrigo, who, as we shall see, tried always to be obedient to his sovereign, gave his consent; but the old ballad tells us that:

"When the fair Ximena came forth to plight her hand,
   Rodrigo gazing on her, his face could not command.

"He stood and blushed before her; thus at the last said he—
   'I slew thy sire, Ximena, but not in villainy:

" 'In no disguise I slew him, man against man I stood:
   There was some wrong between us and I did shed his blood.

" 'I slew a man, I owe a man; fair lady, by God's grace,
   An honored husband thou shalt have in thy dead father's place.' "

This was a very delicate way of putting it, saying only, "There was some wrong between us"—when the wrong had been solely on the part of the Count Don Gomez; and if anything could reconcile us to the thought of such a match, it would be the feeling that Rodrigo was only doing the lady justice in giving her a protecter in place of the one she had lost at his hands.

To give an idea of the festivities that accompanied Rodrigo's marriage, I quote from a ballad describing the occasion:

"The King had taken order that they should rear an arch,
   From house to house all over, in the way where they must march;
   They have hung it all with lances, and shields, and glittering helms,
   Brought by the Campeador from out the Moorish realms.

"They have scattered olive branches and rushes on the street,
And the ladies fling down garlands at the Campeador's feet;
With tapestry and broidery their balconies between,
To do his bridal honor, their walls the burghers screen.

"They lead the bulls before them, all covered o'er with trappings;
The little boys pursue them, with hootings and with clappings;
The fool, with cap and bladder, upon his ass goes prancing
Amidst troops of captive maidens with bells and cymbals dancing."

STORY OF THE LEPER

When Rodrigo was married, he took his wife home to his mother, and bade them love each other for his sake, and then, the King sending for him, he went forth to engage in the royal service; but first he gained the King's consent to go on a pilgrimage to Compostella and do homage to St. Mary.

Like all the noblemen of the time, Rodrigo traveled with a band of knights, and on this occasion he had twenty. The King had given him lands and gifts at the time of his wedding, so that he was now quite rich, and no doubt traveled in great state; nevertheless, he was mindful of the needs of others, and all along the way he distributed alms to the poor and sympathized with them. It happened that among these was a leper who had fallen into a quagmire, and who called upon the horsemen to help him out. Now, leprosy was a terrible disease and made of its victim a most disgusting-looking object; and most people would have turned away and left the poor creature help himself as best he could. This, in fact, was what the knights of Rodrigo's company did; but the Cid was a hero not only on the battlefield, and his great heart was stirred with pity for this loathsome thing that needed his aid. So he alighted from his steed, and helped the leper out of the quagmire, and to the great indignation of the knights took him up before him on his horse and carried him thus to the inn where they were all to spend the night. At supper, when the knights with scowling looks kept themselves as far as possible from the sick man, Rodrigo gave them a lesson in true knighthood by sharing the meal with him. This so offended the company that they left the room. But the Cid did even more, in the goodness of his heart. He ordered beds prepared for all his band, and a chamber to be made ready for himself and the leper. It was done, and the two men lay down to sleep; and when Rodrigo thought of his beautiful young wife, his fine health, his wealth, and favor with the King, and contrasted all these with the lot of the homeless, friendless, stricken beggar beside him, I am sure he felt a glow at his heart that he had been able to do something toward lightening the burden of the outcast.

About midnight he awoke, feeling a breath as of cold air blow right through him from his back to his breast, and he put his hand back to touch his companion, but in vain, for the leper was gone. This frightened him, for, like all the people of that time, he believed and feared evil spirits; so he arose and called for a light, and looked everywhere in the room but could not find anyone; then, lest the thing, whatever it was, should return, he left the light burning and went back to bed, but could not sleep. And after awhile, the legend says, he saw standing before him a form in white garments, and it said to him, "Sleepest thou, or wakest thou, Rodrigo?" And he said, "I do not sleep; but who art thou that bringest with thee such brightness and so sweet an odor?" and the form answered, "I am St. Lazarus. Know thou that I was the leper to whom thou didst so much good and so great honor for the love of God; and because thou didst this for His sake, hath God now granted thee a great gift." Then he went on to say that no matter where Rodrigo might be, whenever he felt that cold breath blow through him he might know by that that whatever work he had in hand would be sure to succeed. His name was to gain in honor every day, he was to be feared in battle by his enemies and to die an honorable death in his own home when he should be full of years. Praying him to persevere in doing good, St. Lazarus left him, and Rodrigo fell upon his knees and prayed. The next morning he proceeded on his pilgrimage, giving out alms and kind words as before.

The first work that was given to the Cid to perform after this was a trial by combat with a famous knight in the service of the

King of Aragon, and the point to be decided was whether a certain city belonged to that King or to King Don Ferrando. Although his opponent was held to be "the best knight in all Spain," Rodrigo was the winner in the contest, and the city belonged thereafter to his King.

Like most successful men, Rodrigo had enemies who were jealous of his rising fame, and some of them tried to injure him. They agreed with the Moors to engage in a mock battle to which Rodrigo should be summoned to fight, and in which he was to be killed by the latter; but among the Moors to whom notice of this plot was sent were the five kings whom in former years he had set at liberty. These showed their gratitude now in a very substantial way by sending to the Cid the letters containing the plot. Rodrigo thought that such falsity deserved to be exposed to the King, and showed him the letters. The King was shocked, and ordered the conspirators to leave his dominions, and Rodrigo to see that they did so, since he himself was going on a pilgrimage. But the wife of one of the chief plotters was a kinswoman of Rodrigo, and came to him in great grief, imploring a letter to some king under whom she and her lord might seek protection; so the Cid, who would not allow his cousin to kneel to him as she would fain have done, gave her very readily a letter to the King of Cordova. This King welcomed the lady and her husband, the Count Don Garcia Ordoñez, for the Cid's sake, and gave them the estate of Cabra to live upon; but the disposition of the Count was not improved by this kindness, for he afterwards made war upon the King from this very estate, until Rodrigo was compelled to take it from him.

Up to this time the Cid had not belonged to the order of knights; and he was very anxious to be knighted by the King's hand. An opportunity soon came. The city of Coimbra, which was held by the Moors, had been besieged six months by the Castilian hosts under King Don Ferrando and the Cid, and finally yielded, the Moors being allowed to depart in safety. Their great mosque was changed to a Christian church and dedicated to St. Mary, and in it was the ceremony performed of knighting the Cid. The King girded on his sword, and gave him the kiss, but not the blow with the hand upon the neck as was customary. This blow was always accompanied with the words, "Awake, and sleep not in the affairs of knighthood," and a Spanish writer says that the King omitted these words and the blow because he knew well that the Cid did not need any such injunction. After this, the Queen, to do him more honor, gave him his horse, and the Infanta (that is, the Princess) Doña Urraca fastened on his spurs—and he was called thereafter Ruy Diaz. The King then commanded him to knight nine nobles for his squires, which he did—and the ceremony was over.

Shortly after, the King and Ruy Diaz were at Zamora, when the five Moorish kings sent messengers with tribute to the Cid, and they delivered their messages in the King's presence. Ruy Diaz offered to the King one-fifth of the tribute, but the King would not receive it, but ordered that from that time Ruy Diaz should be called the Cid, because it was the name given him by the Moors.

After many years of wars in which he was nearly always triumphant, thanks to the leadership of the Cid, King Don Ferrando drew near his death. In the opinion of those times, his life had been well spent; most of his wars had been against the Moors, who were not Christians and were therefore thought fit subjects for expulsion from Spanish territory, he had enriched the churches and monasteries with the spoils taken in battle, and he had made a great many pilgrimages. When he found that he could not live many days longer, he began to arrange for the disposition of his kingdom. According to the old Gothic law, the kingdom was never to be divided, but to remain under one lord, and this would make it the inheritance of Don Sancho, the King's eldest son. But the Old King loved all his children, and was afraid such an arrangement would cause trouble among them; so he parceled out the kingdom among his three sons and two daughters, and thought he was doing a very wise thing.

The Infante Don Sancho considered himself robbed of his rights, however, and said so to his father, and many in the kingdom took sides with him, while others thought that as the King had won most of his dominions he had a right to dispose of them as suited him.

Among the last acts of his life, King Don Ferrando commended to his oldest son the Cid Ruy Diaz, and some days after he breathed his last, having reigned thirty-one years.

EXILE OF THE CID

For some years after this there was nothing worthy of special mention in the career of the Cid. He went on, making the usual number of conquests among the Moors and gaining spoil for himself and the King, and at the same time making enemies by his success. After each of his victories the nobles came up to the Cid and offered him their congratulations when all the while many of them were burning with envy and jealousy of him. These feelings only waited for an opportunity to burst forth, and it came in this way. The Cid was ill at home, and King Don Alfonso was forced to go against the Moors with all his army. And while he was absent a great Moorish force entered the land upon the other side, and the Cid, who was growing better, arose and went against it, and he followed the Moors as far as Toledo, trespassing on the lands of King Alimaymon, against whom King Don Alfonso had sworn never to fight. Here the envious knights saw an opening for their wedge. They persuaded the King that the Cid had broken faith with the King of Toledo in order that the Moors of that city might have a chance to fall upon the Spanish forces and slay them. He went in haste to Burgos and sent for the Cid to meet him there, but the meeting was finally had between Burgos and Bivar.

When the Cid would have kissed the hand of his sovereign, the latter withdrew it, and said to him angrily, "Ruy Diaz, quit my land!" The *Chronicle* says that the Cid thereupon clapped spurs to his mule and vaulted into another piece of ground which was his own, and answered, "Sir, I am not in your land, but in my own." Then said the King still more angrily, "Go out of my kingdoms without delay," and when the Cid asked for the customary thirty days, the King answered that he should have nine days, and no more, and if he was not gone then, he, the King, would come and look for him. The enemies of the Cid had accomplished their end—they had made a breach between him and the King, and one they thought not easily repaired, for when one is exiled one is apt to find the old proverb true, "Out of sight, out of mind." We shall see if they failed in their reckoning.

The Cid himself was sorrowful, but perhaps more indignant than sorrowful; and the people round about were much grieved. When Ruy Diaz asked how many of his friends, kinsmen, and vassals would follow him into banishment, his cousin, Alvar Fañez, answered for all and said, "Cid, we will all go with you, through desert and through peopled country, and never fail you." Then the Cid thanked them all, and said that some day perhaps he should be able to reward them.

This time the decree of exile was not countermanded, and Ruy Diaz had to leave his home and country. The *Chronicle* says that tears came to the Cid's eyes as he looked back and saw "his hall deserted, the household chests unfastened, the doors open, no cloaks hanging up, no seats in the porch, no hawks upon the perches," and we can easily believe it, for it is just such strong, brave men as the Cid who have the warmest love for home and all that goes with it. As he rode away with his followers, he gave orders to Alvar Fañez to see that no wrong be done to the poor along the road. An old woman standing in her doorway said as he passed, "Go in a lucky minute and make spoil of whatever you wish," and in going out from Bivar they saw a crow on their right hand and on coming into Burgos a crow upon their left. These they regarded as good omens, and the Cid feigned to be of good cheer, and said, "Friends, by God's good pleasure we shall return to Castile with great honor and great gain."

At Burgos, the town where he was born, the people were all weeping because of his exile, and yet not one of them dared offer him a night's lodging; for King Don Alfonso in his anger had sent letters to the city forbidding the people to shelter the Cid, under penalty of losing all their goods and having their eyes put out. It was given to a little girl nine years old to come out and make this known to Ruy Diaz, who, when he had heard it, turned away and went to the shrine of St. Mary to pray, for the King could not prevent him from doing that. Then they rode out of the town and pitched their tents upon the sands, where they spent the first night of their exile. The Cid's nephew, Martin Antolinez, had followed his uncle and taken great store of bread and wine, so that there was plenty for all the company, which was a good thing, for the King had forbidden the people of Burgos to give or sell food to the exiles. But more than one day's provisions would be needed for his company, and the Cid had but little money, most of his wealth being in lands, so he set about arranging a plan for obtaining money for his use until he should be able to live by the spoils he hoped to gain.

A very daring and not very honest scheme occurred to him as the only one that could be carried out in so short a time, and he confided its execution to his nephew. Near Burgos lived two Jews to whom the Cid had always been accustomed to sell such of his spoils as he could not use, and they had confidence in him and would not be likely to suspect him of trickery. The Cid sent to them by his nephew to know what they would advance him on two chests of treasure which he wished to leave with them, but which they must come for at night, lest robbers should attack them. The Jews offered six hundred marks, which the Cid thought sufficient. He made a condition, however, that the chests were not to be opened for a year, for he was sure that within that time he could redeem them. The Jews were so glad to have made such a bargain, for the chests were very heavy, that they readily consented not to examine them for a year, and the Cid received the six hundred marks and a present besides for Martin Antolinez, who had been his agent in the transaction. Now, the chests contained nothing in the world but sand, and the Cid felt that he was doing a dishonest thing, for he said to his nephew, "I do this thing more of necessity than of wilfullness; but by God's good help I shall redeem all." As it happened, he did one day repay the Jews, but it was a dangerous risk to take, nevertheless.

The wife of Ruy Diaz, with her women and her two little daughters, was at the monastery of St. Peter, beyond Burgos. They had heard of the Cid's exile, and were praying for him in the early morning when he and his company rode up to the door. Of course, they were all rejoiced to see him, though he had come on a sorrowful errand, and the Cid caught up his little girls and cried over them just as a good father would do nowadays if he were leaving his children, perhaps for years and perhaps for his lifetime. The little family grouped together in the courtyard, in the flaming, smoky light of the torches and tapers held by the good monks, must have made a touching picture. The Abbot made a great feast for the Campeador that day, and they all tried to make merry and drive away all thoughts of the near parting. Meanwhile, the news of the Cid's banishment had flown over all Castile, and the people were both indignant and dismayed, and many left their homes and the offices which they held in order to follow him.

One night at the monastery and then the company must be off. The Cid gave into the Abbot's keeping a sum of money for the support of his wife and children and the waiting women, and a smaller sum for the monastery; and after Mass the next morning he bade farewell to them all. He embraced and blessed Doña Ximena and the little girls, and the *Chronicle* says, "the parting between them was like separating the nail from the quick flesh, and he wept and continued to look round after them." One hundred and fifty knights waited outside to join his already large band of retainers, and they left word with the Abbot as to what route they would take, in case any should come afterwards, wishing to join the company.

They had many miles to go before they should be out of Castile, the Douro River to cross on rafts, and the Sierra de Miedes, a range of wild mountains, to traverse, and all the way along adventurers came to enlist under the Cid's banner, so that before he left Castile he could count three hundred mounted knights, beside foot soldiers.

On the eighth night, the Cid had a vision in which the Angel Gabriel appeared to him and told him to go on and fear nothing, that all his undertakings should end well, and he should be rich and honorable. And the Cid was much rejoiced, and gave thanks for his vision.

RETURN FROM EXILE

The next that we hear of Ruy Diaz is a succession of battles with the Moors in which he almost invariably came off victorious.

But we notice this, that in almost every case he released the Moors who were taken prisoners and let them go where they would, sometimes even giving them a share of what he had fairly won from them in battle. The *Chronicle* says that at one place he gave back to the Moors a castle he had taken, and departed leaving them blessing him for this bounty. And among the first things that he did, he sent Alvar Fañez back to Castile with a portion of the spoils taken, to be given to the King, and with money for the church of St. Mary, at Burgos, in which he was also to hang up the banners of the Moors they had overcome. The good Abbot of St. Peter's and the Cid's family were not forgotten in the distribution, and, indeed, it seemed as if Ruy Diaz had no use for treasure except to give it away.

King Don Alfonso accepted the gifts sent him and was glad he said, that the Cid was faring so well; but he did not think it becoming a king to allow his anger to cool so quickly, so he would not forgive the Campeador just yet or revoke his sentence of banishment; nevertheless, he granted Alvar Fañez's prayer so far as to restore to all the Cid's followers the possessions which their exile had caused to fall to the crown. Alvar Fañez was forced to be content, and went away saying:

"Sir, you have done this now, and you will do the rest hereafter."

Many seemed to have joined him on his return to the Cid, for when he reached Zaragoza, where Ruy Diaz was staying with the Moorish King, he had two hundred horsemen, and foot soldiers without number. But it was not so much on this account as because he brought tidings from the wives and families of the exiles that he was so welcome and that the Cid met him with an embrace.

In one of his battles, where the Cid was opposed by Moorish forces headed by Count Don Ramon Berenguer, Count of Barcelona, who claimed to be lord of the Moors in those parts, Ruy Diaz came by his good sword Colada, which he prized always very highly, and of which we shall hear more hereafter; and he took Count Ramon prisoner at the same time. The Count was so mortified to have his fine horsemen beaten by such a set of ragged fellows, as he called the Cid's forces, that he would not eat for three days; but the Cid finally told him he must eat if he wished to be set free and furnished with means to go back into his own country. This caused him to change his mind and he ate and drank with a relish, and the same day was set free with two of his kinsmen. He could not understand this generosity, and rode away at a rapid pace, looking back often to make sure that no one was coming to retake him, "which," says the *Chronicle* with fine scorn, "the Perfect One would not have done for the whole world, for never did he do disloyal things."

Soon after this, in treating with the Moors who held the castle of Rueda, the King met with treachery from them by which he lost several of his best knights and nobles, and not knowing where else to turn, he sent for the Cid, who was in that region, and consulted with him and took him again into favor, and asked him to come back to Castile. The Campeador thanked the King, but said he could accept the recall on certain conditions only. And what do you think those conditions were? That he himself should receive amends for his banishment in the shape of money, or lands, or titles? Not at all. That the King should make a public confession of his hastiness and promise never to treat Ruy Diaz so in the future? Nor this. In fact, the Cid seemed to have forgotten that he had been unjustly dealt with or that he had any personal wrongs to be salved over; but he saw that here was an opportunity to obtain a great good for all the people; and he demanded three things: first, that in time to come, when a nobleman should be banished for whatever cause, he should have the thirty days the law allowed for preparation; that neither noble nor citizen should be proceeded against till he had been fairly and lawfully heard; that the King should not violate the charters of any town or other place, or impose unjust taxes upon it, or, at any rate, if he did this, it should be lawful for the town to defend itself with arms.

This, we should think, would be a bitter pill for a king to swallow when administered by a subject, but the fact that Don Alfonso took it without so much as winking proves that he began to know the real value of the Cid and wanted his support at any price. When this was agreed on, the King wanted the Cid to return with him to Castile, but Ruy Diaz would not go until he had taken the castle of

Rueda and punished the treachery of the Moors therein. The castle secured and its holders sent as prisoners to King Don Alfonso, the Cid with great riches and honor set out for Castile. Seven castles, gifts from the King's hand, awaited him, and the promise that all places which he might hereafter win from the Moors should belong to him and his heirs forever. However, this was not the last quarrel between the King and the Cid, or rather it was not the last time that the King was disposed to quarrel, for so far as Ruy Diaz was concerned, we find him always obedient to the King, working for the royal interest and defending the royal honor. But there was no serious talk of exile after this, and the Cid's course continued for some time to be a series of triumphs over the Moors, which reflected great glory on his sovereign and Castile.

SIEGE OF VALENCIA BY THE MOORS

The winter passed quietly in Valencia and nothing came to mar the peaceful and happy family life of the Cid. But early in the spring came the news that King Yucef of Morocco was coming across the sea with fifty thousand men, to lay siege to Valencia. Immediately, the Cid began to make preparations for a long siege, laying in great store of provisions, strengthening the walls and the towers and looking to the arms of the citizens, so that by the time King Yucef appeared before the walls everything was in readiness. Doña Ximena and her daughters had never seen the Cid's prowess in battle, and he wished them to know how war was carried on; so when the first party of horsemen sallied forth from the city, the ladies were taken up to the highest tower to watch the engagement. Doña Ximena, when she saw the great power of the Moors, and heard the uproar made by their tambours and their shouting, was very much dismayed, but her husband reassured her, saying that the Moors should furnish a dowry or wedding-portion for her daughters, and that their tambours should soon be hung up as trophies in the churches of Valencia; and he added, "My heart kindles because you are here." When the Moors entered the gardens around the town, the Cid sent out two hundred horse under a knight named Alvar Salvadores, and bade him show Doña Ximena and her daughters the good will he had toward them. This sent Alvar Salvadores off in haste, and he and his forces soon fell upon the Moors and did great execution. The ladies, up on the tower, were standing watching, but they trembled so that the Cid made them sit down where they could not see the fight.

D. J. Luis Pellicer

Provisioning Valencia for a long siege.

Alvar Salvadores, however, did not know this, and supposing that he was followed constantly by their bright eyes, fought so well and was so unconscious of anything but the need of distinguishing himself, that the first thing he knew he found himself in advance of his men, and surrounded by the enemy, who carried him to the Moorish tents. The next day the Cid intended to send out a large force and to have a real battle with the assailants; so he commanded all to be up before cockcrow, to hear Mass at the church, make confession and take communion, for in this way did all the people of that time who made any claim to be religious prepare themselves for a battle. After these ceremonies they felt assured that their souls would go straight to heaven if they themselves were slain on the field.

When the Cid left the city at last, he had only four thousand men to fight against fifty thousand; but by dint of good generalship and hard fighting his side gained the day, and the *Chronicle* says that of the fifty thousand Moors only about fifteen thousand escaped.

When the battle was over the Valencians took a great deal of treasure that was left on the field, and in King Yucef's tent they were rejoiced to find Alvar Salvadores, who had been taken the day before. King Yucef's sword, Tizona, or "The Fire-brand," the Cid kept for himself, but the tent, which was very elegant and supported by two pillars wrought in gold, he ordered preserved with care until he could send it to King Don Alfonso.

Every man received his share of the spoils, even the Moors of the surrounding region being allowed to help themselves, and the Cid, who, among his vassals, had much the same rights as a king, gave his wife's ladies in marriage to some of his bravest knights, and gave them a dowry in silver. As the *Chronicle* says that the ladies were very glad, I suppose we must be satisfied, though it seems a rather high-handed proceeding, this of deciding other people's fates. Alvar Fañez, the Cid's favorite messenger, was sent with others to carry to King Don Alfonso a portion of the spoils, and they found him at Valladolid, whence he came out to meet them in great state.

Alvar Fañez delivered the Cid's message, consisting of his thanks for the kindness shown his wife and daughters, and the news of the great victory over the Moors, and then commanded the gifts for the King to be brought forward; and two hundred horses, each led by a child, and with a sword hanging from the left side of the saddle, were led past, after which was presented the handsome tent of King Yucef. King Don Alfonso was greatly pleased, and said that though he had taken many a tent, he had never taken one like this; and as to the horses, he frankly admitted that never before had Spanish king received such a gift from any vassal. He gave orders that the messengers should be provided for handsomely until time for their return, when they should receive from him full suits of armor. Among those who assisted the King at this interview was Don Garcia Ordoñez, the Cid's inveterate foe, and he and some of his kinsmen talked bitterly among themselves, and said the Cid had sent this present to put them to shame, and they thirsted more and more to humiliate him in some way. There were also in the company the Infantes of Carrion, called Diego and Ferrando Gonzalez, who are to play great part in this chronicle. These two younger men were of ancient family, but that did not signify anything in their case, for they were selfish and cowardly and cruel. But these things are not written on people's foreheads, and so they were held in very good estimation. When they saw the spoil which the Cid had sent to the King as part of the treasure taken in one battle only, when they heard that he had become lord of Valencia and that his riches were constantly increasing, they consulted together and decided to ask the King for the Cid's daughters in marriage. For they agreed in thinking that the Cid would certainly do well by his daughters, and their dowry would make rich whoever should marry them. So the Infantes betook themselves to the King and made their request; and the King thought a while, but scarcely dared promise, for he knew how dearly the Cid loved his children, and thought that perhaps he was not yet ready to part with them.

Marriages in those days and in those southern countries were contracted when the parties were very young, and probably the Cid's daughters were not more than thirteen or fourteen, so it was left to the discretion of the parents or the King as to whom and when they should marry. However, the King told the Infantes that if the Cid approved the match it should meet with his favor, and he offered to make the proposition to Ruy Diaz' messengers to be carried to their lord.

Alvar Fañez received the message, therefore, and replied that he was certain the Cid would carry out the King's wishes in the matter, and that if the King desired the Cid would come to treat with him on the subject. Then, kissing the King's hand, the messengers took their leave.

THE INFANTES OF CARRION

When the Cid saw his messengers returning he went joyfully out to meet them; but his joy was soon turned to thoughtfulness by the message which they brought and which was entirely unexpected. He did not seem to trust his own judgment, but asked the messengers what they thought, and when they answered like dutiful vassals, "even as it shall please you," he went to his wife and laid the whole matter before her. They agreed in thinking that while the Infantes of Carrion were of very good family, they were also uncomfortably proud of the fact, and the Campeador and his wife hardly liked the idea of having them for sons-in-law; nevertheless, as Doña Ximena said, that was not the question, for if the King favored the match they could not help themselves. So the Cid sent word to the King that he would meet him and would do what the King wished. The place appointed was upon the banks of the river Tagus, and the time three weeks from then. "Then there was hurrying to and fro," both in the Castilian court and in Valencia. Whoever had handsome clothes got them out and furbished them up, in order that no tarnished spot should mar the general brightness. Horses and mules were brought out, richly caparisoned, and put through their paces, and, in short, nobody thought of anything but the approaching festivities. The King sent supplies of food to the place of meeting, enough to last many days. As to the Infantes of Carrion, being young and more or less vain, they spent their time in devising rich toilets for themselves, and the *Chronicle* says naïvely, "Some they paid for, and some they went in debt for."

When the Cid, after his splendid preparations were finished, finally took leave of his family, he ordered them to stay strictly in the palace while he was gone, lest harm should come to them; and he bade Alvar Salvadores and some others to stay in the city and guard the palace, for in it were his wife and daughters, "in whom he had his heart and soul." I dare say these knights were greatly disappointed, for they had counted on going with the Cid, but the pill was not without sugar for Alvar Salvadores, who was always inspired to do his best, you remember, when there were ladies in the case. The

Cid had a large company, even without these gentlemen, over a thousand horsemen following him through the gates. All their horses, says the *Chronicle,* had been won by the Cid and not given to him.

King Don Alfonso arrived first at the rendezvous, and went out to meet the Cid. Their meeting was very cordial, which inspired a friendly feeling among the followers of both, save only two of the Cid's enemies who were with the king. That day the Cid and his people dined with the King, who had been there longer and had all things in readiness, and the next day the compliment was returned. King Don Alfonso asked the Cid to sit at his table, but the Cid could not make up his mind to this honor, and so he and the father of the Infantes of Carrion were placed at a table by themselves. The King could scarcely eat for looking at the Cid and marveling at his beard, which had grown to a great length, for it was a long time since the two men had met and they found each other greatly changed. When it came the Cid's turn to play the part of host, he had such a banquet spread that all agreed they had not seen a better for three years. The King and the chief guests had plates of gold, and the rest ate from silver. The Infantes were quite dazzled by this display, and were more anxious than ever to enter a family of such magnificence.

On the third day, after Mass, the King arose before the whole assembly and formally requested, in behalf of the Infantes of Carrion, the hands in marriage of Doña Elvira and Doña Sol. He made it very plain that he would approve such a match, and the Cid felt bound to consent, not really knowing any facts to the disadvantage of the young men; but he tried to plead in excuse that his children were too young to marry. To this the King would not listen for a moment, and bade him make up his mind and give them an answer. There was not much room for choice on the Cid's part, for when the King sent for him first he knew what he would have to say sooner or later, so he said the King might do as he pleased in the matter, and he (the Cid) would be suited.

The Infantes then did homage to the Cid as their father-in-law, and the King gave them into his charge to be taken to Valencia for the marriage; and he also caused it to be well understood that it was he who had made the match and not the Cid. Eight days longer the festivities lasted, and when at length it was time for all to depart, the Cid distributed gifts among the company and made everybody very glad to have been his guest. To the King he gave fifty beautiful horses with rich trappings. Then he begged the King to appoint some one his deputy to give Doña Elvira and Doña Sol to the Infantes, since His Majesty could not be present to do it in person, and the King appointed the trusty Alvar Fañez.

The Cid mounted his horse Babieca, but before he rode away he said to the company that if any would go with him to the wedding they would get something by it, and he besought the King to let all go who wished. The King consenting, the people did not require persuasion, and when the two parties separated more went with the Cid than with the King. Feeling that the happiness of his daughters was in question, the Cid wanted to know more about his prospective sons-in-law, and he appointed two faithful men of his household to ride in their company, and give him an honest opinion of their character. With the Infantes was their uncle, Don Suero Gonzalez, who afterwards made great trouble in the Cid's family. He had been the caretaker of the Infantes, and trained them up to be very proud and scornful; and he himself was a great boaster. When the Cid's men reported this state of affairs, the Cid would have been very glad to break off the match, and was sorry he had ever consented to it; but as the King had made it, he was obliged to submit. Perhaps he hoped that he could make good sons-in-law of them as he had made a good knight of Martin Pelaez. Anyway, he had gone too far to turn back.

When they reached Valencia, he placed the Infantes and their company in the suburb of Alcudia, and he went on to the palace.

The next day the Cid rode out to Alcudia and escorted the Infantes to the palace, where Doña Ximena had her daughters all ready to receive them. The *Chronicle* says that since midnight the ladies had been up, "prinking and pranking." When the company arrived the ladies met and welcomed them in the great hall of the palace. Then the Cid took his seat, with an Infante on each side of him, and all his chief vassals sat in their accustomed seats, and there was silence for awhile. Then Alvar Fañez arose and delivered the young ladies, his cousins, to the Infantes, in the name of the King: Doña Elvira to the Infante Diego and Doña Sol to the Infante Ferrando. After this the Bishop espoused them and they exchanged rings, and all sat down again and "solaced" themselves awhile, that is, were merry and entertained one another. The marriage proper was to be the next day, and was to be performed with great magnificence, so that all who came from Castile to the wedding should always have something to tell of.

The wedding came off in due season, and the festivities lasted fifteen days. They consisted of banquets, bull-fights, target-shooting, cane-throwing, and recitations by the joculars or minstrels, and various other sports; and each guest was sent home with so many gifts that he was looked upon with envious eyes by those who had not gone to the wedding.

THE CID'S VICTORY OVER TWENTY-NINE MOORISH KINGS

Two years passed in peace and quiet, during which the Infantes and their wives and their uncle, Don Suero Gonzalez (more's the pity), lived in Valencia with the Cid; and then one morning news was brought to the palace that the brother of King Yucef was coming with twenty-nine other Moorish kings to avenge King Yucef's death; for that monarch died of grief and shame after his disgraceful defeat. On this same morning, and in connection with this news, an incident happened which made great trouble afterwards between the Infantes and their father-in-law. It seems that the Cid had a pet lion which he had kept until it grew so large that a strong cage had to be made and three keepers appointed for it; and this cage was in an upper story of the palace, out of which opened a court in which the lion was sometimes allowed to walk about; but the doors between the court and the palace were then kept closed. This morning, however, when the keepers had finished cleaning the court they heard shouts that the Moors were coming, and after unlocking the door of the cage they ran down in great haste to know if the news were true—in such haste, indeed, that they forgot to shut the door they ran through, between the court and the palace. It is possible that the lion thought he, too, would like to verify the report; at any rate, he found his way very soon into the hall where the Cid and his sons were, with several knights. The Cid had just held a council with his vassals and decided what to do in regard to the expected attack, and then had lain down on a seat and gone to sleep; and the Infantes and others were playing chess. It must have been something of a shock to look up and find a lion standing near, glaring at them; but, shock or not, it would be a very mean sort of man that would do as the Infantes did. They never thought of the sleeping Cid, or even of each other, but each tried to save his own precious self. Ferrando, the younger, scrambled under the Cid's bench with such speed that he burst his doublet and tore his mantle; while Diego whined, "I shall never see Carrion again!" and, running to a door which opened down into a courtyard, he jumped, and rolled over among the lees from a wine press there, and was covered with them from head to foot. Both of them spoiled their clothes, which was quite punishment enough for two young men so vain of their appearance. With the other occupants of the room, the first thought was of the Cid's safety, and they all wrapped their cloaks about them and stood around the seat. The lion began to walk toward them, when, fortunately, the Cid awoke. Seeing the beast coming, he lifted his hand in surprise, saying "What is this?" and the lion, hearing a familiar and masterly voice, stood still until the Cid took him by the mane and led him back to his cage. It was some time before Ferrando, pale and trembling, left his retreat, and Diego, wet and dirty, came in from the courtyard; but when they did appear, the whole company began to laugh and make fun of them until the Cid bade them stop. The two brothers went out to make fresh toilets, and both were very angry; and of what do you think they accused the Cid? They actually said he had purposely ordered the lion to be loosed in order to see them show the white feather before the other knights. And they swore they would be revenged, not on the Cid directly, they did not dare try that, but on his daughters, who were defenseless women. I can scarcely write civilly about these men, they are so despicable! They consulted their uncle as to how they should take their revenge, and he advised them to wait until this affair with the Moors was over, when they could demand permission of the Cid to take their wives and go to their own home, that Carrion which Diego was afraid he should never see again. And when they were away, and there was no one to protect Doña Elvira and Doña Sol, they could wreak on them the vengeance they thought they owed the Cid. This evil advice pleased the Infantes, and they could hardly wait to carry it into effect; but first, the Moorish kings had to be welcomed, as only the Cid could welcome them. Before meeting the Campeador again it was agreed by the Infantes and their uncle that they should laugh at all allusion to the lion and take in good part all jokes on the subject, that no one might suspect them of harboring resentment.

When the Moors had finally pitched their tents—and there were five thousand pavilions beside common tents—the Cid took the Infantes and Don Suero to the top of the palace and showed them the sight, and they were afraid, though they tried to hide it. On the way down one of the Cid's knights heard them saying together that if they went into battle they should never see Carrion again, and he repeated the saying to the Cid. Ruy Diaz was greatly grieved that his sons-in-law should be such cowards, and to allay their fears and save their reputation, he bade them remain in the city to guard the palace; but they were ashamed, thinking he must have overheard them, and insisted on going into battle.

They did not distinguish themselves there more than we should expect. Diego saw a stout Moor coming at him, and turned and fled till he heard himself called by name. Looking back, he saw Felez Muñoz, the nephew of the Cid, holding the Moor's horse, while its owner lay dead on the ground. Muñoz told Diego to take the horse and pretend he had slain its rider, and the Cid, coming up at this moment, thought this was the way of it and was quite proud of his son-in-law. Well, by means of such feats as this of Felez Muñoz, for none of which we may give credit to the Infantes, the Valencians gained the day, and seventeen of the twenty-nine kings lay dead on the battlefield when the strife was over. There was so much spoil everybody was made rich, and the Infantes received a large portion.

Whenever there was any talk about this battle, and the young knights were mentioned who had carried themselves well on the field, nobody named the Infantes; at the same time, no one criticized their behavior, for all had too great a regard for the Cid's feelings. But the Infantes knew the meaning of the general silence, and suspected that they were a secret laughing-stock, and they were in haste to go away. So they resolved to set on foot the wicked design counseled by their uncle.

TREACHERY OF THE INFANTES OF CARRION

The Infantes knew well in what form to make their request to the Cid, and when they reminded him that they had not seen their home or their parents for two years and had heard no news of them, when they spoke of the dower awaiting their wives in Carrion, and their desire that Doña Elvira and Doña Sol should be made known to their kinsmen there, the Cid felt that the demand was reasonable. The thought of losing his children troubled him, and he said, "When ye take away my daughters ye take away my very heartstrings; nevertheless, it is fitting that ye do as ye have said." Doña Ximena's consent was not readily obtained. She did not feel at all sure of the good intentions of the Infantes, who had shown themselves false of heart more than once; and Alvar Fañez, too, suspected treachery. But the Cid, who was as unsuspicious as he was brave, could not imagine why they should feel so. He cited the noble lineage of the Infantes, and said that the fact that the King made the match would prevent them from ill-treating their wives, if nothing else would. Finally, he bade them say no more about it, for God would not let such a wrong thing happen. So there was nothing to be done but to arrange for the departure of the Infantes and their wives and retainers, and they went loaded down with gifts. The Cid rode with them a league, and he noticed the birds and saw that the omens were bad. He began to think that there might be some reason for the presentiments of his wife and Alvar Fañez; and he called Felez Muñoz and told him to go with the company all the way to Carrion and see what possessions were given to Doña Elvira and Doña Sol, and to come back and report. He had no thought of any greater wrong than that his daughters might be defrauded of their dower. Then he bade them farewell, and the poor young things cried bitterly as if they knew what was in store.

The first night they stayed with the rich Moor Abengalvon, who was friendly to the Cid, and the next day he pressed costly gifts upon them and rode with them part of the way; and the Infantes, seeing that he had great possessions, conspired to kill him and enrich themselves. A Moor who overheard and understood them told Abengalvon, who rode up to the Infantes, surrounded by his men, and charged them with the plot, and he said if it were not for the sake of the Cid they should never reach Carrion. Then, bidding good-bye to the ladies, he turned and rode back home.

The next night the party came to a beautiful oak forest called the Oak-wood of Corpes, and here they prepared to spend the night. The trees were very thick, round about, but there was a clear, green spot in the midst of the forest with a cool fountain near by, and for this reason the place was chosen for the encampment. The mountains around were very wild, however, and there were savage beasts prowling about, but they did not dare come in sight of such a company. At sunrise the next day the mules were loaded and the cavalcade arranged in marching order, when the Infantes gave directions for all to move on except themselves and their wives, saying they would follow soon. In a short time the four were left alone together, and the party had ridden out of sight and hearing. Doña Elvira asked why they had remained there alone, and her husband answered sternly that she would soon see.

Then these inhuman creatures seized their wives by the hair and were about to beat them with their saddle-girths; and the poor things begged them to take the swords Colada and Tizona, which the Cid had given them, and finish their evil work at once. But the Infantes paid no attention, and beat them with the girths and kicked them with their spurs, until they were all lacerated and bloody, and swooned away. Then, with their usual meanness, the brothers carried away the ermine furs and the rich mantles of their wives.

Felez Muñoz had ridden on with the rest, at the Infantes' orders, but not liking the look of things, he went aside into the edge of the forest and waited there to see his cousins pass; and after a while he saw the Infantes go by alone and heard them talking about what they had done and glorying in it. He rode back to the fountain in great haste and found his cousins lying on the ground senseless. He tried to arouse them so that they might get away from so perilous a place, for there was danger lest the Infantes should miss him from their company and come back and kill them all. When the ladies revived they begged for water, and he brought some to them in his hat. Then he placed them on his horse, covered them with his cloak, and leading them into the depths of the forest, away from the road, he made a bed of leaves and grass. When they had lain down he put his cloak over them again, and then, strong man as he was, sat down and cried, for he did not know which way to turn, and it seemed likely they should all die of starvation. If he left his cousins all covered with wounds as they were, they would attract wild beasts, and if he stayed with them there was no one to tell the Cid what had happened.

When the Infantes rejoined their company their bloody spurs were noticed, and the knights began to suspect some villainy; and one hundred of them went up to the Infantes in a body and demanded of them what they had done with their wives. The Infantes said they had left them safe and sound in the Oak-wood near the fountain, that they had not hurt them, but had simply resolved to leave them and have nothing more to do with them. The knights were indignant that the Cid's daughters had been cast off in this manner, and warned the Infantes that some day they would be made to pay for it. Then, leaving the brothers to go their way, the party turned back to the fountain. Here they found no one, but were shocked to see marks of blood on the ground, and began to call loudly on the ladies and make great lamentation. Muñoz and his cousins thought the Infantes were seeking them, with evil intentions, and they made no answer to the calls, so that the company could not find them.

The knights then took counsel together, and agreed to follow up the Infantes and take vengeance on them for killing their wives, for so they supposed they had done; and if they could not find the brothers, they were to ride on to King Don Alfonso, who was then at Palencia, and lay the case before him. They were so determined to have justice done that they vowed not to leave the King's palace until the wrong had been righted as nearly as possible.

So, first, they rode after the Infantes, but, fearing pursuit, the brothers had ridden away at full speed and could not be found; and the next thing was to go to the King. When King Don Alfonso heard their report he was very much grieved, and felt as if it were partly his fault, he having brought about the unhappy marriage. He thought, however, that complaint ought to come from the Cid, and had no doubt it would be presented, so he delayed action until he should hear further in the matter.

THE RESCUE OF DOÑA ELVIRA AND DOÑA SOL

When the sound of voices had died away, Felez Muñoz ventured to come out from the hiding in the forest and go to the nearest village, in order to get food for the ladies; and for seven days and nights this devoted man took care of his cousins in this way until he was able to do something better for them. In the village he became acquainted with a husbandman who lived there with his wife and grown children, and one day, turning the conversation on the Cid, Muñoz found that his chief had at one time in his wanderings been the guest of this old man, and that he was looked upon with great reverence by the whole family, to whom he had given rich presents at leaving. So Muñoz thought the husbandman a safe person in whom to confide, and told him the story of the poor young wives and their hiding place. The old man was sorely grieved at such a tale, but only too glad to do something for the Cid's daughters; and he and his sons went out to the forest at night and brought the ladies into the village to his house. The whole family waited upon them tenderly and made them as comfortable as they could, keeping their presence a profound secret from the rest of the village; and now, having put them into such good keeping, Muñoz felt that he might safely leave them and carry the news to the Cid. But, lest his strange story should seem too monstrous to be true, the ladies gave him a letter to their father, written with the blood from their wounds, which they thought would be proof and to spare of the truth of this report.

On his way he met in the town of Santesteban one Diego Tellez, a follower of the Cid, and to him Muñoz told his story, and agreed with him that it would be better for Doña Elvira and Doña Sol to be moved to Santesteban, where they could be healed of their wounds. Diego accordingly saw to their removal, and before long the ladies had recovered from their hurts.

Still farther on, Muñoz met Alvar Fañez' company carrying to the King a great share of the spoil taken in the battle with King Bucar; and to them, too, he told his errand. Alvar Fañez, as you may imagine, felt more grieved than the others, remembering that by the King's order he had given the Cid's daughters to the Infantes, and he vowed that he would demand justice from the King as soon as he reached Valladolid, where the court was staying.

So Muñoz went on to Valencia, and the others proceeded to the King, and, after delivering their gifts, made known to him all that Muñoz had told them. King Don Alfonso, who had supposed that the Cid's daughters were dead, was greatly rejoiced to find that they were still living, and recovering from their wounds; for if they had been dead all the vengeance in the world would have done them no good, but, living, some reparation might still be offered them for their wrongs. He promised to hold a Cortes in Toledo in three months, and to summon to it the Infantes, and desired Alvar Fañez to bear a message to the Cid, inviting him to be present with as many of his retainers as he thought best. Then, giving orders to have two mules, richly caparisoned, delivered to Alvar Fañez for the use of the ladies, the King dismissed the messengers, who started back to Valencia. On the way they passed the Oak-wood of Corpes and made great lamentation when they saw the place of the crime; but when they came to the village where the old husbandman lived who had been so kind to Doña Elvira and her sister, it seemed as if they could hardly find means to express their gratitude to these good people. They gave rich presents to the old man and his wife, and with their consent, took the sons and daughters to Valencia and married the daughters to rich men in the Cid's company.

When the cavalcade reached Santesteban there was a pathetic meeting between the messengers and the Cid's daughters. Alvar Fañez tried to console his cousins by saying, "You have lost one marriage and may gain a better," but I think the ladies did not find much comfort in this, and were not anxious to make a second trial.

Taking his cousins under his protection, Alvar Fañez journeyed on till he came to the house of the Moor Abengalvon, whose kindness on the outward journey had been so badly repaid by the Infantes; and here the ladies halted to gain strength for the rest of the trip, while Pero Bermudez went on to tell the Cid of their coming. Bermudez found the Cid and Doña Ximena informed of the affair, since Felez Muñoz had reached Valencia some time before, and the parents were anxiously awaiting further news. But when Bermudez pressed the Cid to take speedy vengeance on the Infantes, Ruy Diaz replied that nothing sped well for hurrying, and though he expected justice, he wanted it to come through the Cortes, which was the proper channel, and he begged Bermudez not to stir up any more anger than he already felt, for Muñoz' story had done enough.

The Moor Abengalvon accompanied the ladies all the way to Valencia, and did not leave them until they were safe in their father's palace. The Cid came out two leagues to meet them, and though he had wept at the story of Bermudez, and the whole company burst into lamentations now when they saw him approaching, the old warrior greeted his daughters with cheerful smiles instead of tears, and soothed them, saying, "Ye are come, my children, and God will heal you"; and then he made the same promise that Alvar Fañez had made by way of comfort, that they should be better mated next time. Inside Valencia the lamentations lasted three days, even the Moors that accompanied Abengalvon taking part.

As soon as this was over the Cid began to make great preparations to appear at the Cortes in Toledo, and in order that he might know with exactly what wrongs to charge the Infantes, he had his daughters recount all that had happened to them; and their pitiful story and the scars that confirmed it made him determined to have justice done at all hazards. When he left Valencia, having placed his family and the city in charge of the bishop and of Martin Pelaez, the one-time coward but now bravest of brave knights, he was followed by nine hundred mounted knights and five hundred noble squires, besides many common footmen, and all were well equipped for peace or for war, as the case might require.

The Infantes had been duly summoned to the Cortes and warned that they should no longer be accounted the King's vassals if they did not come. Guessing what this summons might mean, and fearing the Campeador, the Infantes begged to be excused from the Cortes; but the King very quickly sent word that it was partly on their account that the Cortes was to be held, and that the Campeador would certainly be there to exact justice from them, and commanded them finally to be present or to leave his kingdoms.

So the Infantes got together as many followers as possible, thinking to awe the Cid, and in company with their troublesome uncle set out for Toledo, where they arrived earlier than the company of Ruy Diaz.

THE CORTES AT TOLEDO

When King Don Alfonso received word that the Cid was drawing near, he went to meet him to offer him quarters in the royal palace; but the Cid thanked the King and said he should not go into Toledo that night, but would hold a vigil in the church of St. Servans. So the King left him, and the Cid ordered his men to pitch their tents on the hills near by, and he himself with "other good ones" went into the church, where lighted candles had been placed upon the altar, and spent the night in prayer, with occasional conversation.

In the meantime, the King had given orders that the palaces of Galiana should be fitted up properly for the Cortes, and all the walls were hung with cloth of gold and the floors covered with rich carpets; and the splendid chair of the former kings of Toledo was set in the highest place and around it were placed seats for the court.

The Cid heard of these preparations and remembered that he too had a handsome chair of ivory of delicate workmanship, one that belonged to the kings of Valencia, and he ordered a young nobleman of his party to take this chair and place it in the palace, and to guard it all night long lest some of his enemies should try to injure it. The young noble took a hundred squires with him, and they kept guard over the ivory seat all night and until the Cid appeared next day.

When the courtiers came in the next morning they began to make fun of the Cid's throne and to ask the King for what great lady the seat was intended. Upon this the fiery young knight in charge drew his sword and dared them to fight with him, and there would have been serious trouble if the King had not interfered, and assured his court that the Cid should sit in the ivory chair or anywhere else he liked, for that none of his vassals had ever done him such honor as Ruy Diaz. The Cid's immediate followers all put on armor before going to the Cortes, but hid it with ermine, and as for the Cid himself, he must have made a magnificent appearance. The *Chronicle* tells us that he wore "hose of fine cloth and richly-worked shoes, a shirt as white (i.e., dazzling) as the sun, with fastenings of gold and silver, a *bridal* (a sort of shirt) of gold tissue, and over all a red skin with points of gold. A coif of scarlet, wrought with gold," covered his hair, and his long beard was bound with a cord.

At starting he ordered his men neither to do nor say anything unseemly, and, if trouble should arise, to do his bidding promptly, minding no one else except the King. And so they rode off.

Ruy Diaz did not intend to put himself forward by taking the ivory chair without the King's permission, and when he entered the Cortes with a grave step, surrounded by his men, he paused before the King, who rose to receive him, and asked where he should sit. The King offered him a seat beside the throne, but the Cid declined such honor and was then told to take the ivory seat. And the King ordered that thereafter none but king and prelate should be counted worthy to sit with the Cid. All in the Cortes keep looking at Ruy Diaz and marveling at his long beard, save only the Infantes, who, strange to say, had enough shame to sit with their eyes cast down. For a short time there was silence in the hall, and then the Cid rose and said that he hoped the King and nobles would hear what he had to say, and that no one would be allowed to interrupt him, for he was not a man who knew how to make speeches, and interruptions would make it still harder for him to speak as he should. Upon this the King commanded that the Cid should be heard and that no one should disturb the Cortes. He appointed two Alcaldes, or judges,

D. J. Luis Pellicer

The Cid arose to speak.

and they were sworn to judge between the Cid and the Infantes, according to the laws of Castile and Leon. After this, the Cid rose again and made his first demand, without wasting words, for his swords, Tizona and Colada, explaining how they came to be in the keeping of the Infantes; and the Alcaldes decided that the swords must be given back to him. The Infantes talked apart with Count Don Garcia, the Cid's old foe, and decided that if this were the only claim the Cid expected to make, they were well out of the affair. So they brought the swords into the Cortes and delivered them to the King, and he to the Cid; and Ruy Diaz took them out of their sheaths and found that they were really Tizona and Colada, and he was so glad to get them again that he talked to them as if they had been friends who could understand him. Then he handed them over to Alvar Fañez and Pero Bermudez for safe-keeping.

The Infantes hoped this was the end, but they were disappointed, for the Cid soon rose again and made a claim upon them for the treasure he had given them at the time of their departure from Valencia. This had been given, of course, on account of their wives, but as they no longer acknowledged that they had wives, the treasure must be forfeited. This claim, too, the Alcaldes decided to be a just one, but the Infantes, while admitting that they had received the treasure, claimed that it had been expended in the King's service. However, after some discussion, they agreed to raise the amount if the Cid would give them fifteen days for the purpose. This was granted, and when the Infantes came to make up their account with the King it was found that only two hundred marks had been spent in his service, and two thousand eight hundred marks remained for them to pay. Within the fifteen days the sum was made up and delivered to the Cid, and the Infantes were sure that now they were clear of the affair; but again they were mistaken.

When the Cortes reassembled and the Cid arose to speak the third time he charged the Infantes with their villainy toward his daughters, and demanded that they give reason for their conduct. His speech was so full of noble indignation I cannot resist quoting a part:

"Sir, praise be to God and your favor, I have recovered my swords and my treasure; now, then, I pray you let this other demand be heard which I have to make against the Infantes. Full hard it is for me to make it, though I have it rooted in my heart! I say then, let them make answer before you, and tell why it was that they besought you to marry them with my daughters, and why they took them away from Valencia, when they had it in heart to dishonor me, and to strike them, and to leave them, as they were left, in the Oakforest of Corpes? Look, sir, what dishonor they did them! They stripped them of the garments which they had not given them, as if they had been bad women and the children of a bad father. With less than mortal defiance I shall not let them go! How had I deserved this, Infantes, at your hands? I gave you my daughters to take with you from Valencia; with great honor and great treasures gave I them unto you; dogs and traitors, ye took them from Valencia when ye did not love them, and with your bridles ye smote and with your spurs ye spurned and wounded them, and ye left them alone in the Oak-forest to the wild beasts and to the birds of the mountains! King Don Alfonso, they neither remembered God nor you, nor me, nor their own good fortune! And here was fulfilled the saying of the wise man, that harder it is for those who have no understanding to bear with good than with evil. I beseech you, give me justice upon them for evil and dishonor which they have done me! And if you and your Cortes will not right me, through the mercy of God and my own good cause, I will take it myself."

After the Cid had said this and more, he made a formal demand through the Cortes that the Infantes should answer to the charge. The only thing that the young men had to say was that their wives had not been of good enough family, and that it was not fitting for the Infantes of Carrion to marry beneath them. It seems strange that they had not thought of this before entering into such a marriage. At any rate, this lame plea was all they had to offer, and no sooner had they made it than there arose a war of words between their followers and those of the Cid, led by some taunting remarks that passed between Count Don Garcia and Ruy Diaz. And Pero Bermudez forgot that he was to await orders, and being a hot-headed man, he took it upon himself to silence Count Don Garcia by knocking him down. Swords were drawn on both sides, and there were cries of "Cabra" and "Grañon" on one side and of "Valencia" and "Bivar" on the other, and many of the counts fled from the hall. But the counts were recalled and reminded that they were not to revile the Cid. It was rather difficult to keep order after this, and there was probably a great deal of angry headshaking and fierce threatening while the King and the Alcaldes were making their decision in a room apart.

PUNISHMENT OF THE INFANTES OF CARRION

When the King and the Alcaldes had made up their minds, they returned to the Cortes and announced the decision. It was that the Infantes and their uncle, Don Suero Gonzales, who had aided and abetted them all along, should do battle with any three of the Cid's followers whom he might choose for his champions. This decision pleased the Cid greatly. The Cid had no difficulty in finding champions, for scarcely had the King spoken when Pero Bermudez, who seemed to have been "spoiling for a fight," begged the privilege of engaging one of the Infantes, and two other knights offered themselves immediately after. But the Infantes drew back when the King appointed the next day for the contest, and wanted time to go home and prepare for battle. The King knew them too well to be willing to let them leave Toledo; nevertheless, at the intercession of some of his nobles, he gave them their wish, the Cid consenting.

While these affairs were being discussed in the Cortes, messengers came riding up with letters for King Don Alfonso and the Cid, from the Kings of Aragon and of Navarre. And what do you think was in the letters? Something that was like balm to the wounded pride of the Cid and his retainers—something that must have been like gall and wormwood to the Infantes and their sympathizers—a request for Doña Elvira and Doña Sol in marriage to the sons of these kings! The messengers were soon sent back with a favorable answer, setting the new marriage-day at three months from that time, when the Infantes of Aragon and Navarre were to come to Valencia to claim their brides.

Feelings were very little considered in those days, and the Cid's daughters, like all the young ladies of the time, were disposed of like goods at auction. Still, we must believe that the Cid did for them what seemed best, and that, after one such experience as he had had with sons-in-law, he would not have given them so readily to the next comers if he had not been sure they would be happy.

When this matter was settled the Cid asked permission of King Don Alfonso to set out for Valencia, leaving the battle in charge of his champions, for he had much to do in acquainting his daughters with their new prospects and in making preparations for the weddings. His request was granted, and after a general distribution of treasure such as usually took place on the Cid's arrival or departure, he took leave of the King, mounted Babieca, and rode away. There was an incident connected with this parting which is told in a little ballad of Lockhart's much more prettily than I could tell it in prose, so I copy the ballad entire:

"The King looked on him kindly as on a vassal true;
Then to the King Ruy Diaz spake after reverence due—
'O King, the thing is shameful that any man beside
The liege lord of Castile himself should Babieca ride;

" 'For neither Spain nor Araby could another charger bring
So good as he, and certes, the best befits my King.
But that you may behold him, and know him to the core,
I'll make him go as was wont when his nostrils smelt the Moor.'

"With that, the Cid, clad as he was in mantle furred and wide,
On Babieca vaulting, put the rowel in his side;
And up and down, and round and round, so fierce was his career,
Streamed like a pennon on the wind Ruy Diaz' minevere.

"And all that saw them praised them—they lauded man and horse,
As matchéd well and rivalless for gallantry and force;
Ne'er had they looked on horsemen might to this knight come near—
Nor on other charger worthy of such a cavalier.

"Thus, to and fro a-rushing, the fierce and furious steed,
He snapt in twain his hither rein:—'God pity now the Cid,'
'God pity Diaz,' cried the lords—but when they looked again,
They saw Ruy Diaz ruling him, with the fragment of his rein;
They saw him proudly ruling with gesture firm and calm,
Like a true lord commanding—and obeyed as by a lamb.

"And so he led him foaming and panting to the King,
But 'No,' said Don Alfonso, 'it were a shameful thing
That peerless Babieca should ever be bestrid
By any mortal but Bivar—mount, mount again, my Cid!' "

So Babieca went home with the Cid and carried him many times afterwards, and was his steed on such a journey as few men ever took before or since. As for the Infantes, the sooner we attend to their

disagreeable affairs the sooner we shall be done with them. King
Don Alfonso was quite certain that they would not appear at the
time appointed, and so resolved to go to Carrion and have the battle there. When the day of combat dawned there were people from

D. J. Luis Pellicer

Doña Ximena and her daughters.

all over Spain to witness the great deeds that were to be done. The
Infantes were assisted to arm themselves, but seeing Tizona and
Colada in the hands of their opponents, sent to the King to ask that
those fearful swords might not be allowed; but the King rightly said
that they should have stipulated that while in the Cortes, and that
now each man might use the best weapon he had.

To make a long story short, the only one of the six combatants who was seriously injured was Ferrando Gonzalez, who received a mortal wound, though it did not appear so at first; and he, his brother, and uncle were all forced to cry for quarter. The Cid's champions received the award of victory and professed themselves satisfied; but the King was so displeased with the cowardice of the Infantes that he ordered his seneschal to take their arms and horses and declare them traitors. The Infantes and their uncle were so put to shame that they fled away, and after the death of their old father, Carrion came into the hands of the King. The *Chronicle* bids them good-bye in these words, "Great was their shame, and the like or worse betide him who abuseth fair lady, and then leaveth her."

Eight days were devoted to rejoicing when the news reached Valencia that the Cid's champions had won the battle, and Doña Ximena and her daughters were so grateful that they would fain have kissed the hands and feet of the men who had saved their names from dishonor.

Beowulf

*The first English poem written down in the Anglo-Saxon
tongue sometime between 800 and 900 A.D.*

BEOWULF FIGHTS GRENDEL

Translated and Adapted by
JOHN HARRINGTON COX

THE DEATH OF SCYLD AND THE BUILDING OF HEOROT

IN ANCIENT DAYS, when nobles performed deeds of strength, the glory of the Spear-Danes was told far and wide. Often Scyld, Son of Sheaf, with bands of warriors, terrified the earls and deprived many tribes of their land rights. In time it came to pass that each of his neighbors over the sea was forced to obey him and to pay tribute. That was a good king.

At last the appointed time came, when Scyld, very old, had to die. His dear companions bore him to the shore of the sea, as he himself had commanded while he was alive. There at the haven stood his long-owned vessel, icy, and ready for an outward journey. The nobles bore their famous lord upon the bosom of the ship and laid him by the mast. They carried thither also great treasures and many ornaments which they had brought from distant ways. I never heard of a ship more fitly adorned with battle weapons and armor. Upon his breast lay the jewels which were to travel far with him into the possession of the flood. In addition to all this, they set a golden banner high over his head. Then, with sad hearts and a mourning mood, they gave him into the keeping of Neptune and let the sea bear him away. Nobody ever knew what became of that ship.

To Scyld had been born a grandson, the high Halfdane, who, aged and battle-fierce, ruled the glad Scyldings. After him Hrothgar, his son, came to the throne. To him battle-success was given, so that his friendly kinsmen obeyed him gladly until the company of young men grew into a mighty kinsman-troop.

For a long time it ran continually in Hrothgar's mind that he would give orders to build a banquet hall, one greater than the children of men had ever heard of. In this hall he intended to divide among young and old whatever God should give him, except the folkshare and the ransom received for the lives of men. So he sent orders far and wide to many tribes of kinsmen, and it happened very quickly that the greatest of hall-buildings, wide between the gables and towering high into the heavens, was all ready. The King, who had power to enforce his words far and wide, named it Heorot.

THE ENMITY OF GRENDEL

The king did not belie his boast, but distributed rings and treasure at the feast. There was heard the sound of the harp and the sweet music of the bard. Thus the noble warriors lived prosperously, in joy, until a grim stranger began to perform terrible deeds. The powerful spirit who dwelt in the dark places could hardly endure, even for a little while, that he should hear loud mirth in the hall. He was called Grendel, a great monster who inhabited the moors, the fens, and the fastnesses. When night came, he departed to visit Heorot to see how the Ring-Danes had arranged themselves in it. He found therein a company of renowned fighting-men, asleep after the feast. They did not know any sorrow or wretchedness of men. Grim and greedy, the demon seized at once thirty of the thanes. Thence, exulting in his booty, he departed quickly to seek his own home.

At the break of day, the warcraft of Grendel was made known. Then there arose lamentation, a tremendous clamor on account of his feast. The renowned prince sat deep in grief when he saw the track of the hostile stranger. He endured great sorrow on account of the death of his thanes. Nor was it longer than about one night that Grendel performed more murder. He was so confirmed in feud and crime that he did not shrink from them at all. The strife was violent, hostile, and long drawn out. Then it was easy to find one who sought a resting place elsewhere, a bed among the bowers, when Grendel's hatred of the thanes was made known by such a clear sign. He who had the good fortune to escape the fiend kept away from the hall and held himself more protected.

So Grendel ruled, strove against right, one against all, until the best of houses stood empty. It was a long while, a time of twelve winters, that the friend of the Scyldings had to endure boundless woe. Therefore it became known to the children of men that Grendel warred against Hrothgar, waged hate-enmities, crime, and continual strife. He would not on account of friendship remove the death penalty from any of the men of the Danes, nor would he settle the feud for money. None of the councilors needed to expect a bright ransom at the hands of the slayer for the men killed.

The terrible monster, the dark death-shadow, kept on pursuing the youth and the warriors. Night after night, he held the misty moors, ensnared and enfettered men. Thus the enemy of mankind, the solitary stranger, often performed humiliations hard to bear and great crimes. He inhabited Heorot, the treasure-adorned hall, in the murky nights, so that Hrothgar might not approach the throne. That was grief of soul to the ruler of the Scyldings. Many strong-hearted ones often sat in council to determine what were best to do against the sudden terrors. At times they vowed war sacrifices at their heathen temples, prayed to the devil that he would help them in their dire misery. Such was their custom, the hope of the heathen, who in their heart remembered hell. They did not know the Creator, nor did they know how to praise the Ruler of Glory.

THE ARRIVAL OF BEOWULF

The deeds of Grendel were told far and wide until Beowulf, a thane of Higelac, heard about them. He was the strongest of men in that day, noble and mighty. He commanded a good ship to be built immediately, saying he wished to seek King Hrothgar, who was in need of help. The wise men whetted his desire and urged him to undertake the journey. He chose, to accompany him, fourteen warriors, the bravest he could find. Among these was a seacrafty man, who was to act as pilot and point out the landmarks.

Time passed quickly. The bark was on the waves, the boat under the cliff. The currents of the ocean swirled; the sea writhed against the sand. The heroes climbed on board. They bore upon the bosom of the ship bright trappings and splendid coats of mail. Then they shoved out upon a willing journey.

The foamy-necked vessel, urged on by the wind, departed over the sea, most like to a bird. By the same time of the second day, the carved prow had traveled so far that the seagoers beheld the shining ocean cliffs, the steep mountains, and the wide headlands. The voyage was at an end. They anchored their boat and climbed up to the plain. Their war-trappings rattled. First of all they returned thanks to God because the sea-journey had been so easy. Then the guard of the Scyldings, whose duty it was to watch the sea cliffs, saw borne over the gangplank glittering shields and ready armor. The thane of Hrothgar was bursting with curiosity to know who these men were, and he made haste to the shore, riding a horse. He shook his spear powerfully and asked with formal words:

"Who are ye, shield-bearing men and protected by coats of mail, who come thus hither driving a deep keel over the sea-street? I hold the sea watch, in order that no hostile force may invade the land of the Danes, with a ship-army. Never so openly came warriors bearing shields without asking leave of Hrothgar. Never did I see a larger earl upon the earth than is one of you, a man in armor and honored with weapons. He is no mere retainer, unless his peerless form belies him. I must know your origin, ere ye go further hence, lying spies, into the land of the Danes. Now, ye far-dwellers, ye sea-travelers, listen to my sincere thought. It is best to make known at once whence your coming is."

To him Beowulf made answer, unlocked his word-hoard:

"We are people of the race of the Goths and hearth-companions of Higelac. My father was called Ecgtheow, a noble chief, and is still remembered by many a councilor throughout the earth. With a good motive we have come to seek thy lord. Be thou gracious in directing us. We have a great errand to the renowned prince of the Danes, nor, as I deem, shall there be of this matter anything secret. Thou knowest if it is true as we heard say, that among the Scyldings some mysterious persecutor manifests terrible enmity in the dark nights. I may teach Hrothgar how to overcome the fiend or else he shall suffer dire distress as long as the best of houses stands upon the high place."

The unterrified sea-guard, sitting on his horse, replied:

"A bold warrior must know how to distinguish between words and works. I understand that your company is friendly to the lord of the Scyldings. Go forth bearing your weapons and your armor. I will direct you. Likewise I will command my attendants to protect your ship until it shall bear you safely back over the sea-streams to the land of the Goths. It shall be granted to him who acts bravely, that he escape the battle-rush without harm."

Leaving the wide-bosomed vessel riding fast at anchor, they departed for Hrothgar's court. The fire-hardened boar-images shone upon the tops of their helmets. The battle-minded men hastened until they could perceive the high-timbered hall, stately and plated with gold. The building in which the powerful king dwelt was the most famous in the world. The light reflected from it shone over many lands. The guide pointed out the splendid court of the proud Hrothgar, so that they might go directly to it. Then he turned his horse and said:

"It is time for me to return. May the Father Almighty, in His mercy, keep you safe in the journey. I must go back to the sea to keep watch against hostile bands."

BEOWULF AND HIS COMPANY REACH THE COURT

The armor glistened, the hard, hand-forged iron sang, as the men marched straight on, in their terrible war-trappings. They set their wide shields against the wall of the building and stood their spears together, the ash-shafts tipped with gray steel. That was an iron host, honored with weapons.

At once a proud hero began to question them concerning their lineage: "Whence bear ye plated shields, gray coats of mail, grim helmets, and a heap of battle-shafts? I am Wulfgar, a messenger and vassal of Hrothgar. I never saw a strange people, thus many men, more proud. I hope that ye have sought Hrothgar out of magnanimity, and not as exiles."

The proud chief of the Goths made answer: "We are table-companions of Higelac; Beowulf is my name. I will declare my errand to the son of Halfdane, if he will permit us to approach and speak to one so good."

Wulfgar replied: "I will question the friend of the Danes, the chief of the Scyldings, concerning this, and make known at once his answer." Then he turned quickly toward the place where Hrothgar, old and very hoary, sat with his company of earls. The bold messenger went forward until he stood at the shoulder of the king of the Danes. He knew well the custom of warriors. Wulfgar spoke to his friendly lord: "Here have come from afar over the expanse of the ocean, a people of the Goths. They call their leader Beowulf, and they are suppliants that they may exchange words with thee. Do not refuse them, gracious Hrothgar, for they seem worthy of the high esteem of earls. Indeed, their leader is doughty, he who conducted the fighting-men hither."

Hrothgar replied, the defense of the Scyldings: "I knew him when he was a child. His good old father was called Ecgtheow, to whom Hrethel of the Goths gave his only daughter. Now his son has come hither to seek a kindly friend. The sailors, who carried the tribute of the Goths, reported formerly that Beowulf had the strength of thirty men in his handgrip. The holy God has graciously sent him to us, as I think, against the terror of Grendel. I shall give treasures to the good one for his daring. Be thou in haste, command them to come in, and say they are welcome to the people of the Danes."

Then Wulfgar went to the door of the hall and said: "The Prince of the Danes commands me to say that he knows your lineage and your coming is according to his will. Now ye may go in your battle-raiment to see Hrothgar. Leave your shields and slaughter-shafts here, to await the issue of words."

BEOWULF ASKS PERMISSION TO CLEANSE HEOROT

Beowulf arose, around him many a warrior, a choice band of thanes. A few remained to guard the weapons. The others hastened together, under the roof of Heorot. The bold leader, keeping his helmet on, went until he stood on the dais, whence he addressed the king:

"Hrothgar, be thou hale! I am a kinsman and thane of Higelac. In youth I performed many great deeds. The persecution by Grendel was made known to me in my native land by the sea-travelers, who say that this hall, the best of buildings, stands empty and useless as soon as the evening light disappears from the sky. The bravest and wisest councilors among my people urged that I should seek thee, Prince Hrothgar, because they knew my strength. They themselves had looked on, when I came back from the conflict, stained with the blood of enemies, where I bound five, slew sea monsters in the waves by night, endured dire distress, and avenged the enmity against the Goths. And now, alone, I shall decide the issue with Grendel. Do not refuse my request, chief of the Bright-Danes, that I and my company of earls may cleanse Heorot. I have learned that the monster, on account of his rashness, disdains the use of weapons. I, therefore, scorn to bear a sword or wide shield, but I shall seize upon the fiend with my handgrip and struggle for life, foe against foe. If Grendel shall rule in the war hall, I expect he, unterrified, will devour me as he so often did the men of the Danes. If death take me, thou wilt not have to set a head-watch, for Grendel will have my body, stained with gore. He will bear away the bloody corpse and eat it unmournfully. Send then to Higelac the armor which protects my breast. It is the best of battle garments, an heirloom of Hrethel, the handiwork of Wayland. Fate goes ever as it must."

Hrothgar made answer: "It is sorrowful for me to say what humiliation and sudden terror Grendel has caused with his deadly hatred. My hall-company is diminished and my war-host has waned. Fate swept them away into the terror of Grendel. God alone may easily restrain the mad foe from his deeds. Often did the warriors boast, when drinking in the hall, that they would await the onset of Grendel with their swords. Then was the floor bloodstained when day broke, and the benches steaming with gore. I possessed less and less of brave warriors, in that death snatched them away.

Sit now at the feast and unlock thy thoughts as thy mind may urge thee."

Then was a bench prepared for the Goths, upon which the bold-hearted ones sat proudly, all together. One of Hrothgar's thanes served them—held in his hand an adorned tankard, and poured the bright mead. At times the bard sang, clear-voiced, in Heorot. There was the joy of heroes, an immense warrior-troop of Danes and Goths.

UNFERTH'S CONTENTION WITH BEOWULF

Unferth, the chief spokesman of Hrothgar, who sat at the feet of the lord of the Scyldings, unbound his battle secrets. The coming of Beowulf was to him a great mortification, because he did not wish to grant that any man under the heavens should obtain more honor than himself.

"Art thou that Beowulf who strove with Breca in swimming on the wide sea, where ye two on account of pride and a foolish boast made trial of the waves and ventured your lives upon the deep water? No man, neither friend nor foe, might dissuade either of you from the sorrowful journey, when you struck out with your hands, measured the sea-streets, glided over the ocean then welling in the surges of winter. Seven nights ye labored in the power of the flood. He overcame thee in the swimming—had more strength. Truly, Breca performed altogether his boast against thee. Therefore, I expect for thee a worse issue if thou darest await Grendel, for the space of a night."

Beowulf replied: "Lo, thou, my friend Unferth, drunken with beer, many things hast thou said about Breca, told about his journey. I reckon it a truth that I possess more sea-strength, more endurance on the waves, than any other man. We two boasted, being only boys, that we would venture out upon the sea with our lives. And so we did. Each had a naked sword in his hand, and thought to defend himself against the whales. Breca was not able to swim away from me and I would not swim away from him. We were together five nights, until the sea drove us apart. The coldest of weather, the darkening night, the grim north wind opposed us. The waves were furious. The anger of the sea-fishes was aroused. Then my armor, made of chain mail and adorned with gold, performed help. One of the dire foes drew me to the bottom, held me in his grip. However, it was granted to me that I should reach the monster with the point of my weapon. The battle-rush through my hand carried him off.

"Often thus the hostile foes boldly oppressed me. I served them with the dear sword, as was fitting, and it was given to me to slay nine. Not at all did the evildoers have joy in devouring me, sitting around the feast, near the bottom of the sea; but in the morning they lay dead upon the shore, put to sleep with the steel. Never again did they dare to hinder the course of the sailors about the deep harbor.

"Light came from the east, the bright beacon of God. The waves subsided so that I might behold the headlands and the windy walls. Fate often preserves an unfated earl, provided his strength avails. Never did I hear of a harder fight under the vaults of the heavens, nor of more wretched men on the sea. Weary of the journey, I escaped the grip of the foes with my life. Then the sea bore me up into the land of the Finns. Neither you nor Breca ever performed such feats with bloody swords, but instead you deserted your brothers in the hour of need and so became their slayer. For this you shall suffer in hell although your wit be good. I say to you, son of Ecglaf, that Grendel had never performed so many terrible deeds in Heorot, if your soul were as battle-grim as you, yourself, suppose. But he has perceived that he need not expect war from any of the Danes, and so he destroys at his pleasure, and spares none. I shall offer him battle at once, and tomorrow anyone who please may go safely to the hall."

The old battle-king was happy when he heard the determined words of Beowulf. Wealtheow, the gold-adorned queen, stepped forth to greet the strangers, and there was high revelry in Hrothgar's hall until he desired to seek his evening rest. Then the troop arose and the King said to Beowulf: "Never before have I trusted the lordly hall of the Danes to any man. Have now and hold the best of houses, be mindful of glory, display courage, watch against the foe. Every wish that you have shall be granted, if you escape the great work with your life."

Then Hrothgar departed with his company of warriors, and Beowulf, surrounded by his brave seamen, sought his hall-rest. Not one of them expected to see his dear homeland again, for he remembered how Grendel had taken away the people of the Danes. But Beowulf, angry and watchful, awaited the issue of battle.

THE BATTLE BETWEEN BEOWULF AND GRENDEL

Then came from the moor, under the misty hills, Grendel, stalking. The evildoer thought to ensnare some one of the men in the high hall. On he came until he could see readily the great wine hall, bright with plated gold. That was not the first time he had sought the home of Hrothgar. Without delay the joyless monster approached. The door, fast in its iron bands, sprang open when he touched it. Furious, and intending evil, he had burst open the mouth of the building. Quickly after that the fiend trod upon the bloodstained floor. From his eyes there stood an uncanny light, most like fire. He saw in the hall a company of kinsmen sleeping together. The grim slayer laughed aloud in the expectation of a full meal, as he thought that before the break of day he should separate the soul and body of each one of them. Beowulf, watching, saw how the fell foe would behave in making his sudden attacks.

The demon did not delay but snatched a sleeping warrior, slit him before he could awake, and drank his blood in streams and swallowed great bits of his flesh. In a twinkling he had devoured all, even the feet and hands.

Then the malignant spirit stepped farther into the hall and seized the greathearted Beowulf in his resting place on the floor. Leaning on one elbow, Beowulf quickly gripped the monster with his free hand. Grendel perceived at once that in all the regions of the earth he had never met a man with a greater handgrip. He was terrified in his heart, but not on that account might he the sooner get away. His soul was eager to be gone, to flee into the darkness, and to seek the company of devils. His way of life was not such as he had found it in former days.

Beowulf stood erect and clutched him fast. The fingers of the fiend burst and he strove to get out. He intended to escape and flee far away into the fen-retreats. That was a sad journey Grendel had taken to Heorot. Both of the mighty combatants were furious. It was a great wonder the wine hall withstood the battle onset. It did not fall to the ground because it was fastened both inside and out with iron bands, made firm by the cunning thoughts of the smith. Many a hand-bench fell down, as I have heard tell, where the angry ones fought. The wise men of the Danes never expected the beautiful Heorot to be broken to pieces by the strife of men, but they thought it would stand until, in the embrace of fire, it should be swallowed up in smoke. Dire terror fell on each one of the Danes, when they heard weeping at the wall. Grendel, the captive of hell, the adversary of God, lamented sorely, chanted his grisly death song. But Beowulf, the strongest of men in that day in the world, held him fast. He did not intend to let him go, for he reckoned not his life useful to anyone.

Then the companions of Beowulf brandished their swords and thought to protect their renowned prince wherever they could. They did not know, when they hewed the monster on every side, seeking his soul, that he had laid a spell upon all weapons so that none of them, however good, could touch him. But nevertheless the end of Grendel should be wretched and he had to travel far into the keeping of the devils. He soon perceived that the proud kinsman of Higelac had him by the hand and that it was not strong enough to endure the strain. A gaping wound appeared on his shoulder, the flesh burst, and the sinews sprang apart. Hurt to the death, Grendel escaped thence into the fen-retreat whither he sought his joyless abode. He knew that the numbering of his days had come and that the end of his life was at hand. It was a clear sign when Beowulf hung up the hand and the arm of the monster under the wide roof.

THE PEOPLE COME TO VIEW THE MONSTER

Then, in the morning, as I have heard, there was around the gift-hall many a battle-chief. They came from far and near throughout the wide ways to view the wonder. They followed the track of Grendel, to the sea of the devils, whither he had fled. There was the water welling in blood, the horrible swing of the waves all mingled with hot gore where he gave up his heathen soul. Hell there received him.

The proud heroes went back from the sea, riding their yellow horses. At times they let them race, wherever the roads seemed good and were known to be excellent. At times they sang the fame of Beowulf, and many a one said that north or south, throughout the wide earth, there was not a better warrior, nor one more worthy of a kingdom. A famous bard composed a lay about the slaying of Grendel, and recalled the fame of Sigemund, who slew the great dragon and carried off the hoard. He also contrasted Beowulf with the fierce Heremod, whom crime assailed. Thus, with song and story, they returned to Hrothgar's court.

By this time, many a stronghearted retainer had gone to the high hall to see the battle-hand. Likewise, the king himself with a mighty troop, well known for its excellence, and the queen, accompanied by a bevy of maidens, trod the path which led to Heorot. Hrothgar stood upon the threshold, saw the steep roof, adorned with gold, and the horrible hand. "Let thanks be given to the All-Wielder," said he, "on account of this sight. I have suffered much hostility at the hand of Grendel, and only a little while ago this best of houses stood stained with blood, and I did not expect any relief from my great woes. Now a retainer has performed that which all of us in our cunning might not bring to pass. Lo! she who gave birth to the man may say, if she yet lives, that the Creator was gracious to her in her child-bearing. Now, Beowulf, best of men, I wish to take thee into my heart as a son. Hold well the new relationship. There shall be to thee no lack of worldly wishes as far as I have control of things. Full often have I given reward to a less keen warrior and one slower in the fight. The deed which thou hast done will cause thy glory to live forever. May the All-Ruler requite thee with good, as he even now did."

Beowulf replied: "We fought the fight gladly, and boldly encountered the strength of Grendel. I had hoped that thou shouldst have seen the fiend himself, death-weary. I thought to ensnare him quickly with my handgrips, so that he should lie tortured in his death throes. The All-Wielder would not grant that I should keep him from getting away. Nevertheless, in order to escape alive, he had to leave behind his hand, arm, and shoulder. He got little consolation by that, however, for he no longer lives burdened by his crimes. The wound seized him closely in its dire grip and ended his wretchedness. Now he awaits the great judgment to see how the Creator shall pass sentence upon him."

Then was Unferth more silent in his boasting of war deeds when the nobles saw over the high roof the hand and fingers of Grendel. Each of the nails of the horrible claw was most like steel. There was no sword in the world, however excellent, that would have cut away that bloody battle-hand.

Then it was quickly ordered to adorn Heorot within. Many there were, both of men and women, who prepared the guest hall. Golden-hued tapestries shone upon the walls, wonderful sights for those who cared to look upon such things. The bright building was badly wrecked and the hinges of the door were torn away. The roof alone remained altogether sound when the monster, wounded to death, twisted and turned in his flight. When the adornment of the hall was finished, the king himself entered accompanied by his band of trained fighting-men. I have never heard of a great kinsmen-troop that bore itself better around its treasure-giver.

The famous men sat upon the benches to partake of the feast. Heorot was filled with friends. The son of Halfdane gave to Beowulf a golden staff-banner, a helmet, a coat of mail, and a renowned sword, as a reward of victory. Beowulf had no need to be ashamed, for never before had one man given to another such magnificent gifts. Then the king commanded to lead into the hall eight horses. Their bridles were covered with plates of gold and upon one of them was a saddle, cunningly bedecked with jewels. That had been the battle-seat of the king when he wished to practice the play of swords. When warriors fought, Hrothgar was always in the van. All these treasures, both horses and weapons, the old king gave to Beowulf, and commanded him to enjoy them well. Thus did the renowned prince reward the battle-rush. To each of those who came with Beowulf he gave an ancient heirloom of great value, and for the one whom Grendel had slain so wickedly, he atoned with gold. There was song and revelry together when the bard of Hrothgar proclaimed mirth in the hall. Then the harp was struck and many a glee composed. There was sung the deathless lay of the fight at Finnsburg, which told how Hnaef of the Scyldings was fated to fall in Frisian land, how Finn himself was slain at his own home and his queen carried away. Their glory was departed.

At last Wealtheow, Hrothgar's queen, approached the place where Beowulf sat between her two sons. To him were bright golden ornaments, two arm-rings, a coat made of steel rings, and a great necklace. "Dear Beowulf," said the queen, "enjoy these treasures and thrive well. Be gracious in teaching and friendly in deeds to my sons. Thou hast brought it to pass that far and near men honor thee, even as far as the sea bends round the windy walls. Be, while thou livest, a prosperous earl."

Then she went to her seat. The men drank wine and thought not of fate, grim destiny, as it had happened to many a one. Evening came. Hrothgar departed to his own court and left a numberless host of warriors to guard Heorot as they had often done. They cleared away the benches and spread the floor with beds and bolsters. They set at their heads the bright battle-shields. Above them were clearly seen the tall helmet, the bright armor, and the powerful spear. It was their custom to be ready for battle both at home and in the field at any time their lord should have need.

BEOWULF FIGHTS THE DRAGON

Translated and Adapted by
JOHN HARRINGTON COX

Illustration by Henry Pitz

THE HOARD PLUNDERED

FOR FIFTY WINTERS, Beowulf ruled the kingdom well. Then in the dark nights, a dragon that had guarded an ancient hoard in a cave of the mountains for three hundred years began to contest his power. I know not what bondslave it was that penetrated the hoard and plundered the heathen treasure. He took away a handbowl of red gold, so that the dragon, while sleeping near the fire, was robbed by the craft of a thief. Not of his own free will did he seek the cave, but, tormented by the consequences of crime, and fleeing from the vengeance of his master, he accidentally fell therein. Terror seized upon him when he saw the jewels and the heirlooms, which had been hidden there by I know not whom.

The cave stood near the sea and was already to receive the treasure placed there by some ancient man. He was the last of his race and as he carried the jewels and heirlooms into the cave, he spoke a few words:

"Hold now, earth, this treasure which formerly good men took from thee. Pitiless death has taken away all my people. No one is left to bear a sword or to burnish the precious vessels. The hard helmet, adorned with gold, must be deprived of its plates. The polishers, who should keep the battle-masks in good condition, sleep. Likewise the armor, which received the stroke of the sword over the breaking of shields, molders with the hero who bore it. The ring-mail no longer travels far by the side of the warrior. There is no more the sound of the harp. No good hawk swings through the hall, and no longer does the swift horse paw the courtyard. Relentless fate has carried them off." Thus sad-minded, one lamented for all, day and night, until the finger of death touched him at heart.

The dragon, the old twilight-flyer, surrounded by fire, and dreaded by the land-dwellers, found the hoard standing open. It is the duty of a dragon to seek a hoard in the earth, where he may guard the heathen gold, nor is he ever any the better for it. So this dragon, for three hundred winters, had watched the cave until a certain bondslave had angered him in his mind. The thief bore the plated vessel to his lord and asked for a peace protection. The boon was granted to the wretched man, and his lord viewed the ancient work of men for the first time.

THE DRAGON WAGES WAR AGAINST BEOWULF

When the dragon awoke, strife was renewed. The stronghearted one smelt long the stone and perceived the track of the enemy. He sought eagerly for the man who had robbed him while sleeping. Angrily he turned hither and thither on the outside of the mound, but could not find anyone in the waste. The thief in his dark craft had got too far away. At times the dragon reëntered the cave and examined the treasure. He readily perceived that somebody had stolen a part of it.

The keeper of the hoard, swollen with anger, could hardly await the coming of night, for he wished to repay with fire the theft of the precious drinking-vessel. Joyfully he watched the departure of day; then he would no longer remain on the mountain. The beginning of the strife was fearful to the land-dwellers, and vengeance fell quickly and sorely upon their treasure-giver. The dragon began to spew forth coals of fire and to burn the bright dwellings. The gleams terrified the people, for they saw that the hostile air-flyer intended to leave nothing alive. The warfare of the dragon was seen far and near, how the destroyer hated and harmed the people of the Goths. Before the break of day he shot back to his secret cavern, having surrounded the land-folk with fire and brand. He trusted in his mound, in his prowess in war, and in his wall. His trust, however, deceived him.

BEOWULF PREPARES TO FIGHT THE DRAGON

Then was it quickly made known to Beowulf that his own palace, the best of dwellings, the gift-seat of the Goths, was burning. That to him was the greatest of sorrows. He thought that in some way unknown he had angered the eternal Lord, and his breast welled with dark thoughts as was not customary for him. The firedrake, making his attack from the waterside, had destroyed the stronghold of the people. On account of that, the war-king devised vengeance. He commanded to be made a wonderful shield, entirely of iron, for he knew that a linden one would not protect him against fire. The old king scorned to seek the wide-flyer with a great host. He cared not for the dragon's warfare, his strength, and his courage, because he himself had endured many hard battles. Not the least of these was the one in which he slew Dayraven, the champion of the Hugs, in a hand-to-hand conflict. In that expedition to Frisian land, Higelac lost his life, and Beowulf swam across the sea where Hygd offered him wealth and a crown. She did not trust in Heardred, her son and heir, that he could hold the empire against hostile bands. Beowulf would not accept the kingdom, neither would he be lord over Heardred, but he upheld the youth with friendly counsel until he was capable of ruling the Goths. When Heardred lost his life in battle, Beowulf succeeded to the throne. That was a good king.

THE CHALLENGE

Thus the lord of the Goths had escaped safely every danger until that day upon which he was to do battle with the dragon. Then he, one of twelve, swollen with anger, went to look upon the old twilight-flyer. He had learned the cause of the feud, since the stolen cup had come into his possession through the hand of the finder. The thief who had started the strife was the thirteenth man of the company. Sick at heart, he went against his will, a captive, because he alone knew where the cavern was that held the hoard. To get that treasure from the old firedrake was not an easy task for any man. Beowulf sat upon the headland while he bade farewell to his hearth-companions. He was at the point of death, and fate, immeasurably nigh, was soon to approach and plunder his soul. Sorrowfully he said:

"Well do I remember all the battle-rushes I escaped in my youth. I was seven winters old when my grandfather Hrethel took me at the hands of my father. He remembered fittingly our kinship, nor was I less dear to him than his own sons, Herebald, Haethcyn, and my beloved Higelac. When Higelac became king, he gave me treasures, land, and a dwelling place. I repaid him for all these by fighting, and was always foremost in the host, alone in the van. Now I shall strive with the dragon for the hoard."

Then he greeted each one of his dear companions for the last time. "Not at all," said he, "would I bear a weapon against the firedrake if I knew how else I might slay him, as I did Grendel of old. But in this case I expect fire, hot breath, and poison. Therefore I have protected myself with a shield and a coat of mail. I shall not flee from the keeper of the mound the space of a foot, but shall await at the wall, whatever fate may be in store. Abide here on the mountain, for this is not your venture, but mine alone. I shall win the gold by my valor, or battle shall destroy your lord."

The renowned warrior arose with his shield and walked forward under the stony cliff. He trusted in his own strength, which is not the way of a coward. There he saw by the wall an arch of stone standing, out of which a stream flowed. The flood of that stream was hot with battle-fire. He was not able to remain near the hoard, unburned, even for a little while, on account of the terrible heat. Raging with anger, the stronghearted one stormed and sent his clear-sounding war cry in under the gray stone. Hate was aroused. The keeper of the hoard recognized the voice of a man and there was no longer any time to ask for peace. Immediately there came forth out of the cave the hot breath of the firedrake. The earth trembled.

BEOWULF FIGHTS THE DRAGON

The hero brought up his shield with a quick motion against the dragon when he coiled himself for the onset. On he came, like a

curved bow, hastening to his fate. The shield protected well the life
of the great prince for a shorter time than he expected. Fate did not

Henry Pitz

The dragon poured out his deadly breath.

grant victory to him in the beginning of the contest. The lord of
the Goths raised his hand and struck the grisly terror a mighty blow;

the edge of the bright sword turned and bit the bone less keenly than the warrior had need of. Then was the keeper of the mound furious on account of that battle-stroke. He cast forth deadly fire, and the flames spread far and wide. The king of the Goths did not boast of victory, for the naked sword failed him in the conflict, as it should not have done.

It was not long until they met again. The dragon poured out his deadly breath and surrounded Beowulf closely with fire. Not at all did his companions stand around their king with battle-valor, but they fled to the wood to save their lives. In one of them only, did the heart surge for sorrow. Friendship never changes in him who thinks well.

WIGLAF COMES TO THE RESCUE

The dear shield-warrior was called Wiglaf. He saw his lord suffering in the deadly heat, and could not forbear seizing his shield and drawing his sword. That was the first time the young champion should engage in the storm of war in company with his noble lord. His courage did not fail nor his sword weaken in the fight, as the dragon soon perceived.

Sad in heart, Wiglaf said many fitting words to his cowardly companions:

"I remember well how we, drinking mead in the hall, promised our lord to repay him for these battle-equipments, should occasion ever arise. On account of this promise, he chose us from the host to accompany him. He reckoned us good spearmen and keen helm-bearers, although he intended to accomplish this great work alone.

"The time has come when he has need of good fighters. Let us go to help him while the grim fire-terror is upon him. It were a disgrace for us to go back home bearing our shields, except we first strike down the foe and save the life of the prince of the Goths. It is not right that he alone should endure sorrow and fall in the conflict. To him and me shall be sword and helm, armor and mail-defense, in common."

WIGLAF JOINS IN THE FIGHT

Then he waded through the deadly reek to the aid of his lord and said a few words: "Dear Beowulf, perform all well. Remember your boast in youth that you would not let your glory fail as long as life lasted. Now you must defend yourself with all your might. I will help you."

Immediately after these words the dragon came again to attack the hated men with flashing fire. The shield of Wiglaf was burned entirely, and his armor failed to protect him, but the young warrior, undaunted, hastened under the shield of his kinsman. Then the war-king remembered his fame and struck such a mighty blow, that his blade stood fixed in the dragon's head. Naegling, Beowulf's old, gray-etched sword, snapped asunder. The strength of Beowulf's hand was so great that no sword, however hard, could endure its swing. Therefore he was none the better for having a weapon.

The firedrake, for the third time, was mindful of the feud, and rushed upon the hero when the opportunity came. Hot and battle-fierce, he enclosed the entire neck of Beowulf with his sharp teeth. The blood sprang forth with waves and the old king was covered with gore.

BEOWULF AND WIGLAF SLAY THE DRAGON

Then, as I have heard, Wiglaf, rising to his full height, showed the great strength and courage that were natural to him. He paid no attention to the head of the dragon, but struck the malicious brute somewhat lower down, so that the bright sword plunged in and the fire began to abate. Then the king himself, still retaining consciousness, drew his short sword, keen and battle-sharp, and severed the dragon through the middle.

Thus the kinsmen-nobles slew the firedrake. As a thane should be to a prince in his need, so was Wiglaf to Beowulf.

Immediately the wound that the earth-dragon had made upon the king, began to swell and burn. He soon perceived that deadly poison was welling within him. He took a seat by the wall and looked upon the work of the giants, the stone arches, which, supported by pillars, held the everlasting earth-dwelling. Then Wiglaf, the devoted thane, unloosened his helmet and bathed him.

THE DEATH OF BEOWULF

Beowulf spoke, notwithstanding his wound. He knew well that he had reached the end of worldly joy, that the number of his days had gone, and that death was immeasurably nigh.

"Now would I give battle-raiments to my son, had one been given me. Fifty years have I ruled my people, and not one of the kings living around dared oppress me with terror or attack me with weapons. In my home, I awaited the hour of destiny, held well what was mine, sought no treacherous quarrels, nor swore false oaths. For all this, sick as I am with a deadly wound, I may have joy, and the Ruler of men cannot blame me for the murder of kinsmen, when my life parts from the body. Now go quickly to view the hoard under the gray stone, dear Wiglaf, since the dragon is dead, bereft of his treasure. Be in haste, that I may see the gold and look upon the bright gems. Then may I the more easily give up my life and lordship, which I have held so long."

Wiglaf hastened to obey his wounded lord and disappeared under the roof of the mound. There he saw many treasure-jewels, gold, glittering on the ground, and the den of the old twilight-flyer. Strewn around, were the flagons of ancient men, their polishers gone, and their ornaments fallen away. Many a helmet, old and rusty, and many an arm-ring, curiously twisted, hung upon the walls. Standing over the hoard was a standard, all golden, the greatest of hand-wrought wonders. From it there arose a light, so that he could see the floor and examine the jewels. There was no sign of the dragon, for the sword had taken him away.

Then, as I have heard, Wiglaf plundered the hoard, the old work of the giants. He loaded himself with cups and dishes at his will. Likewise he took the banner, the brightest of beacons. He was in haste, urged on by the possession of the treasures. Anxiety tormented him as to whether his prince were still alive. In the place where he had left him, Wiglaf found Beowulf, bleeding, and at the end of life, and he cast water upon him until he spoke. Aged, and full of sorrow, the old king gazed upon the gold, and said:

"I give thanks to the Lord, to the King of Glory, that I have been able to win for my folk all these treasures which I now look upon. I have bought this hoard with my aged life, and now you must fulfill the needs of the nation. I may not be here longer. Command warriors to raise a bright mound, after the funeral fire, at the headland of the sea. Towering high upon the Whale's Ness, it shall be a remembrance to my people, so that the sailors, who drive the tall ships afar over the mists of the ocean, may call it Beowulf's Mound."

The brave-hearted prince took from his neck the golden ring and gave it to Wiglaf, together with his gold-plated helmet and his armor; bade him use them well. "Thou art the last of our race," said he, "the last of the Waegmundings. Fate has swept away all my kinsmen at the appointed time. I must after them."

That was the last word of the aged king. His soul departed from his breast to seek the doom of the just. Wiglaf was most wretched when he saw his beloved lord upon the earth, gasping in death. His slayer, the terrible firedrake, likewise lay dead, overcome by strife. No longer might the ring-bowed dragon keep the hoard, for the edge of the iron had taken him off; the wide-flyer fell upon the mound near the treasure-cave. No more did he wheel sporting in the air at midnight, proud in his possessions. He had fallen by the handwork of the war-chiefs. No man in the land ever thrived, according to my information, however doughty he were, in making attack against the poisonous breath, or in disturbing with his hands the treasure hall, if he found the dragon awake upon the mountain. So Beowulf paid the penalty of his rashness, and he and the old twilight-flyer lay dead together.

THE RETURN OF THE COWARDS

It was not long until the ten cowards, who did not dare to use their weapons in the defense of their lord, came out from the wood.

In shame they bore their shields and war-harness, and fixed their eyes upon Wiglaf where he sat, wearied, near the shoulders of his king, trying to revive him with water. The effort was unavailing. He could not keep the life in his chieftain, nor could he change the will of the Almighty. The doom of God governed the fate of men, even as it does yet.

Then was a grim answer easily gotten from the young man, by those who had lost their courage.

With sorrow in his heart, Wiglaf looked upon his unloved companions and said:

"Lo! he may say, who will speak the truth, that the chief who gave you those battle-equipments, wherein you are now standing, when on the ale-bench he bestowed helmets and mail-coats, utterly and cursedly threw them away. When war overtook him, not at all could the folk-king boast of his army-companions. However, God granted to him that he should avenge himself, when need came. Although I tried to help, I could give him but little protection in the battle. Whenever I struck with my sword, the life-destroyer was always weaker and the fire gushed forth from his head less violently. But at the moment of crisis, too few fighters thronged about the prince. Now shall the acceptance of treasure and gifts of swords, all home-joy and abiding-place, cease to your race. Every one of your land-rights shall be taken from you when your enemies from afar shall learn of your flight, your cowardly deed. Death is better for every earl than a life of shame."

PREPARATIONS FOR THE FUNERAL

At once Wiglaf sent a messenger to announce the battle-deed at the inclosure upon the sea cliff. There the sad-minded warriors sat all the long morning, waiting the return of their lord, or the news of his death. The herald kept nothing back but told them truthfully:

"Now is the lord of the Goths, the joy-giver of his people, fast in his death-bed through the deeds of the dragon. Lying dead by his side is his destroyer, put to sleep with the knife-wounds. Wiglaf sits near Beowulf, one hero by another, and, weary at heart, keeps head-watch over friend and foe."

The troop all arose and with welling tears went under the Eagle's Ness to view the wonder. There they found him dead who in former times had given them rings. They saw also the strange creature, the dragon, lying on the plain, opposite Beowulf. The firedrake, the grim terror, was fifty feet long as he lay stretched out. He had used his earth-cave for the last time. By them stood cups and flagons; dishes were scattered around, and precious swords, eaten through with rust, as though they had been in the bosom of the earth a thousand winters.

Wiglaf spoke: "Many an earl must often endure misery on account of one, as has happened to us. We were not able to persuade our dear king that he should not seek the guardian of the gold, but that he should let the dragon lie there in his dwelling until the end of the world. He held to his high destiny, for the fate was too strong that enticed him thither. Many things he said, and in sadness commanded to greet you. He asked that you build upon the place of the funeral pyre a high mound, great and glorious, in keeping with the deeds of your king, who was the worthiest warrior throughout the wide earth.

"Now, let us hasten to view and to ransack the heap of treasure under the wall. I will direct you, in order that you may see near at hand the rings and the broad gold. When we come out, let the bier be quickly prepared and we will bear our beloved lord where he shall long remain in the keeping of the Almighty."

Then Wiglaf commanded many warriors to bring wood from far and near for the funeral pyre. From the company of the king's thanes he selected seven, the very best, and went with them under the hostile roof. The one who led the van carried in his hand a torch. Ruthlessly they plundered the hoard, and in all haste took out the costly treasures. They shoved the old dragon over the cliff into the bosom of the flood and let the waves bear him away. The twisted gold of every kind, a quantity beyond estimate, was loaded upon a wagon, and, with the hoary battle-king, was conveyed to the Whale's Ness.

BEOWULF'S FUNERAL PYRE

There the people of the Goths prepared a firm pyre, hung with helmets, shields, and shining armor, as Beowulf had commanded. In the midst of it, the weeping warriors laid the famous prince, their dear lord. Then they kindled upon the mountain the greatest of funeral fires. The wood smoke mounted up, black, over the burning pile. The wind ceased its roaring and the crackling flames mingled with the weeping, until the body was destroyed. The heavens swallowed up the smoke.

Upon the cliff, the people of the Goths raised a mound. Ten days they were in building the beacon for the hero, high and broad, and seen far and wide by sea-travelers. Within the mound they placed all the treasures that had been taken from the hoard, and surrounded the place with a wall, such as cunning men might devise. There they left the gold in the ground, as useless to men as it was before. Then twelve of the nobles, sons of earls, rode around the mound, lamenting their king and praising his heroic deeds.

Thus did the Goths mourn the fall of their lord. They said that he was a world-king, the mildest of men and the most gentle, to his people most gracious, and of praise, most eager.

King Arthur

KING ARTHUR

The famous cycle of stories built around a half-legendary, half-historic king of early Britain.

KING ARTHUR AND THE ROUND TABLE

By BEATRICE CLAY

Illustrations by Dora Curtis

OF ARTHUR'S BIRTH, AND HOW HE BECAME KING

LONG years ago, there ruled over Britain a king called Uther Pendragon. A mighty prince was he, and feared by all men; yet, when he sought the love of the fair Igraine of Cornwall, she would have nought to do with him, so that, from grief and disappointment, Uther fell sick, and at last seemed like to die.

Now in those days, there lived a famous magician named Merlin, so powerful that he could change his form at will, or even make himself invisible; nor was there any place so remote but that he could reach it at once, merely by wishing himself there. One day, suddenly he stood at Uther's bedside, and said: "Sir King, I know thy grief, and am ready to help thee. Only promise to give me, at his birth, the son that shall be born to thee, and thou shalt have thy heart's desire." To this the king agreed joyfully, and Merlin kept his word: for he gave Uther the form of one whom Igraine had loved dearly, and so she took him willingly for her husband.

When the time had come that a child should be born to the King and Queen, Merlin appeared before Uther to remind him of his promise; and Uther swore it should be as he had said. Three days later, a prince was born and, with pomp and ceremony, was christened by the name of Arthur; but immediately thereafter, the King commanded that the child should be carried to the postern-gate, there to be given to the old man who would be found waiting without.

Not long after, Uther fell sick, and he knew that his end was come; so, by Merlin's advice, he called together his knights and barons and said to them: "My death draws near. I charge you, therefore, that ye obey my son even as ye have obeyed me; and my curse upon him if he claim not the crown when he is a man grown." Then the King turned his face to the wall and died.

Scarcely was Uther laid in his grave before disputes arose. Few of the nobles had seen Arthur or even heard of him, and not one of them would have been willing to be ruled by a child; rather, each thought himself fitted to be king, and, strengthening his own castle, made war on his neighbors until confusion alone was supreme, and the poor groaned because there was none to help them.

Now when Merlin carried away Arthur—for Merlin was the old man who had stood at the postern-gate—he had known all that would happen, and had taken the child to keep him safe from the fierce barons until he should be of age to rule wisely and well, and perform all the wonders prophesied of him. He gave the child to the care of the good knight Sir Ector to bring up with his son Kay, but revealed not to him that it was the son of Uther Pendragon that was given into his charge.

At last, when years had passed and Arthur was grown a tall youth well skilled in knightly exercises, Merlin went to the Archbishop of Canterbury and advised him that he should call together at Christmas time all the chief men of the realm to the great cathedral in London; "For," said Merlin, "there shall be seen a great marvel by which it shall be made clear to all men who is the lawful King of this land." The Archbishop did as Merlin counseled. Under pain of a fearful curse, he bade barons and knights come to London to keep the feast, and to pray heaven to send peace to the realm.

The people hastened to obey the Archbishop's commands and, from all sides, barons and knights came riding in to keep the birth-feast of our Lord. And when they had prayed, and were coming forth from the cathedral, they saw a strange sight. There, in the open space before the church, stood, on a great stone, an anvil thrust through with a sword; and on the stone were written these words: "Whoso can draw forth this sword, is rightful King of Britain born."

At once there were fierce quarrels, each man clamoring to be the first to try his fortune, none doubting his own success. Then the Archbishop decreed that each should make the venture in turn, from the greatest baron to the least knight; and each in turn, having put forth his utmost strength, failed to move the sword an inch, and drew back ashamed. So the Archbishop dismissed the company, and having appointed guards to watch over the stone, sent messengers through all the land to give word of great jousts to be held in Lon-

Dora Curtis
With Sir Ector and Sir Kay rode young Arthur.

don at Easter, when each knight could give proof of his skill and courage, and try whether the adventure of the sword was for him.

Among those who rode to London at Easter was the good Sir Ector, and with him his son, Sir Kay, newly made a knight, and the young Arthur. When the morning came that the jousts should begin, Sir Kay and Arthur mounted their horses and set out for the lists; but before they reached the field, Kay looked and saw that he had left his sword behind. Immediately Arthur turned back to fetch it for him, only to find the house fast shut, for all were gone to view the tournament. Sore vexed was Arthur, fearing lest his brother Kay should lose his chance of gaining glory, till, of a sudden, he bethought him of the sword in the great anvil before the cathedral. Thither he rode with all speed, and the guards having deserted their posts to view the tournament, there was none to forbid him the adventure. He leaped from his horse, seized the hilt, and instantly drew forth the sword as easily as from a scabbard; then, mounting his horse and thinking no marvel of what he had done, he rode after his brother and handed him the weapon.

When Kay looked at it, he saw at once that it was the wondrous sword from the stone. In great joy he sought his father, and showing it to him, said: "Then must I be King of Britain." But Sir Ector bade him say how he came by the sword, and when Sir Kay told how Arthur had brought it to him, Sir Ector bent his knee to the boy and said: "Sir, I perceive that ye are my King, and here I tender you my homage"; and Kay did as his father. Then the three sought the Archbishop, to whom they related all that had happened; and he, much marveling, called the people together to the great stone, and bade Arthur thrust back the sword and draw it forth again in the presence of all, which he did with ease. But an angry murmur arose from the barons, who cried that what a boy could do, a man could do; so, at the Archbishop's word, the sword was put back, and each man, whether baron or knight, tried in his turn to draw it forth, and failed. Then, for the third time, Arthur drew forth the sword. Immediately there arose from the people a great shout: "Arthur is King! Arthur is King! We will have no King but Arthur"; and, though the great barons scowled and threatened, they fell on their knees before him while the Archbishop placed the crown upon his head, and swore to obey him faithfully as their lord and sovereign.

Thus Arthur was made King; and to all he did justice, righting wrongs and giving to all their dues. Nor was he forgetful of those that had been his friends; for Kay, whom he loved as a brother, he made Seneschal and chief of his household, and to Sir Ector, his foster father, he gave broad lands.

THE ROUND TABLE

Thus Arthur was made King, but he had to fight for his own; for eleven great kings drew together and refused to acknowledge him as their lord, and chief amongst the rebels was King Lot of Orkney, who had married King Arthur's sister, Bellicent.

By Merlin's advice, Arthur sent for help overseas, to Ban and Bors, the two great Kings who ruled in Gaul. With their aid, he overthrew his foes in a fierce battle near the river Trent; and then he passed with them into their own lands and helped them drive out their enemies. So there was ever great friendship between Arthur and the Kings Ban and Bors, and all their kindred; and afterwards some of the most famous Knights of the Round Table were of that kin.

Then King Arthur set himself to restore order throughout his kingdom. To all who would submit and amend their evil ways, he showed kindness; but those who persisted in oppression and wrong he removed, putting in their places others who would deal justly with the people. And because the land had become overrun with forest during the days of misrule, he cut roads through the thickets, that no longer wild beasts and men, fiercer than the beasts, should lurk in their gloom, to the harm of the weak and defenseless. Thus it came to pass that soon the peasant plowed his fields in safety, and where had been wastes, men dwelt again in peace and prosperity.

Amongst the lesser kings whom Arthur helped to rebuild their towns and restore order, was King Leodegrance of Cameliard. Now Leodegrance had one fair child, his daughter Guinevere; and from the time that first he saw her, Arthur gave her all his love. So he sought counsel of Merlin, his chief adviser. Merlin heard the King sorrowfully, and he said: "Sir King, when a man's heart is set, he may not change. Yet it had been well if he had loved another."

So the King sent his knights to Leodegrance, to ask of him his daughter; and Leodegrance consented, rejoicing to wed her to so good and knightly a King. With great pomp, the princess was conducted to Canterbury, and there the King met her, and they two were wed by the Archbishop in the great cathedral, amid the rejoicings of the people.

On that same day did Arthur found his Order of the Round Table, the fame of which was to spread throughout Christendom and endure through all time. Now the Round Table had been made for

King Uther Pendragon by Merlin, who had meant hereby to set forth plainly to all men the roundness of the earth. After Uther died, King Leodegrance had possessed it; but when Arthur was wed, he sent it to him as a gift, and great was the King's joy at receiving it. One hundred and fifty knights might take their places about it, and for them Merlin made sieges or seats. One hundred and twenty-eight did Arthur knight at that great feast; thereafter, if any sieges were empty, at the high festival of Pentecost new knights were ordained to fill them, and by magic was the name of each knight found inscribed, in letters of gold, in his proper siege. One seat only long remained unoccupied, and that was the Siege Perilous. No knight might occupy it until the coming of Sir Galahad; for, without danger to his life, none might sit there who was not free from all sin.

With pomp and ceremony did each knight take upon him the vows of true knighthood: to obey the King; to show mercy to all who asked it; to defend the weak; and for no worldly gain to fight in a wrongful cause; and all the knights rejoiced together, doing honor to Arthur and to his Queen. Then he rode forth to right the wrong and help the oppressed, and by their aid, the King held his realm in peace, doing justice to all.

OF THE FINDING OF EXCALIBUR

Now when Arthur was first made King, as young knights will he courted peril for its own sake, and often would he ride unattended by lonely forest ways, seeking the adventure that chance might send him. All unmindful was he of the ruin to his realm if mischief befell him; and even his trusty counselors, though they grieved that he should thus imperil him, yet could not but love him the more for his hardihood.

So, on a day, he rode through the Forest Perilous where dwelt the Lady Annoure, a sorceress of great might, who used her magic powers but for the furtherance of her own desires. And as she looked from a turret window, she descried King Arthur come riding down a forest glade, and the sunbeams falling upon him made one glory

of his armor and of his yellow hair. Then, as Annoure gazed upon
the King, her heart grew hot within her, and she resolved that, come
what might, she would have him for her own, to dwell with her
always and fulfill all her behests. And so she bade lower the draw-
bridge and raise the portcullis, and sallying forth accompanied by
her maidens, she gave King Arthur courteous salutation, and prayed
him that he would rest within her castle that day, for that she had a
petition to make to him; and Arthur, doubting nothing of her good
faith, suffered himself to be led within.

Then was a great feast spread, and Annoure caused the King to
be seated in a chair of state at her right hand, while squires and
pages served him on bended knee. So when they had feasted, the
King turned to the Lady Annoure and said courteously: "Lady,
somewhat ye said of a request that ye would make. If there be aught
in which I may pleasure you, I pray you let me know it, and I will
serve you as knightly as I may." "In truth," said the lady, "there is
that which I would fain entreat of you, most noble knight; yet suffer,
I beseech you, that first I may show you somewhat of my castle and
my estate, and then I will crave a boon of your chivalry." Then the
sorceress led King Arthur from room to room of her castle, and ever
each displayed greater store of beauty than the last. In some, the
walls were hung with rich tapestries, in others they gleamed with
precious stones; and the King marveled what might be the petition of one that was mistress of such wealth. Lastly, Annoure
brought the King out upon the battlements, and as he gazed around
him, he saw that, since he had entered the castle, there had sprung
up about it triple walls of defense that shut out wholly the forest
from view. Then turned he to Annoure, and gravely said: "Lady,
greatly I marvel in what a simple knight may pleasure one that is
mistress of so wondrous a castle as ye have shown me here; yet if
there be aught in which I may render you knightly service, right
gladly would I hear it now, for I must forth upon my way to render
service to those whose knight I am sworn." "Nay, now, King Arthur," answered the sorceress mockingly, "ye may not think to
deceive me; for well I know you, and that all Britain bows to your
behest." "The more reason then that I should ride forth to right

wrong and succor them that, of their loyalty, render true obedience to their lord." "Ye speak as a fool," said the sorceress; "why should one that may command be at the beck and call of every hind and slave within his realm? Nay, rest thee here with me, and I will make thee ruler of a richer land than Britain, and give thee to satisfy thy every desire." "Lady," said the King sternly, "I will hear and judge of your petition here and now, and then will I forth upon my way." "Nay," said Annoure, "there needs not this harshness. I did but speak for thine advantage. Only vow thee to my service, and there is naught that thou canst desire that thou shalt not possess. Thou shalt be lord of this fair castle and of the mighty powers that obey me. Why waste thy youth in hardship and in the service of such as shall render thee little enough again?"

Thereupon, without ever a word, the King turned him about and made for the turret stair by which he had ascended, but nowhere could he find it. Then said the sorceress, mocking him: "Fair sir, how think ye to escape without my good will? See ye not the walls that guard my stronghold? And think ye that I have not servants enow to do my bidding?" She clapped her hands and, forthwith, there appeared a company of squires who, at her command, seized the King and bore him away to a strong chamber where they locked him in.

And so the King abode that night, the prisoner of that evil sorceress, with little hope that day, when it dawned, should bring him better cheer. Yet lost he not courage, but kept watch and vigil the night through lest the powers of evil should assail him unawares. And with the early morning light, Annoure came to visit him. More stately she seemed than the night before, more tall and more terrible; and her dress was one blaze of flashing gems so that scarce could the eye look upon her. As a queen might address a vassal, so greeted she the King, and as condescending to one of low estate, asked how he had fared that night. And the King made answer: "I have kept vigil as behooves a knight who, knowing him to be in the midst of danger, would bear himself meetly in any peril that should offer." And the Lady Annoure, admiring his knightly courage, desired more earnestly even than before to win him to her will, and she said: "Sir

Arthur, I know well your courage and knightly fame, and greatly do I desire to keep you with me. Stay with me and I promise you that ye shall bear sway over a wider realm than any that ever ye heard of, and I, even I, its mistress, will be at your command. And what lose ye if ye accept my offer? Little enough, I ween, for never think that ye shall win the world from evil and men to loyalty and truth." Then answered the King in anger: "Full well I see that thou art in league with evil and that thou but seekest to turn me from my purpose. I defy thee, foul sorceress. Do thy worst; though thou slay me, thou shall never sway me to thy will"; and therewith, the King raised his cross-hilted sword before her. Then the lady quailed at that sight. Her heart was filled with hate, but she said: "Go your way, proud King of a petty realm. Rule well your race of miserable mortals, since more it pleasures you than to bear sway over the powers of the air. I keep you not against your will." With these words, she passed from the chamber, and the King heard her give command to her squires to set him without her gates, give him his horse, and suffer him to go on his way.

And so it came to pass that the King found himself once more at large, and marveled to have won so lightly to liberty. Yet knew he not the depths of treachery in the heart of Annoure; for when she found she might not prevail with the King, she bethought her how by mortal means she might bring the King to dishonor and death. And so, by her magic art, she caused the King to follow a path that brought him to a fountain, whereby a knight had his tent, and, for love of adventure, held the way against all comers.

Now this knight was Sir Pellinore, and at that time he had not his equal for strength and knightly skill, nor had any been found that might stand against him. So, as the King drew nigh, Pellinore cried, "Stay, knight, for none passes this way except he joust with me." "That is no good custom," said the King; "it were well that ye followed it no more."

"It is my custom and I will followed it still," answered Pellinore; "if ye not like it, amend it if ye may." "I will do my endeavor," said Arthur, "but, as ye see, I have no spear." "Nay, I seek not to have you at advantage," replied Pellinore, and bade his squire give Arthur a spear. Then they dressed their shields, laid their lances in rest, and rushed upon each other.

Now the King was wearied by his night's vigil, and the strength of Pellinore was as the strength of three men; so at the first encounter, Arthur was unhorsed. Then said he: "I have lost the honor on horseback, but now will encounter thee with my sword and on foot." "I, too, will alight," said Pellinore; "small honor to me were it if I slew thee on foot, I being horsed the while." So they encountered each other on foot, and so fiercely they fought that they hewed off great pieces of each other's armor and the ground was dyed with their blood. But at the last, Arthur's sword broke off short at the hilt, and so he stood all defenseless before his foe. "I have thee now," cried Pellinore; "yield thee as recreant or I will slay thee." "That will I never," said the King, "slay me if thou canst." Then he sprang on Pellinore, caught him by the middle, and flung him to the ground, himself falling with him. And Sir Pellinore marveled, for never before had he encountered so bold and resolute a foe; but exerting his great strength, he rolled himself over, and so brought Arthur beneath him. Then had Arthur perished, but at that moment Merlin stood beside him, and when Sir Pellinore would have struck off the King's head, stayed his blow, crying: "Pellinore, if thou slayest this knight, thou puttest the whole realm in peril; for this is none other than King Arthur himself." Then was Pellinore filled with dread, and cried: "Better make an end of him at once; for if I suffer him to live, what hope have I of his grace, that have dealt with him so sorely?" But before Pellinore could strike, Merlin caused a deep sleep to come upon him; and raising King Arthur from the ground, he staunched his wounds and recovered him of his swoon.

But when King Arthur came to himself, he saw his foe lie, still as in death, on the ground beside him; and he was grieved, and said: "Merlin, what have ye done to this brave knight? Nay, if ye have slain him, I shall grieve my life long; for a good knight he is, bold and a fair fighter, though something wanting in knightly courtesy." "He is in better case than ye are, Sir King, who so lightly imperil your person and thereby your kingdom's welfare; and, as ye say, Pellinore is a stout knight and hereafter shall he serve you well.

Have no fear. He shall wake again in three hours and have suffered naught by the encounter. But for you, it were well that ye came where ye might be tended for your wounds." "Nay," replied the King, smiling, "I may not return to my court thus weaponless; first will I find means to purvey me of a sword." "That is easily done," answered Merlin; "follow me, and I will bring you where ye shall get you a sword, the wonder of the world."

So, though his wounds pained him sore, the King followed Merlin by many a forest path and glade, until they came upon a mere, bosomed deep in the forest; and as he looked thereon, the King beheld an arm, clothed in white samite, shoot above the surface of the lake, and in the hand was a fair sword that gleamed in the level rays of the setting sun. "This is a great marvel," said the King, "what may it mean?" And Merlin made answer: "Deep is this mere, so deep indeed that no man may fathom it; but in its depths, and built upon the roots of the mountains, is the palace of the Lady of the Lake. Powerful is she with a power that works ever for good, and she shall help thee in thine hour of need. For thee has she wrought yonder sword. Go now, and take it."

Then was Arthur aware of a little skiff, half hidden among the bulrushes that fringed the lake; and leaping into the boat, without aid of oar, he was wafted out into the middle of the lake, to the place where, out of the water, rose the arm and sword. And, leaning from the skiff, he took the sword from the hand, which forthwith vanished, and immediately thereafter, the skiff bore him back to land.

Arthur drew from its scabbard the mighty sword, wondering the while at the marvel of its workmanship, for the hilt shone with the elfin light of twinkling gems—diamond and topaz and emerald, and many another whose name none knows. And as he looked on the blade, Arthur was aware of mystic writings on the one side and the other, and calling to Merlin, he bade him interpret them. "Sir," said Merlin, "on the one side is written 'Keep me,' and on the other 'Throw me away.'" "Then," said the King, "which does it behoove me to do?" "Keep it," answered Merlin; "the time to cast it away is not yet come. This is the good brand Excalibur, or Cut Steel, and well shall it serve you. But what think ye of the scabbard?" "A fair cover for so good a sword," answered Arthur. "Nay, it is more than that," said Merlin, "for, as long as ye keep it, though ye be wounded never so sore, yet ye shall not bleed to death." And when he heard that, the King marveled the more.

Then they journeyed back to Caerleon, where the knights made great joy of the return of their lord. And presently, thither came Sir Pellinore, craving pardon of the King, who made but jest of his own misadventure. And afterwards Sir Pellinore became of the Table Round, a knight vowed not only to deeds of hardihood but also to gentleness and courtesy; and faithfully he served the King, fighting ever to maintain justice and put down wrong, and to defend the weak from the oppressor.

SIR LAUNCELOT DU LAC

Now, as time passed, King Arthur gathered into his Order of the Round Table knights whose peers shall never be found in any age; and foremost among them all was Sir Launcelot du Lac. Such was his strength that none against whom he laid lance in rest could keep the saddle, and no shield was proof against his sword dint; but for his courtesy even more than for his courage and strength, Sir Launcelot was famed far and near. Gentle he was and ever the first to rejoice in the renown of another, and in the jousts, he would avoid encounter with the young and untried knight, letting him pass to gain glory if he might.

It would take a great book to record all the famous deeds of Sir Launcelot, and all his adventures. He was of Gaul, for his father, King Ban, ruled over Benwick; and some say that his first name was Galahad, and that he was named Launcelot du Lac by the Lady of the Lake who reared him when his mother died. Early he won renown by delivering his father's people from the grim King Claudas who, for more than twenty years, had laid waste the fair land of Benwick; then, when there was peace in his own land, he passed into Britain, to Arthur's Court, where the King received him gladly, and made him knight of the Round Table and took him for his trustiest friend. And so it was that, when Guinevere was to be brought to Canterbury, to be married to the King, Launcelot was chief of the knights sent to wait upon her, and of this came the sorrow of later days. For, from the moment he saw her, Sir Launcelot loved Guinevere, for her sake remaining wifeless all his days, and in all things being her faithful knight. But busy-bodies and mischief-makers spoke evil of Sir Launcelot and the Queen, and from their talk came the undoing of the King and the downfall of his great work. But that was after long years, and after many true knights had lived their lives, honoring the King and Queen, and doing great deeds whereby the fame of King Arthur and his Order passed through all the world.

THE ADVENTURE OF THE CHAPEL PERILOUS

Now on a day, as he rode through the forest, Sir Launcelot met a damsel weeping bitterly, and seeing him, she cried, "Stay, Sir Knight! By your knighthood I require you to aid me in my distress." Immediately Sir Launcelot checked his horse and asked in what she needed his service. "Sir," said the maiden, "my brother lies at the point of death, for this day he fought with the stout knight, Sir Gilbert, and sorely they wounded each other; and a wise woman, a sorceress, has said that nothing may staunch my brother's wounds unless they be searched with the sword and bound up with a piece of cloth from the body of the wounded knight who lies in the ruined chapel hard by. And well I know you, my lord Sir Launcelot, and that, if ye will not help me, none may." "Tell me your brother's name," said Sir Launcelot. "Sir Meliot de Logris," answered the damsel. "A knight of our Round Table," said Sir Launcelot; "the more am I bound to your service. Only tell me, gentle damsel, where I may find this Chapel Perilous." So she directed him, and, riding through forest byways, Sir Launcelot came presently upon a little ruined chapel, standing in the midst of a churchyard, where the tombs showed broken and neglected under the dark yews. In front of the porch, Sir Launcelot paused and looked, for thereon hung upside down, dishonored, the shield of many a good knight whom Sir Launcelot had known.

As he stood wondering, suddenly there pressed upon him from all sides thirty stout knights, all giants and fully armed, their drawn swords in their hands and their shields advanced. With threatening looks, they spoke to him, saying, "Sir Launcelot, it were well ye turned back before evil befall you." But Sir Launcelot, though he feared to have to do with thirty such warriors, answered boldly, "I turn not back for high words. Make them good by your deeds." Then he rode upon them fiercely, whereupon instantly they scattered and disappeared, and, sword in hand, Sir Launcelot entered the little chapel. All was dark within, save that a little lamp hung from the roof, and by its dim light he could just espy how on a bier before the altar there lay, stark and cold, a knight sheathed in armor. And drawing nearer, Sir Launcelot saw that the dead man lay on a blood-stained mantle, his naked sword by his side, but that his left hand had been lopped off at the wrist by a mighty sword-cut. Then Sir Launcelot boldly seized the sword and with it cut off a piece of the bloody mantle. Immediately the earth shook and the walls of the chapel rocked, and in fear Sir Launcelot turned to go. But, as he would have left the chapel, there stood before him in the doorway a lady, fair to look upon and beautifully arrayed, who gazed earnestly upon him and said: "Sir Knight, put away from you that sword lest it be your death." But Sir Launcelot answered her: "Lady, what I have said, I do; and what I have won, I keep." "It is well," said the lady; "Had ye cast away the sword, your life days were done. And now I make but one request. Kiss me once." "That may I not do," said Sir Launcelot. Then said the lady: "Go your way, Launcelot; ye have won, and I have lost. Know that had ye kissed me your dead body had lain even now on the altar bier. For much have I desired to win you; and to entrap you, I ordained this chapel. Many a knight have I taken, and once Sir Gawain himself hardly escaped, but he fought with Sir Gilbert and lopped off his hand, and so got away. Fare ye well; it is plain to see that none but our lady, Queen Guinevere, may have your services." With that, she vanished from his sight. So Sir Launcelot mounted his horse and rode away from that evil place till he met Sir Meliot's sister, who led him to her brother where he lay, pale as the earth, and bleeding fast. And when he saw Sir Launcelot, he would have risen to greet him; but his strength failed him, and he fell back on his couch. Sir Launcelot searched his wounds with the sword, and bound them up with the bloodstained cloth, and immediately Sir Meliot was sound and well, and greatly he rejoiced. Then Sir Meliot and his sister begged Sir Launcelot to stay and rest, but he departed on his adventures, bidding them farewell until he should meet them again at Arthur's court.

As for the sorceress of the Chapel Perilous, it is said she died of grief that all her charms had failed to win for her the good knight Sir Launcelot.

THE ADVENTURES OF SIR GARETH

Gareth was the youngest of the sons of Lot and Bellicent, and had grown up long after Gawain and Mordred left their home for King Arthur's court; so that when he came before the King, all humbly attired, he was known not even by his own brothers.

King Arthur was keeping Pentecost at Kink Kenadon on the Welsh border and, as his custom was, waited to begin the feast until some adventure should befall. Presently there was seen approaching a youth who, to the wonderment of all that saw, leaned upon the shoulders of two men, his companions; and yet as he passed up the hall, he seemed a goodly youth, tall and broad-shouldered. When he stood before the king, suddenly he drew himself up and after due greeting, said: "Sir King, I would ask of you three boons; one to be granted now and two hereafter when I shall require them." And Arthur, looking upon him, was pleased, for his countenance was open and honest. So he made answer: "Fair son, ask of me aught that is honorable and I will grant it." Then the youth said: "For this present, I ask only that ye will give me meat and drink for a year and a day." "Ye might have asked and had a better gift," replied the King; "tell me now your name." "At this time, I may not tell it," said the youth.

Now King Arthur trusted every man until he proved himself unworthy, and in this youth he thought he saw one who should do nobly and win renown; so laughing, he bade him keep his own counsel since so he would, and gave him in charge to Sir Kay, the Seneschal.

Now Sir Kay was but harsh to those whom he liked not, and from the first he scorned the young man. "For none," said he, "but a low-born lout would crave meat and drink when he might have asked for a horse and arms." But Sir Launcelot and Sir Gawain took the youth's part. Neither knew him for Gareth of the Orkneys, but both believed him to be a youth of good promise who, for his own reasons, would pass in disguise for a season.

So Gareth lived the year among the kitchen boys, all the time mocked and scorned by Sir Kay, who called him Fairhands because his hands were white and shapely. But Sir Launcelot and Sir Gawain showed him all courtesy, and failed not to observe how, in all trials of strength, he excelled all his comrades, and that he was always present to witness the feats of the knights in the tournaments.

So the year passed, and again King Arthur was keeping the feast of Pentecost with his knights, when a damsel entered the hall and asked his aid: "For," said she, "my sister is closely besieged in her castle by a strong knight who lays waste all her lands. And since I know that the knights of your court be the most renowned in the world, I have come to crave help of your mightiest." "What is your sister's name, and who is he that oppresses her?" asked the King. "The Red Knight he is called," replied the damsel. "As for my sister, I will not say her name, only that she is a highborn lady and owns broad lands." Then the King frowned and said: "Ye would have aid but will say no name. I may not ask knight of mine to go on such an errand."

Then forth stepped Gareth from among the serving men at the hall end and said: "Sir King I have eaten of your meat in your kitchen this twelve month since, and now I crave my other two boons." "Ask and have," replied the King. "Grant me then the adventure of this damsel, and bid Sir Launcelot ride after me to knight me at my desire, for of him alone would I be made knight." "It shall be so," answered the King. "What!" cried the damsel, "I ask for a knight and ye give me a kitchen-boy. Shame on you, Sir King."

And in great wrath she fled from the hall, mounted her palfrey and rode away. Gareth but waited to array himself in the armor which he had kept ever in readiness for the time when he should need it, and mounting his horse, rode after the damsel.

But when Sir Kay knew what had happened, he was wroth, and got to horse to ride after Gareth and bring him back. Even as Gareth overtook the damsel, so did Kay come up with him and cried: "Turn back, Fairhands! What, sir, do ye not know me?" "Yes," answered Gareth, "I know you for the most discourteous knight in Arthur's court." Then Sir Kay rode upon him with his lance, but Gareth turned it aside with his sword and pierced Sir Kay through the side so that he fell to the ground and lay there without motion. So Gareth took Sir Kay's shield and spear and was about to ride away, when seeing Sir Launcelot draw near, he called upon him to joust. At the first encounter, Sir Launcelot unhorsed Gareth, but quickly helped him to his feet. Then, at Gareth's desire, they fought together with swords, and Gareth did knightly till, at length, Sir Launcelot said laughing: "Why should we fight any longer? Of a truth you are a stout knight." "If that is indeed your thought, I pray you make me knight," cried Gareth. So Sir Launcelot knighted Gareth, who, bidding him farewell, hastened after the damsel, for she had ridden on again while the two knights talked. When she saw him coming, she cried: "Keep off! Ye smell of the kitchen!" "Damsel," said Sir Gareth, "I must follow until I have fulfilled the adventure." "Till ye accomplish the adventure, Turnspit? Your part in it shall soon be ended." "I can only do my best," answered Sir Gareth.

Now as they rode through the forest, they met with a knight sore beset by six thieves, and him Sir Gareth rescued. The knight then bade Gareth and the damsel rest at his castle, and entertained them right gladly until the morn, when the two rode forth again. Presently, they drew near to a deep river where two knights kept the ford. "How now, kitchen knave? Will ye fight or escape while ye may?" cried the damsel. "I would fight though there were six instead of two," replied Sir Gareth. Therewith, he encountered the one knight in midstream and struck him such a blow on the head that he fell, stunned, into the water and was drowned. Then, gaining the land, Gareth cleft in two helmet and head of the other knight, and turned to the damsel, saying: "Lead on; I follow."

But the damsel mocked him, saying: "What a mischance is it that a kitchen-boy should slay two noble knights! Be not overproud, Turnspit. It was but luck, if indeed ye did not attack one knight from behind."

"Say what you will, I will follow," said Sir Gareth.

So they rode on again, the damsel in front and Sir Gareth behind, till they reached a wide meadow where stood many fair pavilions; and one, the largest, was all of blue, and the men who stood about it were clothed in blue, and bore shields and spears of that color; and of blue, too, were the trappings of the horses. Then said the damsel: "Yonder is the Blue Knight, the goodliest that ever ye have looked upon, and five hundred knights own him lord." "I will encounter him," said Sir Gareth; "for if he be good knight and true as ye say, I fear him not." "Fie!" said the damsel, "For a dirty knave, ye brag loud. And even if ye overcome him, his might is as nothing to that of the Red Knight who besieges my lady sister. So get ye gone while ye may." "Damsel," said Sir Gareth, "ye are but ungentle so to rebuke me; for, knight or knave, I have done you good service, nor will I leave this quest while life is mine." Then the damsel was ashamed, and, looking curiously at Gareth, she said, "I would gladly know what manner of man ye are. For I heard you call yourself kitchen-knave before Arthur's self, but ye have ever answered patiently though I have chidden you shamefully; and courtesy comes only of gentle blood." Thereat Gareth laughed, and said: "He is no knight whom a maiden can anger by harsh words."

So talking, they entered the field, and there came to Sir Gareth a messenger from the Blue Knight to ask him if he came in peace or in war. "As your lord pleases," said Sir Gareth. So when the messenger had brought back this word, the Blue Knight mounted his horse, took his spear in his hand and rode upon Sir Gareth. At the first encounter, their lances shivered to pieces, and such was the shock that their horses fell dead. So they rushed on each other with sword and shield, cutting and slashing till the armor was hacked from their bodies; but at last, Sir Gareth smote the Blue Knight to the earth. Then the Blue Knight yielded, and at the damsel's entreaty, Sir Gareth spared his life.

So they were reconciled, and at the request of the Blue Knight, Sir Gareth and the damsel abode that night in his tents. As they sat at table, the Blue Knight said: "Fair damsel, are ye not called Linet?" "Yes," answered she, "and I am taking this noble knight to the relief of my sister, the Lady Liones." "God speed you, Sir," said the Blue Knight, "for he is a stout knight whom ye must meet. Long ago might he have taken the lady, but that he hoped that Sir Launcelot or some other of Arthur's most famous knights, coming to her rescue, might fall beneath his lance. If ye overthrow him, then are ye the peer of Sir Launcelot and Sir Tristram." "Sir Knight," answered Gareth, "I can but strive to bear me worthily as one whom the great Sir Launcelot made knight."

So in the morning they bade farewell to the Blue Knight, who vowed to carry to King Arthur word of all that Gareth had achieved; and they rode on till, in the evening, they came to a little ruined hermitage where there awaited them a dwarf sent by the Lady Liones with all manner of meats and other store. In the morning, the dwarf set out again to bear word to his lady that her rescuer was come. As he drew near the castle, the Red Knight stopped him, demanding whence he came. "Sir," said the dwarf, "I have been with my lady's sister, who brings with her a knight to the rescue of my lady." "It is lost labor," said the Red Knight; "even though she brought Launcelot or Tristram, I hold myself a match for him." "He is none of these," said the dwarf, "but he has overthrown the knights who kept the ford, and the Blue Knight yielded to him." "Let him come," said the Red Knight; "I shall soon make an end of him, and a shameful death shall he have at my hands, as many a better knight has had." So saying, he let the dwarf go.

Presently there came riding toward the castle Sir Gareth and the damsel Linet, and Gareth marveled to see hang from the trees some forty knights in goodly armor, their shields reversed beside them. When he inquired of the damsel, she told him how these were the bodies of brave knights who, coming to the rescue of the Lady Liones, had been overthrown and shamefully done to death by the Red Knight. Then was Gareth shamed and angry, and he vowed to make an end of these evil practices. So at last they drew near to the castle walls and saw how the plain around was covered with the Red Knight's tents, and the noise was that of a great army. Hard by was a tall sycamore tree, and from it hung a mighty horn, made of an elephant's tusk. Spurring his horse, Gareth rode to it, and blew such a blast that those on the castle walls heard it; the knights came forth from their tents to see who blew so bold a blast, and from a window of the castle, the Lady Liones looked forth and waved her hand to her champion. Then, as Sir Gareth made his reverence to the lady, the Red Knight called roughly to him to leave his courtesy and look to himself; "For," said he, "she is mine, and to have her, I have fought many a battle." "It is but vain labor," said Sir Gareth, "since she loves you not. Know too, Sir Knight, that I have vowed to rescue her from you." "So did many another who now hangs on a tree," replied the Red Knight, "and soon ye shall hang beside them."

Then both laid their spears in rest and spurred their horses. At the first encounter, each smote the other full in the shield and, the girths of their saddles bursting, they were borne to the earth, where they lay for awhile as if dead. But presently they rose and, setting their shields before them, rushed upon each other with their swords, cutting and hacking till the armor lay on the ground in fragments. So they fought till noon and then rested; but soon they renewed the battle and so furiously they fought that often they fell to the ground together. Then, when the bells sounded for evensong, the knights rested again awhile, unlacing their helms to breathe the evening air. But looking up to the castle windows, Gareth saw the Lady Liones gazing earnestly upon him; then he caught up his helmet and calling to the Red Knight, bade him make ready for the battle; "And this time," said he, "we will make an end of it." "So be it," said the Red Knight. Then the Red Knight smote Gareth on the hand that his sword flew from his grasp, and with another blow he brought him groveling to the earth. At the sight of this, Linet cried aloud, and hearing her, Gareth, with a mighty effort, threw off the Red Knight, leaped to his sword, and got it again within his hand. Then he pressed the Red Knight harder than ever, and at the last bore him to the earth, and unlacing his helm, made ready to slay him; but the Red Knight cried aloud: "Mercy! I yield." At first, remembering the evil deaths of the forty good knights, Gareth was unwilling to spare him; but the Red Knight besought him to have mercy, telling him how, against his will, he had been bound by a vow to make war on Arthur's knights. So Sir Gareth relented, and bade him set forth at once to Kink Kenadon and entreat the King's pardon for his evil past. And this the Red Knight promised to do.

Then amidst much rejoicing, Sir Gareth was borne into the castle. There his wounds were dressed by the Lady Liones, and there he rested until he recovered his strength. And having won her love, when Gareth returned to Arthur's court the Lady Liones rode with him, and they too were wed with great pomp in the presence of the whole Fellowship of the Round Table; the King rejoicing much that his nephew had done so valiantly. So Sir Gareth lived happily with Dame Liones, winning fame and the love of all true knights. As for Linet, she came again to Arthur's court and wedded Sir Gareth's younger brother, Sir Gaheris.

THE COMING OF SIR GALAHAD

Many times had the great Feast of Pentecost come round, and many were the knights that Arthur had made since first he founded the Order of the Round Table; yet no knight had appeared who dared claim the seat named by Merlin the Siege Perilous. At last, one vigil of the great feast, a lady came to Arthur's court at Camelot and asked Sir Launcelot to ride with her into the forest hard by, for a purpose not then to be revealed: Launcelot consenting, they rode together until they came to a nunnery hidden deep in the forest; and there the lady bade Launcelot dismount, and led him into a great and stately room. Presently, there entered twelve nuns and with them a youth, the fairest that Launcelot had ever seen. "Sir," said the nuns, "we have brought up this child in our midst and now that he is grown to manhood we pray you to make him knight, for of none worthier could he receive the honor." "Is this thy own desire?" asked Launcelot of the young squire; and when he said that so it was, Launcelot promised to make him knight after the great festival had been celebrated in the church next day.

So on the morrow, after they had worshipped, Launcelot knighted Galahad—for that was the youth's name—and asked him if he would ride at once with him to the king's court; but the young knight excusing himself, Sir Launcelot rode back alone to Camelot, where all rejoiced that he was returned in time to keep the feast with the whole Order of the Round Table.

Now, according to his custom, King Arthur was waiting for some marvel to befall before he and his knights sat down to the banquet. Presently, a squire entered the hall and said: "Sir King, a great wonder has appeared. There floats on the river a mighty stone, as it were a block of red marble, and it is thrust through by a sword, the hilt of which is set thick with precious stones." On hearing this, the King and all his knights went forth to view the stone and found it as the squire had said; moreover, looking closer, they read these words: "None shall draw me hence, but only he by whose side I must hang; and he shall be the best knight in all the world." Immediately, all bade Launcelot draw forth the sword, but he refused, saying that the sword was not for him. Then, at the king's command, Sir Gawain made the attempt and failed, as did Sir Percivale after him. So the knights knew the adventure was not for them and, returning to the hall, took their place about the Round Table.

No sooner were they seated than an aged man, clothed all in white, entered the hall, followed by a young knight in red armor, by whose side hung an empty scabbard. The old man approached King Arthur and bowing low before him, said: "Sir, I bring you a young knight of the house and lineage of Joseph of Arimathea, and through him shall great glory be won for all the land of Britain." Greatly did King Arthur rejoice to hear this and welcomed the two right loyally. Then when the young knight had saluted the King, the old man led him to the Siege Perilous and drew off its silken cover; and all the knights were amazed, for they saw that where had been engraved the words, "The Siege Perilous," was written now in shining gold: "This is the Siege of the noble prince, Sir Galahad."

Straightway the young man seated himself there where none other had ever sat without danger to his life; and all who saw it said, one to another: "Surely this is he that shall achieve the Holy Grail." Now the Holy Grail was the blessed dish from which Our Lord had eaten the Last Supper, and it had been brought to the land of Britain by Joseph of Arimathea; but because of men's sinfulness, it had been withdrawn from human sight, only that, from time to time, it appeared to the pure in heart.

When all had partaken of the royal banquet, King Arthur bade Sir Galahad come with him to the river's brink; and showing him the floating stone with the sword thrust through it, told him how his knights had failed to draw forth the sword. "Sir," said Galahad, "it is no marvel that they failed, for the adventure was meant for me, as my empty scabbard shows." So saying, lightly he drew the sword from the heart of the stone and lightly he slid it into the scabbard at his side. While all yet wondered at this adventure of the sword, there came riding to them a lady on a white palfrey who, saluting King Arthur, said: "Sir King, Nacien the hermit sends thee word that this day shall great honor be shown to thee and all thine house; for the Holy Grail shall appear in thy hall and thou and all thy fellowship shall be fed therefrom." And to Launcelot she said: "Sir Knight, thou hast ever been the best knight of all the world; but another has come to whom thou must yield precedence." Then Launcelot answered humbly: "I know well I was never the best." "Ay, of a truth thou wast and art still, of sinful men," said she, and rode away before any could question her further.

So that evening, when all were gathered about the Round Table, each knight in his own siege, suddenly there was heard a crash of thunder so mighty that the hall trembled, and there flashed into the hall a sunbeam brighter far than any that had ever before been seen and then, draped all in white samite, there glided through the air what none might see, yet what all knew to be the Holy Grail. And all the air was filled with sweet odors, and on every one was shed a light in which he looked fairer and nobler than ever before. So they sat in an amazed silence, till presently King Arthur rose and gave thanks to God for the grace given to him and to his court. Then up sprang Sir Gawain and made his avow to follow for a year and a day the Quest of the Holy Grail, if perchance he might be granted the vision of it. Immediately other of the knights followed his example, binding themselves to the Quest of the Holy Grail until, in all, one hundred and fifty had vowed themselves to the adventure.

Then was King Arthur grieved, for he foresaw the ruin of his noble Order. And turning to Sir Gawain, he said: "Nephew, ye have done ill, for through you I am bereft of the noblest company of knights that ever brought honor to any realm to Christendom. Well I know that never again shall all of you gather in this hall, and it grieves me to lose men I have loved as my life and through whom I have won peace and righteousness for all my realm." So the King mourned and his knights with him, but their oaths they could not recall.

THE VISION OF THE HOLY GRAIL

Sir Galahad rode on his way till nightfall, when he sought shelter at a little hermitage. Thither there came in the night a damsel who desired to speak with Sir Galahad; so he arose and went to her. "Galahad," said she, "arm you and mount your horse and follow me, for I am come to guide you in your quest." So they rode together until they had come to the seashore, and there the damsel showed Galahad a great ship into which he must enter. Then she bade him farewell and he, going on to the ship, found there already the good knights Sir Bors and Sir Percivale, who made much joy of the meeting. They abode in that ship until they had come to the castle of King Pelles, who welcomed them right gladly. Then, as they all sat at supper that night, suddenly the hall was filled with a great light, and the holy vessel appeared in their midst, covered all in white samite. While they all rejoiced, there came a voice saying: "My knights whom I have chosen, ye have seen the holy vessel dimly. Continue your journey to the city of Sarras and there the perfect Vision shall be yours."

Now in the city of Sarras had dwelt long time Joseph of Arimathea, teaching its people the true faith, before ever he came into the land of Britain; but when Sir Galahad and his fellows came there after long voyage, they found it ruled by a heathen king named Estorause, who cast them into a deep dungeon. There they were kept a year, but at the end of that time, the tyrant died. Then the great men of the land gathered together to consider who should be their King; and, while they were in council, came a voice bidding them take as their King the youngest of the three knights whom Estorause had thrown into prison. So in fear and wonder they hastened to the prison, and releasing the three knights, made Galahad king as the voice had bidden them.

Thus Sir Galahad became King of the famous city of Sarras, in far Babylon. He had reigned a year, when, one morning early, he and the other two knights, his fellows, went into the chapel, and there they saw, kneeling in prayer, an aged man, robed as a bishop, and round him hovered many angels. The knights fell on their knees in awe and reverence, whereupon he that seemed a bishop turned to them and said: "I am Joseph of Arimathea, and I am come to show you the perfect Vision of the Holy Grail." On the instant there appeared before them, without veil or cover, the holy vessel, in a radiance of light such as almost blinded them. Sir Bors and Sir Percivale, when at length they were recovered from the brightness of that glory, looked up to find that the holy Joseph and the wondrous vessel had passed from their sight. Then they went to Sir Galahad where he still knelt in prayer, and behold, he was dead; for it had been with him even as he had prayed; in the moment when he had seen the vision, his soul had gone back to God.

So the two knights buried him in that far city, themselves mourning and all the people with them. And immediately after, Sir Percivale put off his arms and took the habit of a monk, living a devout and holy life until, a year and two months later, he also died and was buried near Sir Galahad. Then Sir Bors armed him, and bidding farewell to the city, sailed away until, after many weeks, he came again to the land of Britain. There he took horse, and stayed not till he had come to Camelot. Great was the rejoicing of Arthur and all his knights when Sir Bors was once more among them. When he had told all the adventures which had befallen him and the good knights, his companions, all who heard were filled with amaze. But the King, he caused the wisest clerks in the land to write in great books this Quest of the Holy Grail, that the fame of it should endure unto all time.

THE FAIR MAID OF ASTOLAT

At last the Quest of the Holy Grail was ended, and by ones and twos the knights came back to Camelot, though many who had set out so boldly were never seen again about the Round Table.

Great was the joy of King Arthur when Sir Launcelot and Sir Bors returned, for, so long had they been away, that almost he had feared that they had perished. In their honor there was high festival for many days in London, where Arthur then had his court; and the King made proclamation of a great tournament that he would hold at Camelot, when he and the King of Northgalis would keep the lists against all comers.

So, one fair morning of spring, King Arthur made ready to ride to Camelot and all his knights with him, save Launcelot who excused himself, saying that an old wound hindered him from riding. But when the King, sore vexed, had departed, the Queen rebuked Sir Launcelot, and bade him go and prove his great prowess as of old. "Madam," said Sir Launcelot, "in this, as in all else, I obey you; at your bidding I go, but know that in this tournament I shall adventure me in other wise than ever before."

The next day at dawn, Sir Launcelot mounted his horse and, riding forth unattended, journeyed all that day till, as evening fell, he reached the little town of Astolat, and there, at the castle, sought lodgment for that night. The old Lord of Astolat was glad at his coming, judging him at once to be a noble knight, though he knew him not, for it was Sir Launcelot's will to remain unknown.

So they went to supper, Sir Launcelot and the old Lord, his son, Sir Lavaine, and his daughter Elaine, whom they of the place called the Fair Maid of Astolat. As they sat at meat, the Baron asked Sir Launcelot if he rode to the tournament. "Yea," answered Launcelot; "and right glad should I be if, of your courtesy, ye would lend me a shield without device." "Right willingly," said his host; "ye shall have my son, Sir Tirre's shield. He was but lately made knight and was hurt in his first encounter, so his shield is bare enough. If ye will take with you my young son, Sir Lavaine, he will be glad to ride in the company of so noble a knight and will do you such service as he may." "I shall be glad indeed of his fellowship," answered Sir Launcelot courteously.

Now it seemed to the fair Elaine that never had she beheld so noble a knight as this stranger; and seeing that he was as gentle and courteous as he was strong, she said to him: "Fair Knight, will ye wear my favor at this tournament? For never have I found knight yet to wear my crimson sleeve, and sure am I that none other could ever win it such honor." "Maiden," said Sir Launcelot, "right gladly would I serve you in aught; but it has never been my custom to wear lady's favor." "Then shall it serve better for disguise," answered Elaine. Sir Launcelot pondered her words, and at last he said: "Fair maiden, I will do for you what I have done for none, and will wear your favor." So with great glee, she brought it to him, a crimson velvet sleeve embroidered with great pearls, and fastened it in his helmet. Then Sir Launcelot begged her to keep for him his shield until after the tournament, when he would come for it and tell them his name. The next morn, Sir Launcelot took his departure with Sir Lavaine and, by evening, they were come to Camelot. Forthwith Sir Lavaine led Sir Launcelot to the house of a worthy burgher, where he might stay in privacy, undiscovered by those of his acquaintance. Then, when at dawn the trumpets blew, they mounted their horses and rode to a little wood hard by the lists, and there they abode some while; for Sir Launcelot would take no part until he had seen which side was the stronger. So they saw how King Arthur sat high on a throne to overlook the combat, while the King of Northgalis and all the fellowship of the Round Table held the lists against their opponents led by King Anguish of Ireland and the King of Scots.

Then it soon appeared that the two Kings with all their company could do but little against the Knights of the Round Table, and were sore pressed to maintain their ground. Seeing this, Sir Launcelot said to Sir Lavaine: "Sir Knight, will ye give me your aid if I go to the rescue of the weaker side? For it seems to me they may not much longer hold their own unaided." "Sir," answered Lavaine, "I will gladly follow you and do what I may." So the two laid their lances in rest and charged into the thickest of the fight and, with one spear, Sir Launcelot bore four knights from the saddle. Lavaine, too, did nobly, for he unhorsed the bold Sir Bedivere and Sir Lucan the Butler. Then with their swords they smote lustily on the left hand and on the right, and those whom they had come to aid rallying to them, they drove the Knights of the Round Table back a space. So the fight raged furiously, Launcelot ever being in the thickest of the press and performing such deeds of valor that all marveled to see him, and would fain know who was the Knight of the Crimson Sleeve. But the knights of Arthur's court felt shame of their discomfiture, and, in especial, those of Launcelot's kin were wroth that one should appear who seemed mightier even than Launcelot's self. So they called to each other and, making a rally, directed all their force against the stranger knight who had so turned the fortunes of the day. With lances in rest, Sir Lionel, Sir Bors, and Sir Ector, bore down together upon Sir Launcelot, and Sir Bors spear pierced Sir Launcelot and brought him to earth, leaving the spear head broken off in his side. This Sir Lavaine saw, and immediately, with all his might, he rode upon the King of Northgalis, unhorsed him and took his horse to Sir Launcelot. Now Sir Launcelot felt as he had got his death wound, but such was his spirit that he was resolved to do some great deed while yet his strength remained. So, with Lavaine's aid, he got upon the horse, took a spear and laying it in rest, bore down, one after the other, Sir Bors, Sir Lionel, and Sir Ector. Next he flung him into the thickest of the fight, and ere the trumpets sounded the signal to cease, he had unhorsed thirty knights.

Then the Kings of Scotland and Ireland came to Sir Launcelot and said: "Sir Knight, we thank you for the service done us this day. And now, we pray you, come with us to receive the prize which is rightly yours; for never have we seen such deeds as ye have seen this day." "My fair lords," answered Sir Launcelot, "for aught that I have accomplished, I am like to pay dearly; I beseech you, suffer me to depart." With these words, he rode away at a full gallop, followed by Sir Lavaine; and when he had come to a little wood, he called Lavaine to him, saying: "Gentle knight, I entreat you, draw forth this spear head, for it nigh slayeth me." "Oh! my dear lord," said Lavaine, "I feel sore to draw it forth lest ye die." "If ye love me, draw it out," answered Launcelot. So Lavaine did as he was bidden, and, with a deathly groan, Sir Launcelot fell in a swoon to the ground. When he was a little recovered, he begged Lavaine to help him to his horse and lead him to a hermitage hard by where dwelt a hermit, who, in bygone days, had been known to Launcelot for a good knight and true. So with pain and difficulty they journeyed to the hermitage, Lavaine oft fearing that Sir Launcelot would die. And when the hermit saw Sir Launcelot, all pale and besmeared with blood, he scarce knew him for the bold Sir Launcelot du Lac; but he bore him within and dressed his wounds and bade him be of good cheer, for he should recover. So there Sir Launcelot abode many weeks and Sir Lavaine with him; for Lavaine would not leave him, such love had he for the good knight he had taken for his lord.

Now when it was known that the victorious knight had departed from the field sore wounded, Sir Gawain vowed to go in search of him. So it chanced that, in his wanderings, he came to Astolat, and there he had a hearty welcome of the Lord of Astolat, who asked him for news of the tournament. Then Sir Gawain related how two stranger knights, bearing white shields, had won great glory, and in especial one, who wore in his helm a crimson sleeve, had surpassed all others in knightly prowess. At these words, the fair Elaine cried aloud with delight. "Maiden," said Gawain, "know ye this knight?" "Not his name," she replied; "but full sure was I that he was a noble knight when I prayed him to wear my favor." Then she showed Gawain the shield which she had kept wrapped in rich broideries, and immediately Sir Gawain knew it for Launcelot's. "Alas!" cried he, "without doubt it was Launcelot himself that we wounded to the death. Sir Bors will never recover the woe of it."

Then, on the morrow, Sir Gawain rode to London to tell the court how the stranger knight and Launcelot were one; but the Fair Maid of Astolat rose betimes, and having obtained leave of her father, set out in search for Sir Launcelot and her brother Lavaine. After many journeyings, she came one day upon Lavaine exercising his horse in a field, and by him she was taken to Sir Launcelot. Then, indeed, her heart was filled with grief when she saw the good knight to whom she had given her crimson sleeve thus laid low; so she abode in the hermitage, waiting upon Sir Launcelot and doing all within her power to lessen his pain.

After many weeks, by the good care of the hermit and the fair Elaine, Sir Launcelot was so far recovered that he might bear the weight of his armor and mount his horse again. Then, one morn, they left the hermitage and rode all three, the Fair Maid, Sir Launcelot, and Sir Lavaine, to the castle of Astolat, where there was much joy of their coming. After brief sojourn, Sir Launcelot desired to ride to court, for he knew there would be much sorrow among his kinsmen for his long absence. But when he would take his departure, Elaine cried aloud: "Ah! my lord, suffer me to go with you, for I may not bear to lose you." "Fair child," answered Sir Launcelot gently, "that may not be. But in the days to come, when ye shall love and wed some good knight, for your sake I will bestow upon him broad lands and great riches; and at all times will I hold me ready to serve you as a true knight may." Thus spoke Sir Launcelot, but the fair Elaine answered never a word.

So Sir Launcelot rode to London where the whole court was glad of his coming; but from the day of his departure, the Fair Maid drooped and pined until, when ten days were passed, she felt that her end was at hand. So she sent for her father and two brothers, to whom she said gently: "Dear father and brethren, I must now leave you." Bitterly they wept, but she comforted them all she might, and presently desired of her father a boon. "Ye shall have what ye will," said the old Lord; for he hoped that she might yet recover. Then first she required her brother, Sir Tirre, to write a letter, word for word as she said it; and when it was written, she turned to her father and said: "Kind father, I desire that, when I am dead, I may be arrayed in my finest raiment, and placed on a bier; and let the bier be set upon a barge, with one to steer it until I be come to London. Then, perchance, Sir Launcelot will come and look upon

Dora Curtis

Slowly the barge floated down the river.

[See page 283]

me with kindness." So she died, and all was done as she desired; for they set her, looking as fair as a lily, in a barge all hung with black, and an old dumb man went with her as helmsman.

Slowly the barge floated down the river until it had come to Westminster; and as it passed under the palace walls, it chanced that King Arthur and Queen Guinevere looked forth from a window. Marveling much at the strange sight, together they went forth to the quay, followed by many of the knights. Then the King espied the letter clasped in the dead maiden's hand, and drew it forth gently and broke the seal. And thus the letter ran: "Most noble knight, Sir Launcelot, I, that men called the Fair Maid of Astolat, am come hither to crave burial at thy hands for the sake of the unrequited love I gave thee. As thou art peerless knight, pray for my soul."

Then the King bade fetch Sir Launcelot, and when he was come, he showed him the letter. And Sir Launcelot, gazing on the dead maiden, was filled with sorrow. "My lord Arthur," he said, "for the death of this dear child I shall grieve my life long. Gentle she was and loving, and much was I beholden to her; but what she desired I could not give." "Yet her request now thou wilt grant, I know," said the King; "for ever thou art kind and courteous to all." "It is my desire," answered Sir Launcelot.

So the Maid of Astolat was buried in the presence of the King and Queen and of the Fellowship of the Round Table, and of many a gentle lady who wept, that time, the fair child's fate. Over her grave was raised a tomb of white marble, and on it was sculptured the shield of Sir Launcelot; for, when he had heard her whole story, it was the King's will that she that in life had guarded the shield of his noblest knight, should keep it also in death.

HOW MORDRED PLOTTED AGAINST LAUNCELOT

Before Merlin passed from the world of men, imprisoned in the great stone by the evil arts of Vivien, he had uttered many marvelous prophecies, and one that boded ill to King Arthur; for he foretold that, in the days to come, a son of Arthur's sister should stir up bitter war against the King, and at last a great battle should be fought in the West, when many a brave knight should find his doom.

Now, among the nephews of Arthur was one most dishonorable; his name was Mordred. No knightly deed had he ever done, and he hated to hear the good report of others because he himself was a coward and envious. But of all the Round Table there was none that Mordred hated more than Sir Launcelot du Lac, whom all true knights held in most honor; and not the less did Mordred hate Launcelot that he was the knight whom Queen Guinevere held in most esteem. So, at last, his jealous rage passing all bounds, he spoke evil of the Queen and of Sir Launcelot, saying that they were traitors to the King. Now Sir Gawain and Sir Gareth, Mordred's brothers, refused to give ear to these slanders, holding that Sir Launcelot, in his knightly service of the Queen, did honor to King Arthur also; but by ill-fortune, another brother, Sir Agravaine, had ill will to the Queen and professed to believe Mordred's evil tales. So the two went to King Arthur with their ill stories.

Now when Arthur had heard them he was wroth; for never would he lightly believe evil of any, and Sir Launcelot was the knight whom he loved above all others.

Sternly then he bade them begone and come no more to him with unproven tales against any, and, least of all, against Sir Launcelot and their lady the Queen.

The two departed, but in their hearts was hatred against Launcelot and the Queen, more bitter than ever for the rebuke they had called down upon themselves; and they resolved, from that time forth, diligently to watch if, perchance, they might find aught to turn to evil account against Sir Launcelot.

Not long after, it seemed to them that the occasion had come. For King Arthur having ridden forth to hunt far from Carlisle, where he then held court, the Queen sent for Sir Launcelot to speak with her in her bower. Then Agravaine and Mordred got together twelve knights, friends of Sir Gawain, their brother, and persuaded them to come with them for they would do the King a service. So with the twelve knights they watched and waited in a little room until they saw Sir Launcelot, all unarmed, pass into the Queen's chamber; and when the door was closed upon him, they came forth, and Sir Agravaine and Sir Mordred thundered on the door, crying so that all the court might hear: "Thou traitor, Sir Launcelot, come forth from the Queen's chamber. Come forth, for thy treason against the King is known to all!"

Then Sir Launcelot and the Queen were amazed and filled with shame that such a clamor should be raised where the Queen was. While they waited and listened in dismay, Sir Mordred and Sir Agravaine took up the cry again, the twelve knights echoing it: "Traitor Launcelot, come forth and meet thy doom; for thy last hour is come." Then Sir Launcelot, wroth more for the Queen than for himself, exclaimed: "This shameful cry will kill me; better death than such dishonor. Lady, as I have ever been your true knight, since the day when my lord, King Arthur, knighted me, pray for me if now I meet my death." Then he went to the door and cried to those without: "Fair lords, cease this outcry. I will open the door, and then ye shall do with me as ye will." With the word, he set open the door, but only by so much that one knight could enter at a time. So a certain Sir Colgrevance of Gore, a knight of great stature, pushed into the room and thrust at Sir Launcelot with all his might; but Sir Launcelot, with the arm round which he had wrapped his cloak, turned aside the sword and, with his bare hand, dealt Colgrevance such a blow on the helmet that he fell groveling to the earth. Then Sir Launcelot thrust to and barred the door, and stripping the fallen knight of his armor, armed himself in haste with the aid of the Queen and her ladies.

All this while, Sir Agravaine and Sir Mordred continued their outcry; so when he was armed, Sir Launcelot called to them to cease their vile crys and the next day he would meet any or all of them in arms and knightly disprove their vile slander. Now there was not one among those knights who dared meet Sir Launcelot in the open field, so they were resolved to slay him while they had the advantage over him. When Sir Launcelot understood their evil purpose, he set wide the door and rushed upon them. At the first blow, he slew Sir Agravaine, and soon eleven other knights lay cold on the earth beside him.

Only Mordred escaped, for he fled with all his might; but, even so, he was sore wounded.

Then Sir Launcelot spoke to the Queen. "Madam," said he, "here may I no longer stay, for many a foe have I made this night. And when I am gone, I know not what evil may be spoken of you for this night's work. I pray you then, suffer me to lead you to a place of safety." "Ye shall run no more risk for my sake," said the Queen; "only go hence in haste before more harm befall you. But as for me, here I abide. I will flee for no traitor's outcry."

So Sir Launcelot, seeing that at that time there was nought he might do for Queen Guinevere, withdrew with all his kin to a little distance from Carlisle, and awaited what should befall.

THE TRIAL OF THE QUEEN

When Mordred escaped Sir Launcelot, he got to horse, all wounded as he was, and never drew rein until he had found King Arthur, to whom he told all that had happened.

Then great was the King's grief. Despite all that Mordred could say, he was slow to doubt Sir Launcelot, whom he loved, but his mind was filled with forebodings; for many a knight had been slain, and well he knew that their kin would seek vengeance on Sir Launcelot, and the noble fellowship of the Round Table be utterly destroyed by their feuds.

All too soon, it proved even as the King had feared. Many were found to hold with Sir Mordred; some because they were kin to the knights that had been slain, some from envy of the honor and worship of the noble Sir Launcelot; and among them even were those who dared to raise their voice against the Queen herself, calling for judgment upon her as leagued with a traitor against the King, and as having caused the death of so many good knights. Now in those days the law was that if anyone were accused of treason by witnesses, or taken in the act, that one should die the death by burning, be it man or woman, knight or churl. So then the murmurs grew to a loud clamor that the law should have its course, and that King Arthur should pass sentence on the Queen. Then was the King's

woe doubled; "For," said he, "I sit as King to be a rightful judge
and keep all the law; wherefore I may not do battle for my own
Queen, and now there is none other to help her." So a decree was
issued that Queen Guinevere should be burnt at the stake outside the
walls of Carlisle.

Forthwith, King Arthur sent for his nephew, Sir Gawain, and
said to him: "Fair nephew, I give it in charge to you to see that all
is done as has been decreed." But Sir Gawain answered boldly: "Sir
King, never will I be present to see my lady the Queen die. It is of
ill counsel that you have consented to her death." Then the King
bade Gawain send his two young brothers, Sir Gareth and Sir
Gaheris to receive his commands, and these he desired to attend the
Queen to the place of execution. So Gareth made answer for both:
"My Lord the King, we owe you obedience in all things, but know
that it is sore against our wills that we obey you in this; nor will we
appear in arms in the place where that noble lady shall die"; then
sorrowfully they mounted their horses and rode to Carlisle.

When the day appointed had come, the Queen was led forth to a
place without the walls of Carlisle, and there she was bound to the
stake to be burnt to death. Loud were her ladies' lamentations, and
many a lord was found to weep at that grievous sight of a Queen
brought so low; yet was there none who dared to come forward as
her champion, lest he should be suspected of treason. As for Gareth
and Gaheris, they could not bear the sight and stood with their faces
covered in their mantles. Then, just as the torch was to be applied
to the fagots, there was a sound as of many horses galloping, and the
next instant a band of knights rushed upon the astonished throng,
their leader cutting down all who crossed his path until he had
reached the Queen, whom he lifted to his saddle and bore from the
press. Then all men knew that it was Sir Launcelot, come knightly
to rescue the Queen, and in their hearts they rejoiced. So with little
hindrance they rode away, Sir Launcelot and all his kin with the
Queen in their midst, till they came to the castle of the Joyous Garde
where they held the Queen in safety and all reverence.

But of that day came a kingdom's ruin; for among the slain were
Gawain's brothers Sir Gareth and Sir Gaheris. Now Sir Launcelot

loved Sir Gareth as if he had been his own younger brother, and himself had knighted him; but, in the press, he struck at him and killed him, not seeing that he was unarmed and weaponless; and in like wise, Sir Gaheris met his death. So when word was brought to King Arthur of what had passed, Sir Gawain asked straightway how his brothers had fared. "Both are slain," said the messenger. "Alas! my dear brothers!" cried Sir Gawain; "how came they by their death?" "They were both slain by Sir Launcelot." "That will I never believe," cried Sir Gawain; "for my brother, Sir Gareth, had such love for Sir Launcelot there was naught he could ask that he would not do." But the man said again: "He is slain, and by Sir Launcelot."

Then from sheer grief, Sir Gawain fell swooning to the ground. When he was recovered, he said: "My lord and uncle, is it even as this man says, that Sir Launcelot has slain my brother Sir Gareth?" "Alas!" said the King, "Launcelot rode upon him in the press and slew him, not seeing who he was or that he was unarmed." "Then," cried Gawain fiercely, "here I make my avow. Never, while my life lasts, will I leave Sir Launcelot in peace until he has rendered me account for the slaying of my brother." From that day forth, Sir Gawain would not suffer the King to rest until he had gathered all his host and marched against the Joyous Garde. Thus began the war which broke up the fellowship of the Round Table.

HOW KING ARTHUR AND SIR GAWAIN WENT TO FRANCE

Now King Arthur was loath to war upon Sir Launcelot, and seeing this, Sir Gawain upbraided him bitterly. "I see well it is nought to you that my brother, Sir Gareth, died fulfilling your behest. Little ye care if all your knights be slain, if only the traitor Launcelot escape. Since, then, ye will not do me justice nor avenge your own nephew, I and my fellows will take the traitor when and how we may. He trusts in his own might that none can encounter with him; let see if we may not entrap him."

Thus urged, King Arthur called his army together and bade collect a great fleet; for rather would he fight openly with Sir Launcelot than that Sir Gawain should bring such dishonor upon himself as to slay a noble knight treacherously. So with a great host, the King passed overseas to France, leaving Sir Mordred to rule Britain in his stead.

When Sir Launcelot heard that King Arthur and Sir Gawain were coming against him, he withdrew into the strong castle of Benwick; for unwilling, indeed, was he to fight with the King, or to do an injury to Sir Gareth's brother. The army passed through the land, laying it waste, and presently encamped about the castle, besieging it closely; but so thick were the walls and so watchful the garrison that in no way could they prevail against it.

One day, there came to Sir Launcelot seven brethren, brave knights of Wales, who had joined their fortunes to his, and said: "Sir Launcelot, bid us sally forth against this host which has invaded and laid waste your lands, and we will scatter it; for we are not wont to cower behind walls." "Fair lords," answered Launcelot, "it is grief to me to war on good Christian knights and especially on my lord, King Arthur. Have but patience and I will send to him and see if, even now, there may not be a treaty of peace between us, for better far is peace than war." So Sir Launcelot sought out a damsel and, mounting her upon a palfrey, bade her ride to King Arthur's camp and require of the King to cease warring on his lands, proffering fair terms of peace. When the damsel came to the camp, there met her Sir Lucan the Butler. "Fair damsel," said Sir Lucan, "do ye come from Sir Launcelot?" "Yea, in good truth," said the damsel; "and, I pray you, lead me to King Arthur." "Now may ye prosper in your errand," said Sir Lucan. "Our King loves Sir Launcelot dearly and wishes him well; but Sir Gawain will not suffer him to be reconciled to him." So when the damsel had come before the King, she told him all her tale, and much she said of Sir Launcelot's love and good will to his lord the King, so that the tears stood in Arthur's eyes. But Sir Gawain broke in roughly: "My lord and uncle, shall it be said of us that we came hither with such a host to hie us home again, nothing done, to be the scoff of all men?" "Nephew," said the King, "methinks Sir Launcelot offers fair and generously. It were well if ye would accept his proffer. Nevertheless, as the quarrel is yours, so shall the answer be." "Then, damsel," said Sir Gawain, "say unto Sir Launcelot that the time for peace is past. And tell him that I, Sir Gawain, swear by the faith I owe to knighthood that never will I forego my revenge."

So the damsel returned to Sir Launcelot and told him all. Sir Launcelot's heart was filled with grief nigh unto breaking; but his knights were enraged and clamored that he had endured too much of insult and wrong, and that he should lead them forth to battle. Sir Launcelot armed him sorrowfully and presently the gates were set open and he rode forth, he and all his company. But to all his knights he had given commandment that none should seek King Arthur; "For never," said he, "will I see the noble King who made me knight, either killed or shamed."

Fierce was the battle between those two hosts. On Launcelot's side, Sir Bor and Sir Lavaine and many another did right well; while on the other side, King Arthur bore him as the noble knight he was, and Sir Gawain raged through the battle, seeking to come at Sir Launcelot. Presently, Sir Bors encountered with King Arthur and unhorsed him. This Sir Launcelot saw and, coming to the King's side, he alighted and raising him from the ground, mounted him upon his own horse. Then King Arthur, looking upon Launcelot, cried: "Ah! Launcelot, Launcelot! That ever there should be war between us two!" and tears stood in the King's eyes. "Ah! my Lord Arthur," cried Sir Launcelot, "I pray you stay this war." As they spoke thus, Sir Gawain came upon them and, miscalling Sir Launcelot traitor and coward, had almost ridden upon him before Launcelot could provide him of another horse. Then the two hosts drew back, each on its own side to see the battle between Sir Launcelot and Sir Gawain; for they wheeled their horses and, departing far asunder, rushed again upon each other with the noise of thunder, and each bore the other from his horse. Then they put their shields before them and set on each other with their swords; but while ever Sir Gawain smote fiercely, Sir Launcelot was content only to ward off blows, because he would not, for Sir Gareth's sake, do any harm to Sir Gawain. But the more Sir Launcelot forebore him the more furiously Sir Gawain struck, so that Sir Launcelot had much ado to defend himself and, at the last, smote Gawain on the helm so mightily that he bore him to the ground. Then Sir Launcelot stood back from Sir Gawain. But Gawain cried: "Why do ye draw back, traitor knight? Slay me while ye may, for never will I cease to be your enemy while my life lasts." "Sir," said Launcelot, "I shall withstand you as I may; but never will I smite a fallen knight." Then he spoke to King Arthur: "My Lord, I pray you, if but for this day, draw off your men. And think upon our former love if ye may; but, be ye friend or foe, God keep you." Thereupon Sir Launcelot drew off with his men into his castle and King Arthur and his company to their tents. As for Sir Gawain, his squires bore him to his tent where his wounds were dressed.

MORDRED THE TRAITOR

So Sir Gawain lay healing of the grim wound which Sir Launcelot had given him, and there was peace between the two armies, when there came messengers from Britain bearing letters for King Arthur; and more evil news than they brought might not well be, for they told how Sir Mordred had usurped his uncle's realm. First, he had caused it to be noised abroad that King Arthur was slain in battle with Sir Launcelot and, since there be many ever ready to believe any idle rumor and eager for any change, it had been no hard task for Sir Mordred to call the lords to a Parliament and persuade them to make him king. But the Queen could not be brought to believe that her lord was dead, so she took refuge in the Tower of London from Sir Mordred's violence, nor was she to be induced to leave her strong refuge for aught that Mordred could promise or threaten.

This was the news that came to Arthur as he lay encamped about Sir Launcelot's castle of Benwick. Forthwith, he bade his host make ready to move and, when they had reached the coast, they embarked and made sail to reach Britain with all possible speed.

Sir Mordred, on his part, had heard of their sailing and hasted to get together a great army. It was grievous to see how many a stout knight held by Mordred, ay, even many whom Arthur himself had raised to honor and fortune; for it is the nature of men to be fickle. Thus it was that, when Arthur drew near to Dover, he found Mordred with a mighty host waiting to oppose his landing. Then there was a great sea fight, those of Mordred's party going out in boats, great and small, to board King Arthur's ships and slay him and his men or ever they should come to land. Right valiantly did King Arthur bear him, as was his wont, and boldly his followers fought in his cause, so that at last they drove off their enemies and landed at Dover in spite of Mordred and his array. For that time, Mordred fled and King Arthur bade those of his party bury the slain and tend the wounded.

So as they passed from ship to ship, salving and binding the hurts of the men, they came at last upon Sir Gawain, where he lay at the bottom of a boat, wounded to the death, for he had received a great blow on the wound that Sir Launcelot had given him. They bore him to his tent and his uncle, the King, came to him, sorrowing beyond measure. "Methinks," said the King, "my joy on earth is done; for never have I loved any men as I have loved you, my nephew, and Sir Launcelot. Sir Launcelot I have lost, and now I see you on your deathbed." "My King," said Sir Gawain, "my hour is come and I have got my death at Sir Launcelot's hand; for I am smitten on the wound he gave me. And rightly am I served, for of my willfulness and stubbornness comes this unhappy war. I pray you, my uncle, raise me in your arms and let me write to Sir Launcelot before I die."

Thus, then, Sir Gawain wrote: "To Sir Launcelot, the noblest of all knights, I, Gawain, send greeting before I die. For I am smitten on the wound ye gave me before your castle of Benwick in France, and I bid all men bear witness that I sought my own death and that ye are innocent of it. I pray you, by our friendship of old, come again into Britain and, when ye look upon my tomb, pray for Gawain of Orkney. Farewell."

So Sir Gawain died and was buried in the Chapel at Dover.

THE BATTLE IN THE WEST

The day after the battle at Dover, King Arthur and his host pursued Sir Mordred to Barham Down where again there was a great

King Arthur gives Excalibur to Sir Bedivere.

[See page 295]

Dora Curtis

King Arthur gives Excalibur to Sir Bedivere.

[See page 303]

battle fought, with much slaughter on both sides; but, in the end, Arthur was victorious, and Mordred fled to Canterbury.

Now by this time, many that Mordred had cheated by his lying reports, had drawn unto King Arthur, to whom at heart they had ever been loyal, knowing him for a true and noble King and hating themselves for having been deceived by such a false usurper as Sir Mordred. Then when he found that he was being deserted, Sir Mordred withdrew to the far West, for there men knew less of what had happened and so he might still find some to believe in him and support him; and being without conscience, he even called to his aid the heathen hosts that his uncle, King Arthur, had driven from the land in the good years when Launcelot was of the Round Table.

King Arthur followed ever after, for in his heart was bitter anger against the false nephew who had brought woe upon him and all his realm. At the last, when Mordred could flee no further, the two hosts were drawn up near the shore of the great western sea; and it was the Feast of the Holy Trinity.

That night, as King Arthur slept, he thought that Sir Gawain stood before him, looking just as he did in life, and said to him: "My uncle and my King, God in his great love has suffered me to come unto you, to warn you that in no wise ye fight on the morrow; for if ye do, ye shall be slain and with you the most part of the people on both sides. Make ye, therefore, treaty for a month and within that time, Sir Launcelot shall come to you with all his knights and ye shall overthrow the traitor and all that hold with him." Therewith Sir Gawain vanished. Immediately, the King awoke and called to him the best and wisest of his knights, the two brethren, Sir Lucan the Butler and Sir Bedivere, and others, to whom he told his dream. Then all were agreed that on any terms whatsoever, a treaty should be made with Sir Mordred, even as Sir Gawain had said; and with the dawn, messengers went to the camp of the enemy to call Sir Mordred to a conference. So it was determined that the meeting should take place in the sight of both armies, in an open space between the two camps, and that King Arthur and Mordred should each be accompanied by fourteen knights. Little enough faith had either in the other, so when they set forth to the meeting they bade their hosts join battle if ever they saw a sword drawn. Thus they went to the conference.

Now as they talked, it befell that an adder, coming out of a bush hard by, stung a knight in the foot; and he, seeing the snake, drew his sword to kill it and thought no harm thereby. But on the instant that the sword flashed, the trumpets blared on both sides, and the two hosts rushed to battle. Never was there fought a fight of such bitter enmity, for brother fought with brother, and comrade with comrade, and fiercely they cut and thrust, with many a bitter word between; while King Arthur himself, his heart hot within him, rode through and through the battle, seeking the traitor Mordred. So they fought all day till at last the evening fell. Then Arthur, looking around him, saw of his valiant knights but two left, Sir Lucan and Sir Bedivere, and these sore wounded; and there, over against him, by a great heap of the dead, stood Sir Mordred, the cause of all this ruin. Thereupon the King, his heart nigh broken with grief for the loss of his true knights, cried with a loud voice. "Traitor! now is thy doom upon thee!" and with his spear gripped in both hands, he rushed upon Sir Mordred and smote him that the weapon stood out a fathom behind. And Sir Mordred knew that he had his death wound. With all the might that he had, he thrust him up the spear to the haft and, with his sword, struck King Arthur upon the head that the steel pierced the helmet and bit into the head; then he fell back, stark and dead.

Sir Lucan and Sir Bedivere went to the King where he lay, swooning from the blow, and bore him to a little chapel on the sea shore. As they laid him on the ground, Sir Lucan fell dead beside the King, and Arthur, coming to himself, found but Sir Bedivere alive beside him.

THE PASSING OF ARTHUR

So King Arthur lay wounded to the death, grieving, not that his end was come, but for the desolation of his kingdom and the loss of his good knights. And looking upon the body of Sir Lucan, he sighed and said: "Alas! true knight, dead for my sake! If I lived, I should ever grieve for thy death, but now mine own end draws nigh." Then turning to Sir Bedivere, who stood sorrowing beside him, he said: "Leave weeping now, for the time is short and much to do. Hereafter shalt thou weep if thou wilt. But take now my sword Excalibur, hasten to the waterside and fling it into the deep. Then watch what happens and bring me word thereof." "My Lord," said Sir Bedivere, "your command shall be obeyed"; and taking the sword, he departed. But as he went on his way, he looked on the sword, how wondrously it was formed, and the hilt all studded with precious stones; and, as he looked, he called to mind the marvel by which it had come into the King's keeping. For on a certain day, as Arthur walked on the shore of a great lake, there had appeared above the surface of the water a hand brandishing a sword. On the instant the King had leaped into a boat, and, rowing into the lake, had got the sword and brought it back to land. Then he had seen how, on one side the blade, was written, "Keep me," but on the other, "Throw me away," and sore perplexed, he had shown it to Merlin, the great wizard, who said: "Keep it now. The time for casting away has not yet come." Thinking on this, it seemed to Bedivere that no good, but harm, must come of obeying the King's word; so hiding the sword under a tree, he hastened back to the little chapel. Then said the King:

"What saw'st thou?" "Sir," answered Bedivere, "I saw nought but the waves, heard nought but the wind." "That is untrue," said King Arthur; "I charge thee, as thou art true knight, go again and spare not to throw away the sword."

Sir Bedivere departed a second time and his mind was to obey his lord; but when he took the sword in his hand, he thought: "Sin it is and shameful, to throw away so glorious a sword." Then hiding it again, he hastened back to the King. "What saw'st thou?" said Sir Arthur. "Sir, I saw the water lap on the crags." Then spoke the King in great wrath: "Traitor and unkind! Twice hast thou betrayed me! Art dazzled by the splendor of the jewels, thou that till now hast ever been dear and true to me? Go yet again, but if thou fail me this time, I will arise and with mine own hands slay thee."

Then Sir Bedivere left the King and, that time, he took the sword quickly from the place where he had hidden it and, forbearing even to look upon it, he twisted the belt about it and flung it with all his force into the water. A wondrous sight he saw, for, as the sword touched the water, a hand rose from out the deep, caught it, brandished it thrice and drew it beneath the surface.

So Bedivere hastened back to the King and told him what he had seen. "It is well," said Arthur; "now, bear me to the water's edge and hasten, I pray thee, for I have tarried overlong and my wound has taken cold." So Sir Bedivere raised the King on his back and bore him tenderly to the lonely shore, where the lapping waves floated many an empty helmet and the fitful moonlight fell on the upturned faces of the dead. Scarce had they reached the shore when there hove in sight a barge, and on its deck stood three tall women, robed all in black and wearing crowns on their heads. "Place me in the barge," said Arthur, and softly Sir Bedivere lifted the King into it. And these three Queens wept sore over Arthur, and one took his head in her lap and chafed his hands, crying: "Alas! my brother, thou hast been overlong in coming and I fear me thy wound has taken cold." Then the barge began to move slowly from the land. When Sir Bedivere saw this, he lifted up his voice and cried with a bitter cry: "Ah! my Lord Arthur, thou art taken from me! And I, whither shall I go?" "Comfort thyself," said the King, "for in me is no comfort more. I pass to the Valley of Avalon, to heal me of my grievous wound. If thou seest me never again, pray for me."

So the barge floated away out of sight and Sir Bedivere stood straining his eyes after it till it had vanished utterly. Then he turned him about and journeyed through the forest until, at daybreak, he reached a hermitage. Entering it, he prayed the holy hermit that he might abide with him and there he spent the rest of his life in prayer and holy exercise.

But of King Arthur is no more known. Some men, indeed, say that he is not dead, but abides in the happy Valley of Avalon until such time as his country's need is sorest, when he shall come again and deliver it. Others say that, of a truth he is dead and that, in the far West, his tomb may be seen and written on it these words:

"Here lies Arthur, once King and King to be."

The Mabinogion

The Mabinogion

*Knightly legends of Wales, translated from the
manuscript book, "Red Book of Hergest," and
called the Mabinogion.*

THE HUNTING OF THE BOAR

By PADRAIC COLUM

Illustration by Wilfred Jones

HOW THE YOUTH KILHUCH CAME TO KING ARTHUR'S COURT

THUS the youth rode to the Court of King Arthur; the horse that was under him was of four winters old, firm of limb, with head of dappled gray, with shell-formed hoofs, having a bridle of linked gold on its head, and on its back a saddle of gold. In the youth's hands were two spears of silver, sharp and well-tempered, of an edge to wound the wind, and swifter than the fall of a dewdrop from the blade of reed-grass upon the earth when the dew of June is at its heaviest. A gold-hilted sword was upon his thigh, the blade of which was of gold, bearing a cross of inlaid gold of the hue of the lightning of heaven, and his war-horn was of ivory. Before him were two brindled, white-breasted greyhounds, having strong collars of rubies about their necks. And the hound that was on his left side bounded across to the right side, and the one on his right to his left, and like two sea-swallows they sported around him. His horse, as it coursed along, cast up four sods with its four hoofs, like four swallows in the air, about his head, now above, now below. About him was a four-cornered cloth of purple, and an apple of gold was at each corner, and every one of the apples was of the value of a hundred kine. And there was precious gold of the value of three hundred kine upon his shoes, and upon his stirrups, from his knee to the tip of his toe. And the blade of grass bent not beneath him, so light was his courser's tread as he journeyed toward King Arthur's palace.

When he came before the palace, the youth called out, "Open the gate." "I will not open it," said the porter. "Wherefore not?" asked the youth. "The knife is in the meat, and the drink is in the horn, and there is revelry in Arthur's hall, and none may enter therein except the son of a King of a privileged country, or a craftsman bringing here his craft. Stay thou outside. There will be refreshment for thy hounds and for thy horse, and for thee there will be collops of meat cooked and peppered, and luscious wine, and mirthful songs. A lady shall smooth thy couch for thee and lull thee with her singing; and early in the morning, when the gate is open for the multitude that came hither today, for thee it shall be opened first, and thou mayest sit in the place that thou shalt choose in Arthur's hall." Said the youth, "That I will not do. If thou openest the gate for me, it is well. But if thou dost not open it, I will set up three shouts at this very gate, and these shouts will be deadly to all." "What clamor soever thou mayest make," said the porter, "against the law of King Arthur's palace thou shalt not enter until I go first and speak with the King."

So the porter went into the hall. The King said to him when he came near, "Hast thou news from the gate?" The porter said, "Half my life is past, and half of thine. I have seen with thee supreme sovereigns, but never did I behold one of equal dignity with him who is now at thy gate." Then said King Arthur to him, "If walking thou didst enter, return thou running. It is unbecoming to keep such a one as thou sayest he is outside in wind and rain." Then said the knight Kay who was in Arthur's hall at the time, "By the hand of my friend, if thou wouldst follow my counsel, thou wouldst not break the laws of thy court because of him." "Not so, blessed Kay," said Arthur. "The greater our courtesy, the greater will be our renown, and our fame, and our glory." And by this time the porter was back at the gate.

He opened the gate before the youth who had been waiting before it. Now, although all comers dismounted upon the horse block that was at the gate, yet did he not dismount, but he rode right in on his horse. "Greeting be unto thee, sovereign ruler of the Island," he said, "and be this greeting no less unto the lowest than unto the highest, and be it equally unto thy guests, and thy warriors, and thy chieftains—let all partake of it equally with thyself. And complete be thy favor, and thy fame, and thy glory throughout all this Island." "Greeting be unto thee also," said King Arthur. "Sit thou between two of my warriors, and thou shalt have minstrels before thee, and thou shalt enjoy the privileges of a King born to a throne, as long as thou remainest here." Said the youth, "I came not to consume meat and drink; but if I obtain the boon that I have come seeking, I will requite it thee." Then said Arthur: "Since thou wilt not remain here, Chieftain, thou shalt receive the boon whatsoever thy tongue may name, as far as the wind dries, and the rain moistens, and the sun revolves, and the sea encircles, and the earth extends; any boon thy tongue may name save only my ship and my mantle, my sword and my lance, my shield and my dagger, and Guinevere, my wife. By the truth of Heaven, thou shalt have it cheerfully, name what thou wilt. For my heart warms unto thee, and I know thou art of my blood." "Of thy blood I am indeed," said the youth, "for my mother was thy mother's sister, Prince Anlod's daughter." Thereupon he told the King of his birth and his upbringing.

Kilhuch he was called, and he was given that name because he was born in a swine's pen. Before he was born, his mother became wild, and she wandered about, without habitation. Then she came to a mountain where there was a swineherd, keeping a herd of swine; there she stayed, and in the swine's pen her son was born. The swineherd took the boy, and brought him to the palace of his father, and there he was christened. Afterwards he was sent to be reared in another place.

His mother died soon afterwards. When she knew she was going to die, she sent for the Prince, her husband, and she said to him, "I charge thee not to take a wife until thou seest a briar with two blossoms growing out of my grave." And she asked him to have the grave tended, day by day, and year by year, so that nothing might grow on it. This he promised her, and soon after she died.

For seven years the Prince sent an attendant every morning to dress her grave and to see if anything were growing upon it. But at the end of the seventh year he neglected to do that which he had promised to his wife. Then one day he went hunting. He passed by the place of burial and he saw a briar growing out of his wife's grave. He knew then that the time had come for him to seek another wife. He sought for one, and he married again, and brought another lady into his palace.

A day came when the lady he married went walking abroad. She came to the house of an old crone, and going within she said to the woman, "Old woman, tell me that which I shall ask thee. Where are the children of the man who has married me?" "Children he has none," said the crone. "Woe is me," said the lady, "that I have come to one who is childless." "Children he has none," said the crone, "but a child he has. Thou needst not lament."

Then the lady returned to the palace, and she said to her husband, "Wherefore hast thou concealed thy child from me?" The Prince said, "I will do so no longer." He sent messengers for Kilhuch, and the youth was brought into the palace.

Now when his stepmother saw him she was fearful that he would take the whole of his father's possessions away from her own child, for it was predicted to her by the crone that she would have a son. So she said to him when she looked on him, "It were well for thee to have a wife." The youth answered, "I am not yet of an age to wed," but although he said this he was well grown at the time. His stepmother said to him, "I declare to thee that it is thy destiny not to be suited until thou obtain Olwen, the daughter of Yspaddaden, the Chief of the Giants, for thy wife."

Hearing that name the youth blushed, and the love of the maiden named was diffused through all his frame, although he had never seen her. He went to his father and he told him that it had been declared to him that he would never be suited until he had obtained the daughter of Yspaddaden for his wife. "That will not be hard for thee to do," said his father, "for King Arthur is thy cousin, and he will aid thee. Go to Arthur, therefore. And ask him to cut thy hair, as great lords cut the hair of youths who are dear to them. And as he cuts thy hair ask it of him as a boon that he obtain for thee Olwen, the daughter of Yspaddaden." Then Kilhuch mounted his steed and rode off to the Court of King Arthur.

"I crave it as a boon," said Kilhuch, "that thou, King Arthur, cut my hair." "That shall be granted thee," said the King. "Tomorrow I will do it for thee." Then, on the morrow, King Arthur took a golden comb, and scissors whereof the loops were of silver, and he made ready to cut Kilhuch's hair.

All King Arthur's warriors and chieftains were in the hall, and Guinevere, Arthur's wife, was there also, when the King did honor to Kilhuch by cutting his hair for him.

HOW THEY SOUGHT THE MAID OLWEN

And now Killhuch's hair was cut by the hand of Arthur. Then all the champions and warriors in the hall gathered around them to hear what boon the youth would ask of the King. "Whatsoever boon thou mayest ask, thou shalt receive it, be it what it may that thy tongue shall name," said King Arthur. "Pledge the truth of Heaven and the faith of thy kingdom thereon," said Kîlhuch. "I pledge it thee, gladly." "I crave of thee then, that thou obtain for me Olwen, the daughter of Yspaddaden, and this boon I seek likewise at the hands of thy warriors. I seek it from Kay and Bedour, and the hundred others who are here."

Then said Arthur, "I have never heard of the maiden of whom thou speakest, nor of her kindred, but I will gladly send messengers in search of her. Give me time to seek her for thee." The youth then said, "I willingly grant from this night to that at the end of the year."

King Arthur thereupon sent messengers to every land to seek for the maiden who was named Olwen. At the end of the year the messengers returned without having gained any more knowledge or intelligence concerning her than on the day they went forth.

And when the year had come to its end Kilhuch said: "Everyone has received his boon, and yet I lack mine. I will depart from this place, and the blame for my going will be upon King Arthur." Then said Kay: "Rash youth! Dost thou lay blame on Arthur? Go with us, and we will not part from each other until thou dost confess that the maiden exists not in the world, or until we obtain her for thee." Kay rose up, and thereupon King Arthur called upon Bedour, who never shrank from any enterprise upon which Kay was bound. None was equal to him in swiftness throughout the Island. And although he was one-handed, three warriors could not shed blood faster than he on the field of battle. Another quality he had: his lance could produce a wound equal to those of nine opposing lances. And Arthur called upon Gwalchmai, because he never returned home without achieving the adventure of which he went in quest. He was the best of footmen and the best of knights. He was nephew to Arthur, the son of his sister and his cousin. And Arthur called upon his guide to go with them; as good a guide was he in a land which he had never seen as he was in his own. And he called upon one who knew all tongues to go with them also, and he called upon another, who, if they were in a savage country, could cast a charm and an illusion over them, so that none might see them whilst they could see everyone. And so, with Kay, and Bedour, and Gwalchmai, with the guide, and the one who knew all tongues, and the one who could cast a charm and an illusion, the youth Kilhuch went forth from Arthur's Court in quest of Olwen, the daughter of Yspaddaden.

They went on until they came to a vast open plain. They saw a castle in the middle of it, and it seemed to them to be the fairest castle in the world. They went toward it; that day they journeyed until evening, and when they thought they were nigh the castle, they were no nearer to it than they had been in the morning. And the second and third day they journeyed, and even then scarcely could they reach so far. But at last they came nigh it. And when they were before the castle they beheld a vast flock of sheep, a flock boundless and without end. And upon the top of a mound there was a herdsman keeping the sheep.

They went nearer, and they saw that a mantle of skins was upon the man, and that by his side there was a shaggy mastiff, larger than a steed of nine winters old. And all the trees that were dead and burnt on the plain that mastiff had burnt with his breath down to the very ground.

Then said Kay to the one who knew all tongues: "Go thou and salute yonder man." "Kay," said he in reply, "I engaged not to go farther than thou thyself." "Let us go together then," said Kay. Said the man of spells who was with them: "Fear not to go thither, for

I will cast a spell upon the hound, so that he shall injure no one."
And this he did.

They went up to the mound where the herdsman was, and they
said to him: "How dost thou fare, O herdsman! Whose are the sheep
that thou dost keep, and to whom does yonder castle belong?"
"Stupid are ye, truly," said the herdsman. "Through the whole
world it is known that this is the castle of Yspaddaden." "And who
art thou?" they asked. "I am Custennin, and my brother is Yspaddaden," said the herdsman, "but he oppressed me because of my
possessions. And ye, also, who are ye?" "We are men on an embassy
from King Arthur, and we have come to seek Olwen, the daughter
of Yspaddaden." "O men, the mercy of Heaven be upon you, do
not do that for all the world. None who ever came hither upon
that quest has returned alive."

Then Kilhuch went to the herdsman and told him who he was,
and told him who his father and mother were. Also he gave unto
him a ring of gold. The herdsman sought to put it on his finger,
but it was too small for him, so he put it in his glove. When he
went into his house he gave the glove to his wife to keep; she took
the ring from the glove that was given her, and she said: "Whence
came this ring? Thou art not wont to have good fortune." And he
said: "Kilhuch, the son of the daughter of Prince Anlod, gave it to
me; thou shalt see him here in the evening. He has come to seek
Olwen as his wife." When he said that the herdsman's wife was
divided between joy and sorrow, joy because Kilhuch was her sister's
son and was coming to her, and sorrow because she had never
known anyone depart alive who had come on that quest.

They came to the gate of Custennin's dwelling, and when she
heard their footsteps approaching, the woman ran with joy to meet
them. They entered the house, and they were all served, and soon
after they went forth to amuse themselves. Then the woman opened
a stone chest that was before the chimney corner, and out of it rose
a youth with yellow curling hair. Said one: "It is a pity to hide this
youth. I know that it is not his own crime that is thus visited upon
him." "This is but a remnant," said the woman, Custennin's wife.
"Three and twenty of my sons has Yspaddaden slain, and I have no

more hope of this one than of the others." Then said Kay: "Let him come and be a companion with me, and he shall not be slain unless I also am slain with him." It was agreed that the youth would go with Kay; then they ate.

Said the woman: "Upon what errand come you here?" "We come to seek Olwen for this youth," said Kay. Then said the woman: "In the name of Heaven, since no one from the castle hath yet seen you, return again whence you came." "Heaven is our witness that we will not return until we have seen the maiden," said they.

Said Kay: "Does Olwen ever come hither, so that she may be seen?" "She comes here every Saturday to wash her head," said the woman, "and in the vessel where she washes, she leaves all her rings, and she never either comes herself or sends any messengers to fetch them." "Will she come here if she is sent for?" "Unless you pledge me your faith that you will not harm her, I will not send for her," said the woman. "We pledge our faith," said all of them. So a message was sent, and Olwen came.

The maiden was clothed in a robe of flame-colored silk, and about her neck was a collar of ruddy gold, on which were precious emeralds and rubies. More yellow was her head than the flower of the broom, and her skin was whiter than the foam of the wave, and fairer were her hands and her fingers than the blossoms of the wood anemone amidst the spray of the meadow fountain. The eye of the trained hawk, the glance of the three-mewed falcon, was not brighter than hers. Her bosom was more snowy than the breast of the white swan, her cheek was redder than the reddest roses. Whoso beheld her was filled with love. Four white trefoils sprang up wherever she trod. And therefore was she called Olwen, the Maiden of the White Footprints.

She entered the house, and sat beside Kilhuch upon the foremost bench; and as soon as he saw her he knew her. And Kilhuch said unto her: "Ah! maiden, thou art she whom I have loved; come away with me. Many a day have I loved thee." "I cannot go with thee, for I have pledged my faith to my father not to go without his counsel, for his life will only last until the time of my espousal. But I will give thee advice if thou wilt take it. Go, ask me of my father,

Wilfred Jones

Olwen, Maiden of the White Footprints.

[See page 306]

and that which he shall require of thee, grant it, and thou wilt obtain me; but if thou deny him anything, thou wilt not obtain me, and it will be well for thee if thou escape with thy life." "I promise all this," said Kilhuch.

Olwen returned to her chamber; then Kilhuch and all his friends set out for Yspaddaden's castle.

They came to the castle; they slew the nine guards that were at the nine gates, and they died in silence; they slew the nine watch-dogs without one of them barking. They went through the gates and they went into the hall of Yspaddaden's castle.

"The greeting of Heaven and of man be unto thee, Yspaddaden," said they, when they went in. "And you," said the enchanter, rising up, "wherefore have you come?" "We have come to ask thy daughter Olwen, for Kilhuch." "Where are my pages and my servants? Raise up the forks beneath my two eyebrows which have fallen over my eyes, that I may see the fashion of him who would be my son-in-law." And his pages and servants did so, and Yspaddaden looked at them. "Come hither tomorrow, and you shall have an answer," he said.

They rose to go forth. Then Yspaddaden seized one of the three poisoned darts that lay beside him, and threw it after them. Bedour caught it, and flung it, and pierced the enchanter grievously with it through the knee. "A cursed ungentle son-in-law, truly," said he. "I shall ever walk the worse for this rudeness, and shall ever be with-out a cure. This poisoned iron pains me like the bite of a gadfly. Cursed be the smith who forged it, and the anvil whereon it was wrought! So sharp it is!"

That night Kilhuch and his friends stayed in the house of Custen-nin the Herdsman. The next day with the dawn they arrayed them-selves and proceeded to the castle. They entered the hall, and they said: "Yspaddaden, give us thy daughter in consideration of the dower which we will pay to thee. And unless thou wilt do so, thou shalt meet with thy death on her account." Then said he: "Her four great-grandmothers and her four great-grandfathers are yet alive, and it is needful that I take counsel of them." "Be it so," answered they. They rose up to leave the hall. And as they rose up, he took the second dart that was beside him, and cast it after them. And the man who could work all spells caught it, and flung it back at him, and wounded him in the center of the breast, so that it came out at the small of his back. "A cursed ungentle son-in-law, truly," said he, "the hard iron pains me like the bite of a horseleech. Cursed be the hearth whereon it was heated, and the smith who formed it! So sharp it is! Henceforth, whenever I go up a hill, I shall have a scant in my breath, and pain in my chest." By this time, Kilhuch and his friends had gone from the hall.

The third day they returned to the palace. And Yspaddaden said to them: "Shoot not at me again unless you desire death. Where are my attendants? Lift up the forks of my eyebrows which have fallen over my eyeballs, that I may see the fashion of the man who would be my son-in-law." Then they arose, and, as they did so, Yspaddaden took the third poisoned dart and cast it at them. And Kilhuch caught it and threw it vigorously, and wounded him through the eyeball. "A cursed ungentle son-in-law, truly," said the enchanter. "As long as I remain alive, my eyesight will be worse. Whenever I go against the wind, my eyes will water; and peradventure my head will burn, and I shall have a giddiness every new moon. Cursed be the fire in which it was forged. Like the bite of a mad dog is the stroke of this poisoned iron."

By this time Kilhuch and his friends had gone from the hall.

The next day they came again to the palace, and they said: "Shoot not at us any more, unless thou desirest such hurt, and harm, and torture as thou now hast, and even more." And after that Kilhuch went to him and said: "Give me thy daughter, and if thou wilt not give her, thou shalt receive thy death because of her." Yspaddaden said to him: "Come hither where I may see thee." They placed a chair for Kilhuch, and he sat face to face with the enchanter.

Said Yspaddaden: "Is it thou that seekest my daughter?" "It is I," said Kilhuch. "I must have thy pledge that thou wilt not do toward me otherwise than is just," said Yspaddaden, "and when I have gotten that which I shall name, my daughter thou shalt have." "I promise thee that willingly," said Kilhuch, "name what thou wilt."

"I will name now," said the enchanter, "what I will have to get from thee for her dowry."

Then said Yspaddaden, the father of Olwen, "It is needful for me to wash my head, and shave my beard on the day of my daughter's wedding, and I require the tusk of the boar Yskithyrwyn to shave myself withal, neither shall I profit by its use if it be not plucked out of the boar's head alive."

Said Kilhuch, remembering that Olwen had told him that he must agree to do everything that her father asked him to do, "It will be easy for me to compass this, although thou mayest think it will not be easy."

"Though thou get this," said Yspaddaden, the Chief of the Giants, "there is yet that which thou wilt not get. There is no one in the world who can pluck the tusk out of the boar's head except Odgar, the son of Aedd, King of Ireland."

"It will be easy for me to bring Odgar, the son of Aedd, to the hunt of the boar and get him to pluck the tusk out of the boar's head."

"Though thou do that, there is yet that which thou wilt not do. I will not trust anyone to guard the tusk except Gado of North Britain. Of his own free will he will not come out of his kingdom, and thou wilt not be able to compel him."

"It will be easy for me to bring Gado to the hunt, although thou mayest think it will not be easy."

"Though thou get him to come, there is yet that which thou wilt not get. I must spread out my hair in order to have it shaved, and it will never be spread out unless I have the blood of the Jet Black Sorceress, the daughter of the Pure White Sorceress from the Source of the Stream of Sorrow on the bounds of Hell."

"It will be easy for me to compass this, although thou mayest think it will not be easy."

"Though thou get this, there is yet that which thou wilt not get. Throughout the whole of the world there is not a comb nor a razor nor a scissors with which I can arrange my hair, on account of its growth and its rankness, except the comb and razor and scissors that are between the two ears of the great boar that is called Truith."

"It will be easy for me to get the comb and razor and scissors from the boar Truith, although thou mayest think it will not be easy."

"It will not be possible to hunt the boar Truith without Drudwin, the Little Dog of Greit."

"It will be easy for me to bring to the hunting Drudwin, the Little Dog of Greit."

"Though thou get the Little Dog of Greit, there is yet that which thou wilt not get. Throughout the world there is no huntsman who can hunt with this dog, except Mabon, the son of Modron. He was taken from his mother when three nights old, and it is not known where he is now, nor whether he is living or dead."

"It will be easy for me to bring Mabon to the hunting, although thou mayest think it will not be easy."

"Though thou get Mabon, there is yet that which thou wilt not get. Gwynn, the horse that is as swift as the wave, to carry Mabon, the son of Modron, to the hunt of the boar Truith. His owner will not give the horse of his own free will, and thou wilt not be able to compel him."

"It will be easy for me to compass this, although thou mayest think it will not be easy."

"Though thou get the horse that is as swift as the wave, there is yet that which thou wilt not get. Thou wilt not get Mabon, for it is known to none where he is, unless it is known to Eidoel, his kinsman."

"It will be easy for me to find him, although thou mayest think it will not be easy."

"Though thou get him, there is that which thou wilt not get. Thou wilt have to have a leash made from the Beard of Dillus the Bearded, for that is the only leash that will hold the hound. And the leash will be of no avail unless it be plucked from the beard of Dillus while he is alive. While he lives he will not suffer this to be done, and the leash will be of no use should he be dead, because it will be brittle."

"It will be easy for me to compass this, although thou mayest think it will not be easy."

"Though thou get this, there is yet that which thou wilt not get. The boar Truith can never be hunted without the son of Alun Dyved; he is well skilled in letting loose the dogs."

"It will be easy for me to compass this, although thou mayest think it will not be easy."

"And the boar Truith can never be hunted unless thou get the hounds Aned and Aethlem. They are as swift as the gale of wind, and they were never let loose upon a beast that they did not kill it."

"It will be easy for me to bring these hounds to the hunting, although thou mayest think it will not be easy."

"Though thou get them, there is yet that which thou wilt not get —the sword of Gurnach the Giant; he himself will never be slain except with his own sword. Of his own free will he will not give the sword to thee, either for a price or as a gift, and thou wilt never be able to compel him."

"It will be easy for me to compass this, although thou mayest think it will not be easy."

"Difficulties thou shalt meet with, and nights without sleep, in seeking these things, and if thou obtain them not, neither shalt thou obtain my daughter."

"Horses shall I have, and chivalry; and my lord and kinsman Arthur will aid me in obtaining these things. And I shall gain thy daughter, and thou shalt lose thy life."

"Go forward. And when thou hast compassed all these marvels, thou shalt have my daughter Olwen for thy wife."

HOW THEY PERFORMED THE TASKS SET BY THE CHIEF OF THE GIANTS

They returned to the palace, and they told King Arthur of the tasks that Yspaddaden, Chief of the Giants, had set the youth Kilhuch. Then Arthur sent messengers to find out where the boar was, and the messengers found him in Ireland, in the forests around the Seskin Mountain. And the messengers found that the boar Truith had with him seven pigs that were nearly as fierce as he.

When these tidings were brought back, Arthur summoned all the warriors that were in the Island of Britain, and all the warriors that were in France, and in Armorica, and in Normandy, and he summoned all his chosen footmen and all his valiant horsemen. With all these he went into Ireland. And in Ireland there was great fear and terror on account of his coming with that great host. When he landed, there came to him the saints of Ireland, and they besought his protection. And Arthur granted protection to them, and they gave him their blessing.

Then Arthur sent a messenger to find out if the precious things that Yspaddaden spoke of were still between the ears of the boar, since it would be useless to encounter him if they were not there. Arthur's messenger went to seek the boar; he took the form of a bird, and in that form he descended on the top of the boar's lair. He saw that the precious things were between his ears, and he strove to snatch them away. But the boar rose up angrily and shook himself so that some of his venom fell upon Arthur's messenger, and the messenger was never well from that time forth.

Then Arthur, with his hounds and his huntsmen, went to the Seskin Mountain. The dogs were let loose on Truith and his seven pigs from all sides. The men of Ireland went out and fought against the boar. But in spite of dogs and men he was able to lay waste the fifth part of Ireland. The next day the household of Arthur strove with him; but Arthur's household were worsted by the boar, and they got no advantage over him. On the third day Arthur encountered Truith; he fought for nine days and nine nights, and he did not even kill one of the seven pigs that were with the boar.

After that Arthur sent his messenger again, the messenger who took the form of a bird. The messenger alighted on the top of the lair where Truith was with his seven pigs. He said to the boar: "By him who turned you into this form, speak, if one of you can speak." Then one of the seven pigs—the one whose bristles were like silver so that, whether he went through the wood or across the plain, he could be traced by the glittering of his bristles—made answer. "By him who turned us into these forms," said he, "we will not speak with Arthur. That we have been transformed is enough for us to suffer, without a host coming here to fight with us." "I will tell you," said the messenger, "that Arthur has come but for the comb,

and the razor and the scissors that are between the ears of Truith."
Said the other: "Except he first take his life, Arthur will never get
these precious things from Truith. And we will arise up now, and
go into Arthur's country, and there we will do all the mischief
we can."

On account of his threat, Arthur and his host, and his horses and
his dogs, had to go out of Ireland without delay. . . .

HOW KING ARTHUR MET THE JET BLACK SORCERESS

Messengers came to Arthur to tell him that the boar Truith was
nigh with his seven pigs. Arthur arose; with his household and his
hounds he went to the chase.

All wasted was the country that Truith and his seven pigs had
gone through. They came upon the seven pigs. Two of the huntsmen went against them and they were killed by the pigs. Then
Arthur came up to where two of the pigs were, and he let loose the
whole pack of his dogs upon them. The shouting of the men, and
the barking of the dogs, and the grunting of the pigs brought the
boar Truith to the help of the pigs.

From the time that Truith had crossed the Irish Sea, Arthur had
not looked upon the boar until then. He set his men and his dogs
upon the great-tusked, fiery-eyed boar. Thereupon Truith started
off, his seven pigs with him. They went on, with the great company
of men and dogs keeping them in chase. At the next place where
they made a stand one of the pigs was killed. Again the chase went
on. Where they made a stand next, Lawin and Gwis, two of the pigs,
were killed. Again the chase went on. They made a stand at another
place, and there two pigs more, Banu and Benwig, were killed by
the dogs and the men. And the two pigs that were left parted from
Truith there.

And of these two pigs, one went to Garth Gregin, and there he
slew many men. And the other went on until he was met by the
men of Armorica. In that encounter the pig slew the King of
Armorica, and slew King Arthur's two uncles, and there the pig
was slain.

But the boar Truith kept southward, and southward, too, went Arthur and his men in pursuit of him. The King summoned all Cornwall and Devon to meet him. To the estuary of the River Severn they came, and Arthur, looking on the warriors of the Island of the Mighty, said, "The boar Truith has slain many of my men, but, by the valor of warriors, while I live he shall not go into Cornwall. I will not follow him any longer; I will bring him to bay, and oppose him life to life." Then the warriors of the Island of the Mighty said that all of them would oppose their lives to the boar.

Arthur then sent a body of men with dogs to a certain place, instructing them to return thence to the Severn, and he sent tried warriors to traverse the Island, and force the boar into the River Severn.

Kilhuch was with the men who went to do this. Mabon, the son of Modron, was there, mounted on the horse that was swift as the wave. Kilhuch with four others, all mighty warriors, dashed upon the great-tusked, fiery-eyed boar; they seized hold of him; catching him by the feet they plunged him into the Severn. Its waters overwhelmed him. On one side Mabon, the son of Modron, spurred up his steed, and snatched the razor from between the boar's ears. Kilhuch snatched the scissors. But before they could obtain the comb, Truith had regained the ground. From the moment that he reached the shore, neither dog, nor man, nor horse could overtake him until he entered Cornwall.

Then Arthur and his men went through Cornwall seeking the boar that still had the comb between his ears. And then Kilhuch came upon him. And Kilhuch was holding Drudwin, the Little Dog of Greit, by the leash that had been made out of the beard of Dillus the Robber. He unloosed the dog. The boar flung off the comb that was between his ears. The Little Dog of Greit rushed at him and drove him straight forward and into the deep sea. All the warriors watched Truith plunge into the sea. Thenceforthward it was never known where he went. But wherever he went, Drudwin, the Little Dog of Greit, went, too.

So Kilhuch gained the comb, the last of the precious things that was between Truith's ears; he had the scissors, and the razor that

Mabon, the son of Modron, had taken was given him. He had, too, the tusk of the lesser boar. Then with Arthur and his companions, and Goreu, the son of Custennin the Herdsman, he went to the castle of Yspaddaden, Chief of Giants.

Olwen was in the hall when the porter let them in. She was there and Kilhuch looked upon her, but her father drove her out of the hall. "Have you brought all that is needful for the washing of my head and the shaving of my beard?" he asked roughly, when he saw them before him.

Then Kilhuch showed him the tusk of Yskithyrwyn; he showed him the comb, and the razor, and the scissors that had been between the ears of the boar Truith. Yspaddaden looked on all of them. "Tomorrow," he said, "we will examine all of these things and see if it is fitting that you should have my daughter for your wife." And then he said, "Tonight I would have you join in revelry in my hall." So Yspaddaden feasted King Arthur and his companions and feasted Kilhuch, the youth who had come to claim his daughter for wife. After they had feasted they all went to rest.

The next morning when they came together again Yspaddaden said, "The tusk of Yskithyrwyn you have brought me, and the comb and scissors and razor that were between the ears of the boar Truith. But I must spread out my hair in order to have it shaved, and it will never be spread out unless I have the blood of the Jet Black Sorceress, the daughter of the Pure White Sorceress from the Source of the Stream of Sorrow at the confines of Hell. This you have not brought me. And I declare before all of you that I will not yet myself be cheated in this way."

Then it seemed to Kilhuch that in spite of all the labors that had been done he would not gain Olwen for his wife. But King Arthur rose up, and he declared by his confession to Heaven, that he would bring the blood of the Jet Black Sorceress to them, and that he would force Yspaddaden, Chief of Giants, to give Olwen to Kilhuch for his wife.

King Arthur went without. And there was Gwyn ab Nudd who had come with Arthur's companion. He asked Gwyn to give him counsel as to how he might come to where the Jet Black Sorceress, the daughter of the Pure White Sorceress, was. And Gwyn advised the King to mount his mare Lamrei and to ride to the cave that he would guide him to, the cave that opened to where was the Source of the Stream of Sorrow. When they came to that cave, Gwyn advised Arthur to send his two servants in, "For it would not be fitting or seemly," he said, "to have you, King Arthur, struggle with a sorceress."

The two servants went within the cave. But no sooner did they go within than they became rooted to the ground. "What has happened to my servants?" said Arthur. "I know now," said Gwyn, "that your servants cannot move backward or forward, and neither can anyone else unless he is mounted on your mare Lamrei." Arthur, hearing this, rode into the cave. He lifted up his servants on Lamrei, his mare. As he did, the Sorceress dashed at him. With his dagger he struck at her, and she fell in two halves. Then Gwyn ab Nudd took the blood of the Sorceress and kept it.

Arthur with Gwyn came into the castle of Yspaddaden. The hair of the Chief of the Giants was spread out, and Goreu, Custennin's son, went to him. And Goreau shaved his beard, and cut him from ear to ear. "Art thou shaved, man?" said Goreu. But the Chief of Giants did not answer; terror at seeing Goreu whose brothers he had slain, at seeing Goreu come to him with the sharp things in his hands, made Yspaddaden die.

Then Arthur and those who were with him took possession of that vast castle and all the treasures that were in it. Goreu, the son of Custennin the Herdsman, lived in it henceforth. Olwen became the bride of Kilhuch, and she and he were happy together for as long as they lived. Those who were with Arthur left the castle then, each man going to his own place. And thus did Kilhuch obtain Olwen, the daughter of Yspaddaden, Chief of Giants.

Celtic Heroes

FINN

CUCHULAIN

CUCHULAIN — FINN

The ancient epic literature of Ireland is divided into three great cycles: the Mythological, the Ulster or Red Branch, and the Finn or Ossianic cycle. For inclusion in this volume, stories of the second and third cycles have been chosen. The story of Cuchulain is from the Ulster cycle and that of Finn from the Ossianic.

FINN AND OISIN

By T. W. ROLLESTON

Illustration by Warren Chappell

THE BOYHOOD OF FINN MAC CUMHAL

IN IRELAND long ago, centuries before the English appeared in that country, there were kings and chiefs, lawyers and merchants, men of the sword and men of the book, men who tilled their own ground and men who tilled the grounds of others, just as there are now. But there was also, as ancient poets and historians tell us, a great company or brotherhood of men who were bound to no fixed calling, unless it was to fight for the High King of Ireland whenever foes threatened him from within the kingdom or without it. This company was called the Fianna of Erinn. They were mighty hunters and warriors, and though they had great possessions in land, and rich robes, and gold ornaments, and weapons wrought with beautiful chasing and with colored enamels, they lived mostly a free outdoor life in the light hunting booths which they made in the woods where the deer and the wolf ranged. There were then vast forests in Ireland, which are all gone now, and there were also, as there still are, many great and beautiful lakes and rivers, swarming with fish and waterfowl. In the forests and on the mountain sides roamed the wild boar and the wolf, and great herds of deer, some of giant size, whose enormous antlers are sometimes found when bogs are being drained. The Fianna chased these and the wolves with great dogs, whose courage and strength and beauty were famous throughout Europe, and which they prized and loved above all things. To the present day in Ireland there still remain some of this breed of Irish hounds but the giant deer and the wolf are gone, and the Fianna of Erinn live only in the ancient books that were written of them, and in the tales that are still told of them in the winter evenings by the Irish peasant's fireside.

The Fianna were under the rule of one great captain or chief, and at the time I tell of his name was Cumhal, son of Trenmor. Now a tribe or family of the Fianna named the Clan Morna, or Sons of Morna, rose in rebellion against Cumhal, for they were jealous and greedy of his power and glory, and sought to have the captaincy for themselves. They defeated and slew him at the battle of Cnucha, which is now called Castleknock, near the city of the Hurdle Ford, which is the name that Dublin still bears in the Irish tongue. Goll, son of Morna, slew Cumhal, and they spoiled him of the Treasure Bag of the Fianna, which was a bag made of a crane's skin and having in it jewels of great price, and magic weapons, and strange things that had come down from far-off days when the Fairy Folk and mortal men battled for the lordship of Ireland. The Bag with its treasures was given to Lia, the chief of Luachar in Connacht, who had the keeping of it before, for he was the treasurer of Cumhal, and he was the first man who had wounded Cumhal in the battle when he fell.

Cumhal's wife was named Murna and she bore him two sons. The elder was named Tulcha, and he fled from the country for fear of Goll and took service with the King of Scotland. The younger was born after Cumhal's death, and his name was called Demna. And because his mother feared that the son of Morna would find him out and kill him, she gave him to a Druidess and another wise woman of Cumhal's household, and bade them take him away and rear him as best they could. So they took him into the wild woods on the Slieve Bloom Mountains, and there they trained him to hunt and fish and to throw the spear, and he grew strong, and as beautiful as a child of the Fairy Folk. If he were in the same field with a hare he could run so that the hare could never leave the field, for Demna was always before it. He could run down and slay a stag with no dogs to help him, and he could kill a wild duck on the wing with a stone from his sling. And the Druidess taught him the learning of the time, and also the story of his race and nation, and told him of his right to be captain of the Fianna of Erinn when his day of destiny should come.

One day, while still a boy, he was roaming through the woods when he came to the mansion of a great lord, where many boys, sons of the chief men of Ireland, were being trained in manly arts and exercises. He found them playing at hurling, and they invited him to join them. He did so, but the side he was on won too easily, so they divided again, and yet again, giving fewer and fewer to Demna's side, till at last he alone drove the ball to the goal through them all, flashing among them as a salmon among a shoal of minnows. And then their anger and jealousy rose and grew bitter against the stranger, and instead of honoring him, as gallant lads of gentle blood should have done, they fell upon him with their hurling clubs and sought to kill him. But Demna felled seven of them to the ground and put the rest to flight, and then went his way home. When the boys told what had happened the chief asked them who it was that had defeated and routed them single-handed. They said, "It was a tall shapely lad, and very fair (*finn*)." So the name of Finn, the Fair One, clung to him thenceforth, and by that name he is known to this day.

By and by Finn gathered round him a band of youths who loved him for his strength and valor and for his generous heart, and with them he went hunting in the forests. And Goll, and the sons of Morna, who were now captains of the Fianna under the High King, began to hear tales of him and his exploits, and they sent trackers to inquire about him, for they had an inkling of who this wonderful fair-haired youth might be. Finn's foster-mothers heard of this. "You must leave this place," they said to him, "and see our faces no more, for if Goll's men find you here they will slay you. We have cherished the blood of Cumhal," they said, "and now our work is done. Go, and may blessing and victory go with you." So Finn departed with naught but his weapons and his hunting gear, very sorrowful at leaving the wise and loving friends who had fostered his childhood; but deep in his heart was a wild and fierce delight at the thought of the trackless ways he would travel, and the wonders he would see; and all the future looked to him as beautiful and dim as the mists that fill a mountain glen under the morning sun.

Now after the death of Cumhal, his brother Crimmal and a few others of the aged warriors of the Fianna, who had not fallen in the fight at Cnucha, fled away into Connacht, and lived there in the deepest recesses of a great forest, where they hoped the conquerors might never find them. Here they built themselves a poor dwelling of tree branches, plastered with mud and roofed with reeds from the lake, and here they lived on what game they could kill or snare in the wild wood; and harder and harder it grew, as age and feebleness crept on them, to find enough to eat, or to hew wood for their fire. In this retreat, never having seen the friendly face of man, they were one day startled to hear voices and the baying of hounds approaching them through the wood, and they thought that the sons of Morna were upon them at last, and that their hour of doom was at hand. Soon they perceived a company of youths coming toward their hut, with one in front who seemed to be their leader. Taller he was by a head than the rest, broad shouldered, and with masses of bright hair clustering round his forehead, and he carried in his hand a large bag made of some delicate skin and stained in patterns of red and blue. The old men thought when they saw him of a saying there was about the mighty Lugh, who was brother to the wife of Cumhal, that when he came among his army as they mustered for battle, men felt as though they beheld the rising of the sun. As they came near, the young men halted and looked upon the elders with pity, for their clothing of skins was ragged and the weapons they strove to hold were rusted and blunt, and except for their proud bearing and the fire in their old eyes they looked more like aged and worthless slaves in the household of a niggardly lord than men who had once been the flower of the fighting men of Erinn.

But the tall youth stepped in front of his band and cried aloud: "Which of ye is Crimmal, son of Trenmor?" And one of the elders said, "I am Crimmal." Then tears filled the eyes of the youth, and he knelt down before the old man and put his hands in his.

"My lord and chief," he said, "I am Finn, son of Cumhal, and the day of deliverance is come." So the youth brought in the spoils of their hunting, and yet other spoils than these; and that night there was feasting and joy in the lonely hut. And Crimmal said:

"It was foretold to us that one day the blood of Cumhal should be avenged, and the race of Cumhal should rule the Fianna again. This was the sign that the coming champion should give of his birth and destiny; he was to bear with him the Treasure Bag of Cumhal and the sacred things that were therein."

Finn said, "Ye know the Bag and its treasures, tell us if these are they." And he laid his skin bag on the knees of Crimmal.

Crimmal opened it, and he took out the jewels of sovranty and the magic spearhead made by the smiths of the Fairy Folk, and he said, "These be the treasures of Cumhal; truly the ripeness of the time is come."

And Finn then told the story of how he had won these things. "But yesterday morning," he said, "we met on our way a woman of noble aspect, and she knelt over the body of a slain youth. When she lifted her head as we drew near, tears of blood ran down her cheeks, and she cried to me, 'Whoever thou art, I bind thee by the bonds of the sacred ordinances of the Gael that thou avenge my wrong. This was my son Glonda,' she said, 'my only son, and he was slain today wantonly by the Lord of Luachar and his men.' So we went, my company and I, to the Dun of the Lord of Luachar, and found an earthen rampart with a fence of oaken posts interlaced with wattles, and over this we saw the many-colored thatch of a great dwelling-house, and its white walls painted with bright colors under the broad eaves. So I stood forth and called to the Lord of Luachar and bade him make ready to pay an eric to the mother of Glonda, whatsoever she should demand. But he laughed at us and cursed us and bade us begone. Then we withdrew into the forest, but returned with a great pile of dry brushwood, and while some of us shot stones and arrows at whoever should appear above the palisade, others rushed up with bundles of brushwood and laid it against the palisade and set it on fire, and the Immortal Ones sent a blast of wind that set the brushwood and palisade quickly into a blaze, and through that fiery gap we charged in shouting. And half the men of Luachar we killed and the rest fled, and the Lord of Luachar I slew in the doorway of his palace. We took a great spoil then, O Crimmal— these vessels of bronze and silver, and spears and bows, smoked bacon and skins of Greek wine; and in a great chest of yewwood we found this bag. All these things shall now remain with you, and my company shall also remain to hunt for you and protect you, for ye shall know want and fear no longer while ye live."

And Finn said, "I would fain know if my mother Murna still lives, or if she died by the sons of Morna."

Crimmal said, "After thy father's death, Finn, she was wedded to Gleor, Lord of Lamrigh, in the south, and she still lives in honor with him, and the sons of Morna have let her be. Didst thou never see her since she gave thee, an infant, to the wise women on the day of Cnucha?"

"I remember," said Finn, "when I was, as they tell me, but six years old, there came one day to our shieling in the woods of Slieve Bloom a chariot with bronze-shod wheels and a bronze wolf's head at the end of the pole, and two horsemen riding with it, besides him who drove. A lady was in it, with a golden frontlet on her brow and her cloak was fastened with a broad golden brooch. She came into our hut and spoke long with my foster mothers, and me she clasped in her arms and kissed many times, and I felt her tears on my face. And they told me afterwards that this was Murna of the White Neck, and my mother. If she have suffered no harm at the hands of the sons of Morna, so much the less is the debt that they shall one day pay."

Now it is to be told what happened to Finn at the house of Finegas the Bard. Finn did not deem that the time had come for him to seize the captaincy of the Fianna until he had perfected himself in wisdom and learning. So on leaving the shelter of the old men in the wood he went to learn wisdom and the art of poetry from Finegas, who dwelt by the River Boyne, near to where is now the village of Slane. It was a belief among the poets of Ireland that the place of the revealing of poetry is always by the margin of water. But Finegas had another reason for the place where he made his dwelling, for there was an old prophecy that whoever should first eat of the Salmon of Knowledge that lived in the River Boyne, should become the wisest of all men. Now this salmon was called Finntan in ancient times and was one of the Immortals, and he might be eaten and yet live. But in the time of Finegas he was called the Salmon of the Pool of Fec, which is the place where the fair river broadens out into a great still pool, with green banks softly sloping upward from the clear brown water. Seven years was Finegas watching the pool, but not until after Finn had come to be his disciple was the salmon caught. Then Finegas gave it to Finn to cook, and bade him eat none of it. But when Finegas saw him coming with the fish, he knew that something had chanced to the lad, for he had been used to have the eye of a young man but now he had the eye of a sage. Finegas said, "Hast thou eaten of the salmon?"

"Nay," said Finn, "but it burnt me as I turned it upon the spit and I put my thumb in my mouth." And Finegas smote his hands together and was silent for a while. Then he said to the lad who stood by obediently, "Take the salmon and eat it, Finn, son of Cumhal, for to thee the prophecy is come. And now go hence, for I can teach thee no more, and blessing and victory be thine."

THE COMING OF FINN

And now we tell how Finn came to the captaincy of the Fianna of Erinn.

At this time Ireland was ruled by one of the mightiest of her native kings, Conn, son of Felimy, who was surnamed Conn of the Hundred battles. And Conn sat in his great banqueting hall at Tara, while the yearly assembly of the lords and princes of the Gael went forward, during which it was the inviolable law that no quarrel should be raised and no weapon drawn, so that every man who had a right to come to that assembly might come there and sit next his deadliest foe in peace. Below him sat at meat the provincial kings and the chiefs of clans, and the High King's officers and fighting-men of the Fianna, with Goll and the sons of Morna at their head. And there, too, sat modestly a strange youth, tall and fair, whom no one had seen in that place before. Conn marked him with the eye of a king that is accustomed to mark men, and by and by he sent him a horn full of wine from his own table and bade the youth declare his name and lineage. "I am Finn, son of Cumhal," said the youth, standing among them, tall as a warrior's spear, and a start and a low murmur ran through the Assembly while the captains of the Fianna stared upon him like men who see a vision of the dead. "What seek you here?" said Conn, and Finn replied, "To be your man, O King, and to do you service in war as my father did." "It is well," said the King. "Thou art a friend's son and the son of a man of trust." So Finn put his hand in the King's and swore fealty and service to him, and Conn set him beside his own son Art, and all fell to talking again and wondering what new things that day would bring forth, and the feasting went merrily forward.

Now at this time the people of the royal burg of Tara were sorely afflicted by a goblin of the Fairy Folk, who was wont to approach the place at nightfall, there to work what harm to man, or beast, or dwelling that he found in his evil mind to do. And he could not be resisted for as he came he played on a magic harp a strain so keen and sweet, that each man who heard it must needs stand entranced and motionless until the fairy music had passed away. The King proclaimed a mighty reward to any man who would save Tara from the goblin, and Finn thought in his heart, "I am the man to do that." So he said to the King, "Shall I have my rightful heritage as captain of the Fianna of Erinn if I slay the goblin?" Conn said, "I promise thee that," and he bound himself by the sureties of all the provincial Kings of Ireland and of the Druid Kithro and his magicians.

Now there was among the following of Conn a man named Fiacha, who had been as a youth a trusty friend and follower of Cumhal. He came to Finn and brought with him a spear having a head of dark bronze with glittering edges, and fastened with thirty rivets of Arabian gold, and the spearhead was laced up within a leathern case. "By this weapon of enchantment," said Fiacha, "you shall overcome the enchanter," and he taught Finn what to do with it when the hour of need should come.

So Finn took the spear, and left the strings of the case loose, and paced with it toward nightfall around the ramparts of Tara. And when he had once made the circuit of the rampart, and the light had now almost quite faded from the summer sky, and the wide low plains around the Hill of Tara were a sea of white mist, he heard far off in the deepening gloom the first notes of the fairy harp. Never such music was made by mortal hand, for it had in it sorrows that a man has never felt, and joys for which man has no name, and it seemed as if a man listening to that music might burst from time into eternity and be as one of the Immortals forevermore. And Finn listened, amazed and rapt, till at last as the triumphant melody grew nearer and louder he saw dimly a Shadow Shape playing as it were on a harp, and coming swiftly toward him. Then with a mighty effort he roused himself from dreams, and tore the cover from the spearhead and laid the metal to his brow. And the demoniac energy that had been beaten into the blade by the hammers of unearthly craftsmen in ancient days thrilled through him and made him fighting-mad, and he rushed forward shouting his battle cry, and swinging the spear aloft. But the Shadow turned and fled before him, and Finn chased it northward to the Fairy Mount of Slieve Fuad, and there he drove the spear through its back. And what it was that fell there in the night, and what it was that passed like the shadow of a shadow into the Fairy Mound, none can tell, but Finn bore back to him next day a pale, sorrowful head on the point of Fiacha's spear, and the goblin troubled the folk of royal Tara no more.

But Conn of the Hundred Battles called the Fianna together, and he set Finn at his right hand and said:

"Here is your Captain by birthright and by sword right. Let who will now obey him henceforward, and who will not, let him go in peace and serve Arthur of Britain or Arist of Alba, or whatsoever King he will."

And Goll, son of Morna, said, "For my part I will be Finn's man under thee, O King," and he swore obedience and loyalty to Finn before them all. Nor was it hard for any man to step where Goll had gone before, so they all took their oaths of Fian service to Finn mac Cumhal.

And thus it was that Finn came to the captaincy of the Fianna of Erinn, and he ruled the Fianna many a year till he died in battle with the Clan Urgrenn at Brea upon the Boyne.

THE BIRTH OF OISIN

One day as Finn and his companions and dogs were returning from the chase to their Dun on the Hill of Allen, a beautiful fawn started up on their path and the chase swept after her, she taking the way which led to their home. Soon, all the pursuers were left far behind save only Finn himself and his two hounds Bran and Sceolaun. Now these hounds were of strange breed, for Tyren, sister of Murna, the mother of Finn, had been changed into a hound by the enchantment of a woman of the Fairy Folk, who loved Tyren's husband Ullan; and the two hounds of Finn were the children of Tyren, born to her in that shape. Of all hounds in Ireland they were the best, and Finn loved them much, so that it was said he wept but twice in his life, and once was for the death of Bran.

At last, as the chase went on down a valley side, Finn saw the fawn stop and lie down, while the two hounds began to play round her and to lick her face and limbs. So he gave commandment that none should hurt her, and she followed them to the Dun of Allen, playing with the hounds as she went.

The same night Finn awoke and saw standing by his bed the fairest woman his eyes had ever beheld.

"I am Saba, O Finn," she said, "and I was the fawn ye chased today. Because I would not give my love to the Druid of the Fairy Folk, who is named the Dark, he put that shape upon me by his sorceries, and I have borne it these three years. But a slave of his, pitying me, once revealed to me that if I could win to thy great Dun of Allen, O Finn, I should be safe from all enchantments and my natural shape would come to me again. But I feared to be torn in pieces by thy dogs, or wounded by thy hunters, till at last I let myself be taken by thee alone and by Bran and Sceolaun, who have the nature of man and would do me no hurt." "Have no fear, maiden," said Finn, "we the Fianna are free and our guest-friends are free; there is none who shall put compulsion on you here."

So Saba dwelt with Finn, and he made her his wife; and so deep was his love for her that neither the battle nor the chase had any delight for him, and for months he never left her side. She also loved him as deeply, and their joy in each other was like that of the Immortals in the Land of Youth. But at last word came to Finn that the warships of the Northmen were in the bay of Dublin, and he summoned his heroes to the fight, "for," he said to Saba, "the men of Erinn give us tribute and hospitality to defend them from the foreigner, and it were shame to take it from them and not to give that to which we, on our side, are pledged." And he called to mind that great saying of Goll mac Morna when they were once sore bested by a mighty host—"a man," said Goll, "lives after his life but not after his honor."

Seven days was Finn absent, and he drove the Northmen from the shores of Erinn. But on the eighth day he returned, and when he entered his Dun he saw trouble in the eyes of his men and of their fair womenfolk, and Saba was not on the rampart expecting his return. So he bade them tell him what had chanced, and they said:

"Whilst thou, our father and lord, wert afar off smiting the foreigner, and Saba looking ever down the pass for thy return, we saw one day as it were the likeness of thee approaching, and Bran and Sceolaun at thy heels. And we seemed also to hear the notes of the Fian hunting-call blown on the wind. Then Saba hastened to the great gate, and we could not stay her, so eager was she to rush to the phantom. But when she came near, she halted and gave a loud and bitter cry, and the shape of thee smote her with a hazel wand, and lo, there was no woman there any more, but a deer. Then those hounds chased it, and ever as it strove to reach again the gate of the Dun they turned it back. We all now seized what arms we could and ran out to drive away the enchanter, but when we reached the place there was nothing to be seen, only still we heard the rushing of flying feet and the baying of dogs, and one thought it came from here, and another from there, till at last the uproar died away and all was still. What we could do, O Finn, we did; Saba is gone."

Finn then struck his hand on his breast but spoke no word, and he went to his own chamber. No man saw him for the rest of that day, nor for the day after. Then he came forth, and ordered the matters of the Fianna as of old, but for seven years thereafter he went searching for Saba through every remote glen and dark forest and cavern of Ireland, and he would take no hounds with him save Bran and Sceolaun. But at last he renounced all hope of finding her again, and went hunting as of old. One day as he was following the chase on Ben Gulban in Sligo, he heard the musical bay of the dogs change of a sudden to a fierce growling and yelping as though they were in combat with some beast, and running hastily up he and his men beheld, under a great tree, a naked boy with long hair, and around him the hounds struggling to seize him, but Bran and Sceolaun fighting with them and keeping them off. And the lad was tall and shapely, and as the heroes gathered round he gazed undauntedly on them, never heeding the rout of dogs at his feet, The Fians beat off the dogs and brought the lad home with them, and Finn was very silent and continually searched the lad's countenance with his eyes. In time, the use of speech came to him, and the story that he told was this:

He had known no father, and no mother save a gentle hind with whom he lived in a most green and pleasant valley shut in on every side by towering cliffs that could not be scaled, or by deep chasms in the earth. In the summer he lived on fruits and suchlike, and in the winter, store of provisions was laid for him in a cave. And there came to them sometimes a tall dark-visaged man, who spoke to his mother, now tenderly, and now in loud menace, but she always shrunk away in fear, and the man departed in anger. At last there came a day when the Dark man spoke very long with his mother in all tones of entreaty and of tenderness and of rage, but she would still keep aloof and give no sign save of fear and abhorrence. Then at length the Dark Man drew near and smote her with a hazel wand; and with that he turned and went his way, but she, this time, followed him, still looking back at her son and piteously complaining. And he, when he strove to follow, found himself unable to move a limb; and crying out with rage and desolation he fell to the earth and his senses left him. When he came to himself he was on the mountain side, on Ben Gulban, where he remained some days, searching for that green and hidden valley, which he never found again. And after a while the dogs found him; but of the hind his mother and of the Dark Druid, there is no man knows the end.

Finn called his name Oisin, and he became a warrior of fame, but far more famous for the songs and tales that he made; so that of all things to this day that are told of the Fianna of Erinn, men are wont to say, "So sang the bard, Oisin, son of Finn."

OISIN IN THE LAND OF YOUTH

It happened that on a misty summer morning as Finn and Oisin with many companions were hunting on the shores of Loch Lena they saw coming toward them a maiden, beautiful exceedingly, riding on a snow-white steed. She wore the garb of a queen; a crown of gold was on her head, and a dark brown mantle of silk, set with stars of red gold, fell around her and trailed on the ground. Silver shoes were on her horse's hoofs, and a crest of gold nodded on his head. When she came near she said to Finn, "From very far away I have come, and now at last I have found thee, Finn, son of Cumhal."

Then Finn said, "What is thy land and race, maiden, and what dost thou seek from me?"

"My name," she said, "is Niam of the Golden Hair. I am the daughter of the King of the Land of Youth, and that which has brought me here is the love of thy son Oisin." Then she turned to Oisin and she spoke to him in the voice of one who has never asked anything but it was granted to her, "Wilt thou go with me, Oisin, to my father's land?"

And Oisin said, "That will I, and to the world's end"; for the fairy spell had so wrought upon his heart that he cared no more for any earthly thing but to have the love of Niam of the Head of Gold.

Then the maiden spoke of the Land Oversea to which she had summoned her lover, and as she spoke a dreamy stillness fell on all things, nor did a horse shake his bit nor a hound bay, nor the least breath of wind stir in the forest trees till she had made an end. And what she said seemed sweeter and more wonderful as she spoke it than anything they could afterwards remember to have heard, but so far as they could remember it, it was this:

"Delightful is the land beyond all dreams,
Fairer than aught thine eyes have ever seen.
There all the year the fruit is on the tree,
And all the year the bloom is on the flower.

"There with wild honey drip the forest trees;
The stores of wine and mead shall never fail.
Nor pain nor sickness knows the dweller there,
Death and decay come near him never more.

"The feast shall cloy not, nor the chase shall tire,
Nor music cease forever through the hall;
The gold and jewels of the Land of Youth
Outshine all splendors ever dreamed by man.

"Thou shalt have horses of the fairy breed,
Thou shalt have hounds that can outrun the wind;
A hundred chiefs shall follow thee in war,
A hundred maidens sing thee to thy sleep.

"A crown of sovranty thy brow shall wear,
And by thy side a magic blade shall hang.
Thou shalt be lord of all the Land of Youth,
And lord of Niam of the Head of Gold."

As the magic song ended, the Fians beheld Oisin mount the fairy steed and hold the maiden in his arms, and ere they could stir or speak she turned her horse's head and shook the ringing bridle, and down the forest glade they fled, as a beam of light flies over the land when clouds drive across the sun; and never did the Fianna behold Oisin, son of Finn, on earth again.

Yet what befell him afterwards is known. As his birth was strange so was his end, for he saw the wonders of the Land of Youth with mortal eyes and lived to tell them with mortal lips.

When the white horse with its riders reached the sea it ran lightly over the waves and soon the green woods and headlands of Erinn faded out of sight. And now the sun shone fiercely down, and the riders passed into a golden haze in which Oisin lost all knowledge of where he was or if sea or dry land were beneath his horse's hoofs. But strange sights sometimes appeared to them in the mist, for towers and palace gateways loomed up and disappeared, and once a hornless doe bounded by them chased by a white hound with one red ear, and again they saw a young maid ride by on a brown steed, bearing a golden apple in her hand, and close behind her followed a young horseman on a white steed, a purple cloak floating at his back and a gold-hilted sword in his hand. And Oisin would have asked the princess who and what these apparitions were, but Niam bade him ask nothing nor seem to notice any phantom they might see until they were come to the Land of Youth.

At last the sky loomed above them, and Niam urged their steed faster. The wind lashed them with pelting rain, thunder roared across the sea and lightning blazed, but they held on their way till at length they came once more into a region of calm and sunshine. And now Oisin saw before him a shore of yellow sand, lapped by the ripples of a summer sea. Inland, there rose before his eye wooded hills amid which he could discern the roofs and towers of a noble city. The white horse bore them swiftly to the shore and Oisin and the maiden lighted down. And Oisin marveled at everything around him, for never was water so blue or trees so stately as those he saw, and the forest was alive with the hum of bees and the song of birds, and the creatures that are wild in other lands, the deer and the red squirrel and the wood-dove, came, without fear, to be caressed. Soon, as they went forward, the walls of a city came in sight, and folk began to meet them on the road, some riding, some afoot, all of whom were either youths or maidens, all looking as joyous as if the morning of happy life had just begun for them, and no old or feeble person was to be seen. Niam led her companion through a towered gateway built of white and red marble, and there they were met by a glittering company of a hundred riders on black steeds and a hundred on white, and Oisin mounted a black horse and Niam her white, and they rode up to a stately palace where the King of the Land of Youth had his dwelling. And there he received them, saying in a loud voice that all the folk could hear, "Welcome, Oisin, son of Finn. Thou art come to the Land of Youth, where sorrow and weariness and death shall never touch thee. This thou hast won by thy faithfulness and valor and by the songs that thou hast made for the men of Erinn, whereof the fame is come to us, for we have here indeed all things that are delightful and joyous, but poesy alone we had not. But now we have the chief poet of the race of men to live with us, immortal among immortals, and the fair and cloudless life that we lead here shall be praised in verses as fair; even as thou, Oisin, didst praise and adorn the short and toilsome and checkered life that men live in the world thou hast left forever. And Niam my daughter shall be thy bride, and thou shalt be in all things even as myself in the Land of Youth."

Then the heart of Oisin was filled with glory and joy, and he turned to Niam and saw here eyes burn with love as she gazed upon him. And they were wedded the same day, and the joy they had in each other grew sweeter and deeper with every day that passed. All that Niam had promised in her magic song in the wildwood when first they met, seemed faint beside the splendor and beauty of the life in the Land of Youth. In the great palace they trod on silken carpets and ate off plates of gold; the marble walls and doorways were wrought with carved work, or hung with tapestries, where forest glades, and still lakes, and flying deer were done in colors of unfading glow. Sunshine bathed that palace always, and cool winds wandered through its dim corridors, and in its courts there played fountains of bright water set about with flowers. When Oisin wished to ride, a steed of fiery but gentle temper bore him wherever he would through the pleasant land; when he longed to hear music, there came upon his thought, as though borne on the wind, crystal notes such as no hand ever struck from the strings of any harp on earth.

But Oisin's hand now never touched the harp, and the desire of singing and of making poetry never waked in him, for no one thing seemed so much better than the rest, where all perfection bloomed and glowed around him, as to make him long to praise it and to set it apart.

When seven days had passed, he said to Niam, "I would fain go a-hunting." Niam said, "So be it, dear love; tomorrow we shall take

order for that." Oisin lay long awake that night, thinking of the
sound of Finn's hunting horn, and of the smell of green boughs
when they kindled them to roast the deer-flesh in Fian ovens in the
wildwood.

So next day Oisin and Niam fared forth on horseback, with their
company of knights and maidens, and dogs leaping and barking
with eagerness for the chase. Anon they came to the forest, and the
hunters with the hounds made a wide circuit on this side and on
that, till at last the loud clamor of the hounds told that a stag was on
foot, and Oisin saw them streaming down an open glen, the stag
with its great antlers laid back and flying like the wind. So he
shouted the Fian hunting-cry and rode furiously on their track. All
day long they chased the stag through the echoing forest, and the
fairy steed bore him unfaltering over rough ground and smooth, till
at last as darkness began to fall the quarry was pulled down, and
Oisin cut its throat with his hunting knife. Long it seemed to him
since he had felt glad and weary as he felt now, and since the woodland air with its odors of pine and mint and wild garlic had tasted so
sweet in his mouth; and truly it was longer than he knew. But when
he bade make ready the wood oven for their meal and build a bothy
of boughs for their repose, Niam led him seven steps apart and
seven to the left hand, and yet seven back to the place where they
had killed the deer, and lo, there rose before him a stately Dun with
litten windows and smoke drifting above its roof. When they entered, there was a table spread for a great company, and cooks and
serving-men busy about a wide hearth where roast and boiled meats
of every sort were being prepared. Casks of Greek wine stood open
around the walls, and cups of gold were on the board. So they all
ate and drank their sufficiency, and all night Oisin and Niam slept
on a bed softer than swansdown in a chamber no less fair than that
which they had in the City of the Land of Youth.

Next day, at the first light of dawn, they were on foot; and soon
again the forest rang to the baying of hounds and the music of the
hunting horn. Oisin's steed bore him all day, tireless and swift as
before, and again the quarry fell at night's approach, and again a
palace rose in the wilderness for their night's entertainment, and all

things in it even more abundant and more sumptuous than before. And so for seven days they fared in the forest, and seven stags were slain. Then Oisin grew wearied of hunting, and as he plunged his sharp black hunting knife into the throat of the last stag, he thought of the sword of magic temper that hung idly by his side in the City of Youth, or rested from its golden nail in his bed-chamber, and he said to Niam, "Has thy father never a foe to tame, never a wrong to avenge? Surely the peasant is no man whose hand forgets the plow, nor the warrior whose hands forgets the sword hilt." Niam looked on him strangely for a while and as if she did not understand his

Warren Chappell

In the glimmering dawn Oisin and Niam rode forth.

words, or sought some meaning in them which yet she feared to find. But at last she said, "If deeds of arms be thy desire, Oisin, thou shalt have thy sufficiency ere long." And so they rode home, and slept that night in the palace of the City of Youth.

At daybreak on the following morn Niam roused Oisin, and she buckled on him his golden-hilted sword and his corselet of blue steel inlaid with gold. Then he put on his head a steel and gold helmet with dragon crest, and slung on his back a shield of bronze wrought all over with cunning hammer-work of serpentine lines that swelled and sank upon the surface, and coiled in mazy knots, or flowed in long sweeping curves like waves of the sea when they gather might and volume for their leap upon the sounding shore. In the glimmering dawn, through the empty streets of the fair city, they rode forth alone and took their way through fields of corn and by apple orchards where red fruit hung down to their hands. But by noontide their way began to mount upward among blue hills that they had marked from the city walls toward the west, and of man's husbandry they saw no more, but tall red-stemmed pine trees bordered the way on either side, and silence and loneliness increased. At length they reached a broad table-land deep in the heart of the mountains, where nothing grew but long coarse grass, drooping by pools of black and motionless water, and where great boulders, bleached white or stained with slimy lichens of livid red, lay scattered far and wide about the plain. Against the sky the mountain line now showed like a threat of bared and angry teeth, and as they rode toward it Oisin perceived a huge fortress lying in the throat of a wide glen or mountain pass. White as death was the stone of which it was built, save where it was streaked with black or green from the foulness of wet mosses that clung to its cornices and battlements, and none seemed stirring about the place nor did any banner blow from its towers.

Then said Niam, "This, O Oisin, is the Dun of the giant Fovor of the Mighty Blows. In it he keeps prisoner a princess of the Fairy Folk whom he would fain make his bride, but he may not do so, nor may she escape, until Fovor has met in battle a champion who will undertake her cause. Approach, then, to the gate, if thou are fain to undertake this adventure, and blow the horn which hangs thereby, and then look to thy weapons, for soon indeed will the battle be broken upon thee."

Then Oisin rode to the gate and thrice he blew on the great horn which hung by it, and the clangor of it groaned drearily back from the cliffs that overhung the glen. Not thus indeed sounded the *Dord* of Finn as its call blew lust of fighting and scorn of death into the hearts of the Fianna amid the stress of battle. At the third blast the rusty gates opened, grinding on their hinges, and Oisin rode into a wide courtyard where servitors of evil aspect took his horse and Niam's, and led them into the hall of Fovor. Dark it was and low, with moldering arras on its walls, and foul and withered rushes on the floor, where dogs gnawed the bones thrown to them at the last meal, and spilt ale and hacked fragments of flesh littered the bare oaken table. And here rose languidly to greet them a maiden bound with seven chains, to whom Niam spoke lovingly, saying that her champion was come and that her long captivity should end. And the maiden looked upon Oisin, whose proud bearing and jeweled armor made the mean place seem meaner still, and a light of hope and of joy seemed to glimmer upon her brow. So she gave them refreshment as she could, and afterwards they betook them once more to the courtyard, where the place of battle was set.

Here, on the farther side, stood a huge man clad in rusty armor, who when he saw Oisin rushed upon him, silent and furious, and swinging a great battle-ax in his hand. But doubt and languor weighed upon Oisin's heart, and it seemed to him as he were in an evil dream, which he knew was but a dream, and would be less than nothing when the hour of awakening should come. Yet he raised his shield and gripped the fairy sword, striving to shout the Fian battle-cry as he closed with Fovor. But soon a heavy blow smote him to the ground, and his armor clanged harshly on the stones. Then a cloud seemed to pass from his spirit, and he leaped to his feet quicker than an arrow flies from the string, and thrusting fiercely at the giant his sword-point gashed the under side of Fovor's arm when it was raised to strike, and Oisin saw his enemy's blood. Then the fight raged hither and thither about the wide courtyard with trampling of feet and clash of steel and ringing of armor and shouts of onset as the heroes closed; Oisin, agile as a wild stag, evading the sweep of the mighty ax and rushing in with flickering blade at every unguarded moment, his whole soul bent on one fierce thought, to drive his point into some gap at shoulder or neck in Fovor's coat of mail. At length, when both were weary and wounded men, with hacked and battered armor, Oisin's blade cut the thong of Fovor's headpiece and it fell clattering to the ground. Another blow laid the giant prostrate and Oisin leaned, dizzy and panting, upon his sword, while Fovor's serving-men took off their master in a litter, and Niam came to aid her lord. Then Oisin stripped off his armor in the great hall, and Niam tended to his wounds, healing them with magic herbs and murmured incantations, and they saw that one of the seven rusty chains that had bound the princess hung loose from its iron staple in the wall.

All night long Oisin lay in deep and healing slumber, and next day he arose, whole and strong, and hot to renew the fray. And the giant was likewise healed and his might and fierceness returned to him. So they fought till they were breathless and weary, and then to it again, and again, till in the end Oisin drove his sword to the hilt in the giant's shoulder where it joins the collar bone, and he fell a-swoon, and was borne away as before. And another chain of the seven fell from the girdle of the captive maiden.

Thus for seven days went on the combat, and Oisin had seven nights of healing and rest, with the tenderness and beauty of Niam about his couch; and on the seventh day the maiden was free, and her folk brought her away, rejoicing, with banners and with music that made a brightness for a while in that forlorn and evil place.

But Oisin's heart was high with pride and victory, and a longing uprose in his heart with a rush like a springtide for the days when some great deed had been done among the Fianna, and the victors were hailed and lauded by the home-folk in the Dun of Allen, men and women leaving their toil or their pleasure to crowd round the heroes, and to question again and again, and to learn each thing that had passed; and the bards noting all to weave it into a glorious tale for after days; and more than all the smile and the look of Finn as he learned how his children had borne themselves in the face of death. And so Oisin said to Niam, "Let me, for a short while, return to the land of Erinn, that I may see there my friends and kin and tell them of the glory and joy that are mine in the Land of Youth." But Niam wept and laid her white arms about his neck, entreating him to think no more of the sad world where all men live and move under a canopy of death, and where summer is slain by winter, and youth by old age, and where love itself, if it die not by falsehood and wrong, perishes many a time of too complete a joy. But Oisin said, "The world of men compared with thy world is like this dreary waste compared with the city of thy father; yet in that city, Niam, none is better or worse than another, and I hunger to tell my tale to ignorant and feeble folk that my words can move, as words of mine have done of old, to wonder and delight. Then I shall return to thee, Niam, and to thy fair and blissful land; and having brought over to mortal men a tale that never man has told before, I shall be happy and at peace forever in the Land of Youth."

So they fared back to the golden city, and next day Niam brought to Oisin the white steed that had borne them from Erinn, and bade him farewell. "This our steed," she said, "will carry thee across the sea to the land where I found thee, and withersoever thou wilt, and what folk are there thou shalt see, and what tale thou hast to tell can be told. But never for even a moment must thou alight from his back, for if thy foot once touch again the soil of the earth, thou shalt never win to me and to the Land of Youth again. And sorely do I fear some evil chance. Was not the love of Niam of the Head of Gold enough to fill a mortal's heart? But if thou must go, then go, and blessing and victory be thine."

Then Oisin held her long in his arms and kissed her, and vowed to make no long stay and never to alight from the fairy steed. And then he shook the golden reins and the horse threw its head aloft and snorted and bore him away in a pace like that of flowing water for speed and smoothness. Anon they came to the margin of the blue sea, and still the white steed galloped on, brushing the crests of the waves into glittering spray. The sun glared upon the sea and Oisin's head swam with the heat and motion, and in mist and dreams he rode where no day was, nor night, nor any thought of time, until at last his horse's hoofs plowed through wet, yellow sands, and he saw black rocks rising up at each side of a little bay, and inland were fields green or brown, and white cottages thatched with reeds, and men and women, toil-worn and clad in earth-colored garments, went to and fro about their tasks or stopped gazing at the rider in his crimson cloak and at the golden trappings of his horse.

But among the cottages was a small house of stone such as Oisin had never seen in the land of Erinn; stone was its roof as well as the walls, very steep and high, and near-by from a rude frame of timber there hung a bell of bronze. Into this house there passed one whom from his shaven crown Oisin guessed to be a druid, and behind him two lads in white apparel. The druid having seen the horseman turned his eyes again to the ground and passed on, regarding him not, and the lads did likewise. And Oisin rode on, eager to reach the Dun upon the Hill of Allen and to see the faces of his kin and his friends.

At length, coming from the forest path into the great clearing where the Hill of Allen was wont to rise broad and green, with its rampart enclosing many white-walled dwellings, and the great hall towering high in the midst, he saw but grassy mounds overgrown with rank weeds and whin bushes, and among them pastured a peasant's kine. Then a strange horror fell upon him, and he thought some enchantment from the land of Faery held his eyes and mocked him with false visions. He threw his arms abroad and shouted the names of Finn and Oscar, but none replied, and he thought that perchance the hounds might hear him, and he cried upon Bran and Sceolaun, and strained his ears if they might catch the faintest rustle or whisper of the world from the sight of which his eyes were holden, but he heard only the sigh of the wind in the whins. Then he rode in terror from that place, setting his face toward the eastern sea, for he meant to traverse Ireland from side to side and end to end in the search for some escape from his enchantment. But when he came near to the eastern sea and was now in the place which is called the Valley of the Thrushes,[1] he saw in a field upon the hillside a crowd of men striving to roll aside a great boulder from their tilled land, and an overseer directing them. Toward them he rode, meaning to ask them concerning Finn and the Fianna. As he came near, they all stopped their work to gaze upon him, for to them he appeared like a messenger of the Fairy Folk or an angel from heaven. Taller and mightier he was than the men-folk they knew, with sword-blue eyes and brown ruddy cheeks; in

---

[1] Glanismole, near Dublin.

his mouth, as it were, a shower of pearls, and bright hair clustered beneath the rim of his helmet. And as Oisin looked upon their puny forms, marred by toil and care, and at the stone which they feebly strove to heave from its bed, he was filled with pity, and thought to himself, "not such were even the churls of Erinn when I left them for the Land of Youth," and he stooped in his saddle to help them. His hand he set to the boulder, and with a mighty heave he lifted it from where it lay and set it rolling down the hill. And the men raised a shout of wonder and applause, but their shouting changed in a moment into cries of terror and dismay, and they fled, jostling and overthrowing each other to escape from the place of fear, for a marvel horrible to see had taken place. For Oisin's saddle girth had burst as he heaved the stone, and he fell headlong to the ground. In an instant the white steed had vanished from their eyes like a wreath of mist, and that which rose, feeble and staggering, from the ground was no youthful warrior but a man stricken with extreme old age, white-bearded and withered, who stretched out groping hands and moaned with feeble and bitter cries. And his crimson cloak and yellow silken tunic were now but coarse homespun stuff tied with a hempen girdle, and the gold-hilted sword was a rough oaken staff such as a beggar carries who wanders the roads from farmer's house to house.

When the people saw that the doom that had been wrought was not for them they returned, and found the old man prone on the ground with his face hidden in his arms. So they lifted him up and asked who he was and what had befallen him. Oisin gazed round on them with dim eyes, and at last he said, "I was Oisin the Son of Finn, and I pray ye tell me where he now dwells, for his Dun on the Hill of Allen is now a desolation, and I have neither seen him nor heard his hunting horn from the Western to the Eastern Sea."

Then the men gazed strangely on each other and on Oisin, and the overseer asked, "Of what Finn dost thou speak, for there be many of that name in Erinn?" Oisin said, "Surely of Finn mac Cumhal mac Trenmor, captain of the Fianna of Erinn." Then the overseer said, "Thou art daft, old man, and thou hast made us daft to take thee for a youth as we did a while a-gone. But we at least have now our

wits again, and we know that Finn son of Cumhal and all his gen-
eration have been dead these three hundred years. At the battle of
Gowra fell Oscar, son of Oisin, and Finn at the battle of Brea, as
the historians tell us; and the lays of Oisin, whose death no man
knows the manner of, are sung by our harpers at great men's feasts.
But now the Talkenn[1], Patrick, has come into Ireland and has
preached to us the One God and Christ His Son, by whose might
these old days and ways are done away with, and Finn and his
Fianna, with their feasting and hunting and songs of war and of
love, have no such reverence among us as the monks and virgins
of holy Patrick, and the psalms and prayers that go up daily to
cleanse us from sin and to save us from the fire of judgment." But
Oisin replied, half hearing and still less comprehending what was
said to him, "If thy God have slain Finn and Oscar, I would say that
God is a strong man." Then they all cried out upon him, and some
picked up stones, but the overseer bade them let him be until the
Talkenn had spoken with him, and till he should order what was
to be done.

So they brought him to Patrick, who entreated him gently and
hospitably, and to Patrick he told the story of all that had befallen
him. But Patrick bade his scribes write all carefully down, that the
memory of the heroes whom Oisin had known, and of the joyous
and free life they had led in the woods and glens and wild places of
Erinn, should never be forgotten among men. And Oisin, during the
short span of life that yet remained to him, told to Patrick many
tales of the Fianna and their deeds, but of the three hundred years
that he had spent with Niam in the Land of Youth he rarely spoke,
for they seemed to him but as a vision or a dream of the night, set
between a sunny and a rainy day.

---

[1] Talkenn or "Adze-head" was a name given to St. Patrick by the Irish. Probably it referred
to the shape of his tonsure.

THE BOYHOOD OF CUCHULAIN

By ELEANOR HULL

(Cormac and Fergus, chiefs of Ulster in exile in Connaught, sat in the tent door around the fire, telling Queen Meave of the prowess of young Cuchulain, then a lad of six or seven years.)

HOW CUCHULAIN GOT HIS NAME

AND Cormac said: "In Ulster, near Cuchulain's country, was a mighty artificer and smith, whose name was Culain. Now the custom is, that every man of means and every owner of land in Ulster, should, once in a year or so, invite the King and his chiefs to spend a few days, it may be a week or a fortnight, at his house, that he may give them entertainment. But Culain owned no lands, nor was he rich, for only the fruit of his hammer, of his anvil and his tongs, had he. Nevertheless he desired to entertain the King at a banquet, and he went to Emain to invite his chief. But he said, 'I have no lands or store of wealth; I pray thee, therefore, to bring with thee but a few of thy prime warriors, because my house cannot contain a great company of guests.'

So the King said he would go, bringing a small retinue with him.

"Culain returned home to prepare his banquet, and when the day was come, toward evening the King set forth to reach the fort of Culain. He assumed his light, convenient traveling garb, and before starting he went down to the green to bid the boy-corps farewell.

"There he saw a sight so curious that he could not tear himself away. At one end of the green stood a group of a hundred and fifty youths, guarding one goal, all striving to prevent the ball of a single little boy who was playing against the whole of them, from getting in; but for all that they could do, he won the game, and drove his ball home to the goal.

"Then they changed sides, and the little lad defended his one goal against the hundred and fifty balls of the other youths, all sent at

344

once across the ground. But though the youths played well, following up their balls, not one of them went into the hole, for the little boy caught them one after another just outside, driving them hither and thither, so that they could not make the goal. But when his turn came round to make the counterstroke, he was as successful as before; nay, he would get the entire set of a hundred and fifty balls into their hole, for all that they could do.

"Then they played a game of getting each other's cloaks off without tearing them, and he would have their mantles off, one after the other, before they could, on their part, even unfasten the brooch that held his cloak. When they wrestled with each other, it was the same thing: he would have them on the ground before all of them together could upset him, or make him budge a foot.

"As the King stood and watched all this, he said: ' 'Tis well for the country into which this boy has come! A clever child indeed is he; but were his acts as a grown man to come up to the promise of his youth, he might be of some solid use to us; but this is not to be counted upon.' "

"Then," Fergus said, breaking in upon the tale, "I was vexed because the King seemed to doubt the child, whether his after deeds would equal the promise of his youth; and I spoke up and said, 'That, O King, I think not wisely said; have no fear for this boy, for as his childish deeds outstrip the acts of childhood, so will his manly feats outshine the deeds of heroes and great men.' Then the King said to me, 'Have the child called, that we may take him with us to the banquet.'

"So when Setanta came, the King invited him; but the boy said, 'Excuse me now awhile; I cannot go just now.' 'How so?' said the King, surprised. 'Because the boy-corps have not yet had enough of play.' 'I cannot wait until they have,' replied the King: 'the night is growing late.' 'Wait not at all,' replied the child; 'I will even finish this one game, and will run after you.' 'But young one, knowest thou the way?' asked the King. 'I will follow the trail made by your company, the wheels of their chariots and hoofs of the horses on the road,' he replied."

"Thereupon," continued Cormac, "Conor starts; and in time for the banquet he reaches Culain's house, where, with due honor, he is received. Fresh rushes had been strewn upon the floor, the tables all decked out, the fires burning in the middle of the room. A great vat full of ale stood in the hall, a lofty candlestick gave light, and round the fires stood servants cooking savory viands, holding them on forks or spits of wood. Each man of the King's guests entered in order of his rank, and sat at the feast in his own allotted place, hanging his weapons up above his head. The King occupied the central seat, his poets, counselors, and chiefs sitting on either hand according to their state and dignity. As they were sitting down, the smith Culain came to Conor and asked him, 'Good now, O King, before we sit at meat I would even know whether anyone at all will follow thee this night to my dwelling, or is thy whole company gathered now within?' 'All are now here,' said the King, quite forgetting the wee boy; 'but wherefore asketh thou?'

"'It is only that I have an excellent watchdog, fierce and strong; and when his chain is taken off, and he is set free to guard the house, no one dare come anywhere within the same district with him; he is furious with all but me, and he has the strength and savage force of a hundred ordinary watchdogs. This dog was brought to me from Spain, and no dog in the country can equal him.' 'Let him be set loose, for all are here,' said Conor; 'well will he guard this place for us.'

"So Culain loosed the dog, and with one spring it bounded forth out of the court of the house and over the wall of the rath, making a circuit of the entire district; and when it came back panting, with its tongue hanging from its jaws, it took up its usual position in front of the house, and there crouched with its head upon its paws, watching the high road to Ewain. Surely an extraordinarily cruel and fierce and savage dog was he.

"When the boy-corps broke up that night, each of the lads returning to the house of his parent or his fosterer or guardian, Setanta, trusting to the trail of the company that went with Conor, struck out for Culain's house. With his club and ball he ran forward, and the distance seemed short on account of his interest in the game. As soon as he arrived on the green of Culain's fort, the mastiff noticed him, and set up such a howling as echoed loud through all the countryside. Inside the house the King and his followers heard, but were struck dumb with fear, nor dared to move, thinking surely to find the little lad dead at the door of the fort. As for the hound himself, he thought with but one gulp to swallow Setanta whole. Now the little lad was without any means of defense beyond his ball and hurley-stick. He never left his play till he came near. Then, as the hound charged open-jawed, with all his strength he threw the ball right into the creature's mouth; and as for a moment the hound stopped short, choking as the ball passed down his throat, the lad seized hold of the mastiff's open jaws, grasping its throat with one hand and the back of his head with the other, and so violently did he strike its head against the pillars of the door, that it was no long time until the creature lay dead upon the ground.

"When Culain and the warriors within had heard the mastiff howl, they asked each other, as soon as they got back their voices, 'What makes the watchdog cry?' 'Alas!' the King said, ''tis no good luck that brought us on our present trip.' 'Why so?' inquired all. 'I mean that the little boy, my foster son and Fergus's, Setanta, son of Sualtach, it is who promised to come after me; now, even now, he is doubtless fallen by the hound of Culain.' Then, when they heard that it was Conor's foster son who was without, on the instant to one man they rose; and though the doors of the fort were thrown wide they could not wait for that, but out they stormed over the walls and the ramparts of the fort to find the boy."

"Quick they were," said Fergus, interrupting, "yet did I oustrip them, and at the rampart's outer door I found the child, and the great hound dead beside him. Without a pause I picked up the boy and hoisted him on my shoulder, and, with all the heroes following, we came to Conor, and I placed him between the monarch's knees."

"Yes, so it was," said Cormac, taking up the story again where he had left it; "but let me tell of Culain. The smith went out to find his dog, and when he saw him lying there, knocked almost to pieces and quite dead, his heart was vexed within him. He went back to the house, and said, ''Twas no good luck that urged me to make this feast for thee, O King; would I had not prepared a banquet. My life is a life lost, and my substance is but substance wasted without my dog. He was a defense and protection to our property and our cattle, to every beast we had and to our house. Little boy,' said he, 'you are welcome for your people's sake, you are not welcome for your own; that was a good member of my family thou didst take from me, a safeguard of raiment, of flocks and herds.' 'Be not vexed thereat,' replied the child, 'for I myself will fix on my own punishment. This shall it be. If in all Ireland a whelp of that dog's breed is to be found, 'tis I myself will rear him up for thee till he be fit to take the watchdog's place. In the meantime, O Culain, I myself will be your hound for defense of your cattle and for your own defense, until the dog be grown and capable of action; I will defend the territory, and no cattle or beast or store of thine shall be taken from thee, without my knowing it.'

"'Well hast thou made the award,' said they all, 'and henceforward shall your name be changed; you shall no longer be called Setanta; Cu-Chulain, or the "Hound of Culain," shall your name be.

"'I like my own name best,' the child objected.

"'Ah, say not so,' replied the magician, 'for one day will be the name of Cuchulain ring in all men's mouths; among the brave ones of the whole wide world Cuchulain's name shall find a place. Renowned and famous shall he be, beloved and feared by all.'

'If that be so, then am I well content,' replied the boy.

"So from that day forth the name Cuchulain clung to him, until the time came when he was no longer remembered as the Hound of Culain's Fort, but as the guardian and watchdog of defense to the Province against her foes; and then men loved best to call him 'The Hound of Ulster.'

"Now," continued Cormac, "it would be reasonable to expect that the little boy, who, at the age of six or seven years slew a dog whom a whole company would not dare to touch when he was at large, would, at the age of a grown youth, be formidable to Ulster's foes."

And Meave was forced to admit that it was likely that he would.

HOW CUCHULAIN TOOK ARMS

When Meave had thought awhile, she said, "Are there yet other stories of this wondrous boy?" "Indeed," cried Fiacra, one of the companions of Cormac, who came with him when he went from Ulster into exile, "the story of his taking arms is not told yet, and I think it more than all the other stories you have heard." "How so?" said Meave; "tell it to us now."

Then Fiacra said, "The very year after Cuchulain got his name, he was playing outside the place where Caffa the magician sat with eight of his pupils teaching them his lore. It chanced that he was telling them, as the magicians and Druids are wont to believe, that certain days were lucky for special acts and other days unlucky. 'And for what,' asked one of the boys, 'would this day at which we now are to be counted lucky?'

"'This is the day,' said Caffa, 'on which any youth who should assume arms, as became a champion of war, should attain eternal fame; beside him, no warrior's name in Ireland should ever more be named, or spoken in the same breath with it, for his glory would transcend them all. For such a youth, however, no happy thing were this, for he should die at an early age, no long-lived warrior he; his life shall be but fleeting, quickly o'er.'

"Outside the house Cuchulain overheard the conversation of the teacher with his boys. Instantly and without a moment's pause he laid aside his hurley and his ball, and put off his playing suit. Then, donning his ordinary apparel, he entered the sleeping house of the King. 'All good be thine, O King,' said he. 'Boy, what hast thou now come to ask of me?' replied the King. 'I desire,' said he, 'to take arms as a warrior and champion today.' 'Who told thee to ask for this?' said the King, surprised. 'My master Caffa, the magician,' answered he. 'If that is so, thou shalt not be denied,' replied the King, and he called on those who were about him to give the lad two spears and sword and shield: for in Emain the King had always ready seventeen complete equipments of weapons and armature; for he himself bestowed weapons on a youth of the boy-corps when he was ready to bear arms, to bring him luck in using them. Cuchulain began to try those weapons, brandishing and bending them to try their strength and fitness to his hand; but one after another they all gave way, and were broken into pieces and little fragments. 'These weapons are not good,' said he; 'they are but the equipment of a common warrior, they suffice me not.' Then when he had tried them all, and put them from him, the King said: 'Here, my lad, are my own two spears, my own sword and shield.' Then Cuchulain took these weapons, and in every way, by bending them from point to hilt, by brandishing them, by thrusting with them, he proved their strength and mettle. 'These arms are good,' said he, 'they break not in my hand. Fair fall the land and country whose King can wield armor and weapons such as these!'

"Just at the moment Caffa came into the tent. Wondering, he asked: 'Is the little boy so soon assuming arms?' 'Ay, so it is,' said the King. 'Unhappy is the mother whose son assumes arms today,' said the magician. 'How now?' cried the King; 'was it not yourself who prompted him?' 'Not so, indeed,' said Caffa. 'Mad boy, what made you then deceive me, telling me that Caffa it was who prompted you to ask for arms?' 'O King of Heroes, be not wroth,' replied the lad. 'No thought, indeed, had I to deceive. When Caffa was instructing his pupils in the house today, I overheard, as I was playing with my ball outside, one of the lads asking him what special virtue lay in this day, and for what was it a lucky day. And he told them that for him who should assume arms this day, his luck should be so great that his fame would outstrip the fame of all Ireland's heroes, and he would be the first of Ireland's men. And for this great reward, no compensating disadvantage would accrue to him, save that his life should be but fleeting.'

" 'True is that, indeed,' said Caffa, 'noble and famous thou shalt be, but short and brief thy life.' 'Little care I for that,' replied the lad, 'nor though my life endured but for one day and night, so only that the story of myself and of my deeds shall last.'

" 'Then get thee into a chariot, as a warrior should, and let us test thy title to a future fame.'

"So a chariot of two horses was brought to Cuchulain, and every way he tried its strength, driving it furiously round and round the green, goading the horses and turning suddenly. But for this usage the chariot was not fit, and it broke beneath him. Twelve chariots were brought to him, and he tested them all in this manner, but all of them he reduced to fragments. 'These chariots of thine, O Conor, are no good at all, they serve me not, nor are they worthy of me, thy own foster son.'

"Then the King cried: 'Fetch me here Ivar, my own charioteer, and let him harness my steeds into the kingly chariot, and bring it here to serve Cuchulain.' Then the kingly chariot of war was brought and Cuchulain mounted, testing it every way; and well it served him at every test. 'The chariot is good, and the steeds are good, they are worthy of me,' said the boy; 'it is my worthy match.'

"'Well, boy, it is time that thou wert satisfied at last; now I will take the horses home and put them out to graze,' said Ivar.

"'Not yet awhile,' said Cuchulain. 'Drive but the horses round the kingly fort.' Ivar did so, and then he said again: 'Be satisfied now, my lad; I go to turn the horses out to grass.' For it was but seldom that King Conor went forth in his war-chariot, because the men of Ulster willed not that the King should expose his person in battle; so Ivar was grown idle, and fat through his idleness, and he liked not at all the unwonted exertion that the wee boy asked of him.

"'Not yet awhile,' said Cuchulain again; 'too early is it to turn in; drive now toward the playing fields that the boy-corps may salute me on this the first day of my taking arms.' They did so, and the boy-corps gathered round. 'These are a warrior's arms that thou hast taken!' cried they all, surprised to see him thus equipped in the King's own warrior gear, and driving in the chariot of the King. 'Just so, indeed,' replied the boy. Then they wished him well in his warrior career. 'May success in winning of spoils, and in blood-drawing, be thine,' they cried. 'But all too soon it is thou leavest us and our boyish sports for deeds of war.' 'In no way do I wish to part with the beloved boy-corps,' replied the lad 'but it was a sign of luck and good fortune that I should take arms today; therefore I thought not well to miss my luck.'

"Then Ivar urged the child again, for he was growing tired of the thing, to let him take the horses out to graze. ''Tis early yet,

O Ivar,' said the boy; 'whither then goes this great Highroad I see?' 'That is the Highroad to the borders of the Province, and to the Ford of Watching or the Lookout Ford,' replied the charioteer. 'Why is it called the Lookout Ford?' asken then the boy. 'Because there, on the extreme limits of the Province, a watcher who is a prime warrior of Ulster always stands, prepared to challenge any stranger, before he pass the ford, of his business in the Province: if he who comes be a bard or peaceful man, to grant him protection and entertainment; but if he be a foe, to challenge him to combat at the ford. And seldom,' said the charioteer, 'does a day pass, but at the ford some enemy is slain. As to the bards who pass in peace, no doubt it is the kindness of that warrior they will praise when once they come to Emain, and stand before the King.' 'Who guards the ford this day, if thou dost know?' inquired Cuchulain. 'Conall the Victorious, Ulster's foremost man of war, it is who holds the ford this day.' 'Away then,' cried the lad, 'goad on they steeds, for we will seek the ford and Conall.'

" 'The horses are already tired, we have done enough for this one day,' quoth Ivar. 'The day is early yet, and our day's labors hardly yet begun,' replied the youth; 'away with you along this road.'

"They come at last to the ford's brink, and there beside the Ford of Watching stood young Conall, then Ulster's foremost man of war.

"When he saw the lad driving fully equipped for war in the chariot of the King, he felt surprise. 'Are you taking arms today, small boy?' he said. 'He is indeed,' said Ivar. 'May triumph and victory and drawing of first blood come with them,' answered Canall, for he loved the little lad, and many a time he had said to his fellows: 'The day will come when this young boy will dispute the championship of Ireland with me.' 'Nevertheless,' said he to Cuchulain, 'it seems to me that oversoon thou hast assumed these arms, seeing that thou art not yet fit for exploits or for war.' The boy heeded not this, but eagerly asked, 'What is it thou doest at the Ford of Watching, Conall?' 'On behalf of the Province I keep watch and ward, lest enemies creep in.' 'Give up thy place to me, for this one day let me take duty,' said Cuchulain. 'Say not so,' replied the champion, 'for as yet thou art not fit to cope with a right fighting-man.'

" 'Then on my own account must I go down into the shallows of
yon lake, to see whether there I may draw blood on either friend or
foe.' 'I will go with thee, then, to protect thee, to the end that on
the border-marshes thou run not into danger.' 'Nay, come not with
me, let me go alone today,' urged the lad. 'That I will not,' said
Conall, 'for, were I to allow thee all alone to frequent these dangerous
fighting grounds, on me would Ulster avenge it, if harm should
come to thee.'

"Then Conall had his chariot made ready and his horses harnessed; soon he overtook Cuchulain, who, to cut short the matter,
had gone on before. He came up abreast with him, and Cuchulain,
seeing this, felt sure that, Conall being there, no chance for deed of
prowess would come his way; for, if some deed of mortal daring
were to be done, Conall himself would undertake the same. Therefore he took up from the road a smooth round stone that filled his
fist, and with it he made a very careful shot at Conall's chariot-yoke.
It broke in two, and the chariot came down, Conall being thrown
forward over his horses' heads. 'What's this, ill-mannered boy?' said
he.

" 'I did it in order to see whether my markmanship were good,
and whether there were the makings of a man-at-arms in me.'
'Poison take both thy shot and thyself as well; and though thy head
should now fall a prize to some enemy of thine, yet never a foot
farther will I budge to keep thee.'

" 'The very thing I asked of thee,' replied the boy, 'and I do so in
this strange manner, because I know it is a custom among the men
of Ulster to turn back when any violence is done to them. Thus
have I made the matter sure.' On that, Conall turned back to his
post beside the Lookout Ford, and the little boy went forward southward to the shallows of the marshy loch, and he rested there till
eveningtide."

OF CUCHULAIN'S FIRST FEATS OF CHAMPIONSHIP

"Then Ivar said, 'If one might venture to make a suggestion to
such a little one, I should rejoice if we might now turn back and

find our way home to Emain again. For at this moment in the hall supper is being carved and the feast has just begun; and though for you your appointed place is kept at Conor's side until you come, I, on the contrary, if I come late must fit in where I may among the grooms and jesters of the house. For this reason I judge it now high time that I were back to scramble for my place.'

" 'Harness the horses and prepare the chariot,' Cuchulain said, and thinking that they now were going home, the charioteer most gladly hastened to obey. 'What mountain is that over there?' inquired the boy. 'Slieve Mourn,' replied the driver. 'Let us go thither,' said the lad. They reach the mountain's foot, and, 'What is that cairn I see upon the top?' said he again. 'The White Cairn is its name,' quoth Ivar sulkily. 'I would like to visit the White Cairn,' said the boy. 'The hill is high, and it is getting late,' replied the charioteer. 'Thou art a lazy loon,' Cuchulain says, 'and the more so that this is my first day's adventure-quest, and thy first day's trip abroad with me.' 'And if it is,' cried Ivar, 'and if we ever get home again, for ever and for ever may it be my last!'

"They gained the topmost peak, and far away descried a stretch of level country. 'Come now, driver,' said the lad, 'describe to me from here the whole of Ulster's wide domain; its forts and dwellings, fords and meadowlands, its hills and open spaces. Name every place in order, that thus I may the better know my way about.

" 'What is yon well-defined plain with hollow glens and running streams before us to the south?' 'Moy Bray,' replied the charioteer. 'The names, again, of all the forts and palaces scattered over it?' Then Ivar pointed out the kingly dwelling places of Tara and Taillte, and the summer palace of Cletty on the river Boyne; the Fairy Mound of Angus Og, the god of Youth and Beauty, and the burial-tomb of the Great God or Dagda Mór. And at the last he showed beneath the hill where lay the fort of the three fierce and warlike sons of Nechtan the Mighty.

" 'Are those the sons of Nechtan of whom I heard it said that the Ulstermen who are yet alive are not so many as have fallen by their hands?' 'The same,' said Ivar. 'Away then, with us straight to Nechtan's fort,' Cuchulain cried. 'Woe waits on him who goes to

Nechtan's fort,' replied the charioteer; 'whoever goes or goes not, I for one will never go.' 'Alive or dead thou goest there, however,' said the boy. 'Alive I go then, but sure it is that dead I shall be left there,' replied the charioteer.

"They make their way then down the hill and reach the green before the fort at the meeting of the bogland and the stream; and in the center of the green they saw an upright pillar-stone, encircled by an iron collar on its top. Words were engraven on the collar forbidding any man-at-arms or warrior to depart off the green, once he had entered it, without challenging to single combat some one of those living within the fort. Cuchulain read the writing, and he took the collar off the pillar-stone, and with all his strength he hurled it down the stream, for it was thus the challenge should be made.

"'In my poor opinion,' said the charioteer, 'the collar was much safer where it was, and well I know that this time, at all events, thou wilt find the object of thy careful search, a quick and violent death.' 'Good, good, O driver, talk not over much, but spread for me the chariot coverings on the ground, that I may sleep a while.'

"Now the charioteer was frightened, for he knew the fierceness and ill-fame of the sons of Nechtan, and he grumbled that Cuchulain should be so rash and foolhardy in a land of foemen as to sleep before their very door; but for all that he dared not disobey, and he took the cushions out of the chariot and spread them on the ground and covered Cuchulain with the skins; and in a moment the little fellow was asleep, his head resting peacefully on his hand. Just then Foll, son of Nechtan, issued from the fort. Ivar would well have liked to waken up Cuchulain, but he did not dare, for the child had said before he fell asleep: 'Waken me up if many come, but waken me not for a few'; and Foll mac Nechtan came alone. At sight of the chariot standing on his lands, the warrior thundered forth, 'Driver, be off at once with those horses; let them not graze upon our ground; unyoke them not.' 'I have not unyoked them,' said the charioteer. 'I hold the reins yet in my hands ready for the road.' 'Whose steeds and chariot are they?' enquired the man. 'The steeds of Conor, King of Ulster,' said Ivar. 'Just as I thought,' said Foll; 'and who has brought them to these borders?' 'A young bit of a little boy,' said Ivar, hoping to hinder Foll from fighting him. 'A high-headed wee fellow, who, for luck, has taken arms today, and come into the marshes to show off his form and skill as though he were a grown champion.' 'Ill luck to him, whoever he is,' said Foll; 'were he a man capable of fight, I would send him back to the King dead.' 'Capable of fight he is not, indeed, nor a man at all,' said Ivar, 'but only a small child of seven years, playing at being a man.'

"Cuchulain in his sleep heard the affront that the charioteer put upon him, and from head to foot he blushed a rosy red. His face he lifted from the ground and said: 'I am not a child at all, but ripe and fit for action, as you will see; this "small child" here has come to seek for battle with a man.' 'I rather hold that fit for action thou art not,' replied Foll, surprised to find the little fellow rising from his sleep and speaking with such boldness. 'That we shall know presently,' replied the boy; 'come down only to the ford, where it is customary in Ireland that combats should take place. But first go home and fetch your arms, for in cowardly guise come you hither, and never will I fight with men unarmed, or messengers, or drivers in their cloaks, but only with full-weaponed men-of-war.'

"'That suits me well,' said Foll, and he rushed headlong for his his arms. 'It will suit you even better when we come to the ford,' said Cuchulain. Then Ivar warned Cuchulain that this Foll was no ordinary foe; 'he bears a charmed life,' said he, 'and only he who slays him with one stroke has any chance of killing him at all. No sword-edge can bite or wound him, he can only be slain by the first thrust of a spear, or blow of a weapon from a distance.' 'Then I will play a special feat on him,' returned the boy; 'surely it is to humble me you warn me thus.' With that he took in his hand his hard-tempered iron ball, and with a strong and exact throw just as Foll was coming forth, full-armored from the fort, he launched the ball, which pierced the warrior's forehead, so that he fell headlong on the ground, uttering his last cry of pain, and with that he died.

"Within the fort his brothers heard that cry, and the second brother rushes out. 'No doubt you think this is a great feat you have done, and one to boast of,' he cried. 'I think not the slaying of any single man a cause to boast at all,' replied the boy; 'but hasten now and fetch your weapons, for in the guise of an unweaponed messenger or chariot-boy come you hither.' 'Beware of this man,' said Ivar; 'Tuacall, or "Cunning" is his name, for so swift and dexterous is he, that no man has ever been able to pierce him with any weapon.'

" 'It is not fitting that you speak like this to me,' said Cuchulain. 'I will take the great spear of Conor, and with it I will pierce his shield and heart, before ever he comes near me.'

"And so he did, for hardly was the Cunning One come forth out of the fort, than Cuchulain threw the heavy spear; it entered his heart and went out behind him. As he fell dead, Cuchulain leaped on him, and cut off his head.

"Then the third son of Nechtan came out, and scoffed at the lad. 'Those were but simpletons and fools with whom thou hast fought hitherto,' he said; 'I challenge thee to come down to the ford, and out upon the middle of the stream, and we will see thy bravery there.' Cuchulain asks him what he means by this, and Ivar breaks in: 'Do you not know that this is Fandall, son of Nechtan, and Fainle or Fandall, a "Swallow," is his name, because he travels over the water with the swiftness of a swallow, nor can the swimmers of the whole world attempt to cope with him. Beware of him and go not to the ford.'

" 'Not fitting are such words to be spoken to me,' replied the lad, 'for do you remember the river we have in Emain, called the Callan? When the boy-corps break off their sports and plunge into the stream to swim, do you not know that I can take one of them on either shoulder or even on my palms, and carry them across the water without wetting so much as their ankles? For another man, your words are good; they are not good for me.'

"Then came Fainle forth, and he and the lad entered the stream together, and swam out and wrestled in deep water. But suddenly by a swift turn, the youngster clasped his arms about him, laid him even with the top of the water, and with one stroke of Conor's sword cut off his head, carrying it shoreward in his hand, while the body floated down the current. Behind him he heard the cry of their mother, the wife of Nechtan, when she saw her three sons slain. Then Cuchulain sent her out of the fort, and he and his charioteer went up and harried it, and set it all in flames; for an evil and a pirate fort had that fort been to Ulster, bringing many of their warriors to death, and spoiling all their lands. Then Cuchulain and Ivar turned to retrace their steps, carrying in their hands the heads of Nechtan's sons. They put their spoils and the three heads into the chariot, sticking the dripping heads upon the chariot-pole that passed out behind, and set out in triumph toward Emain and the palace of the King.

"'You promised us a good run today,' said Cuchulain to the charioteer; 'and we need it now after the contest we have made; away with us across Moy Bray, and round the mountain of Slieve Fuad.' Then Ivar spurred the horses forward with his goad, and so fast did they race onward that they outstripped the wind in speed, and left the flying birds behind them. To while away the time, Cuchulain sent stones speeding before him from his sling; before the stone could reach the ground, the chariot had caught it up and it fell again into the chariot floor.

"At the foot of Slieve Fuad a herd of antlered deer were feeding beside a wood. Never before had Cuchulain seen a herd of deer; he marveled at their branching antlers, and at the speed and lightness with which they moved from place to place. 'What is that great flock of active cattle yonder?' inquired the boy. 'Those are not cattle, but a herd of wild deer that wander in the dark recesses of the hills,' replied the charioteer. 'Which would the men of Ulster think the greatest feat, to capture one dead or to bring one home alive?' 'Assuredly to capture one alive,' said Ivar. 'Dead everyone could bring one down, but seldom indeed can one be captured alive.' 'Goad on the horses,' said the lad; and this the driver did, but the fat horses of the King, unused to such a drive and rate of motion as they had had that day, turned restive and plunged into the bog, where they stuck fast. Eagerly Cuchulain sprang down, and leaving the charioteer to struggle with the horses, he set off after the flying deer, and by sheer running came up to them, caught two of the largest stags by the horns, and with thongs and ropes bound them behind the chariot between the poles.

"Again," on their way to Emain, a flock of swans passed overhead, flying before them. 'What birds are those?' inquired the boy. 'Are they tame birds or wild?' 'Those are wild swans,' said Ivar, 'that fly inland from the rocks and islands of the sea to feed.' 'Would the Ulstermen think better of me if I brought them in dead or if I captured them alive?' again inquired the boy. 'Assuredly to bring them down alive.'

"Then Cuchulain took his sling and with a well-aimed shot he brought down one or two of the swans. Again and again he aimed until several of the birds were lying on the path before them. 'Ivar, go you and fetch the birds alive,' said the boy.

"'It is not easy for me to do that,' he said. 'The horses are become wild and I cannot leave them or leap out in front of them. If then I try to get out at the side, I shall be cut to pieces with the sharp rims of the chariot-wheels; if I get out behind, the stags will gore me with their horns.' 'That is not a warrior's speech, but the speech of a coward,' said the lad. 'But come now, step out fearlessly upon the antler of the deer, for I will bend my eye on him, so that he will not stir or harm you, nor will the horses move when I have overlooked them.' This then was done. Cuchulain held the reins, while Ivar got out and collected the fallen birds. With long cords the birds were fastened to the chariot, and thus they went on to Emain, with the wild stags running behind the chariot, and the flock of birds flying over it, and on the poles the bleeding heads of the three sons of Nechtan the Mighty.

"On the walls of Emain a watchman was at the lookout post. 'A solitary warrior draws near to thee, O Conor, and terribly he comes! Upon the chariot pole are bleeding heads; white birds are flying round the car, and wild unbroken stags are tethered fast behind. Wildly and with fury he draws near, and unless some means be taken to abate his rage, the young men of Emain's fort will perish by his hand.'

"'Warriors will not stay his hand. I know that little boy; it is my foster son, who on this day has taken arms and made his first champion-raid. But before women he is ever courteous and modest; let then the women-folk of Emain's fort, and our noble wives, go forth to meet him, for that will tame his rage.' So the champion's wives and the women of Emain went out in a troop to meet him, and when he saw them come, the fury of war passed from Cuchulain, and he leaned his head upon the chariot-rail, that they might not see the battle rage that was upon his face. For in the presence of women Cuchulain was ever calm and gentle-mannered.

"Yet so warm and ardent was he from his warrior-raid, that the champions of Ulster bathed him in three baths of cold water before his heat and travel-stains were passed away from him. And the water of the baths was heated fiery-hot by his plunge into it. But when he was washed, and arrayed in his hooded tunic and mantle of bright blue, fastened with its silver brooch, the little man's fury had all gone from him; he blushed a beautiful ruddy hue all over, and with his eyes sparkling, and his golden hair combed back, he came to take his place beside the King. And Conor was proud of the boy, and drew him between his knees and stroked his hair; and his place was ever beside the King after that.

"Now a little boy that at the age of seven years—" continued Fiachra, who told the tale—"could kill a man, yea, two or three men, whom all the champions of Ulster feared, and who could do such deeds, it were not wonderful if, in your war with Ulster, O Queen Meave, he should prove a formidable foe."

And Meave said thoughtfully, "It were not wonderful indeed."

Then the company broke up, preparing for the march upon the morrow. But that night Meave said to her spouse: "I think, O Ailill, that this young champion of Ulster is not of the make of mortal men, nor is he quite as other champions. And tho our host is good and sufficient for ordinary war, to meet a foe like this, it seems to me that a great and mighty force is needed; for I am of opinion that the war on which we are now come will not be a battle of a night or a day, but that it will be a campaign of many days and weeks and months against that lad. Therefore, at this time, let us return home again, and when a year or two is out, I shall have gathered such a host that the gods themselves could not withstand it." Thus Meave spoke boastfully, and Ailill was well content, for he liked not the war. So for that time, they all turned home again.

Robin Hood

From the

OLD ENGLISH BALLADS

ROBIN HOOD

The Robin Hood ballads are the earliest form in which are related the legendary adventures of the famous outlaw who lived in the English greenwood.

ROBIN HOOD BALLADS

ROBIN HOOD AND LITTLE JOHN

When Robin Hood was about twenty years old,
With a hey down down and a down
He happened to meet little John,
A jolly brisk blade, right fit for the trade,
For he was a lusty young man.

Tho he was call'd Little, his limbs they were large,
And his stature was seven foot high;
Where-ever he came, they quak'd at his name,
For soon he would make them to fly.

How they came acquainted, I'll tell you in brief,
If you will but listen a while;
For this very jest, amongst all the rest,
I think it may cause you to smile.

Bold Robin Hood said to his jolly bowmen,
"Pray tarry you here in this grove;
And see that you all observe well my call,
While thorough the forest I rove.

"We have had no sport for these fourteen long days,
Therefore now abroad will I go;
Now should I beat, and cannot retreat,
My horn I will presently blow."

Then did he shake hands with his merry men all,
And bid them at present good b'w'ye;
Then, as near a brook his journey he took,
A stranger he chanc'd to espy.

They happened to meet on a long narrow bridge,
And neither of them would give way;
Quoth bold Robin Hood, and sturdily stood,
"I'll show you right Nottingham play."

With that from his quiver an arrow he drew,
A broad arrow with a goose-wing:

The stranger reply'd, "I'll liquor thy hide,
  If thou offerst to touch the string."

Quoth bold Robin Hood, "Thou dost prate like an ass,
  For were I to bend but my bow,
I could send a dart quite thro thy proud heart,
  Before thou couldst strike me one blow."

"Thou talkst like a coward," the stranger reply'd;
  "Well armd with a long bow you stand,
To shoot at my breast, while I, I protest,
  Have nought but a staff in my hand."

"The name of a coward," quoth Robin, "I scorn,
  Wherefore my long bow I'll lay by;
And now, for thy sake, a staff will I take,

Then Robin Hood stept to a thicket of trees,
  And chose him a staff of ground-oak;
Now this being done, away he did run
  To the stranger, and merrily spoke:

"Lo! see my staff, it is lusty and tough,
  Now here on this bridge we will play;
Whoever falls in, the other shall win
  The battel, and so we'll away."

"With all my whole heart," the stranger reply'd;
  "I scorn in the least to give out";
This said, they fell to 't without more dispute,
  And their staffs they did flourish about.

And first Robin he gave the stranger a bang,
  So hard that it made his bones ring:
The stranger he said, "This must be repaid,
  I'll give you as good as you bring.

"So long as I'm able to handle my staff,
  The truth of thy manhood to try."
To die in your debt, friend, I scorn.
Then to it each goes, and follow'd their blows,
  As if they had been threshing of corn.

The stranger gave Robin a crack on the crown,
  Which caused the blood to appear;
Then Robin, enrag'd, more fiercely engag'd,
  And followed his blows more severe.

So thick and so fast did he lay it on him,
   With a passionate fury and ire,
At every stroke, he made him to smoke,
   As if he had been all on fire.

O then into fury the stranger he grew,
   And gave him a damnable look,
And with it a blow that laid him full low,
   And tumbl'd him into the brook.

"I prithee, good fellow, O where art thou now?"
   The stranger, in laughter, he cry'd;
Quoth bold Robin Hood, "Good faith, in the flood,
   And floating along with the tide.

"I needs must acknowledge thou art a brave soul;
   With thee I'll no longer contend;
For needs must I say, thou hast got the day,
   Our battel shall be at an end."

Then unto the bank he did presently wade,
   And pulld himself out by a thorn;
Which done, at the last, he blowd a loud blast
   Straitway on his fine bugle-horn.

The echo of which through the vallies did fly,
   At which his stout bowmen appear'd,
All cloathed in green, most gay to be seen;
   So up to their master they steerd.

"O what's the matter?" quoth William Stutely;
   "Good master, you are wet to the skin."
"No matter," quoth he; "the lad which you see,
   In fighting, hath tumbld me in."

"He shall not go scot-free," the others reply'd;
   So strait they were seizing him there,
To duck him likewise; but Robin Hood cries,
   "He is a stout fellow, forbear.

"There's no one shall wrong thee, friend, be not afraid;
   These bowmen upon me do wait;
There's threescore and nine; if thou wilt be mine,
   Thou shalt have my livery strait.

"And other accoutrements fit for a man;
   Speak up, jolly blade, never fear;

I'll teach you also the use of the bow,
  To shoot at the fat fallow-deer."

"O here is my hand," the stranger reply'd,
  "I'll serve you with all my whole heart;
My name is John Little, a man of good mettle;
  Nere doubt me, for I'll play my part."

"His name shall be alterd," quoth William Stutely,
  "And I will his godfather be;
Prepare then a feast, and none of the least,
  For we will be merry," quoth he.

They presently fetchd in a brace of fat does,
  With humming strong liquor likewise;
They lov'd what was good; so, in the greenwood,
  This pretty sweet babe they baptize.

He was, I must tell you, but seven foot high,
  And, may be, an ell in the waste;
A pretty sweet lad; much feasting they had;
  Bold Robin the christening grac'd,

With all his bowmen, which stood in a ring,
  And were of the Notti[n]gham breed;
Brave Stutely comes then, with seven yeomen,
  And did in this manner proceed:

"This infant was calld John Little," quoth he,
  "Which name shall be changd anon;
The words we'll transpose, so wherever he goes,
  His name shall be called Little John."

Then Robin he took the pretty sweet babe,
  And cloathed him from top to the toe
In garments of green, most gay to be seen,
  And gave him a curious long bow.

"Thou shalt be an archer as well as the best,
  And range in the greenwood with us;
Where we'll not want gold nor silver, behold,
  While bishops have ought in their purse.

"We live here like squires, or lords of renown,
  Without ere a foot of free land;
We feast on good cheer, with wine, ale, and beer,
  And evry thing at our command."

Then musick and dancing did finish the day;
    At length, when the sun waxed low,
Then all the whole train the grove did refrain,
    And unto their caves they did go.

And so ever after, as long as he livd
    Altho he was proper and tall,
Yet nevertheless, the truth to express,
    Still Little John they did him call.

ROBIN HOOD AND ALLEN A DALE

Come listen to me, you gallants so free,
    All you that loves mirth for to hear,
And I will you tell of a bold outlaw,
    That lived in Nottinghamshire.

As Robin Hood in the forrest stood,
    All under the green-wood tree,
There was he ware of a brave young man,
    As fine as fine might be.

The youngster was clothed in scarlet red,
    In scarlet fine and gay,
And he did frisk it over the plain,
    And chanted a roundelay.

As Robin Hood next morning stood,
    Amongst the leaves so gay,
There did he espy the same young man
    Come drooping along the way.

The scarlet he wore the day before,
    It was clean cast away;
And every step he fetcht a sigh,
    "Alack and a well a day!"

Then stepped forth brave Little John,
    And Nick the miller's son,
Which made the young man bend his bow,
    When as he see them come.

"Stand off, stand off," the young man said,
    "What is your will with me?"

"You must come before our master straight,
  Under yon green-wood tree."

And when he came bold Robin before,
  Robin askt him courteously,
"O hast thou any money to spare
  For my merry men and me?"

"I have no money," the young man said,
  "But five shillings and a ring;
And that I have kept this seven long years,
  To have it at my wedding.

"Yesterday, I should have married a maid,
  But she is now from me tane,
And chosen to be an old knight's delight,
  Whereby my poor heart is slain."

"What is thy name?" then said Robin Hood,
  "Come tell me, without any fail:"
"By the faith of my body," then said the young man,
  "My name it is Allen a Dale."

"What wilt thou give me," said Robin Hood,
  "In ready gold or fee,
To help thee to thy true-love again,
  And deliver her unto thee?"

"I have no money," then quoth the young man,
  "Nor ready gold nor fee,
But I will swear upon a book
  Thy true servant for to be."

"How many miles is it to thy true-love?
  Come tell me without any guile:"
"By the faith of my body," then said the young man,
  "It is but five little mile."

Then Robin he hasted over the plain,
  He did neither stint nor lin,
Until he came unto the church
  Where Allen should keep his wedding.

"What dost thou do here?" the bishop he said,
  "I prithee now tell to me:"
"I am a bold harper," quoth Robin Hood,
  "And the best in the north countrey."

"O welcome, O welcome," the bishop he said,
  "That musick best pleaseth me";
"You shall have no musick," quoth Robin Hood,
  "Till the bride and the bridegroom I see."

With that came in a wealthy knight,
  Which was both grave and old,
And after him a finiken lass,
  Did shine like glistering gold.

"This is no fit match," quoth bold Robin Hood,
  "That you do seem to make here;
For since we are come unto the church,
  The bride she shall chuse her own dear."

Then Robin Hood put his horn to his mouth,
  And blew blasts two or three;
When four and twenty bowmen bold
  Came leaping over the lee.

And when they came into the churchyard,
  Marching all on a row,
The first man was Allen a Dale,
  To give bold Robin his bow.

"This is thy true-love," Robin he said,
  "Young Allen, as I hear say;
And you shall be married at this same time,
  Before we depart away."

"That shall not be," the bishop he said,
  "For thy word shall not stand;
They shall be three times askt in the church,
  As the law is of our land."

Robin Hood pulld off the bishops coat,
  And put it upon Little John;
"By the faith of my body," then Robin said,
  "This cloath doth make thee a man."

When Little John went into the quire,
  The people began for to laugh;
He askt them seven times in the church,
  Least three times should not be enough.

"Who gives me this maid?" then said Little John;
  Quoth Robin, "That do I,

And he that doth take her from Allen a Dale
  Full dearly he shall her buy."

And thus having ended this merry wedding,
  The bride lookt as fresh as a queen,
And so they returned to the merry green wood,
  Amongst the leaves so green.

ROBIN HOOD AND THE CURTAL FRIAR

In summer time, when leaves grow green,
  And flowers are fresh and gay,
Robin Hood and his merry men
  Were disposed to play.

Then some would leap, and some would run,
  And some would use artillery:
"Which of you can a good bow draw,
  A good archer to be?

"Which of you can kill a buck?
  Or who can kill a do?
Or who can kill a hart of greece,
  Five hundred foot him fro?"

Will Scadlock he killd a buck,
  And Midge he killd a do,
And Little John killd a hart of greece,
  Five hundred foot him fro.

"God's blessing on thy heart," said Robin Hood,
  "That hath [shot] such a shot for me;
I would ride my horse an hundred miles,
  To finde one could match with thee."

That causd Will Scadlock to laugh,
  He laughed full heartily:
"There lives a curtal frier in Fountains Abby
  Will beat both him and thee.

"That curtal frier in Fountains Abby
  Well can a strong bow draw;
He will beat you and your yeomen,
  Set them all on a row."

Robin Hood took a solemn oath,
  It was by Mary free,
That he would neither eat nor drink
  Till the frier he did see.

Robin Hood put on his harness good,
  And on his head a cap of steel,
Broad sword and buckler by his side,
  And they became him weel.

He took his bow into his hand,
  It was made of a trusty tree,
With a sheaf of arrows at his belt,
  To the Fountains Dale went he.

And coming unto Fountain[s] Dale,
  No further would he ride;
There was he aware of a curtal frier,
  Walking by the water-side.

The frier had on a harniss good,
  And on his head a cap of steel,
Broad sword and buckler by his side,
  And they became him weel.

Robin Hood lighted off his horse,
  And tied him to a thorn:
"Carry me over the water, thou curtal frier,
  Or else thy life's forlorn."

The frier took Robin Hood on his back,
  Deep water he did bestride,
And spake neither good word or bad,
  Till he came at the other side.

Lightly leapt Robin Hood off the friers back;
  The frier said to him again,
"Carry me over this water, fine fellow,
  Or it shall breed thy pain."

Robin Hood took the frier on 's back,
  Deep water he did bestride,
And spake neither good word nor bad,
  Till he came at the other side.

Lightly leapt the frier off Robin Hood's back;
  Robin Hood said to him again,

"Carry me over this water, thou curtal frier,
  Or it shall breed thy pain."

The frier took Robin Hood on's back again,
  And stept up to the knee;
Till he came at the middle stream,
  Neither good nor bad spake he.

And coming to the middle stream,
  There he threw Robin in:
"And chuse thee, chuse thee, fine fellow,
  Whether thou wilt sink or swim."

Robin Hood swam to a bush of broom,
  The frier to a wicker wand;
Bold Robin Hood is gone to shore,
  And took his bow in hand.

One of his best arrows under his belt
  To the frier he let flye;
The curtal frier, with his steel buckler,
  He put that arrow by.

"Shoot on, shoot on, thou fine fellow,
  Shoot on as thou hast begun;
If thou shoot here a summers day,
  Thy mark I will not shun."

Robin Hood shot passing well,
  Till his arrows all were gone;
They took their swords and steel bucklers,
  And fought with might and maine;

From ten oth' clock that day,
  Till four ith' afternoon;
Then Robin Hood came to his knees
  Of the frier to beg a boon.

"A boon, a boon, thou curtal frier,
  I beg it on my knee;
Give me leave to set my horn to my mouth,
  And to blow blasts three."

"That I will do," said the curtal frier,
  "Of thy blasts I have no doubt;
I hope thou'lt blow so passing well
  Till both thy eyes fall out."

Robin Hood set his horn to his mouth,
  He blew but blasts three;
Half a hundred yeomen, with bows bent,
  Came raking over the lee.

"Whose men are these," said the frier.
  "That come so hastily?"
"These men are mine," said Robin Hood;
  "Frier, what is that to thee?"

"A boon, a boon," said the curtal frier,
  "The lik 2 I gave to thee;
Give me leave to set my fist to my mouth,
  And to whute whutes three."

"That will I do," said Robin Hood,
  "Or else I were to blame;
Three whutes in a friers fist
  Would make me glad and fain."

The frier he set his fist to his mouth,
  And whuted whutes three;
Half a hundred good ban-dogs
  Came running the frier unto.

"Here's for every man of thine a dog,
  And I my self for thee:"
"Nay, by my faith," quoth Robin Hood,
  "Frier, that may not be."

Two dogs at once to Robin Hood did go,
  The one behind, the other before;
Robin Hoods mantle of Lincoln green
  Off from his back they tore.

And whether his men shot east or west,
  Or they shot north or south,
The curtal dogs, so taught they were,
  They kept their arrows in their mouth.

"Take up thy dogs," said Little John,
  "Frier, at my bidding be";
"Whose man art thou," said the curtal frier,
  "Comes here to prate with me?"

"I am Little John, Robin Hood's man,
  Frier, I will not lie;

If thou take not up thy dogs soon,
    I 'le take up them and thee."

Little John had a bow in his hand,
    He shot with might and main;
Soon half a score of the friers dogs
    Lay dead upon the plain.

"Hold thy hand, good fellow," said the curtal frier,
    "Thy master and I will agree;
And we will have new orders taken
    With all the haste that may be."

"If thou wilt forsake fair Fountains Dale,
    And Fountains Abby free,
Every Sunday throughout the year,
    A noble shall be thy fee.

"And every holy day throughout the year,
    Changed shall thy garment be,
If thou wilt go to fair Nottingham,
    And there remain with me."

This curtal frier had kept Fountains Dale
    Seven long years or more;
There was neither knight, lord, nor earl
    Could make him yield before.

DEATH OF ROBIN HOOD

When Robin Hood and Little John
    Down a down a down a down
Went o'er yon bank of broom,
    Said Robin Hood bold to Little John,
"We have shot for many a pound.

"But I am not able to shoot one shot more,
    My broad arrows will not flee;
But I have a cousin lives down below,
    Please God, she will bleed me."

Now Robin he is to fair Kirkly gone,
    As fast as he can win;
But before he came there, as we do hear,
    He was taken very ill.

And when he came to fair Kirkly-hall,
   He knockd all at the ring,
But none was so ready as his cousin herself
   For to let bold Robin in.

"Will you please to sit down, cousin Robin," she said,
   "And drink some beer with me?"
"No, I will neither eat nor drink,
   Till I am blooded by thee."

"Well, I have a room, cousin Robin," she said,
   "Which you did never see,
And if you please to walk therein,
   You blooded by me shall be."

She took him by the lily-white hand,
   And led him to a private room,
And there she blooded bold Robin Hood,
   While one drop of blood would run down.

She blooded him in a vein of the arm,
   And locked him up in the room;
Then did he bleed all the live-long day,
   Until the next day at noon.

He then bethought him of a casement there,
   Thinking for to get down;
But was so weak he could not leap,
   He could not get him down.

He then bethought him of his bugle-horn,
   Which hung low down to his knee;
He set his horn unto his mouth,
   And blew out weak blasts three.

Then Little John, when hearing him,
   As he sat under a tree,
"I fear my master is now near dead,
   He blows so wearily."

Then Little John to fair Kirkly is gone,
   As fast as he can dree;
But when he came to Kirkly-hall,
   He broke locks two or three:

Until he came bold Robin to see,
   Then he fell on his knee;

"A boon, a boon," cries Little John,
 "Master, I beg of thee."

"What is that boon," said Robin Hood,
 "Little John, [thou] begs of me?"
"It is to burn fair Kirkly-hall,
 And all their nunnery."

"Now nay, now nay," quoth Robin Hood,
 "That boon I'll not grant thee;
I never hurt woman in all my life,
 Nor men in woman's company.

"I never hurt fair maid in all my time,
 Nor at mine end shall it be;
But give me my bent bow in my hand,
 And a broad arrow I'll let flee
And where this arrow is taken up,
 There shall my grave digged be.

"Lay me a green sod under my head,
 And another at my feet;
And lay my bent bow by my side,
 Which was my music sweet;
And make my grave of gravel and green,
 Which is most right and meet.

"Let me have length and breadth enough,
 With a green sod under my head;
That they may say, when I am dead,
 Here lies bold Robin Hood."

These words they readily granted him,
 Which did bold Robin please:
And there they buried bold Robin Hood,
 Within the fair Kirkleys.

SOURCES OF STORIES IN VOLUME IV

The Departure of Telemachus, from The Odyssey of Homer, translated by George Herbert Palmer. Houghton Mifflin Company.

The Adventures of Odysseus, from The Adventures of Odysseus, and the Tale of Troy, by Padraic Colum. The Macmillan Company.

Rustem and Sohrab, from The Epic of Kings, retold by Helen Zimmern. The Macmillan Company.

The Forging of the Sampo, from The Sampo, by James Baldwin. Charles Scribner's Sons.

Roland and Oliver, from The Story of Roland, by James Baldwin. Charles Scribner's Sons.

The Battle at Roncesvalles, from The Song of Roland, translated by Isabel Butler. Houghton Mifflin Company.

Stories from the Chronicle of the Cid, by Mary Wright Plummer. Henry Holt and Company, Inc.

Beowulf Fights Grendel: Beowulf Fights the Dragon, from Beowulf, translated and adapted by John Harrington Cox. Little, Brown and Company.

King Arthur and the Round Table, from Stories of King Arthur and the Round Table, by Beatrice Clay. J. M. Dent & Sons, Ltd.

The Hunting of the Boar, from The Island of the Mighty, by Padraic Colum. The Macmillan Company.

Finn and Oisin, from The High Deeds of Finn, by Thomas William Rolleston. The Thomas Y. Crowell Company.

The Boyhood of Cuchulain, from Cuchulain, the Hound of Ulster, by Eleanor Hull. The Thomas Y. Crowell Company.

Robin Hood, from English and Scottish Popular Ballads, edited by F. J. Child. Houghton Mifflin Company.